I Love You Just the Way You Are

I Love You Just the Way You Are

Riley Rian

(She/They)

Paperback: 978-1-958423-00-4   eBook: 978-1-958423-02-8
Hardcover: 978-1-958423-01-1   Audio: 978-1-958423-03-5

Library of Congress Control Number: 2022908751
Printed in Maryland

Publisher's Cataloging-in-Publication data

Names: Rian, Riley, author.
Title: I love you just the way you are / Riley Rian.
Series: Rock Canyon Series
Description: Easton, MD: Riley Rian Books LLC, 2022. | Summary: Maddie, trans-girl and Twitch streamer, has just begun presenting as her authentic female self at the beginning of the novel. Kellan, star quarterback and secret manga artist, doesn't recognize her and thinks she's the hot new girl in town.
Identifiers: LCCN: 2022908751 | ISBN: 978-1-958423-01-1 (hardcover) | 978-1-958423-00-4 (paperback) | 978-1-958423-02-8 (ebook)
Subjects: LCSH Transgender people--Fiction. | Sexual minorities--Fiction. | Love--Fiction. | Arizona--Fiction. | High School--Fiction. | Romance fiction. | BISAC YOUNG ADULT FICTION / Romance / LGBTQ+ | YOUNG ADULT FICTION / LGBTQ+
Classification: LCC PS3618.I22 I56 | DDC 813.6--dc23

To Falynn,
It'll always be you.

And to Kai Shappley,
Transgender activist & future president. You rock, girl!

"AT THE WINDOW OF TOMORROW"
Stuart Wilde
– final blog post before his death, May 1st, 2013

At the window of tomorrow
I saw many a yesteryear.
It was easy to see where we'd come
In the intervening time–
How we'd grown, and struggled, and triumphed
Beyond the yesteryear was tomorrow's future
It wasn't much different than today
But a little more was added
–A little more light–
And in this way, we came to transcend
And the yesteryears moved up slowly
And the tomorrows moved down gradually
They joined in the middle and spun around each other
To become Heaven on Earth–
The one we've been promised.

Prologue

Maddie

"Maddie, you're gorgeous. Look at you!"

The mirror in front of me showed a girl that I didn't recognize. Her blue-black hair fell in a diagonal swoop across her right eye and then tapered up to her left eyebrow before lengthening again, coming down to rest in a sharp triangle on her opposite cheek.

Her makeup had turned her into a beautiful little doll, the rouge of her cheeks contrasting the soft paleness of her skin. Her lips were shaped into a small pucker. Her visible pale blue eye was encircled in purple eyeshadow.

The eye blinked and I remembered that I was looking at myself.

"Destiny, what did you do to me?" I said as I tried not to touch my now glowing face.

My best friend... well, my only friend, smiled, closing her eyes and shaking her head, her dreadlocks swishing back and forth. Destiny had been my friend before she knew I was trans. I was afraid that when she found out, she wouldn't want to talk to me anymore. I couldn't have been more pleased to be wrong. She had become the biggest ally I could have ever wished for.

"It wasn't magic, girl. You're a cute little thing already. But when I applied a little artistic flourish here and there, voila! I accentuated your long lashes and filled out your lips a little. I contoured that cute little upturned nose of yours, thinning it just a smidge. The rest is all you, with added color. Those tropical blue eyes are popping against that dark purple eyeshadow. I outdid myself there. Let me tell you, girl, if I didn't already have your number, I'd be asking for it!" she said, her strong hands shaking my shoulders as she laughed.

I turned back to the beautiful pale girl in the mirror, catching myself laughing with her. *For the first time in my life, I look on the outside the way I feel on the inside.*

After years of dysphoric pain, the unusual but pleasurable sensation of my cheeks bumping into my eyes as I smiled was a welcome experience. I reached back and grabbed her hand.

"I don't know how to thank you, Dest. You've helped me so much over the past year, with my new name, new clothes, and now with my makeup... without you... I don't know. I don't think I could have done all this. I mean, especially this!" I pointed a circle around my face. "What did you use, like three brushes, four creams, and I don't know, two powders? I lost count. I know that I won't be able to remember all this," I said, looking bewildered at the umpteen little containers strewn across the desk she had repurposed as a makeup station.

"Don't worry, girl, we'll practice as much as you need to. You'll get it down; it just takes patience. I'm going to help you every step of the way. It's what friends are for, boo. But you're going to have to buy the next round of makeup because I'm about broke after surprising you with this Target haul," Destiny said with a laugh. I cringed thinking about her spending what little money she had on me.

"I owe you like four lunches out and a million lattes for making me look almost as pretty as you. You're the best!" I said as I squeezed her hand again.

"Mm-hmm. Better be large lattes too. You know I don't play when it comes to my coffee."

I giggled, watching my now very red mouth seemingly painted in an unending smile. Destiny had added shape and depth to my lips that I wouldn't have dreamed possible, making them appear larger than they really were. I wished that the makeup was permanent and I would never have to look at myself without it again. I no longer saw a teenage boy in the mirror. I rested my head against the back of the chair and sighed.

"Do you think anyone will recognize me?" I asked as she packed away eyeshadow palettes in a small bag. She examined me, eyes narrowed.

"I don't know. Everything about you is different. I know you like the back of my hand so I can still see you behind the makeup." She pursed her lips and blew me a kiss. "Remember, I did crush on you a little when we first met... before I learned you weren't into girls."

I couldn't help but laugh as I remembered swatting off her initial advances. "I forgive you. I've suffered worse things than a pretty girl checking me out."

She put her hand on her chest and stood up straight. "Who, me? Pretty? Why, thank you," she said, and then doubled over with that wonderfully percussive laughter of hers. That was the first thing I had ever noticed about her when we met. I'd just been pulled out of school for mental health issues, and I was feeling about as confident as a cow in a slaughterhouse. For the first time, I was walking into a homeschool and online students meetup group, not knowing what to expect. She was the first thing I heard when I opened the door, cackling across the room, only stopping to bounce over and be the first one to say hi to me. We had been best friends ever since.

She reached out and tapped my arm.

"But seriously, you told me that no one ever really paid attention to you in school. You somehow made it all the way to the middle of your sophomore year without making any friends. If anybody is going to be able to slip by unnoticed and start a new life, it's going to be you."

She stepped behind me and gently ran her fingers through my hair, braiding a piece halfway down before letting it slip through her hand. She had a habit of doing this. It always made me feel little shivery bubbles of bliss that would run from the top of my head to the tips of my toes. It made up for all those years that I wished I was a little girl at sleepovers with my friends.

"But hey," she said, stepping around me and gently tipping my chin toward her. "Whether they recognize you or not, you be you. Don't let anybody change you. You've come so far, girl. Don't you dare let anybody steal your light. You blind 'em with it. And before you know it, you'll have a boyfriend and you'll be so popular on Twitch that you won't have any time for me." She stuck her bottom lip out in a fake pout.

"Pfft, you know I'll always have time for you. You're my best friend. And now that you're going to be living in Rock Canyon soon, we'll be able to hang out even more."

Destiny sighed and plopped down on her bed. I could see by the smirk and the arched eyebrow that this was still a sore subject.

"Not gonna lie, it's going to be hard leaving Brandon behind. I don't see how we can continue our relationship being over an hour away. And I don't know if my mom is going to have to work once the divorce is final. She's homeschooled me and Kenya all our lives… I don't know how I feel about that possibly coming to an end."

I looked around at her spacious room, with the en-suite bathroom, and the epic African art arrayed across the four pink walls.

"And, yeah, I know I shouldn't be so angry at her for wanting to get far away from Phoenix. It's not like she chose for my dad to sleep with his secretary. But Brandon and I have been together for two years and... well, you know what happened between us the night before my mom told us she was leaving my dad."

We had talked about this before, but every time it came up, I was crushed for her all over again. I didn't know what it was like to have a boyfriend, but I did know what it was like to have your heart broken. The oh-so-wonderful mixture of anger and devastation that makes you alternate between crying your eyes out and breaking shit.

"I know. I'm sorry, Dest. It's not fair. It's not her fault, but it still sucks, and I know why you're angry. But I promise we'll have a great summer. And don't forget the best part! We'll have theatre class together, even if you don't want to get up that early, you sleepyhead," I said, moving to join her on the bed.

She scrunched up her face and fell backward, moaning. "Ugh, yes, I'm going to that. I did promise you. But it's going to be all white kids, isn't it?"

"Yeah, sucks, right? We don't bite too hard though," I said with a snarky smile. I briefly considered holding that expression to look at myself in the mirror, but let it go.

Destiny playfully swatted my arm, sitting back up with a burst of energy. "Alright, alright, enough about me and my troubles. Let's go to the skatepark. I want to see if those kids we've been skating with the past few weeks recognize you."

My heart kicked immediately into a higher gear as I imagined standing in front of the kids at the skatepark. They'd been nothing but nice to me, but this was my first time presenting as female. I was desperate not to get rejected. But I knew I had to start somewhere. I had sat through countless sessions with Dr. "How does that make you feel?" so I could begin hormone replacement therapy and get on with my life. I hadn't gone through all that to sit alone in my room and (hopefully) watch my boobs grow. I needed to get out there and Destiny's idea was as good as any.

"Okay, let's do it," I breathed out. "It would be nice if my knees wouldn't shake every time I think about leaving this room, but one step at a time, right?" I said, hoping Destiny couldn't hear the trepidation in my voice. If she did, she played it off—she's great like that.

"Hey, maybe I'll skate there with you. You can watch me fall on my ass some more. I know that makes you laugh." She flashed a coy smile, and I waved her off.

"Eh, you're getting better. Don't be too hard on yourself. You keep teaching me makeup and I'll keep teaching you how to skate. I'll have you on the halfpipe by summer."

Destiny snorted. "Uh-uh, nope. I'm staying on flat pavement. That's enough for me." She shook her head as she strode out of her bedroom. I followed her after taking a final glance in the mirror. I allowed myself exactly five seconds to make an overly excited face while I screamed in my head, "I look like a girl, I look like a girl!"

It was absolutely necessary, I assure you.

I caught up to her by the front door and rested my hand against her arm. "Hey, thanks. I've always been so alone with my secret, and you've been there so much for me. Taking this leap is both exciting and terrifying, but just knowing that I have you in my corner... I want you to know that it means everything to me."

"Always, boo. Just promise me one thing, okay?" She turned back toward me.

"What's that?" I began to chew at my lip as I do when I'm nervous, but immediately stopped, horrified that I was somehow going to ruin the watermelon lip gloss.

Destiny gently grabbed my right arm, turning it over so that the inside of my forearm faced upward. She ran her index finger down a still angry-looking red wound and swallowed audibly.

"No more hurting yourself. No more cutting, even just a little bit. No more letting yourself get so low you can't call me. We haven't really addressed that night from a few months ago... when you went too far... but you scared the hell out of me. Shoot, you scared the hell out of my mom. Your dad told her that if you would have lost any more blood, you could have..."

She trailed off, her head sinking to her chest, eyes closed. She gripped my arm tight and I closed my throat, choking off the emotion that was threatening to consume me. I leaned into her and wrapped my arm around her waist.

When I could trust myself not to lose it, I looked up into her face.

"I know. I'm sorry. I don't know what happened that night. I just felt so hopeless, like... I was never going to be me. Always going to be *him* and I hated that. I should've done anything but what I did. I didn't mean to hurt you. I wasn't thinking about anybody but myself. I just wanted out."

Destiny opened her eyes and looked down at me. I felt two inches tall when I saw the tears rolling down her cheeks. I knew that I hurt everyone I loved when I tried to take my own life a few months ago. There wasn't a night that went by that I didn't wish I could go back and change that moment.

"Don't cry," I told her softly, wiping her face gently with the back of my hand. "I haven't cut myself or anything since that night. I've been better since starting my therapy and beginning HRT. I mean, I still have my 'attitude,' as my dad likes to remind me almost every day, but that's just me and he'll have to deal," I said and laughed. Destiny giggled with me through her tearful sniffles.

"I don't want you to lose your attitude. I just want you to be happy," she said, stepping back and releasing my arm.

"I am. And I know I need to keep it together if I want to achieve my goals... like more friends, a boyfriend, making an awesome trans-focused Skyrim type of RPG—"

"Oh my God, don't start nerding out on me," Destiny began, her hands up. "I get the point. You're good now that you've got your HRT going and you see a future of possibilities.

I don't need your eyes glazing over as you talk about your gaming. Spare me that, girl, and we're golden."

She pulled me into a close hug as we shared another laugh.

"Seriously though, thanks for asking about that, Dest. I felt like I owed you an apology for that night. I would have died had that been you."

She shrugged. "It's all good. For real. I'm just happy we talked about it. You'll come to me next time, no matter how low you get? Promise?"

She held out her pinky and I couldn't help but giggle as I entwined mine around hers.

"I promise."

"Good. Now let's go taste some asphalt."

Chapter 1
Maddie

"Maddie, you're a natural! Two weeks into this job and you're already making little hearts with the milk foam... though, I'm not quite sure I understand why you only do that with plant milk," my boss, Mark, said, looking at me sideways.

"Oh, that's easy," I replied, pouring the final drink of a large online order. "If you're a kind and thoughtful enough person to drink non-dairy, you get a heart in your drink. If you're unthinking and ignorant and order regular milk, no heart." I spun around with a smug smile and began rinsing out the metal frothing pot for what felt like the hundredth time that shift.

I had scored a summer job at my favorite place in the world—La Pintoresca Café. Or, "The Quaint Café" as it would be called in English. But most people in Rock Canyon just called it The Resca. I had been a loyal customer here since I was a little kid. It was the first place I thought of when my therapist suggested that I pick up a part-time job as a way to become comfortable presenting as female. And it's a good thing that my application was accepted; it was the only place I had applied.

The morning shifts had quickly become my favorite, even though I had to be here at six am. The heavenly smells of fresh bread being pulled from the oven, dancing with the beans as they were roasted and ground on-site was paradise.

My hands would be jittery by nine—the consequence of the 'free coffee for employees' policy that I took full advantage of. Unfortunately, there wasn't a free bread for employees' policy (sucks, I know) but Mark let me have it anyway. I'd wash away the jitters with a few pieces on my break in my favorite corner booth, enjoying the rich desert sunlight pouring in through the floor-to-ceiling glass windows, the old pine floor bathed in an ethereal glow.

As I returned the frothing pot to its station, where it would stay for all of two seconds, I could feel Mark staring a hole into the back of my head. I turned to face him, a cheeky little grin washing over my face. He blinked a few times, his furrow melting away into an amused annoyance. He chuckled and shook his head.

"Well, I guess it's okay if you only want to spruce up the plant milk orders. Who am I to stop you? I just hope no one else has picked up on your little quirk. Last thing we need is a Karen complaining about something else." He shook his head again and looked deliberately up through his eyelids. "You're an intense little thing though, you know that?"

I twirled around and stuck my tongue out, fighting back laughter. I had grown closer to Mark since I started working at The Resca. He had worked or managed the café ever since I could remember. I had always looked up to him as a visible example of the world not ending when a person was openly queer. For years, I had secretly wanted to talk to him about my struggles with gender identity and sexual orientation, but held off until last winter when I was released from in-patient psychological care.

After my accident and subsequent vacation to the psych ward, it was starkly obvious to me that I would need to start living my truth if I was to live at all. So, I confided all my secrets in Mark in the hopes that he would understand.

He more than understood. I was so grateful that I could lean into his strength and wisdom. Mark had come out in high school in the mid-2000s when it was even worse than it is today. He knew exactly the road I was going to have to travel—potholes, bumps, and sharp turns included. But to look at Mark, you wouldn't know he had struggled. All I saw was a happy, healthy, and well-adjusted adult. I wanted to get where he was, and I was willing to go through whatever it took.

Well, at least I thought I was in my initial exuberance.

I remembered the day that I approached him, last winter. The café was quiet and "These Foolish Things," was playing softly in the background. The song stuck with me because it played on his Pandora jazz station just about every other time I was there.

I told him I needed to talk to him about something. He must have already seen all the signs because he just nodded and pulled me into a booth. I told him I was transgender and had always kind of known it, but it had become more and more obvious over the past few years.

To the day that I die, to the very last breath I take, I will never forget what he said to me, his voice as soft and tender as an oat milk latte. He took both of my hands, gently holding them across the table.

"Maddie, no matter who or what you are in this world, there will always be people who are going to reject you. They're going to tell you that you're not good enough, not smart enough, not pretty enough, not *something* enough. And that's everybody's experience, queer or not. It just gets more fun when you add being a transgender girl on top of that."

He smiled, and I smiled back, but it was more of a mirrored expression as I leaned forward with rapt attention, feeling that he was about to tell me something very important and I wanted to be ready to soak it in.

"But you can't let that stop you. Because this is your life as much as it's anybody else's. And if you don't live your truth, you're going to suffer in your lies. It's far easier to take the punches with your head held high than it is to cower in the corner, pretending to be something you're not. That'll kill you from within.

"My advice to you is to come out when you're ready. It's not my place or anyone else's to force you to come out. Don't let anybody, including me, push you into doing something you don't want to do. I'm here for you and we can talk any time you want. 24/7. I'm honored that you chose to share yourself with me first. That's not something that's lost on me. You know, I didn't have anybody to talk to when I was your age and I wish I did. Things would have been a hell of a lot easier."

I started to get emotional thinking about Mark suffering when he was my age. I wondered why the world had to be this way. Why were queer kids forced to bury themselves so that everyone else could feel comfortable? I looked down at the table and blinked back the moisture pooling in my eyes. I felt a jolt of warmth as Mark squeezed my hands.

"Hey, listen!" Mark said, doing his best Navi impression from Ocarina of Time, knowing my love for that video game. I smiled and looked up. It was hard to be sad looking at Mark with his bright pink hair sitting atop his movie star face. When I was little, I used to think he was George Clooney, totally missing the fact that George was decades older than Mark.

"When you've come out," he continued in an even softer voice, "it won't always be sunshine and roses. Don't let me fool you. Coming out is not some panacea that will fix everything inside of you. Sometimes it's still going to be rainy and dark. Especially at your age when you can't really choose who you are around day-to-day.

"But it sure beats being locked away in the closet hiding. In the closet, it's always going to be pitch black and you're always going to feel alone. Coming out puts you in a position to meet other people just like us. Coming out makes it easier to find and connect with them. And then, if it turns out you have to stand in the rain sometimes, you won't be getting soaked alone. You'll have friends and allies standing proud with you."

I don't remember how I made it out of the café that afternoon and back to my bedroom before dissolving into a blubbering puddle. I wrote down what Mark had said in my journal and read it every day until I had the courage to formally come out to my parents, telling them I was going to start presenting as female and asking them to help me get hormone replacement therapy.

I leaned against the counter, lost in memories but still aware enough to be careful not to burn myself on the espresso machine. I closed my eyes, smiling as I remembered my dad wrapping me in a big embrace and calling me Maddie for the first time. It was like being a refugee in a foreign land, with no hope of return, and then, suddenly, I was allowed to come home.

My parents were even supportive of my therapist's suggestion of online school. Since my dad worked at home, he joked that he could keep a good eye on me to make sure I wasn't just sitting on Twitch gaming all the time.

Online school was okay; it was just the same stuff but from home. The biggest perk was not having to sit in a classroom with a bunch of kids you couldn't care less about.

Instead, I got to sit home and figure out what steps I wanted to take next to best express myself. It also opened other opportunities, like being able to attend organized events for homeschoolers and non-traditional students, where I met Destiny.

"Earth to Maddie. Quit spacing out, we've got two customers waiting for you at the counter. I've got to go deal with a vendor dropping off supplies out back, and Lucy has extended her 15 into a 30, it seems." Mark huffed and disappeared through the kitchen door.

When I whirled toward the counter to greet the customers, I stumbled forward a bit, almost tripping over my own feet. I'm not in the habit of being this clumsy; I think this was the first time it ever happened. It's just that when I looked up, I saw a pair of familiar honey-brown eyes peering down at me. I hadn't seen these eyes in the café yet, but I had seen them in my bedroom, with my own eyes closed.

Kellan Davis. The boy that I thought of when I let myself dream. And here he was, looking at me. Smiling at me. The sun streaming in behind him seemed a little brighter as I approached the register.

I belatedly noticed that he wasn't alone. A girl stood next to him, scrolling her finger over her phone screen. From the short bursts of random songs emanating from her phone speaker, I could tell she was scrolling through TikTok.

I didn't have to look hard to know that it was Kate Wilson. Cheerleader. Fake tan. Asshole. And a year older than us if I remembered correctly. I had never talked to her, but I had seen her in action in the hallway last year, teasing a girl for being fat.

I looked back at Kellan. *Please tell me this isn't your girlfriend*, I wanted to ask him.

"Hi, what can I get for you?" I managed to croak out instead, inwardly cringing when I realized how shy I had just sounded.

Kate didn't look up from her phone, and Kellan didn't immediately answer. Instead, he just stood there, his lips parted a little, his hands awkwardly hanging at his sides as if he didn't know what he should do with them. I felt my eyes get bigger and my breathing came to a grinding halt mid-inhale.

Is he checking me out right now? Or does he recognize me? And which is worse?

Kate, her gaze never moving from her phone, nudged Kellan in the ribs and he winced a little.

"Hey, dummy, are you going to order, or do I have to do that for you, too?" she said, her lips snarling.

Kellan glanced at her and then looked at me almost apologetically. "We'll take two large snickerdoodle lattes please," his deep melodious voice rumbled. The way he slid down half an octave on *please* made me imagine that he was tugging at my underwear. I prayed that the vibrations of his voice wouldn't go further than my ears and embarrass me while I was wearing skinny jeans.

After ordering, he looked down and I watched as his long eyelashes fluttered a few times. I took the opening while he wasn't paying attention to gawk at his toned arms, and then travelled the scenic route to the tightness of his chest against his slim-fitting t-shirt. I wondered if he shaved or let it be hairy. I was hoping for the latter.

"That's all," he said, and my eyes nervously sprang back to meet his. I didn't notice any register of surprise on his face, just that same kind smile. I didn't want it to seem like I was just staring at him for no reason, so I asked the question I usually followed up drink orders with.

"Do you want that with almond milk?" my voice quivered, and I hoped it was only obvious to me.

"Ew, gross. Just give us regular milk," Kate said, still not looking up from her phone.

"Yeah, just regular milk. Thanks," Kellan agreed.

I looked down at the register, trying to hide my disappointment.

I guess that figures. The inside can't possibly match the outside... not that you'd actually look at me twice if you knew the truth... and definitely not with Ms. Arizona on your arm. Well, I had my little fantasy. Time to move on.

I rang up their order and went to fulfill it. I could feel Kellan appraising me as I bent over to grab the milk out of the fridge beneath the frothing machine. I spilled a little bit when I poured it, trying my best to stop my hands from shaking. I fought hard to avoid looking back at him, but I failed. He was tanner and even more muscular than when I'd last seen him at school before Christmas. His dark brown, almost black hair was meticulously styled into wavy layers that fell to mid-ear. His lips were fuller than a guy's should be, and I would have been jealous that they weren't mine if I didn't find them so sexy on him.

He had a slight bit of facial hair trailing a god's jawline, and I shivered imagining what it would feel like to trace a finger across it. His nose was a little bit big but it worked on him since he was so freaking tall. I'm only 5'1, so whatever he was, it was at least a foot over me. I wondered if Kate appreciated what it felt like to be held by a guy like Kellan. Probably not, I quickly decided.

I chanced one more glance when I sat the drinks down. He was openly staring at me, his hands now in the pockets of his athletic shorts. He wasn't leaving me much room to consider anything other than the possibility that maybe he had recognized me and was looking closer to make sure.

I wanted to shift out of my trained customer service persona and ask him what his deal was, but I noticed that his eyes were kind, not calculating, and the corners of his mouth were upturned into a slight smile. It wasn't a smile that someone would get when they noticed a major change in a person, like seeing what you always thought of as a boy suddenly dressing like a girl and wearing makeup. That kind of smile would be predatory, the eyes wide, the brow lowered, the teeth bared. This was just a guy with a relaxed, approving smile.

So, that means he's checking me out.

He lingered at the counter for a moment longer than was necessary, and I had to consider that he found me attractive. I wanted to like this moment, I wanted to give in to the butterflies in my stomach that were telling me this was a meet cute.

But I couldn't. Here he was with another girl—a different one than he'd been with the last time I saw him in the school hallways—and he was kinda flirting with me. I supposed that was his reputation. I'd always heard about Kellan's exploits from conversations overheard in the school hallways. It seemed he had made his way through one girl after another, somehow able to convince the next one that it would last longer than a month.

As it began to dawn on me what was happening, the butterflies went away and were replaced by the feeling of needing to take a shower.

"Kellan, come on, what are you waiting for? I'm thirsty," I heard Bottle Blonde yell from across the café. I turned away and grabbed the metal frothing pot to wash it. I didn't want to look at him anymore now that I knew I was being sized up as "the next one."

I took a deep breath and unclenched my jaw. I was determined to see that this situation was, in fact, a gift.

This predatory behavior of his clearly showed that he didn't recognize me. Now, granted, Kellan and I weren't exactly in the same classes. I was honors and AP everything and Kellan... was not. He was too busy being the star quarterback of the stupid football team to worry about the real purpose of school—getting an education. But Kellan lived only a couple of blocks away from me for as long as I could remember; he had to know who I was, if only in passing. We had ridden the bus together since elementary school. He saw me twice a day for, what, 180 days a year? He had literally seen me thousands of times, even if he didn't pay attention.

So, that meant that an attractive boy thought enough of me to stare. He thought I was a 'normal' girl and probably peeked at the rest of my body when I wasn't looking... kinda like I did to him... but that's not the point! The point was that I passed as a girl to a cute boy. I *should* have felt good about this. I was presenting as female and evidently doing a pretty decent job of passing.

But, no. I was going to overanalyze it like usual. My mind rushed in to assist with the immediate reminder that I was trans and Kellan wouldn't actually be interested if he knew. Like that was all that mattered about that moment.

I wanted to punch something, but instead focused on drying the frothing pot. When I had finished and placed it back at its station, I looked at the clock on the wall and realized my shift was already over. I usually wasn't particularly anxious to get out of the café, but today I welcomed it with a twirl and a spin as I danced to the employee area.

I hastily said goodbye to Mark, feeling bad for leaving the register empty but knowing that I needed to get out of there. I yanked off my apron and hung it on a rack by the employee entrance. I grabbed my skateboard and shoved my entire body into the heavy steel door leading out to the service entrance. The heat made me cringe as I walked into the bright oven that was June in central Arizona. I could feel the sweat already forming on my thighs.

I guess that's what I get for wearing black skinny jeans in the summer, I told myself as I brushed my hair back and slammed my skateboard down on the pavement.

I quickly zoomed past a few cacti that had been planted years ago in the little nook behind the café, as I navigated toward the skate park, feeling both the rush of anticipation of being minutes away from catching some air on the halfpipe, and the relief of being miles away from Kellan.

Chapter 2
Kellan

I swatted at the sweat dripping off my brow as I yawned. I was coming to the end of the two-mile walk from my house to La Pintoresca. I was up way earlier than I should have been on a summer day that didn't involve football practice. But there was a girl involved, so whaddya gonna do? I couldn't get her out of my head.

I thought I knew all the girls around my age in this town. I had made a mental note of every hottie that went to North Rock Canyon High, which was my school, and South Rock Canyon High. Perhaps this little thing was from SRCH and I had just overlooked her.

But how was that even possible? It would be like going outside to stargaze and missing the giant meteor streaking toward your house.

Let's just start with her hair. Her perfect, grabbable hair. It was legit manga hair. In my wildest fantasies, I never thought I'd meet a girl that had manga hair.

I'd never told any of my friends this because I knew that they would make fun of me, but when I was not playing football or chasing girls, I liked to watch anime and draw manga. It was my real passion, even above football. I liked football, don't get me wrong, and I knew it was my best way out of town and away from both of my alcoholic parents. But manga? That was my real love.

And here was this girl I had never seen before, and she had hair that made me reconsider whether I was religious or not. I mean, there had to be a God if a girl had hair like that. It was straight black, the thin strands falling to her shoulders, with some of it covering one of those amazingly blue eyes with the little sprinkles of hazel. Those eyes were going to cost me an entirely new set of colored pencils when I drew her because I didn't have anything that could match that.

She had a small and absolutely delicate little mouth that I was afraid I would crush on our first kiss. Her nose was arrow-straight, upturned just so at the tip. I yearned to hold her heart-shaped face between my hands while she raked her multi-colored nails down my back.

There was nothing wrong with checking her out—I was cool with that. But all these thoughts about her... it had been non-stop since I met her yesterday. And why? I had plenty of action with Kate... what did I need to go chasing café chick for? Heck, I didn't even know her name; I was so lost in her face that I forgot to look at her nametag. I had started calling her Manga Girl to fill in the missing blank.

When I opened the door to The Resca, I audibly groaned as the air conditioner wrapped my body in sweet relief. I scanned immediately behind the counter, frowning when I didn't see her. I felt the wind leave my sails when I realized that she might not even be working today. I hadn't considered the fact that she would be on a schedule and may or may not be there at any given moment. I guess I'd been in my little athletic bubble for so long that I didn't even know how the real world worked.

I pulled my sweat-soaked shirt away from my chest and fanned myself back and forth a few times. Deflated, I thought about turning around and leaving but decided against it as I weighed my options. I could either return to the furnace of a desert summer day, or remain in the cool comfort of the café. I chose to stay.

I walked to the register, feeling my shoulders relax, realizing that I didn't have to put on a show for anyone. That was the stress about chasing girls. I always felt as if I had to be the star performer, spreading my feathers out like a peacock. Sometimes I looked forward to being alone, where there was no pressure and no demands.

The café was near-empty and the server behind the counter was an older guy with pink hair. I ordered a simple iced black coffee. Since I had the pleasure of walking here instead of riding with Kate, I was too overheated for milk.

I propped my elbows on the counter at the drink pickup station, tapping my hands against my cheek to the rhythm of the jazz song playing. I could see why Manga Girl liked working here. You could forget about the outside world and get lost in a little cozy bubble of comfort food and drinks.

I jerked upright after a half-hearted glance around the café. Manga Girl was sitting in a corner booth, barely visible, hunched over, furiously writing in what looked like a fancy journal. She was so short, I couldn't see her from the angle at the entrance.

Looking at her, I felt like I was in the tunnel leading out to the football field, our team huddled just before kickoff, itching to hear the announcer call us out. My foot tapped impatiently against the ground as I willed the barista to hurry up and hand me the coffee, afraid her break would be over before I had my chance. When he finally returned with my drink, I grabbed it and began hurtling toward her booth.

"Hi. Is this seat taken?" I said, a little more eager than I wanted to be.

She flinched and looked at me, flustered. I glanced at the nametag. Maddie ♥. I thought the heart next to her name was cute. I was a sucker for a girly girl.

"Umm… I'm just on my break writing… can I… help you?" Her eyebrows were arched, and her lips were pulled to one side of her face. I could see the irritation radiating off her skin like fire. I had the distinct sense that I was about to get burned.

"I saw you here yesterday when I was with my friend and I wanted to say hello. You seemed friendly," I said.

You seemed friendly? That's all I've got? Might as well walk home now.

"Your friend, huh? Looked like a girlfriend to me, Kellan."

My head snapped backward, my eyes growing as big as the café's emblem embroidered on her apron.

"How do you know my name? It's not like I'm wearing it on my shirt like you, Maddie," I said, not sure why I was pointing at her nametag. *She puts it on every day before work,* I told myself. *It's not like she doesn't know it's there.*

"Your girlfriend practically screamed it across the room yesterday when you lingered for too long at the counter. You shouldn't disappoint her." She clicked her tongue a few times and shook her head slowly. I took a mental snapshot of the way her hair fell back and forth across her face so that I could capture it on my sketchpad later.

I gathered my jaw from the floor and shrugged my shoulders in a motion that had become automatic to me since I started wearing football pads when I was eight.

Maddie was already buried back in her journal before I had a chance to respond. I took the opportunity to set my face into the look I called "hunk mode"—the eyes smoldering, the head tilted just slightly, the jaw sucked in just so.

I slid into the booth across from her and she glanced up at me, her inverted eyebrows conveying a clear annoyance at this continued interruption. I waited a few seconds for her to say something, but she didn't. I was about to speak when she slammed her pencil down abruptly and angled her head sideways, puffing out a blast of air. It seemed hunk mode had failed.

"What are you writing?" I asked, trying to sound light and unintimidated by her glare. If I was succeeding on the outside then it was betraying how I felt on the inside.

"I'm using the 26 letters of the English alphabet in various combinations to express my personal, private thoughts in my personal, private journal," she deadpanned. As an artist, I liked to watch mannerisms, and I enjoyed watching how she pursed her lips after finishing a sentence. I wondered how long she'd had that habit.

"Oh, that's interesting. And what are those thoughts, blue eyes?"

Maddie looked at me blankly for a moment and then glanced back at the old clock hanging on an exposed beam above the register. "My break is almost over," she said, sliding out of the booth. "It was not very fun chatting with you, Kellan. Have a nice day." She hurried quickly toward the kitchen door behind the counter.

"Hey, wait. We just started talking. What time do you get off work today?"

Maddie acted as if she didn't hear me, although I knew she must have. It was so quiet in here that you could have heard someone stirring their coffee four booths away.

She disappeared behind the door, not bothering to look back. I fidgeted with my now empty cup for a few minutes, hoping she'd be forced to return to work the register. She didn't return.

Was that... her... rejecting me? Huh.

I stood up and scratched the side of my head. What was it with this girl? I was used to a little bit of resistance at first, maybe to save face so they could say they tried when they inevitably gave in. But I'd never had a girl outright run away from me after showing zero interest. I looked down into my coffee and absentmindedly swirled the melting ice cubes at the bottom of the plastic cup.

Guess she's really not coming back.

I sat the cup down on the table as a reminder to her that I existed. I don't know what made me want to do that. It was probably a dick move on my part. Whatever.

I turned away from the table and headed toward the exit. *I'll come back tomorrow and try again*, I told myself, ignoring the disappointment spreading throughout my body like a virus.

I took a last longing glance at the kitchen door and then made my way back out into the heat.

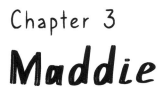

Chapter 3
Maddie

Oh no, you again? When are you going to get the point?

I briefly entertained fleeing into the backroom as I watched Kellan saunter up to the register.

Three weeks had passed since that first day I made lattes for him and the bottle blonde. He hadn't missed a day since then. Sometimes she was with him, and sometimes he was alone. I thought I'd never be excited to see Kate Wilson, but I surprised myself. It was better when he was with her because he was subdued. He couldn't openly hit on me when he was with his girlfriend now, could he?

That first night after seeing him, I had allowed myself to pretend that I was a cisgender girl while thinking about him. Doing this exercise helped me sometimes when I was struggling to discover what was me and what was what I thought I should be.

For example, I tended to go overboard with the feminine stuff, like dresses, which I hated but figured they would make me look more like a girl. I would ask myself: if you were cis, would you wear this? The answer was always *hell no*. So, why wear it out of a sense of external validation? You're female whether you wear the stupid dress or not, I would tell myself.

When I did this mental exercise with Kellan, I immediately knew that I had no interest in him. I didn't want to be chased by a dog who was prone to breaking his leash. *If* I was to be in a relationship at this time—and that was a monster of an if—I would want to be with someone so loyal that they taped their eyes shut around other girls. I already had hard evidence that this wasn't Kellan.

"Hi, Maddie, how are you today?" the mutt himself said, grinning broadly as he stood across from me at the register. He played with the little hairs of his beard in a way that seemed practiced.

I had to try not to laugh at him. I had come to imagine him wearing one of those silly jester hats that had droopy tentacles with tiny bells hanging off the ends. How could he be so peppy after I had rejected him at least a dozen times? I half expected him to back up and start doing the Charleston to whatever old crap Mark had playing.

"How can I help you, Kellan? Can I get you a drink or reject your advances or both?"

"It'll be both. Get me a large snickerdoodle latte with almond milk because I know you only put hearts in the non-dairy drinks," he said, finishing with a wink.

"Huh, so you do notice more than my body?" I said, genuinely surprised. "I couldn't tell by your constantly roving eyes. Here I thought you were a mindless jock with no personality or awareness." I shot him a sarcastic smile.

Kellan feigned indignation, clutching at his heart and knitting his eyebrows together. "Well, I never! I'm just trying to be your friend. And I seem to be doing an awful job of it."

"Yeah, you really are. You've done nothing but hit on me every day for three weeks. I don't think you've missed a shift. It would be impressive if it wasn't so absolutely annoying. I enjoyed working here until you started bothering me," I said.

I almost wanted to tell him who I really was so that maybe he'd just leave me alone. But I wasn't ready for the wider consequences of that, so I resigned myself to verbal fencing for the rest of the summer.

I moved to make his drink, but I hadn't heard the credit card machine beep yet. I glanced back to see if he'd paid and had to look twice to make sure it was Kellan. He was hunched over, looking like a little kid who just had his favorite toy taken away.

Was I that harsh? And was he this sensitive? I felt bad but I was tired of playing this game. I knew he wasn't being rude to me; he was just being a guy. Which might have been cute in an alternative universe where he would know the truth about me and still be interested. But I knew I wasn't in that universe, I was in *this* universe—a place where quarterbacks didn't run around happily dating trans girls.

"I didn't know I bothered you so much. I'm sorry," he said softly as he limped past me toward the pickup station.

He sounded genuine, so I finished his drink with a heart shape and spared him my usual banter.

When I was finished making his drink, I took it to the pickup area but kept holding it. I waited for him to meet my eyes. When he did, I almost melted. The contrived bullshit that was usually there was gone. He was real in this moment. No pose, no cockiness... just soft pools of brown sugar that I wanted to spend the rest of the afternoon wrapped in.

I glanced down, ignoring the warmth in my body and the sudden ache in my heart. This wasn't the time or the place to let myself feel like this, and it certainly wasn't the right guy. I pushed it down into the pile of all the other feelings I had denied myself. One day, I knew they would come charging up and I would have to deal with the mess. I was just glad that it wasn't this day.

I steadied myself and held his gaze. "Look... Kellan... you're a nice enough person. But I know what your intentions are and the answer is no. You come in here with your girlfriend as often as you come in here alone. You're not fooling anybody. You should honor your commitment to her and stop talking to me. Here's your drink. Have a nice day," I said, dying inside as I returned to the register to serve the next customer.

"She's not my girlfriend," he said softly, and I cursed myself for hoping it wasn't the last time I heard his voice in that low, velvety tone.

"Have a nice day, Kellan," I said. "Hi, can I help you?"

I watched him out of the corner of my vision retreat

slowly to the side door. While pouring the next customer's latte, I glanced up and saw him slinking slowly past the front windows, still hunched over. For some reason, I felt more attracted to him this way. I thought maybe it was because I had defeated him but decided that couldn't be it. I wouldn't want a defeated guy. But I did want an authentic guy. And this was Kellan stripped of the armor and posturing. I felt sad thinking this must be a rarity for him.

I handed the customer her latte and tried to smile but I just couldn't bring myself to do it. I attempted to ground myself back in the café by focusing on the smells of the French bread baking in the kitchen, but even that didn't pull me back. All I wanted to do was run home to a warm bath and then crawl into bed.

It killed me seeing Kellan sad, but he was not my problem to solve. My problem would be him getting too close and discovering me. Or worse, *not* realizing that I'm a trans girl who he used to know as somebody else, and then we kiss and he feels me up and... yeah, no. I can't do that to myself.

So, sorry to hurt your feelings, Kellan, but you have got to leave me alone before you figure me out. Stick with your cheerleaders and stop bothering me.

I looked at the long line forming and hollered into the back for some extra help. My shift was only a few more hours, and then I could go home and escape from all this. I planned my music playlist for my post-work bath as I took the next order.

Chapter 4
Kellan

There. That's as close as I can get to your beauty... though I still don't think this does you any justice.

I put the final touches on my latest drawing of Maddie.

"Bruh," my phone said, alerting me that I had a new text message. I had recorded my best friend Tyrell's voice saying, "Bruh," and made it my alert sound. He said it so much that his mom even bought him a dictionary last Christmas, telling him that there were other words he could use to express himself. I grabbed my phone and checked it.

Tyrell: "Hey, bruh, are you partying with us later tonight or what? You've been MIA for a minute."

I cringed and sagged my shoulders. I had been blowing off Tyrell for most of the summer. He was self-absorbed, so he didn't ask too many questions, which was good because I would be far too embarrassed to tell him the truth—that I was blowing him off to draw a girl who kept rejecting me and who refused to even be my friend.

It had been, what, six weeks of this? And almost my entire world had become her. What had started with an "Oh my God, she's so hot, let me get that number," had blossomed into wanting to know everything about her. What her favorite color was, what she did in her free time, where she went to school, how she looked when she woke up in the morning.

I had to wonder on because the truth was plain—I wasn't getting any answers out of Maddie. Every time I tried to ask her about something other than the café, she'd dodge it or outright reject my question with a roll of her eyes. Suffice to say, I had learned a great deal about the food and beverages at The Resca. It was my only option to hear that sultry voice of hers.

I picked up the new set of colored pencils that had finally come in the mail from Europe. Her eyes were such a specific color of blue that I found so enrapturing, and only this particular set of pencils had the captivating shade I needed. There was no way that I was going to settle for anything less than the real deal.

I looked around my tiny bedroom and wished that I could plaster my walls with drawings of her instead of the silly sports posters and video game characters that stared back at me. But I wouldn't know how to explain that to other girls I might bring in here.

I looked at my unmade bed and found it hard to imagine wanting any girl other than Maddie in it. I wondered if she would think my retro lava lamp sitting on the nightstand was cool. Kate just made fun of it.

I stood up and stretched slowly. My eyes happened to fall on the calendar tacked into the wood paneling next to my door. Football would begin in earnest tomorrow and my time for drawing would be cut short. That hurt more than I wanted it to. A big part of me wanted to say the heck with football and invest all my time in drawing. I wanted to pretend that I lived in a world where people celebrated art as much as they celebrated the ability to throw an oddly shaped leather ball.

But football was my way out of town. My GPA was atrocious, hovering around 2.0 in the easiest classes I could manage to find. I showed up to school, chased skirts, and played sports. Sometimes I worried about my lack of academic credentials, but Coach Baker always told me not to worry about all that. "USC scouts don't give a shit whether you have a 4.0 or 1.0 when they see you lighting up the scoreboard," he'd said many times over the past two years.

Football was going to be my life whether I liked it or not. I kicked myself for not focusing more on film study over the summer, knowing that the college scouts would begin actively recruiting me this year. I sighed and looked down, realizing I was still in my underwear. I moved to grab a fresh shirt and shorts from my closet.

I would only be a junior this season, but I had already created something of a buzz within the football world. My recruitment was even talked about on college football news sites. It was comical to think about grown men caring about where some kid goes to college. What was not comical was the ability to get away from here and potentially make millions in the NFL someday.

Get that fat contract, I told myself, *and you'll have plenty of time to focus on art. Right now, it needs to be all about football.*

I strode into the kitchen with a spring in my step, thinking about the way I had captured Maddie's little ears poking through her hair before pausing when I saw my mother heading for the refrigerator. I caught her eye for a second before looking away, the pain of seeing it glazed over too much for me to bear.

"Where are you going this early?" she slurred as she grabbed another beer. One look at the clock told me it was still 9:32 in the morning. Mom worked nights and it wasn't a big deal that she drank while the sun was still rising. At least that's what she told me. I had other thoughts but kept them to myself.

I did the mental math on what number beer she was probably on at this point. Given that she usually got home at seven, she'd be right around eight or nine. A quick glance in the recycling pile proved me right.

I remembered when I was worried that it was three or four every day. Ah, the good times. When can we go back to those?

"I'm going to go for a run and grab a coffee at the café. Need to hit the pavement before it gets too hot to even open the door."

I'd like to stay here and work on my art while I have the time, but I need to get out of here before you get so drunk that you don't even remember my name, I thought to myself but didn't dare say out loud. There was no arguing with her when she was drunk. She'd throw the nearest thing at you if she thought you were being judgmental.

Mom turned and pointed a finger at me over the top of the can as she shuffled back toward the couch.

"I noticed you've been charging a lot of drinks at that café and eating out a lot this week. You know I buy coffee and frozen meals, right? I don't want to keep spending a bunch of money on food. It isn't my fault you're home late every night training for football or running girls or whatever it is you're doing."

I'd moved to stand by the door during her rant, one hand already resting on the doorknob, ready to bounce the moment she was finished. I doubted that she'd remember what she'd even said this morning. We'd probably have this conversation three more times during the week.

I winced as I heard the can crack open. I didn't even drink anything out of a can anymore; every time I'd heard that sound since I was little, I could either feel my father's hands beating me or my mom getting so wasted in front of the TV that she didn't remember where she was.

As I watched her, my face screwed up in disgust. She couldn't even sit up straight. She had slouched across two couch cushions, barely held in place from tumbling over by a couple of old pillows.

Truth is, she'd have a decent point about what I spend on food if she didn't spend triple on alcohol. It was technically her money, but she was supposed to be the responsible parent that could support our little two-person family. With nothing to come home to, I guess I'd been spending more time around town eating out. And with Maddie at the café... well... I couldn't stay away from there.

But I needed to cut down on the eating out so I could fly under the radar. I didn't need my mom's shit during football season. No distractions this year. I needed to be fully focused when the scouts were in the stands.

"Alright, I understand," I said. "I'll try to eat through the freezer this week. It's just been more convenient for me with all that I do to grab food out on my way home."

She looked away from the blaring TV for long enough to cut eyes at me. "We aren't made of money, Kellan. They pay you well as a nurse but when you've got a mortgage and a car and..."

I tuned her out and closed my eyes, her soapbox fading into the background. I noticed that as Mom slid further into alcoholism, she had started to go on these epic rants that never seemed to end. I learned to turn my focus inward when I noticed her winding up, escaping to a happier place.

I liked to imagine myself running out of the tunnel on a Sunday afternoon in early autumn, eighty thousand fans screaming my name, beautiful cheerleaders all focused on me as I jogged onto the field to make my NFL debut. In these fantasies, Tyrell was always with me, and we were about to dominate, doing what we'd always done. I'd throw him perfect pass after perfect pass, and we'd roll up the points for our team.

This time was different though. This time, I imagined going home afterward with Maddie. She'd be grinning at me from ear to ear, telling me how great I was out there. I stopped mid-fantasy and furrowed. Usually, at this point in the fantasy, it would be me going home with a carload full of hot cheerleaders... when did Maddie wiggle her way into it?

I was contemplating this change when I was yanked away by a sharp snorting sound. I looked toward the couch, seeing my mother's eyes closed, the can of beer tipped over, the amber-colored poison spilling onto her stomach. She must have passed out during her monologue and was already snoring.

I cursed softly as I ran to grab the beer, sitting it on the end table next to her. Some had spilled onto the beige carpet at the foot of the couch, but I wasn't going to deal with that now. I was tired of cleaning up after her messes. I was done helping her hide the destructive consequences of her drinking. I wanted her to smell it when she woke up.

I considered waking her up then and there, to scream in her face that she needed to get it together, but I stopped. I wasn't sure what good that would do either one of us. It wasn't my problem. I was out of here in two years. If she kept the bills paid until then, I would figure out living expenses in college. I was certain that any scholarship I received would cover room and board.

I lingered for a moment, thrusting my hands into my pockets. It was painful to look at her, to see how she'd aged rapidly in the past few years. It was even more painful seeing parts of myself in her features. The full lips, the dark brown hair, the prominent nose with the rounded tip, and the sharp cheekbones. But my cheeks weren't pocked and lobster red from being an alcoholic.

I remembered my mom being beautiful when I was younger; I could still see the pretty woman beneath the layer of age, but she had put her body through the wringer since she started drinking. If she didn't stop... well, I didn't want to imagine what would happen.

No distractions this season. Everything will be okay, I've just got to do my thing.

I pulled the blanket down from the back of the couch and gently draped it over her. I remembered that she used to do this when I was little and would fall asleep in front of my PlayStation. I pushed away the ache that had bubbled in my chest and tried not to forget how good life used to be when she was sober and seemed to actually care about my existence.

I tiptoed quietly to the door, although I probably could have stomped out and it wouldn't have mattered. I opened it, glanced back, and then slammed it as hard as I could. I turned toward the sidewalk and broke into a sprint. I needed to get away from this house, away from these thoughts. I loved the island of peace that was my bedroom, but the rest of the house felt like a gloomy sinkhole that would bury me alive if I stayed too long.

I pushed myself as hard as I could until my body had nothing left. When the café was less than a block away, I slowed to a walk, my chest heaving.

I eyed a bench just out of sight of the café's windows and sat down. I racked my brain thinking about what I wanted to say to Maddie, my manga-haired beauty who hated me.

I thought about telling her about my art, thinking maybe I should have brought some with me. But somehow, I didn't think she'd appreciate that I was spending my time drawing her. I could see her face now—her inimitable eyes slashing a cut across my face as she told me in no uncertain terms to get the hell out.

Yeah, I was going to have to find another way to get her to be my friend.

Finding no answers on the bench, I walked into the café. I didn't realize how heavy the feeling was in my chest until I saw her behind the counter. One look at her, even though she was facing away from me, and I felt lighter than air, the events of the morning fading away as I flew like a moth closer to the flame.

She was beautiful no matter what angle you saw her from. From the back, I enjoyed her small round butt pressing against a pair of jeans that I would have sworn were painted on.

"Hi, Maddie. How are you today?" I said without any of the usual bravado that annoyed her. She turned around slowly, but not slow enough for me to miss the eye roll.

"Yep. That's me. Can I help you?" she said, the familiar arch of her eyebrows threatening to bring a smile to my face as I remembered drawing this very expression last week.

"Yeah… actually, I was wondering if you had a break soon. If I could maybe buy you a drink? We haven't exactly got off to the right start. I'd like to get to know you… as a friend. I'm sorry if I've offended you at some point." I started to smile but then stopped when she angled her head sideways and sighed.

"What?" I said, genuinely confused. What could I have possibly said wrong now?

"My shift is almost over. Sorry. Can I make a drink for you?" The way she said it made me feel like she wished I would just turn around and leave without ordering anything. Of all the days for her to be like this toward me… I wished it wasn't this one. It would be so nice to have a friend to talk to other than Tyrell or one of my boys from football. They wouldn't understand the things I was feeling about my life, about my mom, about football, about… anything.

Something told me that she would. *Just a conversation, Maddie, that's all. No games. No tricks.*

"How about lattes for both of us and we could sit outside on the bench and talk? Come on, Maddie, it won't be so bad." I felt like pleading but stopped before I looked like a complete idiot.

She looked away for a few seconds. I followed her gaze to the clock. I felt like every time we talked, she was looking at that damn clock. Probably hoping it was break time or the end of her shift. What was it about me that she despised so much?

When she finally looked at me again, I could tell that she wasn't going to be joining me on the bench.

"Kellan, let me be perfectly clear so we can stop this charade. I'm not interested in hanging out with you, in any capacity, at any time, ever. Please stop trying. Now, I've got a lot going on today and I need to do a few things before I can end my shift. So, can I get you a drink or...?"

I looked down at the counter. The sting of her rejections over the past couple of months had finally reached my eyes. I knew the moisture clouding my vision wasn't just about Maddie but I definitely didn't want her to see it.

"Umm, no thanks. I'm good," I managed to get out, not bothering to look up before turning and walking away. Outside, I returned to the bench. I put my head in my hands and almost begged the sword that she had thrust into my stomach to go ahead and finish me off.

Wow. Outright, look-me-in-the-eye rejection. Is this how girls feel when I'm done with them?

I wished at that moment I had a car like my friends did because I needed to be alone, away from everyone else as soon as possible. I considered running home again, but I knew I didn't have much left in the tank after all the sprinting earlier.

I pulled my phone out of my pocket, checking it without really thinking. I saw a text I had from Kate about something random. Feeling lower than dirt, I clicked the call button. I knew how I was going to put this morning behind me, and I hated myself already.

She answered on the third ring.

"Is this a booty call, Davis? Cause I'm in, just sayin'."

I let out a sarcastic chuckle. "Yeah, it is. I'll be over in 30 minutes."

I let her go. I mean, not really, but I just stayed away. I learned to drink crappy coffee at home. I hung out with Kate and Tyrell in the two seconds I had between practice, lifting weights, watching film for the upcoming football season, and sleeping.

Our team would practice every day of the week except for Sunday until the season started in two weeks. I didn't have time for enigmatic baristas with soul-stealing smirks. I poured myself into all things football so that I wouldn't think about her anymore.

Except that I thought about her constantly. In the cracks of time between running plays, in the last moments of a challenging bench press, in the haze between wakefulness and sleep, she danced across my mind, taunting my efforts to forget.

And then I saw her again. Trust me, I didn't try to. Tyrell was dropping me off after practice and I was making my way up the sidewalk to my house, stopping every few steps to take another big gulp of a protein shake, when I heard the distinctive sound of skateboard wheels on asphalt.

Which was strange. I hadn't seen a kid skating in our neighborhood in a minute. There used to be this quiet kid a couple of blocks over from me, in the richer section of the housing development, that used to skate past every morning. I forgot his name—might have been Jake, or maybe Jeff. I don't know, we weren't friends. But I hadn't seen him in maybe a year. I figured his family must have moved or maybe he just went to the skate park now.

And then I saw the telltale black skinny jeans, the heavy purple eyeshadow encircling pale blue eyes, and the strands of blue-black hair blowing every which direction in the wind. I forgot about that other kid and only thought of her.

It was the first time I had seen her without her work apron on. She was wearing a black t-shirt with the words "Dark Tranquillity" written in a fancy font.

She locked eyes with me for a moment but kept going. I stared after her, watching her dissolve into a tiny speck until she had reached the stop sign and turned out of sight.

In the following days, I made sure I was home at the same time to see if this was a regular routine for her. I would wait excitedly on my front porch, like a kid on the 4th of July waiting for the fireworks to start. I walked circles around my yard, every sound making me freeze in place, trying to figure out if it was her. When it wasn't, I would deflate, only to be reinvigorated by the next sound coming up the road.

She didn't disappoint. Most evenings, she came within 20 minutes of the time I expected. I couldn't figure out what took her past my house. Did she live near me? Was that on the way to or from work? If she lived deeper in this development, she would most likely cruise by here on her way to the skatepark.

I wanted desperately to speak to her again. I'd pace in front of the house, waiting to hear the distinctive gunshot sound of her doing an ollie just before she reached the gently sloping hill in front of my house. I was hoping that maybe she'd miss the ollie one of these days and be forced to slow down and grab her board. That's when I'd planned to make my move.

She never missed one. After the first few nights, she didn't even bother to look at me. I waved anyway. I wanted her to know that I was there, that I was still interested in trying to connect with her. I was still too embarrassed to go back to the café but thought that I should. This standing in the yard waiting for the hot girl to skate by for all of ten seconds nonsense was getting to me. It was weird and, if I'm honest, probably a little creepy. I worked on rallying myself to gather the courage to step back up to the plate.

I wasn't ready to give up.

Chapter 5
Maddie

My final shift ended two days before school started. I could have worked the last day before school, but I was already starting to get super nervous. I would be doing something, feeling perfectly fine, and then suddenly I would lean forward, gripped by panic I couldn't explain. Then I would think about school. I didn't know what awaited me there and it was starting to eat at me. Instead of working, I planned to spend the last 24 hours freaking out in peace.

Mark had been mopey all shift. I could see him glancing at me sideways, clenching his jaw. He didn't want to see our time together come to an end. And now that Kellan had stopped harassing me at work, I was sad to see it come to an end, too. At the end of my shift, we met in the backroom.

"This is the saddest day of my life. I wish you would stay on for just one little itsy-bitsy four-hour shift a week. We've had so much fun working together this summer. I'm going to miss you," he said through watery eyes, his bottom lip jutting forward in an exaggerated pout.

"I know. I'm going to miss you, too. But I'll be by for drinks and to hang out. I'm just going to be so busy with the computer science program at school, and not to mention streaming, that I won't have any time for work," I said and then paused and laughed. "Wow, I sound like a little brat, don't I? Too busy for work."

He waved me off. "Don't worry, it looks good on you. And before you go, I have something for you." He opened his locker and pulled out a small package that was wrapped meticulously in rainbow parchment paper.

"Aww! You bought me a present?" I said, clapping my hands in front of my chest.

Mark scoffed. "Honey, I *made* you a present, I didn't *buy* you a present. Don't you dare insult me!" He arched an eyebrow and mustered his best stern boss face. It was pathetic. Mark was incapable of looking mean. I lightly punched him on the shoulder.

"You're so sweet. I'm going to open it right now!"

I grabbed the present out of his hands and undid the ribbons, tearing apart the delicate paper. I picked up a little knitted pillow that was hiding underneath. It had a light brown background with "Human" stitched across the front in blue, pink, and white. Trans pride colors. I stood there dumbfounded and felt the floodgates start to burst open. Other than Destiny, no one had ever done something so thoughtful for me.

"Whenever you have a hard time at school, just remember that you deserve to be happy, that you deserve to be loved, that you—"

Whatever self-constraint I had managed to summon evaporated, and the waterworks commenced. You know how sometimes you cry, and you feel the emotion first and *then* you feel a fat tear fall slowly out of the side of your eye? Yeah, this wasn't like that. Tears exploded from my eyes like little salty cannonballs. I didn't even give poor Mark a chance to finish his thoughts before I slammed into him, knocking him slightly backward and wrapping my small arms around his body.

"Thank you for everything," I said, the words as blurred as my eyes. "I'm going to miss you so much. You've always been there for me." I kept trying to talk but my words had become unintelligible, lost in a gurgle of sniffles and failed attempts at breathing. If Mark wasn't holding me, I would have fallen onto the ratty old bench next to the back door.

"Aww, you're gonna make me cry now! Stop, girl! I'll always be here, you know that. Anytime you need to talk to somebody, you come see me. You mean the world to me, Maddie. I'm rooting for you. You got this, honey. I know you can do this. You keep your head held high at that school. You hear?"

I nodded and stood back, trying to wrap mental fists around my emotions to contain them. I wiped the tears away from my cheeks and blew my nose. As I threw the tissue away in the wastebasket, I chuckled thinking that if the desert heat didn't ruin my makeup by the end of a day, I could always count on myself to finish the job.

"Come and see me after your first few days, I want to hear how everything is going. Remember that I know where you live!" He stuck a finger out and wagged it in my face. "Don't you big time me! Don't make me come searching for you!"

I laughed and gave him another hug.

"I will. Hey, I've got to get going," I said, taking off my apron for the final time. "I have a streaming thing... but thanks again for this adorable little pillow. I'm going to put this right on my desk so I see it every day." I smiled appreciatively, thinking that while Mark was almost old enough to be my father, he felt like the older brother I never had.

He tussled my hair gently and then somberly accepted my apron. I took one last look around at the backroom, lingering on the chipped water pipe above the bench that I'd spent countless breaks staring at. It was odd—those moments were the ones I'd probably remember 50 years from now. Sitting and staring at a chipped old pipe, daydreaming about what it would be like when school started.

I reached for my skateboard and put a hand on the back door. I looked over my shoulder and started my part of our running joke that we ended our shifts with.

"If only you were younger and not gay," I would start.

"If only you were older and male," he would finish.

It was bittersweet to laugh at that one more time as I opened the door and turned away from the comfort of summer break and the café, and into the harsh glare of the setting sun and the school year to come.

I wasn't in a hurry to get home. Holding my skateboard in my right arm, tucked against my body, I thought about how when I got home, I'd have to prepare for the inevitable freak out that would begin. I didn't do well with change I couldn't control. I mean, who does? All I wanted was to rest in this in-between space for as long as I could.

As I reached the front of the café and considered putting the board down and starting my slow skate home, I heard a familiar voice near the front entrance. Kellan.

He didn't see me, thank God. He was walking and talking to another kid about our age that I recognized as Tyrell. I hadn't spoken to him, but I remembered him from school. He and Kellan had been friends ever since I started noticing boys in elementary school. He was a cute guy, with his cornrows and wide smile. I watched them for a minute, and it was nice to see Kellan happy with his friend. I didn't think he was here looking for me. Maybe he had moved on?

I was grateful that he had stayed away from the café since our awkward interaction a few weeks prior. I felt bad for rejecting him; he did seem like maybe he just wanted to be friends. But I knew that if he got too close, he would eventually see me for who I was and I didn't feel like dealing with that just yet. Not after crushing on him for all those years.

I paused at the edge of the sidewalk, leaning against a telephone pole. I watched the echoes of the sun that had already sunk beneath the nearby courthouse, brandishing the sky in oranges and pinks. I plopped my earbuds in and selected a Purrple Cat playlist on my phone. I thought that the melancholy vibe of the beats would best fit this moment.

I briefly pondered what it would have been like to spend the summer as Kellan's girlfriend. I shuddered immediately, imagining the emptiness of the casual sex and the longing to spend quality time outside of his bedroom. In all my time of watching him from a distance, I had never known him to want anything more from a girl since he hit puberty.

I nodded to myself. I was glad I had rejected him. Even if he had accepted me for who I was, I sure as shit was not going through that.

Sorry, Kellan. Better move on to your next cheerleader. That's what you're really looking for. Someone mindless that can pretend like you're not just hooking up for a few months before you ditch them.

I dropped the skateboard onto the pavement and skated toward the sidewalk, going so slow that I felt like I was being drawn frame by frame in one of those manga books I loved to read.

I cocked my head to the side when I realized that Kellan's annoying pattern of showing up had a silver lining. He looked hard and close and yet he never recognized me. There was a chance, however slim, that no one else would either. That they would see me as the girl I was and treat me accordingly.

A small, yet precious speck of confidence appeared in my mind, and I held onto it with everything I had. Worried that it would evaporate as fast as it had arrived, I thrust my foot down into the pavement, picking up speed and trying to outrun my thoughts.

I concentrated on my upcoming stream on Twitch, the final one of the summer, and told myself that I could live in this in-between space for one more night. The summer was almost behind me; the school year had yet to arrive. I was free of all concerns, and I could let this night be my eternity.

I smiled as I cut through the dry evening air as fast as I dared, creating the wind that tumbled my hair like undulating currents of electricity.

I was going to be okay. Everything was going to be okay.

Chapter 6
Kellan

I spent the final day before school started as I had spent most of August—football practice, lifting weights, and thinking about Maddie. The only thing different about this day was that my dad had texted me in the morning asking if we could get some burgers and talk. For reasons I didn't understand, I didn't make up a story about why I couldn't go. I texted him back and told him to pick me up from practice. The moment I clicked send, I regretted it.

My dad had left us when I was eight. In hindsight that was a good thing for me and my mom. But when you're an eight-year-old boy and your dad packs his bags, his liquor-infused breath telling you that he's leaving and never coming back, it feels like you're going to die. And when the piece of shit does bother to show up in your life four or five times a year at random, only to pick at you and tell you that you're not good enough? You learn to make yourself believe that you don't care anymore.

He would make it to a few games, see me at Christmas, and maybe we would hang out a couple of times in between.

He would tell me he cared but I had long since stopped buying that lie. All he cared about was running women and getting drunk.

"I'm a long-haul trucker, Kellan, it's how I make a living. You can't blame me for not being around more. It hasn't been an easy life," I could hear him telling me when I was 10. At a time when I would have killed to have a father there for me, to play catch, to tell me what it meant when I looked at a girl and felt a warmth spreading across my chest.

By the time I was 12, I had begrudgingly come to accept that he wasn't going to be there for me. Which, ironically, made it all the harder when he was. I heard the exhaust pipes from ten houses away before I saw the old red Chevy pull up. I faked a smile as I climbed into his truck. He turned down the radio and smiled around the cigarette perched on the end of his lips.

"Hey, boy, you ready for the season? Baker tells me there will be scouts from all the major schools here to watch you, including USC. Sent me a link with a write-up about you on some college sports website," he said as I remembered that he and Coach had played together at North Rock Canyon when they were my age. "Don't forget your old man when you hit the big time! You can share some of those college girls with me," he said with a big laugh.

Sure, Dad, I'll remember you like you remembered me, I thought as I kicked the bottle back under the seat that had rolled forward when he gunned the engine.

"Yeah, we're ready," I said, looking out the windshield and ignoring his comment about the college girls. "We won states last year, but we've lost a few guys on defense. It's going to be harder this season, but I think we can repeat."

I could smell my dad's breath as it filled the cabin. I guess hanging out with your kid for a few hours required multiple shots of Jim Beam beforehand. I wanted to roll down the window but thought twice of it. He'd inevitably make some comment and then I'd have to be on the defensive for the rest of the night.

"So, where are we eating? Out at Martin's like usual?" I asked him.

Dad glanced at me sideways, a smirk appearing across his mouth. "Yeah, something wrong with that?"

"No, that's cool. I like their burgers. I was just asking," I said, nodding a few times and trying to play off the fact that I was already hurt, and I hadn't been in his truck for more than five minutes.

Dinner was fine enough. Martin's was a truck stop north of Phoenix on Interstate 17. It smelled of grease and under-showered men, but the food was good. The sounds of laughter and country music filled the place, and I had to admit that if I had bright spots in my childhood, this place was one of them.

Dad couldn't keep his eyes off the young waitresses' ass but that wasn't anything new. I couldn't really be a hypocrite because that's how I was with the girls at my school.

But watching him gave me a new insight about myself. I felt disgusted thinking that there wasn't much difference in how we treated women. I was certain that I didn't want to be Jack Davis—a failed college athlete turned drop-out, turned sleazebag, with a woman in every state.

On the way back home, he asked me between long drags of his cigarette if I wanted to come back to his place with him for a while. I told him it sounded good, but I had to be up early for the first day of school. He laughed and slapped my arm, a little bit of ash falling into my lap as he made some stupid joke about how he wouldn't be able to learn with all those barely dressed girls running around.

After he dropped me off, I ran to the shower, trying to wash more than tobacco smoke off my skin. As I scrubbed my body from head to toe, I thought about all the times I had acted just like my dad. Saying sweet nothings to some girl to get into her pants. Making jokes about getting laid with Tyrell or one of the other boys, with no consideration for how the girl might enjoy being valued for more than just her body.

I sank to the floor of the shower, sobbing. I had been so many firsts for so many girls. I held my hand over my chest, feeling like I was going to throw up. I had never valued a girl for more than the pleasure she could provide me. I was my fucking dad and there was no running from it.

I put a washcloth over my head so that the water didn't pelt me directly in the eyes as I thought about how I wanted desperately to change. I would do anything not to become the asshole that my dad was. And, for some reason, that made me think of Maddie.

It started to make sense why she rejected me. She was smarter than any girl I had ever met. I mean, I didn't really have any evidence to back that statement up, but she seemed like one of those straight-A honors girls. The type of girl that was smart enough not to get tangled up with a guy like me.

I leaned back from the spray. I closed my eyes and rested my head against the shower wall. Thinking of her was painful in its own way, but it was the right kind of pain. It was the kind of pain that urged me to keep going, to keep trying. I pretended that the ripping out of my insides was a purification process, that it was cleansing me of my unthinking, uncaring, toxic behavior.

I clenched my fists as I realized that Maddie might have been interested in me if she thought I wanted more than sex. She might have been more interested in me if... well... I wasn't me in the first place.

I sighed. Feeling sorry for myself wasn't going to help. Nor was dwelling on the past. I shifted my thoughts to the manga book idea I had fleshed out over the past week. Maddie was the main character—a superheroine on a skateboard. I knew what I wanted to do with her as a character, the types of scenes and triumphs I wanted to watch her experience. I wanted to make it and give it to her. I wanted her to see that I cared. I planned to begin the book tonight, but I couldn't come up with what she would be fighting against... other than me.

A big part of me wanted to let the idea go because it felt weird. It was already strange that I had been drawing nothing but her since June. If I showed up in a month or two after not speaking with her and handed her the book, what would she even think? Why the hell would I spend time making something like that about a girl who wanted nothing to do with me and would just reject me again?

The answer pounded like violent surf across my mind. It was simple and direct and impossible to ignore. True, she might not want anything to do with me, and that was fine. I couldn't change that.

But I also couldn't change that I wanted everything to do with her.

Chapter 7
Maddie

Remember how I said everything was going to be okay? Yeah, well, I was wrong... 24 hours later, the in-between space I had embraced the previous night had long since fled, replaced by the "it's only one moment at a time" phase. You know, the thing you tell yourself when you're going through something awful?

Yeah, it was one moment at a time alright, with each moment that passed the curtain of summer break descending a little more, the shadows creeping across my mind like silent black clouds before a storm.

I was sprawled across my bed, my head resting on the wall, slowly rubbing my fingers together as I always do when I'm anxious, when I heard a soft knock on my door.

"It's open," I said and lazily stretched before returning to the same slumped position against the wall.

"Hey, Maddie, mind if I join you?" my twin sister, Charlotte, asked, poking her head in. I glanced over at her blue eyes, blonde hair, and warm smile and I felt a pang of jealousy that she would get to walk into school tomorrow with nothing to worry about. I made a throwing away gesture with my hand, more at my thoughts than her comment.

"Sure, come in," I said.

She bounced in and sat down in my gaming chair. She grabbed my headset and controller and pretended like she was streaming. I couldn't help but laugh. She would definitely rack up the teen boys if she had a Twitch channel.

I had stuffed my room to the brim with professional streaming gear—a big flat-screen mounted on the wall behind my desk, one older CRT television for when I played randomizers of classic video games on original hardware, and two computer monitors so I could keep an eye on chat. The rest of my room was kind of spartan, at least for a teenage girl. I had a few manga and video game posters, an armoire for my clothes, and a large skinny mirror nailed to my closet door.

My favorite part of my room was the four south-facing windows. They were annoying when I streamed, having to use blackout curtains to keep the sun out, but it was nice when I wasn't. I would often lay here on my bed just as I was doing now and gaze out at the sky. It helped me to process whatever was going on inside of my mind... which usually was a lot.

Charlotte nodded her head to the song that was playing through my computer speakers. "What's this? I like it!"

"Tegan and Sara – Walking with a Ghost. I've got one of my epic indie rock playlists going. Wasn't feeling much of anything else tonight."

She moved to join me on the bed. "Oh, cool. It's a good song." I looked up at her and could see past her smile, to the concern evident in her slightly creased eyes.

We had similar features, except hers were more feminine. I mean, of course they would be. She got to be born the right way and I had to figure out what to do with the cards I was dealt. She was born with a pretty face that shined atop a body that was developing the curves and bumps of a beautiful young woman. And I was just a petite little AMAB.

I took a deep breath and shrugged off the sad story my mind was telling me. I loved my sister; it wasn't her fault that my life was this way. I often imagined if things were reversed—if she had been born trans instead of me. She would never be able to pass as a cisgender boy the way I did as a girl. Charlotte looked as if she was created in an old Disney laboratory as the perfect princess.

And I couldn't really be that sore at her. She had attended a charter school for years to pursue her amazing talent in theatre. I felt that the girl was headed for Hollywood someday... not that I'd tell her that. But she had walked away from her arts school to go to North Rock Canyon High with me.

When she first told me of her decision, I interrogated her for days, trying to find out if my parents were making her. She swore on her life that she wanted to do it herself so that she could be there for me. I wasn't satisfied until she admitted that she also knew she'd be a shoo-in for the lead female role in the play. I couldn't blame her for that—must have been really hard getting a leading role at a school where everyone is as talented as you are.

I jumped a little when I felt her hand reach out and gently touch mine. "Hey, I just wondered, how are you doing and everything? I know tomorrow is a big day for you. Are you feeling alright?"

I busted out laughing, unable to control myself at how parental she sounded. "Oh, you know, it's no big deal. Just the first day I'm back in over nine months. I'll be presenting as myself, as female. Not really a big deal at all, yeah? I'm no longer Jeff—that other person with that other name... now I'm me. Maddie. I finally get to be me at school." I smiled and shook my shoulders in mock excitement. "I mean, of course they'll be throwing parties when I get there. Everyone is going to be stoked and there is ZERO chance I'll get made fun of here in the good ole outer suburbs of Phoenix. In reddish-state Arizona. I'm great, actually, thanks for asking."

I sighed, realizing how snarky that sounded. I didn't want her to think I was being snippy. I shifted my head down to the bed and closed my eyes.

"I'm super nervous, I'm not going to lie. I saw at least a dozen kids from school over the summer and none of them recognized me. But they weren't really paying attention, so I don't know what to make of it." I frowned, remembering

Kellan. "Well, that's not entirely true. One guy definitely was paying attention, but he just thought I was some girl he'd never met. I'm hoping I don't run into him at school."

I didn't tell Charlotte that the guy was Kellan. I had confessed my crush on him a few years ago and she had teased me relentlessly until I cussed her out. I didn't think she'd pick at me now, but I was too embarrassed to go there.

When she didn't respond, I glanced up at her and saw that she had pressed her lips together in a smile that bordered on laughter.

"What? I hate that look," I moaned.

She laughed and tapped my leg. "It's just nice that after all these years of feeling forced to be something that you're not, you had an admirer at work when you were being yourself. Doesn't that at least make you excited?"

"It would, I guess, if it wasn't this particular guy," I replied.

"Oh, are you not attracted to him or something? Or is he super creepy?" She wrinkled her nose.

"It's not that he's not attractive, or that he's creepy ... well, maybe a little bit creepy... I don't know. It's just... if he knew I was trans, he wouldn't have kept barking up the tree, you know? That kind of pisses me off. I know it shouldn't, but it does," I said, sitting up.

Charlotte nodded. "I can understand that. But someday that won't be the case. Maybe not with this guy, but I don't think this is a big deal to everyone. Remember all those stories we've read on the internet where trans girls had partners and they were happy?"

I shrugged. "Yeah, but the male-to-female Reddit forum is a cheap substitute for experiencing your own happiness. Right now, I just feel so alone. I know there are a few LGBTQ kids at school, and I want to reach out to them, but I don't think any of them are trans. It would be cool to have someone else to share with, someone who would understand exactly what I'm going through right now."

I pawed at the little rainbow flags on my sheets, struggling to find the right words.

"I don't know. Maybe I need to be the first one in our area to take the plunge and show other kids who are hiding that it's okay, that they're okay, and they don't have to hide anymore," I said, blinking back the moisture that had formed in my eyes. It always hurt when I thought about how alone I really was.

I tapped my lips and continued. "The only problem with all that is... I just want to pass as a cis girl and get through high school without making waves. I don't even want to try to be in any LGBTQ clubs. I don't want anyone to know I'm trans. I just want to make it through the next two years unscathed and untouched. I'm terrified that I won't be able to do that. And I'm ashamed that that's what I want in the first place."

Charlotte scooted over next to me and laid her head against my side. I would have laughed at how funny this probably looked if I wasn't so bummed.

"I know you. I've watched you since your... accident... last year. You're incredibly strong. I look up to you, Maddie. You're willing to walk into that school and take a huge chance because you refuse to live a lie. So, I don't care what anybody says about you. If they find out you're trans and they judge you, it's because they're immature," she said, shaking her head against my arm as she tapped my stomach with her fingers.

I loved when she became animated. She had been overly dramatic since she was born, and I secretly enjoyed watching her when she was upset. I freaked out, sure, but my responses were generic. I'd break something, cuss a bunch, scream... the usual. Charlotte would turn a freak out into a ballet, swirling around in graceful circles, making the most ridiculous faces as her thick blonde braid miraculously stayed in place on one side of her chest.

I closed my eyes for a moment and basked in the glow of her praise. It felt good when my sister stuck up for me. I doubt she ever thought negatively about me being transgender, even privately to herself. She had never been anything but supportive.

"Thanks, Char. I appreciate it," I said, leaning my head into hers. "I needed this tonight. I think I've just been sitting here counting the minutes until I can walk into that school and find out what, if anything, I'm up against. I hate it."

We both heard a small creaking noise and turned. My father was leaning against the doorframe, wearing what he called his "Zoom office attire," an oxford shirt and tie with athletic shorts. I often teased him for his long, wavy hair and scruffy beard, saying that he looked more like Jesus than the vice president of sales for MVidio Tech.

Dad was going to want to give a pep talk and I wasn't going to be able to escape it. I started to sink inside again, feeling the walls closing around me.

I knew he cared deeply about me, about all of us. When Dad wasn't working, he was either helping me through my latest crisis, watching silly old romantic comedies from the 90s and 2000s that Charlotte loved, or playing in the backyard with my little brother, Ryan.

I knew that he was here to try to help, but I just wanted to be left alone. There was nothing anybody could do or say that would make me feel better until I knew what school was going to be like.

"Hey, Char, mind if I talk to Maddie alone for a few minutes?"

"Okay, Dad. Hey, if you want to talk later, I'm here," Charlotte said, sliding off my bed.

I nodded at her retreating figure and turned back to the window.

My father grabbed my gaming chair and slid it over in front of the bed, dropping into it with a loud puff.

"So, Maddie... no Twitch tonight? I thought this was one of your streaming nights. Aren't your friends and fans going to be looking for you?"

"I'm too nervous to stream right now," I said sharply, still hoping he'd get the point that I wasn't in the mood for much of this.

"Don't you have the big Minecraft thing in a couple of weeks?"

He was undaunted by my surliness. I groaned in frustration. *Just let me be! Don't I have enough things to think about?*

"Yeah… I've got a tournament with my team. I'm just… I don't really want to talk right now, okay? I'm kind of stressed out." I laid down and faced toward the wall away from him.

"I understand. Listen, Maddie, if you're not sure about school tomorrow, we can look into some other options. Going to school online worked well last year and we could always do that again. The kids seemed supportive of you in the few extracurricular activities we managed to talk you into."

He paused, waiting to see if I would respond. When I didn't, he leaned forward and put his hand on my shoulder.

"Look, I know we've already talked about all this, but I just wanted to let you know that if at any time you don't feel comfortable, we can do something else."

I scratched the tip of my nose lightly and then looked back at him. "I appreciate what you're trying to do. I'll be okay. I just want to be alone right now. Thanks for trying to help."

Dad nodded and stood up.

"Okay, I can take a hint, even though I don't want to. I just wanted you to know that we're here for you. Please let us know if you're having a hard time. We can do something different."

He brushed my hair once before stepping quietly out of my room. I relaxed a little when I heard the door click shut. I thought about what he said, about how last year had been smooth, and about how the café experiences had been great. Well, minus Kellan.

School would be different, that was for sure. But I wanted to be in the computer science program and I couldn't do that online. It would prepare me to get into a good video game design program in college. I wouldn't say that was my ultimate dream; I think I'd rather be a pro-skater and streamer than design video games. But I'd always wanted to make my own video game too. Even if my streaming or skating took off, I could still work on a side project if I had the skill set.

A rage coursed through my veins as I thought about everything I had to gain by going back to school, and how scared I was. And how shitty it was that I lived in a world where being myself was literally unsafe.

Well, screw that. No way am I letting fear stand in the way of my future. If those kids don't accept me, they can suck hot rocks.

I sat up and raised my fists above my head, clenching my teeth. *I'm walking into that building and I'm torching it with confidence. The hell if I'm going to cower in a corner because someone else might not be able to accept me. It's not my problem!*

I looked at my desk and noticed the little pillow Mark had given me. I jumped off my bed and grabbed it, running my fingers over the little bumps that said "Human."

I could do this. I was going to do this. I remembered what Mark had told me, "You hold your head up high, you hear?"

I wasn't going to let him down. I sat the pillow back on the desk and grabbed my pajamas and headed for the shower.

I got this.

Chapter 8
Kellan

Here she comes! I run out the door but I don't think I'm going fast enough. I'm not going to catch her. Faster, faster, I need to go faster! I feel as if I'm trying to run through molasses, but when I look down, all I see is my sidewalk. Come on, come on, I say to myself, she's going to be here any second!

I hear the crash of the wheels over the asphalt getting louder but I'm only halfway to the road. I look to the right, to the direction that she always comes from, and there she is. She's only wearing a tiny black bikini, and her pale skin shimmers in the rich evening sunlight, the halo aura around her perfect body almost blinding. My heart leaps in my chest and I try to speed toward her, but I trip over my feet and tumble to the ground.

I hear the skateboard stop and I look up. She's walking toward me, one hip at a time, a suggestive smile beneath narrowed eyes. I don't blink, afraid to miss whatever is going to happen next. She stands over me and puts her hands on her hips, just above the little strings keeping her bikini bottom in place. She looks down at me, smirking. She points to her body, making a lazy circle with her finger.

"This isn't for you, silly boy," she says in a singsong voice. "You don't know how to value me. You can look all. you. want... but you'll never touch."

She leans over and sticks her tongue out, running her hands slowly up her inner thighs. She blows me a kiss and then spins around. I hear the skateboard slam back onto the pavement and her laughter cuts me open as she skates away.

I jolted upright, awakened to the sound of a loud crash and a muffled curse. I looked around and realized I was in my room. *It was just a dream, just a dream.*

I placed a hand on my forehead, fighting to regain my breath. I pulled on my covers, growing frustrated as I struggled to get my legs out from under the tangled sheets.

Deep breath, Kellan. Just a strange dream. Been drawing her so much she's taunting you in your sleep.

I stretched and then looked down at my boxers. I couldn't help but laugh at my body's response to a dream about Maddie. I shook my head, yawned, and then fell back onto my pillow with a soft thud.

I heard more banging from the kitchen and figured it was time to get up and get ready for the first day of school. And then it dawned on me.

School! She might be there! If she's new and lives in North Rock Canyon... which she has to! She skates by here on the way to the skatepark or work or whatever the hell she's doing. Why would she skate through here if she didn't live nearby?

I shot up faster than the speed of light, my eyes wide. I couldn't be certain that she would go to our school; after all, it was possible that she went to South Rock Canyon despite the brilliance of my groggy 7 am logic. But what I did know was that if she went to NRCH, I was going to find out by the end of the day.

Now fully awake and feeling ready to tackle anything, I bulleted out of bed to get ready. I could hear the crackling of eggs in a frying pan as I came down the hallway. I moved to give my mom a hug but paused when I smelled the open Coors Light. I glanced around and saw it sitting by the stove.

"Hey, Mom, how was work?" I gave her a quick obligatory hug before reaching for the coffee pot. At least she had thought to make me coffee for my first day of school, knowing I'd probably sleep in until the last minute. I shouldn't be so hard on her.

"I went and it was. Had another overdose come in. Young girl from the other side of town. It's sad. Been happening more lately. Rock Canyon used to be mostly free of hard drugs. But I guess this place is as vulnerable as any other." She cracked another round of eggs over the hot pan.

"You want your usual, Kellan?" she said, taking a big gulp of the beer.

"Sure, Mom, thanks. Hey, how many of those are you going to have today?" I said and then immediately cringed. *Why did I ask her that?*

Staring at her frozen back, I watched her turn toward me slowly, her mouth twisted a nasty snarl. I instinctively turned slightly from her, ready to run.

"You pay the bills here?" she asked with a low growl.

"No, I just—"

"Right. Then it's none of your business how many I'm going to have. Get off my back. I work nights, this is my evening, and I want to unwind. I know what I'm doing."

She belched and I turned away, wanting to vomit. After seeing how my father's drinking affected our family when I was a kid, I never in a million years considered that she might start. All the abuse and terror we went through... and yet here she was. Pounding can after can, day after day. I swallowed the lump in my throat, telling myself it wasn't my business. *Two more years and I'll be gone. Stick with the mantra.*

"Okay, I'm sorry," I said, turning back to face her.

She nodded. "Do you have a ride to school today? I can't let you take the car. I've got to do some grocery shopping later before work."

"Yeah, Tyrell is going to pick me up in like... oh, shit, ten minutes!"

I watched as my mom put the egg between the bread and layered a slice of cheese on top. I grabbed the paper plate and wolfed the sandwich down on my way to the bathroom.

I finished with a final giant bite, then hopped in the shower, soaping and rinsing as fast as I could. I toweled off and felt the smile creeping onto my face.

Maddie might be there!

I grabbed the first t-shirt and pair of jeans I could find. I heard the bark of Ty's horn and ran out the front door, yelling bye to my mom.

When I got to the car and opened the door, the wall of sound rushed to reach me. I didn't even bother to say hi... he wouldn't have heard me.

I looked at him and laughed to myself, his expensive Oakley's making him look like a rockstar as he nodded to the pounding beat. Nobody would ever be as cool as Tyrell was to me. Everybody else played for second place. We fist-bumped and he shifted his Civic into first gear.

"What's Beach House?" he yelled as he pointed over at my t-shirt in between shifting gears.

"A band... but never mind about that," I yelled back. "We're already late. Let's go, man!"

I buckled in and said a silent prayer to whatever god or gods existed, hoping that I could survive a ten-minute car ride with Tyrell. I tried to relax and eventually got into the flow of the Chinese hip-hop he was playing. It was his new thing. He told me it set him apart from the other posers in town, made him cultured.

Whatever, Ty, we all know you're trying to date the new foreign exchange student, Mei Ling. He had met her in his, as he called it, "official capacity" as student ambassador a week ago and they had been together every day after practice, making an uncountable amount of TikTok videos.

When we arrived at school and walked in, the place was abuzz. There were students filling every nook and cranny of the hallway, their nervous excitement taking the form of bodies that didn't quite know how to stand in front of so many other people. I lived to draw people like this—the hands and arms splayed awkwardly at the sides, the fake smiles trying to project a coolness that belied their fear of being socially ridiculed. Yep, it was definitely the first day of high school.

I had expected the atmosphere to be lively, but this was chaos. The din of noise echoed off the tiled walls of the hallway so loudly that you couldn't even hear yourself thinking. I saw people standing in groups, nodding their heads but there was no way they could hear what was being said.

I edged my way through the crowd until I saw my group of guys from the team huddled in a corner of the hallway, just outside the door leading to the cafeteria. I could see that they were laughing and joking about something. I leaned in close.

"Hey, guys, what's going on? Place is really lit up this morning," I said and bumped fists with a massive kid nick-named Big Rude. He was my left tackle, the guy responsible for protecting my blindside on the football field. He always looked a little deranged but this morning he was outdoing himself. He pulled at the bandana stretched across his giant head.

"Dude!" he said and pointed down the hallway.

"What? I need more than that," I said, almost having to yell over the noise. He leaned in.

"Have you seen that kid, Jeff? Remember that little skinny, quiet kid? He went to school with us until like a year ago and then disappeared, I guess. Well, if you hurry up, you can probably see him. He just walked down to his locker. He's changed. Like mega changed, man," Big Rude said, unable to hide the joy in his voice.

I laughed and shook my head. "What's so funny about him?"

Big Rude could hardly contain himself, leaning forward until he was mere inches from my face and I could smell the 15 sausages he had eaten that morning for breakfast. "Well, I'm not sure Jeff is still Jeff. Just go down there and you'll see."

My curiosity piqued, I strolled down the hall, wanting to see what all the fuss was about. I looked around for a skinny kid that looked funny, but I stopped when I saw Maddie.

Oh my God, she's here!

I forgot all about Jeff and focused entirely on her. Her back was to me, and she was wearing a purple shirt that I knew would match the purple eyeshadow she always wore. I belatedly noticed a small crowd murmuring around her, pointing and giggling.

I wasn't sure why they were pointing at her. Did I miss something here? What's funny about a hot new girl? I felt someone next to me and turned to look at a grinning Big

Rude. We were no more than five feet away when he pointed his meaty arm at Maddie's head.

"I told you, man. Jeff is just not Jeff anymore."

He said it loudly as if he didn't care that she could hear him. Most of the hallway quieted down and looked in our direction. I noticed Maddie's hands shaking and I wanted to slap Big Rude for making her nervous.

And then she turned around. She glared at me and it felt like someone had taken a knife and twisted it into my heart.

"Do you see now? That's Jeff, dude!" Big Rude said, slapping me on the back.

It was then that it clicked into place. I understood what he was talking about. Maddie was Jeff, the kid who skated by my house for all those years. The kid I had gone to school with but never really talked to. I hadn't recognized... him... all summer. I had just seen *her*. The girl that I had spent every waking moment making drawings and fantasizing about. And had begun a manga series about. And... oh my God... she's not really a girl.

My mouth must have been at my knees as I was thinking through all this. I closed it and swallowed rapidly, my breath catching as I stared into her eyes. *His* eyes.

It must have only been three seconds at most, but it was one of those moments that stretched into infinity. She was the one who broke eye contact, running as fast as she could down the hallway.

I stared after her, unable to move or speak. I heard the guys from the football team erupting into laughter when Maddie... *Jeff?* tripped and fell at the end of the hallway before getting up and stamping off around the corner.

I felt paralyzed. I didn't know whether to follow or not. I didn't know what had just happened. Was that real? Or another very strange, very cruel dream?

"See? Nice icebreaker for the first day back in school, huh? We all needed that. Awesome of Jeff to help us out," Big Rude said, looking around at the crowd like a gameshow host.

I vaguely thought that I wanted to punch him right in the mouth for talking about Maddie like that, dream or not, but I was still unable to move. I felt another one of my football buddies punch me on the arm. I turned and saw that it was Tyler, my other wide receiver opposite Tyrell.

"You okay, man? Looks like this one shocked you more than the rest of us. Of course I knew she'd be here because my mom's the principal."

I blinked and nervously laughed. "Yeah, I wasn't expecting that. That was... different," I trailed off, lost in my thoughts about Maddie and how I had missed the obvious.

I walked away from the team as they continued making jokes about the person they knew as Jeff. I couldn't stay around for that. I had to process my feelings for Maddie now that I knew she wasn't what I thought she was.

I had been falling in love... I mean, let's face it, that's what was happening while I was agonizing over capturing her face in every last detail on my sketchpad, wondering about her interests, what her hopes and dreams for her life were. Then there were the long, sleepless nights that I spent over the summer dying to know her ideal dream date so that I could make it real and sweep her off her feet, and then finally discover what her lips tasted like.

My vision blurred a little and the sounds of the hallway faded into the background. I felt like I was going to be sick. I hurried to the nearest bathroom and closed myself in a stall. Mercifully, I had the place to myself. My mind was on overload, trying to make any excuses it could for why I found Maddie so irresistible. I felt it reach the tipping point and angled my head for the toilet, closing my eyes so I didn't have to watch the sandwich coming back up. When I was finished, I gasped for air and stumbled toward the sink to clean myself up.

Breathe. It's okay, I told myself. *Jeff did a great job turning himself into a girl. He's got a skinny girl's body, and he doesn't really have a guy's face, either. You got fooled and saw what you wanted to see.*

I put my hand on my forehead and leaned against the bathroom wall. My breath was still ragged, and I wasn't quite ready to head back out into the hallway. I knew classes would be starting soon but I needed these precious few minutes to pull myself together.

Then my mind brought up the real fear that was patiently waiting its turn. *I'm gay.*

I kicked my foot off the wall and started pacing. No, I couldn't be gay. It's just wasn't possible. I mean, it would be okay if I was, but I wasn't. I didn't think about guys like that. Not once. I had slept over at Tyrell's countless times and the one time I had seen him naked, I wanted to hurl. And Ty was ripped. If I liked guys, I would have responded long ago.

I fell for Maddie as a girl. Period. She fooled me, I'll admit it. But nobody else knew about my feelings for Maddie, so it was okay, I told myself. I returned to the sink and washed my hands again.

The hallway was emptying when I re-emerged. I grabbed a bottle of water out of the vending machine and tried to push Maddie out of my mind. I failed. All I could see was her standing behind the cash register at the café, a cute little red bow in her hair. I thought it made her look like a little present, and whoever got to unwrap her would be the luckiest person in the world.

STOP IT! I looked around, afraid someone would be able to see through me, see my desires for another guy and start laughing. I yanked my schedule out of my pocket, trying to remember what my first-period class was. I had to read it three times before my brain finally worked and told me what it said.

"Intro to World Civilization II." I hoped and prayed that Maddie was in AP history, not the dumbed-down version like me. I needed a moment before I saw her again.

I staggered toward my class, not at all sure that I wouldn't wake up at any moment.

Chapter 9

Maddie

I hid at the back of the library, in a quiet little corner surrounded by bookshelves. If I would have felt anything other
than mortified and embarrassed, I would have noticed how
cozy this little area was. Right now, all I saw was a refuge
from the rest of the student body.

I didn't know where else to go. I didn't make it five
minutes at school before getting laughed at, and then I humiliated myself further by tripping and falling. If there was a
disappear button on my body, I would have pressed it.

The little nook in the library that I retreated to had
a small table sat low to the floor and an old loveseat with
tape across one of the cushions. I curled up in the loveseat
and rocked back and forth. I tried to put my mind elsewhere,
thinking about my upcoming Minecraft tournament. But that
just made me sad because while the people I competed with
accepted and supported me, it seemed like everyone here was
only going to laugh at me.

I tried with every ounce of my being not to cry. If I
ruined my makeup, I didn't have a way to fix it. I'd have to

go through the day with streaks of eyeliner and mascara running down my cheeks. Or worse, I'd have to take it all off and look like a—

"Young lady, aren't you supposed to be in your first-period class?"

I looked up wide-eyed, unable to stop myself from trembling. The older woman staring at me softened and moved to sit beside me.

"What's the matter? You look frightened."

I looked down at the thin blue carpet underneath my feet.

"I… I'm just having a rough morning," I said.

"Are you by chance Maddie, our new student?"

My eyes shot to her face, searching it for answers. "How do you know who I am?"

She smiled sweetly and pointed to the trans pride bracelet around my wrist.

"Some of the teachers this past week have been talking about a transgender student named Maddie. Word gets around fast. I know how that goes. I was telling my wife last night that I hoped I would run into you. I had a lot of respect for you before I even met you. You're a brave young woman for not hiding."

"You're… gay?" I asked and then blushed. Of all the things to say in that moment! To act like I was some 'normal' person that was shocked that their school librarian was a lesbian.

She threw her head back and roared. "Among other things, yes, I'm gay. I'm Margaret, by the way. You're meant to call me Mrs. Miller, but if you do, I won't speak to you anymore." She winked and I felt some of the tension from my shoulders easing.

"I'm not going to ask you what happened this morning, it would probably break my old heart. Instead, I'm going to write you a little note that you can take to your first-period class so you won't get in trouble. Are you okay to go there now?"

I studied the blue carpet for a moment, considering my options before looking at her and nodding. There was no sense sitting here and dragging this out. I didn't walk back into the building to run away at the first sign of bullying. That wasn't me and that was not who I was going to become. I could have just stayed home if that was what I was going to do.

"Thank you… Margaret. I appreciate it."

She smiled and then walked toward her desk. She scribbled the note down with a flourish and I thanked her as she handed it to me. Feeling a little bit lighter, I began the walk to the computer lab on the other side of the school.

The hallways were mostly empty, and no one looked at me twice. When I got to the lab, I stood outside the door for at least five minutes. My legs wouldn't stop shaking as I tried to work up the courage to open the door. When I finally did, I must have looked like a frightened deer staring at a pair of headlights. My eyes moved from person to person, resting just long enough to see if anyone was looking at me funny.

There were a few quiet comments, but I couldn't tell if they were about me or not. I tried to relax a little as I gave my note to the teacher and took my assigned seat. The kids sitting on either side of me didn't look up.

I settled down after a few minutes and allowed myself to take in the lab. Where the library was decidedly 20th century, everything in this place looked brand new. There were rows and rows of computers. Each student had a 20" inch monitor and the chairs were similar to my gaming chair.

Somebody on the school budget deserves a really big hug. This is awesome!

Once I felt more comfortable, I focused on catching up. I hadn't missed much... the teacher had just finished dryly reciting the syllabus when I walked in. But I was glad I didn't miss any more of the class because it was quickly apparent that we were being shoved into the deep end on day one. The goal of the two-year program was to learn Python inside and out at a collegiate level. There was no time to waste.

I watched the teacher as he tried to explain the software we would be using, but my mind kept wandering. It was difficult getting immersed into the black and white of computer language when there was an infinite number of grey possibilities waiting for me back in the hallway. I puddled through and forced myself to stop thinking about what was going to happen when class was over. I eventually got into a flow and during the second exercise, I even shared small talk with the girl next to me. *She must have not been in the hallway this morning*, I thought.

When it was lunchtime, I ran to my locker to grab my bag. Being vegan, I didn't trust the school to have very many options for me. In fact, I doubted they had any. So, I had packed a lunch of plant-based protein crackers with hummus to dip them in. It would be enough to tide me over until after school.

But there was one thing that the school did have that I wanted to get my lips on. Lemonade. Really good, really sugary lemonade. Reminded me of the lemonade I used to get at Chic-fil-A before I had my vegan come-to-Jesus moment years ago. If I ever needed sugar, it was today.

I waited in line to get a cup and tried to pretend like I couldn't feel the entire room staring at me. I forgot how fast gossip spreads in school—I should've known that I'd be the star of the show by midday.

I made a quick plan in my head. I'd grab my lemonade, keep my head down, and take my lunch back to that quiet corner of the library. I'd try to slip in unnoticed, but if Margaret caught me, I hoped she'd be okay with me eating there. It would be a lot easier than trying to sit alone at a table with everyone staring at me.

Thank you, school, for not giving me the same lunch period as my sister. How very thoughtful of you.

The line moved slowly, but I finally got up to the lemonade dispenser and grabbed the largest cup I could see, figuring the day warranted it. I paid and began walking back toward the door to exit.

It was then that I felt something greasy and gooey plunk me in the forehead. And then another mushy blob hit me in the cheek. I looked down and saw two chicken nuggets smeared with barbeque sauce laying at my feet. I heard a table full of guys laughing and looked to see them pointing.

"Hey, she's looking at us," one of them started. "Hey, princess, will you be my girlfriend? Can I get your number?"

"Looking good with sauce on your face. Maybe I can add some more sticky stuff to it after school, huh? You'd like that, wouldn't you?"

"You got a surprise for us underneath those skinny jeans, don't cha, Jeff?"

I was shocked at how obscene they were being. Like, really? They didn't even know me, didn't even speak to me last year, but now that I'd made a change in my appearance, it somehow encouraged them to unload on me? And that was funny to them? I knew this would happen but I still didn't understand.

I looked around at the table, appalled at the tears that started to fall. I hated being so weak, but I wasn't prepared for this. This wasn't just normal bullying. This was downright cruel. I had done nothing to any of them and yet they were hurling insult after insult at me without a care in the world. As if I was less than human. As if I deserved it.

And then my heart bottomed out when I saw Kellan. He was laughing. I could feel my face crumbling as we locked eyes. I looked away and bolted for the exit. I knew that trans bullying could get violent fast, so I hurried out of the cafeteria as quickly as I could, making my way toward the library.

How is this happening to me? I'm just going to school, not bothering anybody else. What's so funny about me? And how could *he* let them do that to me? How could he just sit there and watch them throw food and laugh about it? How could he be such a monster after trying to talk to me all summer? And why the hell did I care what Kellan Davis did or thought?

The library looked empty as I scurried over to what I was sure would become my new favorite spot. I slid down into the old loveseat and curled into a tiny ball, sobbing as quietly as I could.

Why did I come back here?

Chapter 10
Kellan

I sank lower into my seat, my head hovering above my tray. Watching Maddie as she ran away from the abuse made me feel like the biggest jerk in the world. I couldn't hide that I laughed. I laughed with my friends because I didn't want to be the only one at the table not laughing. But that wasn't a proper excuse. My cowardly response killed a golden opportunity to do the right thing. Now she would only see me as one of them.

I felt so ashamed that I didn't even talk to anyone for the rest of lunch. I kept replaying her face when she first noticed me watching. It gutted me to know that I had contributed to her suffering, that I approved of their actions by not sticking up for her.

Instead of going to my third-period class after lunch, I went to the bathroom and locked myself in the handicap stall. I tried to tell myself that it didn't matter anymore, that Maddie wasn't a girl, and I didn't need her approval. I didn't have to waste my time trying to get her attention. I wasn't happy with my actions, and I wouldn't participate again, but the fact that she lumped me in with my friends was irrelevant.

I paced around the little area, struggling to get an anchor in the swirling sea of my thoughts.

Trying to push Maddie away didn't feel right. I always knew when something felt right or wrong—that's one of the reasons I was such a great quarterback. I could sense an open man before I even saw him. I couldn't explain in words how that worked, it just did. And I knew that abandoning Maddie wasn't the right choice.

Nobody deserved to be treated that way. It was my place as team captain... no, it was my place as a human being to stand up and tell my friends that what they were doing was wrong. They didn't have to be friends with her, but they should have just left her alone.

But you laughed, Kellan. YOU participated. You are as wrong as they are, remember?

I looked up at the ceiling and stifled a scream. This wasn't what I wanted to be dealing with on the first day of school, with just over 24 hours to go until the first game of the season. I cursed and punched the door open. I jumped when it bounced against its hinges and flew back toward me.

"Goddammit!" I huffed. I didn't ask for any of this. Why is this happening to me right now? I just wanted to impress the scouts, maintain my mediocre GPA, and get through another school year. I didn't come here to take up for... whatever you are, Maddie. I'm sorry you got bullied. It was wrong. I want them to leave you alone so we can all just get on with our lives.

I closed my eyes but all I saw was her face across hundreds of pages of my sketchpad. I swallowed hard.

Why do you have to be so beautiful? I have to move on from you... but I don't know if I can. Like a fool, I've fallen for you. Like a fool, I couldn't bring myself to do anything but laugh when you needed a hero. And like the biggest fool of all, I'm still sitting here thinking about you as if you're a girl.

I sighed and caught my reflection in the mirror. My eyes looked beaten with pain. Pain that I was an asshole who laughed, pain because I knew I needed to apologize, and pain because I was worried about her. I didn't want to care about her anymore. It wasn't healthy now that I knew the truth. Caring would only make life more difficult for me at a time when I needed simplicity.

But I do care. She's been my world for two months. I can't just snap my fingers and let her go.

I washed my hands quickly and avoided my reflection. I'd had enough introspection for one day. I decided that it was time to make this right and then do whatever I needed to do to move on.

I thought about where she might have escaped to. I doubted she would head directly to her next class. In her distraught state, she wouldn't have been able to show up without having to give an explanation. If there was one thing I knew about Maddie after the summer, it was that she didn't provide explanations.

If it were me, I would have gone to the locker room or the football field or someplace that would make me feel comfortable. Where would a loner who wrote in journals go in a situation like this?

The library. I hurried to the center of the school. I approached the open area quietly and surveyed the rows of computers and didn't see her. I scanned slowly over the rest of the open-concept arrangement and saw a cluster of bookshelves toward the back. I walked over and stopped abruptly when I saw her curled in a ball on a small couch, her eyes closed, and her hands wiping gently at her cheeks.

I felt my apprehension melt away, and all I could think about was how it would feel to hold her against my chest. I would gently brush her hair back and tip her head toward mine so I could softly kiss the tears as they fell.

I knew what I was thinking, and I knew who I was thinking about, but I couldn't stop. It felt so right.

I must have audibly sighed because the next thing I knew she was sitting bolt upright, her kaleidoscopic blue eyes bulging. Before I had the chance to say a word, she flashed her middle finger at me and ran out of the library. I started to follow but stopped.

Her first day of school had already been hell. I didn't want to compound it by chasing her down and making her talk to someone she didn't want to talk to in the first place.

After seeing me laugh at lunch, I doubt she would have listened.

But I wanted to apologize. I *needed* to apologize. I remembered that when I knew her as Jeff, she lived a couple of blocks over from me. We rode the same school bus before I started catching rides with older girls.

My bus stop was before hers in the mornings. I could remember seeing... her... run from her house trying to catch the bus before it pulled away.

After practice, I promised myself I would go to her house, look her in the eyes, and make this right.

A quick glance at Tyrell's dashboard told me it was already after six. For once, I was glad that Tyrell was incapable of driving the speed limit. We were at my house in less than five minutes. I leaped out of the car and didn't stop running until I hit my bedroom.

A quick sniff of my armpits told me that I smelled awful from practice, but there was little I could do about that without a shower. And I didn't want to waste any more time before I chickened out and stayed home. I hastily threw on a clean shirt before pausing when I saw the stack of drawings on my desk. My stack of Maddie.

I flipped through them and pulled out what I felt was my best. She was coming around the corner on her skateboard by my house, the sun glinting off the tiny little cluster of freckles on the tip of her nose. On a whim, I tucked it under my arm and carried it with me.

I could feel my heart pounding as I broke out into a sweat at the mere sight of her house. What the hell was I going to say to her? Would she even listen? And how would her parents react? What if her father answered the door?

As I reached the front of her house, I was beginning to think that this was a horrible idea and nearly turned around. As I was deliberating, I heard the distinctive sound of her skateboard coming up behind me. *Oh, shit.*

I turned around and we locked eyes. I could see her jaw clenched from 40 feet away. I couldn't stop myself from feeling excited watching her approach. I swear I could feel the electricity coming off of her and I braced myself to be shocked.

I knew that she was pissed at me and I was probably the last person in the world she wanted to see standing in front of her house. I knew I should be thinking about how I was going to apologize to her and then leave her alone, but that's not what was on my mind as I watched her coming closer, her fists clenched and her mouth a solid line of impenetrable steel.

She's breathtaking, I admitted to myself. *Who are you underneath all this armor?*

I shook the feeling away as she skated up to me. She stopped three feet away, kicking the board up and snatching it out of the air with her right hand in one graceful motion.

"What do you want? Come to laugh again?" she said, snarling at me as she stormed past. Her hair smelled like cinnamon cookies. I hadn't noticed that at the café.

"What? No! I came to apologize. For my friends… and for myself."

She whirled around and leaned her body toward me, her finger pointed inches from my chin, the evening sunlight reflecting off the little silver ring wrapped around it. I'll never forget the way she looked in this moment—her eyes blue-hot with fire, her hair disheveled and covering half of her face.

Please. Let me be your friend.

I jumped in before she had a chance to speak. "Maddie, I'm sorry about today. I didn't know that you were—"

"Trans?" she spat. "Well, I am. What of it, Kellan? It's none of your business."

"Is that what it's called? I didn't know. I'm wrapped in my own world I guess. Look, I'm sorry, okay? I want to be your friend—"

Air whooshed across my face as she interrupted me with a quick swipe of her hand.

"I don't even want to be your friend. I didn't want to talk to you this summer and I don't want to talk to you now. Why can't you leave me alone? What do you want from me?

You laugh at me at school and then you come here trying to be my friend? Go fuck yourself."

She spun back toward the door.

"Maddie, it's not like that. I... I didn't mean to laugh today. It was a mistake. I was shocked at what was happening. I didn't—"

She turned and faced me at the top step leading to her porch, her icy glare silencing me mid-sentence.

"Save it, Kellan. You're the same as them. Just a stupid jock who doesn't care if he hurts other people's feelings. Well, guess what? I don't care about any of you, either." She opened the door and yelled over her shoulder, "Don't ever come back here!"

She slammed it shut and I stared after her. I started to put my hands in my pockets out of habit and then remembered that I had brought the drawing with me. It slipped my mind in the heat of the moment.

I looked down at my shoes after a few awkward moments, not sure what to do next. I thought about leaving the picture near the door, hoping that she would find it, or that her parents would see it and give it to her. Feeling that I had been awkward enough already by coming here, I decided against it. I turned to leave when I heard the door open. I looked back expectantly. A tendril of fear curled like a fist around my heart as a man stepped onto the porch.

Her dad. Shit! Now I'm in for it.

"Hi, Kellan, I take it? Hugh Martin, I'm Maddie's father." He walked over to me and offered his hand.

I shook it and felt intimidated by his firm grip. I tried to force myself to make lasting eye contact with him, but my eyes kept returning to the ground. He was a lot shorter than me, but I felt like a small child in his presence.

"Umm, yeah, I'm Kellan. I, umm… came to apologize for my friends'—and my own—behavior today. They made fun of her… called her, I guess her old name, and I laughed along with them and I'm sorry. I feel awful about it. I know it wasn't right. I had seen Maddie all summer at the café and I didn't realize…" I trailed off, afraid that my blabbering was only going to make things worse.

Hugh put his hand on my shoulder. I looked up, determined to keep eye contact with this man. If he was going to give me hell, I was willing to take it. I deserved it.

"I heard the entire exchange between you two. My home office is right there, on the first floor." He pointed toward an open window.

"Your friends did recognize her correctly. And I understand using the old name. But that isn't her name, not anymore. When you use the old name, it's called deadnaming and it's very offensive. She changed her name to reflect who she authentically is. Calling her the old name is unacceptable."

I could understand that, but I think she was upset about a lot more than just the use of her old name. The things my friends said to her… I wondered if she would hear those things when she was by herself tonight, replaying on a loop. I cringed.

I felt like Hugh was waiting for me to look at him before continuing. My eyes were quivering, thinking about how deep Maddie's hurt must go but I forced myself to look at him.

"Maddie is a female who was born in a male body. She isn't choosing something different than who she is; she's just being herself. It's been very hard for her for years. As her parents, we support her fully and want her to be happy."

Hugh glanced away from me, and I took my first good look at him. I couldn't really see Maddie in his features. He had long hair and glasses, and a small goatee. His eyes were striking in a way that was different from Maddie's. They were the kindest I'd ever seen. They looked alive and vibrant and didn't shift from side to side like I was used to seeing in adults. They were nothing like my father's. They didn't look calculating or cruel or dead. When he held my gaze, I felt nothing but openness and trust.

"I thought it would be rough for her going back to public school," he continued, "but I didn't think the first day would be this bad."

I blushed as red as their front door. "Gosh, I feel absolutely awful. I mean, I honestly thought she was a girl, like, you know, biologically or whatever. I talked to her at the café at least a dozen times over the summer. Thought she was the new kid in the neighborhood. I even drew this picture of her," I pulled it out and handed it to him. "I was going to give it to her, but I didn't really have the chance."

Hugh examined the picture, his hand involuntarily covering his mouth. By the way his eyes scanned it excitedly, I could tell he was impressed. A buzz began building inside of me as I watched Maddie's dad admire my drawing. I couldn't say how good it would be compared to somebody else's, but I knew it was my best. I was so fascinated by how she looked flying around the corner on her skateboard. It was as if an angel descended to Earth, put on a death metal band t-shirt, and hopped on a wooden board with wheels. It took me days to get the drawing where I wanted it, trying to capture all the subtle contours of her pale skin gleaming in the sun.

"Kellan, this is... wow! This is amazing! You have a real talent. Are you pursuing art in school?" He looked at me eagerly and I felt the buzz grow into a warmth that I hadn't felt in a long time.

I'd been given compliments by many people in my life. Girls I'd slept with. My coach and my teammates. Other coaches we'd played against. Even a scout from Arizona State last year. But when Hugh gave me a compliment about my art, I felt like the eight-year-old boy who yearned to have his father come back home, to tell him how much he meant to him and how proud he was to be his dad.

I shifted my weight from foot to foot and looked at Maddie's face on the picture, not trusting myself to look into his eyes just yet. "I draw at night sometimes. No one really knows that I do this. It's something I've always kept to myself. It helps me, I don't know, stay calm I guess? Just something I do," I shrugged and looked down at the ground. "I thought I would share it with Maddie... I was inspired by her courage to be herself, so I wanted to show a piece of myself that I hide, that no one else knows about. Thanks for the compliment, though. I appreciate it, sir."

"Call me Hugh. No need for formality."

I blinked, taken aback. I couldn't imagine anyone calling my father Jack and getting away with it. To call a man anything other than sir or coach hadn't been a part of my experience.

"Okay, Hugh. Well, I guess I should get going. I hope Maddie is okay. If you would, please give that to her and tell her I'm very sorry for hurting her feelings."

Hugh reached out to touch my arm. "It was big of you to come and apologize, Kellan. I'll see that Maddie gets this," he lifted up the picture, "and your apology. Don't take her words to you as final. I think she'll warm up and start to make friends once she gets comfortable in school being herself. And you're welcome here anytime as long as you treat my daughter with respect and kindness."

I nodded my head and found the courage to look the man in the eye one more time before walking back to my house.

When I was halfway home, still reeling from how different Hugh was from my parents, I realized how shitty my dad had been to me all my life. I just had the best experience I'd ever had with a man around my father's age… and it only happened because I participated in making fun of his kid not more than seven hours prior. Wow. I didn't know if that said more about my dad or Hugh.

It was obvious that Maddie didn't have it easy. I wouldn't deny her that or pretend like I understood what she was going through. But she did have a father. And I was really happy about that because she needed all the support she could get.

A surge of what I could only describe as life energy welled inside of me, swirling around my head, making me want to jump. I wanted to be a part of her support team. She didn't have to like me, she didn't have to be my friend, but I wanted to stand up for her. She didn't deserve what had happened at school today. If I could help it, I wasn't going to let it happen again.

I walked into an empty house and ignored the hunger gnawing at my stomach. I sat down on the couch, took out my phone, and Googled "trans."

I was determined to understand her.

Chapter 11
Maddie

"Wow, they actually said to that you? That's awful," Charlotte said in a small voice just above a whisper.

I shrugged and shifted away from the sunlight pouring into my room, the after images of tree branches glued to my mind when I blinked. I was in my usual position for these conversations, slouched across my bed the short way, with my arms hanging limply at my sides. My hands felt fat from the blood pooling in my fingertips, but I didn't care enough to move.

I had tried to reconnect with what Mark had said at the café, that I was enough and that it didn't matter what anyone said, but it was a struggle. All I could feel was the sharp pricks of their laughter when I closed my eyes, the sound cutting me up into a million little pieces in front of the entire cafeteria.

I heard a soft knock on my door but didn't bother to respond. Since it wasn't Charlotte, it was either my mom or dad and I knew they'd come in no matter what I said. Sure enough, the door opened and my mom stuck her head in.

"Hey, Maddie, mind if I come in for a sec?"

You're going to anyway, why ask?

"Yeah, sure, come on in," I said and swept my arm across the room in a sarcastic welcoming motion.

I watched out of the corner of my eye as she shared a silent conversation with Charlotte, Mom arching her eyebrows and mouthing something I couldn't catch.

I hadn't seen that fearful, "verge-of-tears mom" look since last year. The scrunched-up eyes, the mouth that looked like a half-smile, half-frown... if that was even possible. I knew she would be worried that I was going to regress back into my old self-injury patterns. A part of me could understand her fear but a bigger part of me was angry that she didn't trust me.

I turned and looked at her. For a second, I saw an older Charlotte. And what should have been an older me.

"Your dad told me you had a rough day at school. I'm sorry to hear that, sweetie."

I flipped my hands in a shrug. "Eh, I knew it would be hard. Don't worry, I'm not going to like freak out or anything. I didn't get my hopes up too much."

Mom moved to sit on the edge of the bed. She was holding a large sheet of paper but I couldn't tell what was on the other side. Charlotte careened her neck around to get a better view and let out a gasp.

"WOW! Who drew that? That looks just like Maddie!" she yelped, coming closer to the picture.

I sat up abruptly, my heart instantly pounding. "What? Let me see that!"

Mom flipped the picture over and sat it gently on the bed. My eyes must have almost fallen out of my head because I couldn't believe what I was seeing. I pounded the pillow next to me with a clenched fist.

"Who drew this?" I demanded.

"Kellan left it with your dad after your... conversation with him," Mom said, her answer sounding more like a question of whether I could handle this.

I snatched up the picture and stared at it. I could feel the lump in my throat expanding, threatening to erupt at any moment. I wanted to rip the drawing to shreds, but for some reason, I couldn't.

"Wait... hang on a sec... we're not talking about Kellan Davis, are we?" Charlotte asked excitedly. When neither one of us answered, she almost squealed.

"You're kidding, right? Oh my God, Maddie, Kellan Davis drew this for you! I thought you said you had a bad day!" She giggled but stopped when I tossed the picture across the room like a frisbee and sank my head into my hands.

"He must have done this over the summer," I said, my voice muffled. "When he thought I was someone else."

I paused for a moment, and I could hear my mom whispering to Charlotte. I didn't have time for this. I glanced at them.

"Please leave. I just... I can't do this right now. I need to be alone."

I put my head back into my hands and prayed that they wouldn't push me. I clenched my jaw tight and held on. It would be lights out if my mom saw me exploding. No skate park, no Destiny, no nothing until she talked to my therapist.

After an agonizing few seconds, I finally heard them shuffling out of my room. Unlike my dad, my mom was good in these situations. She may not have handled it well when I freaked out, but at least she knew when to give me my space. Dad would push, thinking that I needed to express my feelings and work through it. Sometimes that helped, but most of the time, I just wanted to punch him.

A cold terror swept through my body when I heard the door click. I realized that the drawing was still here. I regretted that I didn't ask my mom to take the damn thing with her.

I squeezed my head between my hands as hard as I could, stifling the urge to scream. I'd have to look at the stupid drawing of myself that the stupid kid I had crushed on for however many stupid years had made. And it hurt all the worse because there was no way he would ever make another one again.

Don't look at it, just throw it under the bed. Shred it. It's a lie. It was made from a lie.

I ignored the voice in my head that was trying to be helpful and scooted off the edge of my bed. I looked across the room and saw my face staring back at me. I walked over and gently picked it up. I smiled, unable to help myself. It was me, manga style. If my boyfriend had done this for me, I think I would have been ready to marry him. But this was Kellan.

I sighed and carried it back to my bed. What the hell was wrong with this guy? I did nothing but push him away all summer and yet he still drew this. Why was he so attracted to me?

I shook my head. No, he must have *been* attracted to me. He certainly wouldn't be into me now. Not after he found out that I was trans. I wrapped my arms around my chest and rocked slowly back and forth.

So, why did he bring this here? What cruel intention is behind it? He's not interested in me anymore... so does he feel sorry for me? Does he think that this will make me feel better? Because it doesn't. It makes me feel awful.

I felt the unmistakable tingling creeping up the skin of my arms. I curled into a ball face-down and buried them underneath my chest. The last time this feeling visited me, I woke up in a hospital with my dad hunched over in a chair, staring at me from less than a foot away, his eyes bloodshot. The only time I'd ever seen him cry was when I woke up in that bed, realizing my attempt to end my life had failed.

I can't go back to that. Anything but that.

I dropped immediately into the breathing exercises that my therapist taught me. I counted my breaths and imagined myself standing in a field of rainbow flowers. I tried to see the unicorns grazing in the distance, tried to see the little capes of fur on their hooves, tried to imagine myself walking over to pet them.

"*You got a surprise underneath those skinny jeans, don't cha, Jeff?*"

Their voices found me even in my safe space. And try as I might, I couldn't keep his voice out either. Or his face. His laughter.

You fucking asshole, to laugh at me, at the things they said, and then you bring this picture here... you bastard!

I leaped off my bed and screamed as loud as I could, the primal howl echoing in my ears long after I had finished. I wanted to scream again, to punch the reflection of myself in the mirror hanging on my closet door, but I heard footsteps flying up the stairs. I looked at my door just as it gashed open.

"MADDIE! What's wrong?" my dad yelled, bursting into the room and grabbing me by the shoulders.

"What do you mean what's wrong? What *isn't* wrong? Everything about my life is wrong!" I retorted, shrugging off his hands and taking a step backward.

"Talk to me. What's going on?" He put his hands on his hips.

"What's going on? You saw the picture. Don't you understand? That's not me. He drew that before he knew what I was. He doesn't see me like that now," I said before looking down and whispering, "because I won't be a girl in his eyes anymore."

I staggered back onto my bed, collapsing in a sobbing heap. The years of trapped hurt burst forth and my skin felt like a barrier for the emotion that was desperately trying to escape. It kept building and building, and I wailed into my pillow, unable to escape the torrent. I could feel my dad's arms wrap around me. I wanted to push him away but I didn't have the strength to fight anymore. He held me while I poured out what seemed like an infinite reservoir of pain.

When you feel hopeless but you don't care, it's not that bad. I mean, it's awful but it's a numb kind of awful. When you feel hopeless but you *still* care, that's hell. Every agonizing moment that passes with nothing changing feels like your heart is going to burst. And then when it doesn't, you start to wish that it would because you don't know how much more you can take.

That was me on my bed. What had started as anger and sadness about a rough day at school morphed into a full-blown dysphoric meltdown.

The drawing was made by a boy. A boy who liked a girl. Except that the girl in his mind wasn't trans. She was just another girl. Why couldn't I just be that girl in the drawing? Why did I have to be me?

I groaned and squeezed my pillow as hard as I could. I snatched breaths between shuddering, wondering if it would ever let up.

When it eventually subsided, my dad slowly let go and sat up next to me. I could hear the soft rustle of paper. I sniffled loudly and propped myself up on my pillows. I grabbed a tissue from the box on my nightstand and wiped my eyes until they were clear enough to see him.

His eyes were gentle and warm when he looked at me. I felt guilty for always wanting to push him away but sometimes it hurt so hard to listen to all that positive crap he would try to tell me. Sometimes I just wanted to deal with my pain for what it was. But this time, I was grateful he was there. I didn't want to think about how it would have ended had he not been there.

He reached out and held my hand.

"Kellan knew about you when he brought the picture, Maddie. He knew you were trans and yet he still brought it. I'm not saying that means he's ready to waltz in and ask you out on a date, but it does mean something. He told me that he wanted to share his art that he kept secret from everyone else because he was inspired by your courage."

I furrowed. "If he thinks that keeping his art secret from his friends is the same as being transgender, he's a bigger ass—"

"No, I don't think he meant that at all," Dad interrupted with a small laugh. "I think he wanted to connect with you. He made a mistake and he felt awful. He probably felt peer pressure to participate. And that doesn't wipe away his behavior or responsibility... but at least he owned it. Who else thought to show up here today? The other kids probably didn't even think twice about you. Kellan did. That says something to me. I hope it says something to you."

I looked down at our hands. Dad had a point, but I didn't want to see it. If I saw it, I'd have to acknowledge that Kellan might not be a jerk. And if I thought he wasn't a jerk, then I'd have to consider talking to him. And if I wanted to talk to him but he didn't really want to talk to me anymore because I was trans... then I'd be in a deeper hole than I am now.

Dad reached out and tucked my hair behind my ear. "Be patient. Allow things to unfold a little before you judge everything. You don't have to be so hard on yourself. The world has come a long way, but it has a lot further to go. You're helping to push the boundaries of what is and isn't accepted. I am so proud of your courageousness to choose to walk into that school as your authentic self. I don't know if I could do that in your shoes. I mean it. You're strong beyond your years, kiddo."

I looked into his eyes, desperate to feel the words and not just hear them. But I didn't feel anything. I was numb to the core after emptying everything I had into that pillow.

"Thanks, Dad." He gave me another hug before walking to the door.

"Are you going to be okay? Do you want me to take the drawing?"

I bit my lip and shook my head. "No, leave it. I'm good. I'm going to get a shower and shake off the rest of this and head to bed early."

"Okay. I love you. Always. If you want to talk, you know where I live."

Against my better judgment of humor, I laughed a little. He was so corny sometimes that his jokes somehow became funny. I took a minute to gather myself after he left, and then stored Kellan's drawing underneath my bed. I still wanted to get rid of it but something told me I would regret it.

I grabbed my pajamas and went into the bathroom. This part of my day was always treacherous. If I could avoid looking at the alien's reflection in the mirror, I would be okay. Tonight, of all nights, I needed to make it into the shower unscathed.

I stripped and turned the water to near full-hot. There were few things I loved more in life than a long, relaxing shower, but it also made me feel bad. Using all that water and energy just to sit there for an extra ten minutes made me feel like an eco-fraud, like I shouldn't be constantly blowing up my socials with climate change facts if I was going to lounge in the shower forever.

But sometimes I needed that extra time. Sometimes it was the difference between being okay and being crushed. The water wrapped me in a warm embrace that was healing. I liked to close my eyes and imagine myself in a grotto behind a waterfall, with my mysterious stranger who would take me in his arms and hold me.

I almost made it past my enemy. I opened the shower curtain, dipping my foot in the running water to see if it was too hot, and then stepped in. As I was closing the curtain, my naked body taunted me in the mirror. I stopped for a few seconds, staring, and then slammed the curtain shut. I collapsed into a fetal position on the floor and started crying again, the tears mixing with the water and streaking toward the drain.

I could feel the stubble on my legs, but I didn't trust myself with a razor tonight. All I could do was let the water surround me like a blanket.

Go to your safe place, I told myself. *He's there. He'll hold you until you feel better.*

Pushing all my thoughts away, I closed my eyes and focused on the sexy stranger in my imagination. Sometimes it felt silly to imagine him, but other times, like tonight, it felt like a lifeline. No one else in the world understood me like he did. And he didn't have to say a word. All he had to do was hold me.

I looked at my phone when I got out of the shower and was embarrassed to discover that it lasted for over 20 minutes. I'd have to make it up by buying carbon offsets with my last paycheck from the café. I had planned to upgrade my mic for streaming but that would have to wait.

I tiptoed back to bed, careful not to make any noise. I didn't want to talk to Charlotte again. Nothing against her but I finally felt calm. All I wanted to do was climb in bed, put the covers over my head, and forget that I had to go to school again in the morning.

I grabbed Mark's pillow and carried it to bed. I snuggled it against my chest and closed my eyes. Within minutes, I was fast asleep.

Chapter 12
Kellan

"There he is! Look at him!" Big Rude squealed. I turned and saw Maddie at her locker. I felt a clutching in my chest and wheeled toward Big Rude.

"Dude, what is your problem? Just leave her alone. She doesn't need our shit," I said, glancing in her direction. Her hand was frozen on a book on the top shelf of her locker. It had been over a week since I stopped by her house to apologize, and I hadn't seen her much in the hallways. When I had seen the football team huddling near her as I entered the building with Tyrell, I practically sprinted over to make sure they weren't harassing her.

"What do you mean she? He's a guy," he said, the humor remaining in his voice.

"She's transgender, man. Just respect her space and let her be. She isn't hurting anybody and it's none of our business." A second glance at Maddie confirmed that she heard every word. She hadn't moved.

He folded his arms over his chest and leaned backward. "Why are you sticking up for her? What's in it for you?" he asked with a shit-eating grin.

I shook my head. "It's not about me. Or you. She's a human being, Paul," I said, jarring him a little with his real name. I doubt anyone had called him Paul since 6th grade. "How would you feel if we all made fun of you because you ate twice as much as the rest of us?"

I must have scratched past the surface because he traded the smile for a scowl.

"What the fuck is going on with you today, dude? Kate didn't come over this morning and help you rise and shine?"

"I don't hang out with her anymore. Someone I met over the summer made me realize that she wasn't my type. But I'm serious about making fun of her. That ends. Now. We're better than that." I took a step forward, getting in his face.

"Man… I don't know what's got into you. This isn't the Kellan I know. I don't need this, I'm outta here," he said and stomped off.

Maddie was still a statue at her locker. I glanced at a few of my other teammates who had watched our interaction. I nodded at them and made my way toward my first-period class.

It felt like there was a magnetic charge trying to pull me back toward Maddie as I walked away. I resisted. It didn't feel like the right time, and I still didn't know what exactly I wanted with her.

But I'm not sure that even mattered because it was crystal clear what she wanted from me—nothing. The two times I had seen her in the hallway since the first day of school felt more like a hallucination than reality. I could understand why she was avoiding me. I had obviously crushed on her over the summer, and she must have assumed my feelings evaporated on the first day of school when I found out about her. Well, she'd be wrong.

It wasn't as easy to her let go as I first thought it would be. After being devastated that she wasn't really a girl, I thought that it might actually work in my favor. I didn't need to fall in love right now. I had two seasons of football left to cement my recruiting status. I would blast out of this town and never come back, headed to USC to become a star, no longer having to watch my mom slowly killing herself each morning. I didn't need to fall in love with somebody and be distracted.

When I reached the door to my class, I paused and leaned against the wall, closing my eyes. I couldn't lie to myself. I was totally distracted. I had been working around the clock on my manga book project. Maddie was still the main character, but I reworked the plot to include her as transgender.

Evil aliens had twisted the minds of the students at North Rock Canyon High, making them fear and hate trans people. Maddie, with her ability to wrap a protective bubble around herself while skating, used her psychokinetic powers to fling the aliens into submission... while wearing skimpy outfits.

So, it was super cheesy, but it was fun drawing her eyes full of fury as she ollied over their little green bodies. I hoped that she would appreciate it if I ever showed it to her.

Every night I had marathon drawing sessions until I couldn't keep my head up. Then I would lay in bed and beat myself hollow trying to find the answer to the most important question of all: do you still want her even though you know she's trans?

Two months ago, the answer would have been easy. Nope, no thank you. But now that Maddie had wrapped herself around my heart with no plans to leave, the answer wasn't so clear at all.

It was easy to look at her and say yes. It was easy to draw her and say yes. It was easy to think about hanging out in my room, talking about nothing but feeling like it was everything, and say yes. It was even easy to think about kissing her, about running my thumb across her bottom lip before sucking it between mine.

Yes.

The answer would slip away when I thought about her naked. Would she really look like a boy? I had to force myself to imagine this because it was so foreign to what I had built up in my mind all summer. Then, it was always her small frame straddling me, the lava lamp illuminating half her body, her hair falling on my chest as my hands reached up her sides to caress her face.

"Hey, Kel. I was looking for you." I felt a finger lightly poking me in the chest and my eyes popped open.

"Jazz, you startled me," I said, nervously laughing.

"You did look a little lost in your thoughts there. I just wanted to tell you that I volunteered as the equipment manager for today's game. I'll be on the bus with you boys." Her mischievous smile twinkled in her eyes. "Sit next to me in the back, 'kay?"

I felt an instant stirring in my jeans that I wished weren't there. I remembered Kate saying that Jasmine had a thing for me, but I had forgotten all about it. If it wasn't for Maddie, I'd be on cloud nine with this little interaction. As it stood, I knew I'd be scrambling later for a way out.

"Okay, sounds good. Hey, we better get to class. Last thing I need is for Hammler to come and slam the door on us and have detention next week. Coach would kill me," I said, heading for my seat in the back of the classroom.

Yep, I was definitely distracted. There was no doubt about it. The second game of the season, a time when I should be locked into football, and it was the furthest thing from my mind.

I looked at the scoreboard. Fourth quarter, a little less than one minute to go. We were down by five. I felt like it was my fault. Here we were, 90 minutes away from home, with scouts in the stands, the only sounds to hear were blowing whistles and hollering coaches, the only sights sweaty guys in football pads... you would think it would be easy to focus, right?

Nope. I thought of Maddie. I wondered what she was doing. I fantasized about getting home late and seeing her sitting in the little chair next to my front door. For all I cared, she could just stay sitting right there, and I'd sit at her feet, talking to her all night until the sun rose.

"Bruh, I think I can get this kid to bite. I've been setting this up all game. Quick pump fake and then airmail me a sweet little present and we'll unwrap it together in the end zone."

Shake it off, Kellan. Focus and let's go.

"I got you. Let's huddle with Baker real quick and get on the same page."

We took the field after talking with Coach and I lined up the team. I took the snap, shuffled three steps backward, and pump-faked to Tyrell. He had cut toward the sidelines and the defender bit perfectly. Had I thrown the pass, it would have likely been intercepted and returned for a touchdown. Instead, I reset and arced a high looping pass to a wide-open Ty, who caught it easily and hustled to the endzone.

He was beside himself on the sidelines. He kept shoving me and I kept trying to dance away.

"Took you long enough to wake up, bruh."

"What do you mean? We've played good all night," I said, a furrow creeping into my smile.

"You know exactly what I mean. I know you're thinking about that bus ride home with Jasmine. That's alright, I feel you. At least you were the Kellan I knew for the final play. Maybe show up a little earlier next time, huh?"

I shook my head. "Whatever, dude. We won. We beat the best team we're going to play until the final game of the year. We just got to execute from here on out."

The locker room was jubilant, guys high-fiving and talking about their weekend plans. I felt like I was watching a movie; I could smile and laugh but I wasn't really in the room with them. I was happy as if it was their accomplishment, not mine. I could care less that we won or that scouts had seen me throw the game-winning touchdown pass. There was only one thing I remotely cared about winning and she might as well have been in another universe.

I slid into a pair of sweatpants and an old t-shirt and quietly slipped out of the visitor's locker room. I stepped onto what I thought was an empty bus and headed for the back.

Jasmine was already waiting for me on the last bench. *Shit! I forgot about this. How do I get out of this?*

I fumbled through my directory of ready-made excuses to get rid of girls and came up empty. I usually started pushing girls away *after* we had spent time together, not before. It was far easier to come up with something when I had grown tired of them. It didn't make sense to my body why I would want to walk away from Jasmine when we hadn't even kissed yet.

I forced myself to acknowledge her beauty before I said no. She had straight, shorter hair that hung like parentheses around her cheeks. She had amazingly full lips, amber eyes, and a body that even baggy clothes couldn't conceal. But she wasn't wearing baggy clothes tonight. She was wearing a short skirt and a tank top that exposed a row of hard abs, which I found wonderful on a girl.

"Hi," she said, scooting toward the window and patting the seat next to her.

"Hey," I said, sitting down. She huddled tightly with me, wrapping our arms together.

"I can't wait until everybody is on the bus. I just want to get moving so we can have our own little space back here," she whispered into my ear.

As she squeezed my arm, the competition began between wanting to get lost in this meltiness and battling against it with the incessant mantra, "She's not Maddie." There was no concealing my racing heartbeat, and I was afraid that Jasmine would notice.

I tried to breathe as my teammates slowly trickled to their seats. Ty took one look at us, gave me a thumbs-up, and grinned. I wanted to burst down the aisle and force the door open.

I remained in place, my breath catching as Jasmine's hand slid across my chest, reaching my face and tilting it toward her. I could see the bus moving through the reflection of the parking lot in her eyes.

"Slouch down with me. You're so tall," she giggled, the strawberry smell of her hair erasing my thoughts temporarily.

I slid lower and closed my eyes, imagining Maddie. I allowed myself to feel that it was her face that was coming closer to mine. I allowed it to be her lips that were soon fighting mine open and gently nibbling before straying to my neck. It was Maddie's hand that slid below my waistband and grabbed me. And it was Maddie stroking me as the bus turned on the highway, the whine of the accelerating engine concealing my soft moaning.

Yes, Maddie, please touch me. I don't care what you are. I want you. Only you.

It was Maddie who whispered sometime later, "You need a ride home tonight?"

It was Maddie's ear that heard me breathlessly answer, "Yes."

It was *not* Maddie's car that I climbed into in the school parking lot. The hazy make-believe of the bus was all but gone as Jasmine raced us toward my house. I vaguely remembered that she knew where I lived because of a few parties I had last year. I would have choked on my words if she needed directions.

I fought the chains squeezing my heart, trying desperately to let go and enjoy the night. Jasmine was a beautiful girl with a great personality—a combination I'd yet to find. She was a huge improvement after the toxicity of Kate. She had always been so sweet whenever we talked. So, why couldn't I enjoy this? Why was I fighting so hard when Maddie wanted nothing to do with me?

Because you're in love with her.

I shot upright in the passenger seat and swallowed hard. Jasmine looked at me sideways for a moment, her eyes still glazed over from the bus. I shot a quick smile at her, barely registering her presence as I swam in this new realization.

I'm... in love? This is what that feels like?

The flicker of a warm glow washed across my heart, beginning to grow into a roaring fire as I became Maddie's boyfriend in my imagination. The fire blazed as we held hands and went on cute dates to cafés and the arcades. I wondered if she liked to eat popcorn at the movies, or if she closed her eyes when she listened to her favorite music like I did, and then I almost laughed out loud.

Did falling in love make you think of the silliest things? Why was it suddenly so important that I know the most irrelevant details about her?

Because nothing about her is irrelevant.

The raging inferno was about to consume me as I thought about her in the dim light of my bedroom. I could see a passing car's headlights illuminate her body for the briefest of seconds and then Jasmine grabbed my hand. The flames vanished in a puff of smoke as I looked over at her eager smile and was plunged back into terror.

We pulled up to my house and I didn't see a way out. If I told her that I didn't want this, what would she think? What would anybody she told think? How could I ever face her again? But I had no idea how I could go through the motions. There was no part of my heart left unclaimed and I had nothing to give anyone else.

I unlocked the door and let Jasmine in first, locking it behind me. When I turned around, my back screamed as I was shoved against the door. She quickly tugged my pants down and started pulling up my shirt, motioning for me to raise my arms.

"I've wanted to do this for so long. You were so busy wasting your time with that white trash. You have no idea what you've missed."

I felt myself involuntarily grow again as she kissed slowly down my stomach. When her chin tapped against me, she giggled.

I've had a handful of moments in my life where it felt like I was standing at a fork in the road. A choice point that would bring irreparable consequences regardless of the path chosen. Last year, it was an older guy from the local college football team that I occasionally trained with. He invited me to a party and offered me cocaine. Even though a hot college girl was smiling and egging me on to try it, I walked out. I knew it was bad news. I knew if I got hooked on that crap, I'd blow my chance to leave this town. I never trained with that guy again.

This moment felt like that. While there was nothing wrong with Jasmine, I didn't want her. And if she wasn't what I wanted, I had no business letting her do this to me.

I closed my eyes and saw Maddie's face as I felt Jasmine's lips on me. I gently pushed her away and stepped to the side.

"I... I can't do this," I said, hiding my face in my hands.

"What's wrong? Did I do something wrong?" She sounded so hurt and I felt like I wanted to cry. I hated that she would likely feel rejected but I had no choice. I had to tell her the truth.

"I'm... in love... with somebody else. I'm sorry. I was confused and honestly didn't realize it until a few moments ago. I don't want to do this and hurt you later."

She stood and stepped back, her eyes narrowed.

"You mean we felt each other up the whole way back from the game, you bring me all the way here, and *now* you tell me?"

I realized my pants were still around my ankles, so I awkwardly pulled them up.

"Yeah, I know. I'm sorry. I didn't know until—"

"So, me touching you made you realize that you're in love with somebody else. Wow, Kellan. I can't believe this! You know, that bitch was right about you. You're a selfish dick." She grabbed her keys off the floor and stormed out.

I expected to feel a massive sense of guilt about letting Jasmine down or even embarrassment about choosing a girl who didn't like me back. But I didn't. I felt relieved, my path cleared to pursue Maddie because I had done the right thing. She didn't even want to speak to me, and yet I cared enough not to betray her. She'd never know about this moment, but I would. And for the first time in my life, that mattered to me.

I decided that I'd worry tomorrow about the fact that she'd probably never talk to me. I welcomed being Maddie's boyfriend back into my mind, enjoying the scenes again as I made my way slowly to my bedroom and closed the door. I grabbed my drawings and flopped across my bed. I cycled slowly through them, stopping when I got to my favorite.

Maddie was wearing only a long t-shirt that came down to her upper thighs. Both of her hands were grabbing her hair and her head was tilted slightly to one side. Her tongue was sticking out. I traced the outline of her legs slowly with my finger.

I chose you tonight, Maddie. I wonder if that would mean anything to you. I know what you are, and still, I chose you. I don't know what it is that you hate so much about me... but I wish you'd talk to me. Will you ever give me a chance?

I sat the pictures down and curled into a ball. Hours or minutes later—I couldn't tell which—I drifted off to sleep, conscious of nothing in the world but her.

Chapter 13
Maddie

I never thought I'd be one of those kids that looked forward to Friday afternoon and the end of the school week. I was the nerd who enjoyed getting lost in the thick weeds of an old poem, trying to figure out the author's intent. I craved learning how to define and declare string variable types in computer science. I yearned to connect the dots between climate change and human activity in earth science class.

Yet here it was, Friday afternoon, and I was one of those people. Celebrating the end of another school week. In my defense, I didn't think most kids experienced the phenomenon of hearing whispers and giggles everywhere they went.

I stepped onto my bus and sat down with a huff next to Charlotte in our usual spot, second bench, right side, close to the door. I didn't want to take a chance on sitting any further back. Not yet.

"Well, you look cheerful. How was your day?" Charlotte quipped.

I slid my backpack between my legs and grimaced. "Peachy. Kellan Davis is still playing savior. I've managed to mostly avoid him the past week, but unfortunately, I left a book in my locker on the first day of school. I brought one of those sapphic romances from Siera Maley when I was naïve enough to think I'd have time to read. When I went to grab it, there he was."

"Oh, no! What happened?" she said, turning toward me. I told her how the kid everyone called Big Rude verbally bullied me and Kellan got on his case. Charlotte looked nonplussed.

"Soooo, the problem is…?" She kept shaking her head slightly with her eyebrows arched and I wanted to smack her.

"I don't need some guy to help me. I'm fine on my own." I stared out the front of the bus window as we started to move.

Charlotte leaned back and pretended to massage a nonexistent beard. "Ahh, I see. The independent girl. Born under the sign of The Warrior." She mimed the gaze of a fierce champion and I cracked up.

"How much Skyrim have you been playing? You're supposed to be the beautiful blonde that sits and twirls her hair and sends pictures she shouldn't to boys," I said as we shared a laugh.

"Besides," I continued, "if I were to be born under a sign, it should have been The Shadow. Each day I would be able to cast a spell and be invisible for 60 seconds. That's long enough to hustle to my locker and get out of there before anybody has a chance to make fun of me."

"Heh, that's funny." Charlotte whacked my arm with the back of her hand. "My character right now is a Khajit, born under The Shadow. And hey, who says I have to sit and twirl my hair and send bikini pics to guys just because I look the part? Who made these rules? What if I just want to sit in my sweatpants and play modded Skyrim?"

I looked at her conspiratorially. "Yeah, you're right. Down with the man! Anarchists, are you with me!?" I thrust rock fingers skyward and Charlotte swatted my arm, giggling.

We sat quietly for a few minutes, and I idly watched each kid get off at their stop. I wondered if they were happy, or confused and miserable like me. Probably the latter, I decided, as I watched one girl walk toward her house, the slouch clearly visible even from twenty feet away.

Charlotte mercifully interrupted my thoughts as they reached the very dangerous "will *I* ever be happy?" territory. I should probably keep her around more.

"Hey, do you mind if I borrow that book?" she asked with a hint of shyness.

"Hmm? Oh, the one from the locker? Sure, here," I said, leaning down and rifling through my pack until I found it. "Trying to connect with me by reading queer romance?" I joked, bumping my shoulder with hers.

"Ego much? No, I need a good read. I'm dry. And how would reading a sapphic romance help me connect with you?"

She had a point. The thought of me being with a girl was a no-go and Charlotte knew that about me since forever. "Okay, okay. Don't blame me when you ugly cry though. *Colorblind* is not for lightweights!"

She tucked the book between her arms and smiled. I looked past her and saw that we had reached our bus stop. I grabbed my pack and stomped back into the heat. I wouldn't be staying in it any longer than necessary. At this time of day, the neighborhood started to smell like a rotten diaper. The town trash service came on Friday, and they were always running late.

"So, what are you up to this weekend? Any good parties I should be aware of?"

I snorted. "Funny. Tonight, I'll be streaming, and then Destiny is coming over tomorrow and staying forever. The plan is to forget that Mondays even are a thing and pretend that the weekend is all that will ever exist. You?"

"I'll be ugly crying in the bathtub, remember?" she said, tapping me with the book.

"That's right. You know, I'm not sure if any two people have ever had more exciting weekend plans. I don't want to push it, but if we want to live extraordinarily dangerously, we can all walk to the café tomorrow and get hopped up on sugary drinks." I made a swooping motion with my arm like someone's goofy dad. Charlotte took a step back, her palms facing me.

"Whoa, this is getting too much for me. I think I'll just start with a bubble bath and take things from there."

I laughed. "Have fun. FYI, I'll be streaming soon. Knock before you enter if you need my wisdom or grace for any reason."

Charlotte huffed as she opened the front door. "God, Maddie, we really do need to work on your ego."

"Nah. It's cute on me."

"Only me and UberHappy left. We started with 20 people on the server, and within an hour, just two left. This is a brutal hide-or-hunt tonight. I've never won a hide-or-hunt. We've gotta win this one. Let's find his base and knock him out!"

It had been two weeks since I'd been on Twitch. During the summer, I streamed at least four nights a week. I'd missed it. I'd missed my community. Tonight, I had over a hundred people watching me play the Minecraft minigame "hide-or-hunt" and chat was blowing up.

> *JustAnotherHappyFace:* "Hey, I'm new here. Can anybody tell me what Hide-or-Hunt is? Looks fun! uwu."

I quickly read the chat feed on a monitor to my right before looking back to the TV. I'd arrived at a narrow space between two cliffs, and I parkoured over a treacherous drop of at least one hundred blocks. With a Cheshire grin on my face, I stalked toward the corner of the map where I thought UberHappy's base was.

I couldn't stop and answer questions in that intense moment. I knew one of my mods would respond. If I lost my focus and Uber got the jump on me, I'd be screwed. I'd played with him before—he was formidable at 1v1 combat and I wouldn't be able to make up the lost damage.

ToryisCute05: "@JustAnotherHappyFace Hi! Welcome to Maddie's channel. So, Hide-or-Hunt is basically a Minecraft game where there are borders around a set portion of the world, and you have to make a secret base with a beacon, you know those things that shoot lights way up into the sky? Well, anyway, you place that somewhere, preferably hidden, and if another player finds it and mines it, you're out. It's also where you spawn when another player kills you."

I heard the telltale dinging sound that notifies me that someone had chatted. I halfway wished I had turned it off today because it was almost nonstop.

I didn't have time to catch all of Tory's reply to the newcomer, but I trusted that she'd covered it. Tory was my first follower and had been my main moderator since I started streaming a couple of years ago. I hated when I said that Destiny was my best friend because while I'd never met Tory in person, we'd been super tight online since the beginning. She was waiting for me the second I went live tonight.

ToryisCute05: "Maddie!!! OMG! I was so worried. No tweets, no Discord, no streaming… giving me a heart attack girl!!!"

I was glad that I was already wearing blush because if I hadn't, it would have been obvious how embarrassed I felt for ditching my friends and fans the past two weeks.

"Yeah… I'm sorry, guys. I had a very rough return to school. Turns out not everyone accepts me for who I am… not like you guys do. I should have been streaming this week… but I was depressed. It was all I could do to make it to my bed after school." I shrugged and put my hands out at my sides.

ToryisCute05: "Aww, I'm sorry to hear that! We've got your back! You're awesome and amazing. Just keep being you! People will come around. The more we stand for trans-rights, the more this bigotry will fade."

"Thanks, Tory. You're the best. You know, I'm just so grateful to be back. When I got a message from Kingfisher earlier this week asking me about a round of hide-or-hunt, it was like a relief. I needed somebody to prod me back on here. The last thing I need is to get rusty before the big tournament next weekend. And, of course… I'm always interested in embarrassing a bunch of boys. Let's goooo!"

I shifted in my chair and reminded myself for the 15th time to breathe and focus on the game. I was so overwhelmed by the support of my community that I doubted I'd be able to sleep that night. I had forgotten that there were decent people in the world.

I swung my sword toward the terrain ahead, pointing. "We've seen Uber come from this direction several times. I feel like his base HAS to be somewhere back here." My eyes scanned rapidly, trying to spot any obvious disturbances in the world.

Players trying to hide their base would go to great lengths to clean up after themselves, making it look as if the terrain had been untouched in the area around their base. As the game wore on, however, it became harder and harder to conceal your position.

If you were killed, you'd respawn at your base. You had to quickly craft the items you needed and get out of there before someone spotted your nametag and discovered your position. It could be dangerous to stick around for too long. You had to weigh your options carefully.

My hope was that Uber had gotten sloppy and left himself vulnerable in the endgame.

I forced myself to take yet another deep breath, the tension choking my airways. My heart felt like a blast beat from a metal song as I spied a suspicious piece of cobblestone underwater, at the bottom of a small lake, where normal stone texture should be. The presence of cobblestone here made it very likely that I was about to find a secret base. I shot up out of my seat excitedly and then quickly realized this was a good way to get killed. I slammed back down in the chair and made my way closer.

I hit F5 on the keyboard to do a quick monologue for the YouTube video I'd post later. My avatar with the name "MakeThisBelievable" appeared. I had a custom skin that made her look like a Viking shieldmaiden.

"Well, well, well… it looks like we've found something interesting. We've passed through here before and I don't remember seeing that,"—I clicked F5 again to return to normal view—"piece of cobblestone at the bottom of this lake. Perhaps when we killed Uber five minutes ago, he didn't have time to patch this up properly? Hmm. Pretty sus if you ask me. Let's investigate!"

I jumped into the water and swam to the bottom, doing the best I could to keep a careful eye out for Uber. There was no sign of him when I reached the bottom, so I switched to my pickaxe and quickly mined the cobblestone block. My butt came out of the chair when I saw a small base, with a furnace, two chests, and Uber's beacon in the corner. My hand was visibly shaking on the mouse as I rushed toward the beacon.

"Oh my God! It's Uber's base! Let's go!" I mined the beacon like my life depended on it and screamed when the game said that I was the winner. I bounced around my room, making rock fingers, headbanging, and generally losing my mind for a solid 15 seconds before collapsing back in my gaming chair in a pile of laughter.

"I bet they didn't expect to lose to a teenage girl at a game I've barely played. Sucks to be them!" I flipped my hair back and tried to play it off cool, but I was far too hyper. I hadn't felt this good since I was back at the café with Mark.

The chat went absolutely mental, as one of my favorite regulars and fellow teenage streamer from the UK would say, DavidinWales. He gifted me $5 in bits and I felt like crying.

> *DavidinWales:* "GGs! Good job, Maddie. You deserved a win after everything you've been through."

"Aww, David! Thanks, you didn't have to do that! Awwww! You make me feel so special! Thanks for both the $5 and the GGs. What are you doing up though, isn't it like, I don't know, 3 or 4 in the morning in Cardiff? I hope you didn't stay up for me!"

> *DavidinWales:* "I wouldn't miss one of your streams for the world, Maddie. It's good to have you back and see you happy. It's worth only getting three or four hours of sleep just to see you smile, tbh."

I read his comment and blushed. I'd watched his streams and he was super cute. Whenever he flirted with me, I always felt validated as a girl.

"Aww, David, you're a sweetheart! That means so much to me. I hope I get to catch you tomorrow. Good luck with your tournament! I'll be rooting for you." I made a heart and blew him a kiss. I smiled so hard that it hurt. I think my cheek muscles must have atrophied since school started.

"Thanks for stopping by, everybody. I'm super hungry... I don't feel like I've eaten in like a week. It's been so stressful lately. I think I'm going to head off for the night. This has been AWESOME! You guys are the best. I'll try to get on again at some point this weekend. I want to get some more practice in before the big Minecraft tournament next weekend, but I'd like to get back to our late-night Lenora's Mask rando stuff, too. I had a blast with that over the summer... well, anyway, have a good night, everyone, see ya guys soon! This is Maddie, signing out." I blew everyone a kiss and closed the stream.

The loneliness was as instantaneous as the flick of a light switch. I went from being in a large room with all my friends to being alone in my bedroom, only the sound of the whirling computer fans keeping the deafening roar of silence at bay.

Deflated, I stared at the blank computer monitors and TV in front of me. Before I could dwell too much on it, I stood up and stretched. It would do no good to sit here and sulk after having such a great night.

It's okay. I have friends. I'm not all alone. I need to remember that.

I turned to leave my room in search of food but stopped when I saw Kellan's manga portrait poking out from underneath my bed. *Why haven't I ripped you to shreds yet?*

I wondered what Destiny would think if she saw it. No, I knew what she'd think. She'd tell me I was being stupid for not hanging out with him. She didn't know him though.

I looked closer at the picture. I felt the stabbing pain rise out of seemingly nowhere, capturing my senses and playing its own game of hide-or-hunt with my heart, threatening to mine it into a thousand pieces.

Damn it! I just wanted to keep the good vibes from the stream. Well, you know what? I am. Screw you, Kellan, and screw all your friends.

I took the picture and shoved it under my bed. We'd have a date later—me, the picture, and a lighter. I didn't need this constant reminder of what I couldn't have. There would be other boys who would like me and do things for me. I didn't need Kellan's drawing magically appearing when I was teetering on the edge of sanity, waiting to push me into the abyss.

I sauntered out toward the kitchen, pushing away the nagging question of why I didn't shred it. I reminded myself that Destiny would be here tomorrow, and it was time to get back to the life I had before school started. No more Kellan, no more drama. Just the computer science program, Destiny, and the skate park.

Chapter 14
Kellan

I wasn't ready for Monday morning. If I slept at all over the weekend, I wasn't aware of it. I dodged texts from Tyrell asking what happened with Jasmine, but that didn't keep him away for long. I heard a car door slam late Saturday afternoon, and when I peeked out the living room window, it was Ty coming up the sidewalk. I hid out of sight until he finally left.

I didn't want to deal with any of that. It was disappointing that Jasmine had immediately run to our friends and talked about what happened. I would have thought she would be embarrassed to have been rejected, especially given what she was about to do to me. Now I'd be on the hook to explain why I didn't sleep with her, and just who exactly I was in love with.

The only bright spot about the morning was that my mom didn't work the previous night, so she was still asleep. I'd be able to prepare for the day without a bunch of unnecessary bullshit.

I grabbed my phone and connected it to the Bluetooth speaker in the kitchen. I made a cup of coffee and then scrolled through the songs I had downloaded, selecting "Beach House — Space Song," and then relaxed on the couch, enjoying the first glimmering rays of sun filtering into the living room. I quickly got lost watching the odd patterns of light and shadow dancing on the carpet. The house plants hanging in the windows created abstract shapes that seemed to match the soundscape coming from the speakers. I thought that it was neat how eerily calm I felt, even though I was faced with impending doom. But I guess without uncertainty, what was there to fear?

I sagged into the couch cushions, closing my eyes and releasing myself into the sonic bliss that was Beach House. "Space Song" felt like it belonged to me and Maddie, the lyrics perfectly encapsulating my feelings for her.

"Who will dry your eyes when it falls apart?"

I had listened to this song on loop all weekend, and each time I heard it, I fell more in love with her. She was so alone, and she must be so scared every second she was in school. She could never be certain what was going to happen. *How does she live like that? How is she so incredibly brave?*

I took my final gulp of coffee as my phone was ringing. It was Tyrell.

"Hey, man, what's up?" I said as if nothing had happened over the weekend.

"Dude, what's going on? You ignored me all weekend. Are you okay? Once I know that you're okay, I want you to know how fucking pissed I am that you didn't return my texts."

I chuckled. "Yeah, I'm okay. And yeah, I saw the texts. I've had a rough weekend, man. Since everybody blew up my phone, I guess you heard what happened Friday night."

"Yeah, man, that's not cool of her. She ought to know better than to kiss and tell. But it sounded like from what we heard, you threw her out of the house and told her you were in love with somebody else."

I let the line go quiet for a few seconds before responding. I didn't really want to go there just yet with Tyrell. I still clung to my "no distractions" motto for football season, even though I knew that ship had sailed.

"You picking me up this morning?" I finally asked.

He snorted. "Yeah, alright. I got you. But I want some answers, bruh. If I'm going to have your back, I need to know what's going on."

That sounded fair to me. I couldn't expect Tyrell to cover for me blindly. I'd have to give him something. "Alright, I'll tell you when you get here. Let me hop off and get some food real quick and then I'll meet you at my mailbox."

I hung up with him and started feeling the panic expanding in my chest. What, exactly, was I going to tell him? Because we didn't lie to each other. We might lie to our parents, to girls, to our coach, to our other friends even... but we never lied to each other. That's not the type of relationship we had. It would be less painful to jump onto a bed of nails than lie to him.

But I'd have to be strategic with the truth. I would have to find a way to tell him what was going on while leaving myself enough personal space to figure out how I was going to pursue Maddie. He didn't need to know directly about her yet.

I gobbled down a couple of protein bars and emptied a glass of water before grabbing my backpack and heading out. Tyrell was already waiting for me.

He turned the music off when I got in the car. For him to turn the music off, he must have been desperate for answers.

"Alright, bruh. We ain't moving until I know the identity of this girl that was worth ditching Jazz for. Spill it or walk."

I sighed, looking down the street in the direction of her house. "So, I met her at The Resca over the summer. I had never seen her before. How did we miss someone our age? You and I have swept this place for years and we missed her. She's the hottest girl I've ever seen. I talked with her dozens of times, and I just fell for her."

He nodded, a slight smile creasing his face. "So, why didn't you tell me about her? Actually, hold up. Let's get real. Why haven't I seen you with her if you've known her for that long? You just keeping her to yourself in your bedroom?"

That's not that far from the truth, Ty, but not in the way you think.

I looked out the passenger window at my house. We still hadn't moved. I didn't mind the interrogation so much—it felt good to talk about her to someone else. But the sadness that I felt about the next answer I had to give made me want to run back to my bedroom, throw the covers over my head, and die. The crackling of the leather seat as I shifted my weight reminded me just how quiet it was in the car.

"She's not interested in me."

"What?! You're joking, right?" he erupted, and I didn't have to look at him to know his eyes would be as big as the hole his mouth would be making.

"Nope," I shook my head, "Not even a little interested. In fact, I think she hates my guts." I turned back toward him. "Funny, huh? All these girls the past few years and the first one I fall for doesn't give a shit about me."

Tyrell sat back in his seat and smacked the steering wheel lightly. "Well, I guess I'm not the only one being shut down right now. Makes me feel a little bit better about myself."

I blinked and then remembered the Chinese foreign exchange student he'd been after. "Oh, Mei Ling isn't interested in you?"

"Oh, nah, that's going good. That's a slow burn. I got that. No, I was talking about Jessica. She just broke up with her boyfriend from South Rock Canyon last week and I was trying to cheer her up Saturday night. She wasn't ready for that." He grinned broadly.

"Ty..." I started and then shook my head laughing. "Alright, bruh, let's get to school before we're late." I put my hand out for a quick fist bump before bracing myself for his Gran Turismo impression.

When we got to school, I avoided Jasmine's eyes and headed for my locker. I didn't really need anything there, but it gave me an excuse to not have to go near her just yet. I couldn't avoid her forever, but if there were points for trying, I'd be earning them.

I glanced down the opposite side of the hallway, away from Jasmine and the football team, and saw Maddie headed for her locker. She was wearing the little red bow in her hair that I remembered from the café, and for a second, the hallway and all the other kids in it disappeared. She was nodding her head rapidly and I assumed she had earbuds in.

That's probably for the best. I don't want you to hear what any of these idiots say about you.

Before she could make it to her locker, a group of younger guys blocked her way. I dropped my stuff in my locker quickly and hustled toward them.

I watched her trying to step around them but they kept blocking her path. I felt like I was back in my dream, where I was running in what felt like invisible molasses trying to get to her.

"I just want one kiss, that's all. I want to know what it feels like to be kissed by a freak," I heard one of the boys say. I was about to jump into the fray when Maddie threw the books she was holding at the kid's face. They smacked into him and then fell in a big spread. I finally reached the kid just as his arm reared back to punch her. I grabbed it and yanked him around to face me. He doppler shifted from smug to piss-in-your-pants scared in less than a second. I didn't recognize him, so he must have been a freshman. I pulled him toward me by his shirt collar.

"Don't you ever bother her again. Don't look at her, don't speak to her, don't even move when you see her. You understand?" I wondered what my face looked like. I wished later that someone had taken a picture. I had never felt so certain as I did at that moment that what I was doing was the right thing.

The kid trembled and nodded his head vigorously. I let him go and he chased after his friends who had already fled. I looked at Maddie, who wouldn't make eye contact with me. I bent to the ground and picked up her books carefully. I noticed one of the books was her journal that I had seen her with at the café, and I made a show of closing it as soon as I noticed it, burying it between her schoolbooks.

I handed the books to her and felt her hand brush mine. I wish I hadn't felt that. My brain grabbed the sensation and it seared into my mind, begging for more. I walked away before I could ruin the moment with words. I needed to go back to my locker, but I wanted what just happened between us to sink in. I wanted her to have no place to run in her mind. I defended her and she'd have to acknowledge that.

I wandered the halls after the other students had gone to their classes. I knew I'd eventually run into the school cop when she went on her rounds or some other teacher and have to explain myself.

I stopped short. *Where were the adults that should be protecting Maddie? Where was the school cop? She should have been there or at least close by. They have to know that she's here... why aren't they keeping an eye on things?*

I spun around and headed for the front office. The principal needed to hear about this. That kid would have cleaned Maddie's clock if I wasn't there. Sure, he would have suffered the consequences after the fact, but that wouldn't have stopped Maddie from getting hurt and being further humiliated.

And from bruising her angelic face.

I balled my fists as I seethed, thinking how this school was letting her down. They were going to be held accountable. They were going to do something to make sure this didn't happen again.

I stormed toward the office, holding the sensation of her skin against mine to steel my resolve.

"Kellan, what a pleasant surprise this morning. Although, I hope you're not cutting class to talk to me," Dr. Walker said with a smile that I wasn't convinced was real. I knew I was in the lion's den, and I had to watch my every word and movement, or she'd pounce.

Dr. Walker was Tyler's mom. Tyler was the other starting wide receiver on the football team, opposite Tyrell. He was a decent enough guy, but his mom was a notorious ballbuster. When you were around her, she treated you as if you were her kid. Which I guess made sense as she probably thought of every kid in school as hers for the seven or so hours we were there every day.

"I'm not purposefully cutting class, ma'am. I was involved in stopping a bullying incident this morning." That brought a solid crease across Dr. Walker's brow. The crease looked like it easily slid into place after many years of practice. She leaned forward and tapped her fingers against her imposing old desk.

"Where did this incident take place?"

"In the hallway, just outside the cafeteria. This girl, her name is Maddie…" I paused for the briefest of moments, noticing Dr. Walker's eye roll. I wanted to punch her but stifled it.

"Umm, yeah, anyway, Maddie was trying to reach her locker when a group of freshmen boys kept blocking her. They weren't letting her get through and one of them looked as if he was about to strike her when I grabbed him and told them to get lost."

Dr. Walker leaned back, the annoyance evident as she pressed her lips together and then blew out a burst of air.

"I knew this was going to be a nuisance this year. Are you aware that the girl involved, Maddie, is transgender?"

"Yes. I found out the first day of school," I said.

"What do you make of that?" she asked, looking at me through narrowed eyes. I wondered where she was going with this.

"I'm sorry, I don't think I understand the question."

What do I make of it? What is there to make of it? It's who she is.

"I mean, how do you feel about that? We didn't have this when I was younger. It seems like your generation has embraced these wild ideas of gender fluidity, being born in the wrong body, and all sorts of other such nonsense. And now we're supposed to devote all our resources to protecting these kids who *choose* these lifestyles. It just makes everything so much harder on the administration."

I was frozen in my chair, shocked at what I was hearing. This was supposed to be a neutral authority figure, there to keep the peace and enforce the rules of the school… which, by the anti-bullying propaganda posted in every hallway, seemed to mean protecting kids like Maddie. If they weren't willing to do that, why were they even there?

I wanted to take my arm and swipe everything off her desk but restrained myself. I ground my shoes into the carpet, squeezing some of my frustration out before I spoke.

"I didn't know anything about this kind of stuff before Maddie. But I don't think that's really important to what happened to her today. No one deserves to be bullied. It isn't for us to accept or reject her—can't others just leave her alone if they disagree? Does she deserve to get bullied because she's transgender?"

I had intended the question to be rhetorical. In most cases, a question of this nature would be rhetorical, with an obvious answer. With Dr. Walker, I let it hang in the air, genuinely curious about her response.

She adopted her slight smile, the painted-on variety of a greasy politician who tells you they're going to do something about an issue that you care about and then does the exact opposite when no one is paying attention.

"Okay, Kellan. We'll make sure someone is stationed in the hallway at all times between classes. I'm not sure why someone wasn't there this morning, but I'll see that it's fixed. Is there anything else I can help you with?" she said, and stood up, indicating that our meeting was over.

I wasn't finished. Remaining seated, I said, "That's it? That's all we can do for her? Who is to say where she is going to get bullied? Or that someone will actually be there watching?"

Dr. Walker adjusted the front of her suit coat, her smile fading as she sat back down. "What else would you have me do Kellan? Oh, that's right, I forgot that you're the one with 20 years of secondary education administrative experience." Her eyes pierced into mine.

I blushed but I wasn't going to be deterred. "I don't know... but something more should be done. Maybe call an assembly and discourage bullying? Threaten severe consequences? I don't know, I just don't want to see her or anyone else get hurt."

She nodded slowly, getting a faraway look in her eyes that scared the hell out of me. "Hmm, I think you might be onto something. Yes, perhaps it would be wise to listen to you. An assembly could be just the thing we need to put an end to this before it becomes something larger."

My head snapped back. "What? Really? You're actually going to listen to me?"

That smile that made me want to take a shower was back again. "Yes, really. Except, I'm not going to be the one speaking at it. You are."

"Wait... what? *Me*? Why me?" I glanced around the room, suddenly feeling trapped.

"Because you had the brilliant idea. I think your peers will listen to you more than they'll listen to me. You're the captain of the football team and one of the most popular kids in school. You have influence and credibility. I'll give you ten minutes to make your case. Don't threaten anything you don't have the power to deliver on. Use this opportunity to defuse the situation. If you can help keep extra paperwork off this desk, I'd be ever so grateful."

"Maddie isn't extra paperwork," I said, abruptly standing.

"That will be all, Kellan, thank you. Meet me in the cafeteria in 20 minutes."

I paced in the little backroom just off the stage. I could hear the steady roar of the entire student body clustered on the other side of the thin wall. Everyone loved an impromptu assembly. It got you out of class and broke up the routine of the day.

Dr. Walker nodded to me, and we walked out on the stage together. She said a few words and then told the school I had a message to deliver, handing me the microphone and stepping aside.

For my part, I had spent the past 20 minutes racking my brain. I had no idea what I was going to say. I had walked into the principal's trap and had no way of escaping. This was going to be off-the-cuff. All I could do was hope that I didn't sound as nervous as I felt.

"Uh, hey, guys. I spoke with the principal this morning because I saw a student getting bullied pretty hard. If I wasn't there, it would have gotten out of hand. I don't think this is right. I think we're better than this at NRCH and I want to do anything I can to put an end to it." Straight to the point. Not bad, but not great. I could do better.

I paused for a few seconds, considering my next words, and I heard someone from the back shout, "We love you,

Kellan!" and half the room laughed. I smiled a little and then waved them off.

"Guys, this is serious. She doesn't deserve this—I mean, no one deserves to be bullied, you know? If you see it, report it. As we all know from the millions of posters strewn across the school, we have a zero-tolerance policy for bullying. One strike and you're out. We've all seen what happens on the news when bullying goes unchecked. We don't want that to happen here. We're all in this together. We don't have to be friends with each other, but we can at least leave each other alone, okay? Just leave her alone."

The second time I slipped and said, "her," brought a look of confusion to some of the faces I saw in the crowd. Students began looking around at each other, wondering who I could be talking about.

I cringed, watching as the general direction of their glances started to move toward the back-right corner of the room. I strained my eyes to see who they were looking at, fearing the worst. I was right.

Her face locked in my vision and I could tell she was pissed. I started to bring the microphone up to my mouth to speak again but she shot up and bolted for the exit before I had the chance.

I threw the microphone down, turning to Dr. Walker and saying, "Let me talk to her, I can handle this," then I sprinted after her. The only sound I heard was the pounding of my shoes against the concrete floor as I hurried out of the room.

I saw her throwing her body at the big steel doors leading to the parking lot. I put my head down and gave it all I had, making the doors in three seconds flat.

I lowered my shoulder and bashed it into one of the doors, blasting it open with a loud bang. She turned back toward me, thrust her arms into the sky, and screamed.

Chapter 15
Maddie

I was running as fast as I could. I had to get out of here. That idiot literally had every kid in the school looking directly at me.

I heard a loud bang behind me, and I spun around. I saw the broad shoulders and brown eyes and hell flew into me.

Of course, it's Kellan, who else would it be? I clenched my fists toward the sky and screamed.

"Are you okay?" he asked, slowing his pace and walking up to me, his hands in front of his chest, trying to motion for me to calm down.

Don't you dare try to control me! You're nothing to me!

"Who the HELL made *YOU* my protector?" I said as I began pacing in a small circle, holding his eyes in mine.

"I don't know, I—"

"You have no right!" I thrust my finger up at his face. "Why did you do this? Why are you bringing even more attention to me?"

He stared disbelievingly at me, making the same face as when he found out I was trans. I wanted to kick him in the balls so hard, he'd never be able to walk again.

"Were you there this morning? Those guys were being aggressive. There were six of them, Maddie. Six. I don't know what they were after, but the one guy was getting ready to punch you after you tossed your books at him. They weren't going to let you get away without a fight. If I wasn't there—"

"If you weren't there, I would have slit their throats and danced in their blood."

He blinked and looked at me incredulously, the faintest hint of his lips curving. "Are you always so morbid and intense?"

I stopped pacing and pursed my lips to blow a stray piece of hair away from my mouth. When it fell back, I shrugged and looked sideways at Kellan.

"I don't know, maybe? Why do you care?"

"I don't know, Maddie. I just do. Look, I'm sorry if I hurt your feelings. I'm trying to help you. You're going to get hurt if someone doesn't put an end to this. I don't know why everyone is threatened by you, but they are. I mean, it's not like you don't see this stuff on TV or the internet—"

"This stuff? *This stuff?* This is my life, Kellan! I—"

"I know, I know. I'm sorry, I didn't mean it like that. I just meant it shouldn't be surprising for people when someone comes to school... looking like you. And a person being different than normal shouldn't be a reason to start laughing every time they walk by. You're just being you. And I'm just trying to help you. Don't you see that?"

I sighed and looked down. I watched him out of the corner of my eye. I saw him relax and take a few steps toward me. There was a tugging on my heart to let go, to let him in, but I needed to put an end to this before I gave in to that temptation. I was not willing to get my heart broken when he came to his senses and decided to reject me. It was time to make this crystal clear so that he'd finally leave me alone.

"How many girlfriends have you had, Kellan?" I crossed my arms together and cocked my hip.

"*What?*" Kellan jerked back as if he'd been shot. Of all the questions he could have expected, this was probably nowhere near the top of the list. He looked perplexed. Can't say I wasn't enjoying it.

"Actually... none." He shifted his weight from side to side. I hated to admit it but I liked making him nervous.

I closed my eyes for a moment and laughed. "No, that's... not quite what I meant. I meant... how many girls have you *been* with?"

"Oh... umm... I don't really know." He blushed and looked down.

"Exactly. It's been one after the other. I haven't been to this school in almost a year and even I know that."

Kellan's gaze was fixed on his shoes. I felt bad, just like I did at the café weeks ago when I thought I was putting an end to this. I appreciated what he did for me at school, I really did. But if he was doing this because he thought he was interested in me, I was going to save us both the inevitable heartache.

"Kellan, this is what has happened. You saw me over the summer. You thought I was something different than what I am. You thought I was the new girl on the block, someone you hadn't met. I wasn't your normal type, but I intrigued you. I was something unique, something not usually on your menu. You got curious and you wanted to try it, to try me. I became your next target."

I paused and brushed back my hair. The wind had picked up, blowing small bits of sand around that stung me in the eyes. I tried to smile even though what I had to say next ripped me apart.

"The really insulting thing is… the part of all this that hurt the most all summer… was realizing that if I had all the attributes of your other girlfriends, and we… hung out and stuff… I'd last for what, three months? Max? Probably a lot less, and then you would have moved on without thinking twice. Go ahead and deny it."

He finally took his eyes off the ground and looked at me like a puppy dog who had just been beaten by his beloved owner. I had the sudden urge to kiss him, but that would be the worst mixed signal to send. I kept my face tight, the emotion locked behind it.

"I'm not like those other girls, Kellan. I'm not interested in being used. You would have broken my heart. I would have just been the next in line. And that really hurts.

But I don't even have what you're looking for anyway. And you know that. So... thanks for helping me. Thanks for standing up for me. I know you think you're doing the right thing. I respect that. But now you can let it go. I'm not what you want... and, Kellan?"

I was terrified that my voice was going to break because I was about to lie to him. But I had to do this. I had to protect myself in the long run. He was going to eventually move on, and I didn't want to be around when he did.

I looked deep into his eyes, hoping he couldn't see through them, to the little girl that was crying inside for him to hold her, to tell her that she didn't have to worry about protecting herself.

The sun was at his back, his muscular body rigid and tensed toward what must have felt like a firing squad. I took a deep breath and squeezed the trigger with a whisper.

"You're definitely not what I want."

I held his eyes for another moment and then slowly turned and began walking away from him, a small part of me dying with each step.

"Wait! Don't!" he shouted at my back, and I could hear the agony in his voice. I stopped but didn't dare turn around. I couldn't. I didn't want him to see me crying.

"Don't what?" I choked out.

"I don't know... just don't walk away. I don't want this to end."

I started walking.

"It never began."

Chapter 16
Kellan

I crawled through the rest of the day. The only thing in the world I truly cared about had told me we were nothing… where did that leave me?

I'll tell you where. Hiding in a bathroom stall, feeling like a piano had fallen on my head, asking myself the same question over and over again.

What is so awful and scary about me that I can't even be your friend?

I had no answer.

I managed to drag myself to practice that night, though all I wanted to do was go home. Ty pulled me aside before we took the field, stopping by the massive old pine that we looped around during our warmup jog. He looked more serious than usual and I braced, afraid he was going to question why I was sticking up for Maddie.

"Good speech today, bruh. I like how you took up for her. Some of the guys were ribbing you at lunch, but I had your back. There aren't too many black people in this town, and I know how it feels to be an outsider sometimes. It could have been me they were making fun of," he said. We clasped and shared a quick bro hug. I was relieved to be wrong. He was just being a good friend.

"Ty, I pity the idiot who decides to make fun of you. I've seen you one time in action. Remember that kid at the basketball court downtown who called you the n-word? That dude's eye was *still* purple two weeks later when he apologized." We both shared a hearty laugh, and I didn't think I'd ever loved him more than at that moment. I needed him to have my back today. I didn't want to feel any more alone than I already did.

"Hey, man, thanks for standing up for me," I said, tapping his arm with the back of my hand. "I just want to see peace in the hallways. Let people be who they are. I'm not trying to change the world, just don't want anybody to get hurt."

He nodded and started bouncing up and down, his nervous energy always getting the best of him. "I always got your back, bruh. By the way, I saw the first 15 plays for Friday. It's a bromance for me and you. No less than eight plays where I get the ball. Coach must know something about their secondary. I smell the endzone and it smells reallll good. This could be a big game for us. Pad our stats out. Let's lock in and get this." He faked like he was going to punch me in the groin, and then took off in a sprint across the field.

Practice was the soothing balm that I needed. I felt sharper than I had since football season began. When I would think about Maddie, my heart would throw up a flare, reminding me that I'd eventually have to leave this field and deal with those feelings, but I kept pushing them away.

When practice was over, and I was alone in the locker room, Maddie returned full force. I gave in to the feelings, not caring if I rolled off the bench and died right there on the cold floor.

I closed my eyes and saw the sad smile she gave me as she told me I wasn't what she wanted. Her eyes were narrowed from the sun, her freckles almost translucent.

I would do anything to see that again. But I'm not going to, am I, Maddie?

I stood up and grabbed my bag. Ty was probably waiting for me, bass booming so loud, they heard it in Phoenix. When I emerged into the athletic parking lot, I gasped. Hugh Martin was leaning against the back of his Volvo, looking toward the sunset.

Oh no, what does he want? Is he going to chew me out? I wonder what Maddie told him.

He flashed me a friendly wave when he saw me, and I nervously walked toward him.

"Hi, Kellan. I heard about the assembly today. I wanted to talk to you. Mind if I give you a ride home?"

I hesitated for a second, unsure whether I wanted to get into a car with a man I barely knew. I shook that feeling off quickly, realizing that anyone who supported their kid as much as Hugh did would have to be a decent guy.

"Sure. Let me say something to my friend who usually gives me a ride." I walked toward the loudest bass I could hear and easily found Tyrell's car. I opened the door and shouted in.

"Hey! I've got another ride. I'm good, man, I'll see you tomorrow." I watched him turn down the radio with a sly smirk.

"Hold on, bruh. Don't tell me. Which hot little babe are we talking about? You make up with Jasmine?"

I laughed. "Actually, it's not like that. Maddie, the girl I called the assembly for... well, I guess her father heard about it and wants to talk. Probably just wants to thank me for taking up for his daughter. They don't live too far from me, so it's cool."

Tyrell frowned but nodded. "Okay, bruh. I'll see you tomorrow then. Come find me on Call of Duty later if you get bored."

I stepped back from his car just in time to save my foot from being run over. *Jesus, Ty, you're going to hurt somebody with your driving someday if you don't start being more careful!*

When I got into Hugh's car, I immediately smelled Maddie and almost fainted from bliss. It was that same amazing cinnamon cookie scent that I picked up on when she brushed past me in her yard on the way to slamming the door in my face. I let myself savor it for as long as I could.

I glanced over at Hugh when I felt the car backing up. He didn't seem angry, which was good because I didn't think I could have handled another lecture.

"You can put that seat back, Kellan. The last person in here was Maddie and, well, obviously you're a tad larger than her." He chuckled. I'm grateful that he started with a joke. I needed it.

"So, I take it you've heard about all the fun we've been having here at NRCH today?" I asked, keeping the tone light.

Hugh glanced at me for a second while making a right turn. There was humor in his eyes, but I could tell he was also seriously concerned by his furrowed brow.

"I got a phone call from the principal around lunchtime just as Maddie was waltzing in through the front door. She wanted to know if I had seen her, that she might have run off the school grounds. When I confronted her, I heard that you held an assembly about bullying and that she took it personally. She said you embarrassed her in front of the entire school, and she felt like she was suffocating and had to get out of there."

"Did she say what happened after she ran out of the school?" I looked expectantly at Hugh.

He frowned. "No, she didn't. That was all I was told before her bedroom door was slammed in my face. You know how that goes." *Yes*, I wanted to say, *I know exactly how it feels to be shut out of Maddie's world. It's like having your heart sucked out and blended up in front of you while you take your last breath.*

"I didn't push her," Hugh continued. "I know better than to push her in the heat of the moment. So, what actually happened?"

I shifted uncomfortably in the seat, my big frame squashed between Maddie's dad and the passenger door like a sardine in a can.

For a second, I considered how much to tell him, and then I said screw it and told him everything. There was no sense hiding anything from him. I could only help Maddie so much—her dad would be able to go directly to the school and push for change. I summed up our interaction in the parking lot, stopping just before the part where Maddie told me I wasn't what she wanted.

"Frankly, I'm scared to death for her. Those kids were willing to fight. And for what? What the HELL is wrong with them?" I realized I was getting worked up and took a breath. "I'm sorry, it's just hard to see it. It's hard to understand it. She's just… being."

I bumped my head on the side of the car as Hugh navigated a sharp turn. I rubbed it and tried to get comfortable again.

"You know what she told me in the parking lot?" I said, and then almost facepalmed. *Why are you going to tell him this? It's her dad, for Christ's sake.*

"No, I don't. What did she say?" he asked, looking concerned. I knew at this point I had to go through with it. I swallowed and looked out the passenger window.

"She said I wasn't what she wanted. I'm not going to lie, that about crushed me. That was the worst moment of my life. I keep asking myself why it hurts so much… but it just does. I'm so confused about everything. I was never confused and then I met Maddie. Now everything is complicated, and I feel like my head is a bag of cats."

I screamed at myself to shut up but was unable to. I was on a roll downhill and figured if I was going to find the bottom, I might as well make the crash spectacular.

"And, you know, it's not only that I'm confused about my feelings toward her... but I'm confused about who I am, who I'm becoming. All I know is I want to protect her. I've never felt so strongly about anything in my life. Not even about football. I feel like there's everybody else and then there's Maddie. And nothing compares to her anymore. I love the way that feels... but I don't understand it in the least bit."

I waited, my breath held for Hugh to say something, anything. I didn't care if it was to ask me about my grades. When he didn't respond, I pulled my foot out of my mouth and spoke again, figuring at this point I had nothing left to lose.

"Please say something because I'm just digging myself into a deeper and deeper hole, telling a girl's father everything I feel about her." I nervously laughed as I looked at him out of the sides of my eyes.

We were close to my house, and I was feeling beyond embarrassed that I'd talked the entire time. But it was so effortless to unload to Hugh. *Is this what it's like to have a real father?*

We pulled up in front of my house and I belatedly realized that he must have known where we lived. I only knew where Maddie lived because she got on the bus after me in the mornings when I used to ride it.

I sat still in the seat, waiting for him to respond. He steepled his fingers beneath his chin, lost in thought. He finally cleared his throat and looked at me.

"You have a genuine interest in her. I appreciate that as her father. If she liked you back, would you pursue her? Would you want to be her boyfriend?" he asked me, his kind eyes unflinching.

I looked away. I knew it was a valid question for him to ask. He probably didn't want his daughter to get hurt and wanted to know my intentions. As I pondered how to respond to that, I noticed a few kids playing basketball further down the street. Nostalgia washed over me for a past that had slipped away.

A past where I ran off the bus at the end of the day and only worried about hanging out with Ty and my other friends. All we had to do was play basketball and dream about which girls we wanted to kiss. Life was getting complicated fast. My mom's drinking, college and scouts, and now falling in love.

Is this what growing up feels like? Is this what self-discovery feels like? No, thanks. I'll take my childhood back.

But that sentiment wasn't entirely true. It was painful at times, yes, but what I felt for Maddie was what I yearned to experience back then. Then I hit puberty and thought everything was about sex, but obviously I was dead wrong. It was easy to get, so I got blinded by it. But what I was really searching for was a connection... for love. And now that I had fallen in love, it wasn't a feeling I ever wanted to give up, even if it wasn't reciprocated.

I sank my head to my chest, aware that Hugh was still waiting patiently for my answer. I took a deep breath and answered him... but maybe even more importantly, I answered myself. I needed my own answer to the question that I'd wrestled with over the past few weeks. I could feel the answer soaring up from within me and erupting in a burst of joy.

"Yeah. Absolutely. There's nobody like her. And I don't mean the transgender part. I mean *her*, you know? Just her. There's something beneath that armor. She hasn't let me in, so I can't be certain, but I can feel it. There's something about her that makes it worth trying in spite of all the rejection. I can't give up. I won't. She's... everything to me. So, yeah, I'd pursue her to be her boyfriend if she was into me... because even though she isn't, that's what I'm already doing.

"And that part about her being transgender?" I could feel the hot tears flowing from my eyes, but I didn't try to hide them. I didn't care. My soul was open wide for the first time in the presence of another human being. I felt safe in this space. Her dad had been there for Maddie when just about any other parent would have told her that she was deluded, that no way was their son going to act like a girl.

But Hugh didn't do that. He supported her when she was honest about who she was, and I trusted he would support me for the same reasons. I was going to reach in all the way and rip out the answer I'd been hiding from myself.

"I don't care that she's transgender. I'm completely fine with that. I accept her 100%." I smiled, the tears having gone from fat drops to a river. The sun caught in my eyes and blurred my vision. That was okay because all I could see was Maddie.

"She's a girl, period... and she's breathtakingly gorgeous," I whispered almost reverently.

I finished and let out a big breath. I had expected to crumble but I felt lighter than air. The glow that enraptured me from within burst forth into laughter and I wiped my eyes and looked at Hugh.

"I'm sorry, I've just asked myself that question over and over again, and I guess it took someone else asking me to get clear."

Hugh smiled and placed his hand on my arm.

"You don't have anything to be sorry about, Kellan. Thanks for being honest with me, and more importantly, yourself. Maddie doesn't have an easy road ahead, and as her father, I try to smooth the road out as much as I can for her."

I shook my head. "No, she doesn't have it easy, that's for sure. And whatever I feel inside... and whatever she feels about me... she doesn't have to like me. She can hate my guts.

That's fine. I mean, it's not fine, but… I don't know, I just want her to be safe, to have a chance to experience life like the rest of us. You know, I half expect her to just not show up one day. To stop trying. But I hope she doesn't. I love seeing her…" I trailed off and looked down at my hands.

Hugh released my arm and shifted in his seat. "I keep waiting for her to come to me each night and say, 'I just want to go back to online school.' But I hope she doesn't, either. She wants to be there to take the computer science program to prepare for college. She wants to be a video game designer. Did you know that?"

"No," I said, my eyes widening. "I didn't know that. That's really cool. I hope she makes it. It would be so cool to play a game she made one day."

I looked at Hugh and he smiled at me like I always wished my dad would when I was a little kid. It was a proud and happy smile.

"Kellan, you're one of the best things that has ever happened to Maddie. I know she's being hard on you right now. She's scared, and she doesn't understand why anyone would want to help her. I understand if you eventually stop trying, but I'm rooting for you. I'd love to see you two as friends. The way you just described what happened at school today, and your feelings toward her… I know you genuinely care. And that's all any father can ask for. Thanks for telling me your side of the story. I didn't really believe what Maddie said about you."

I threw my head back and bumped it against the ceiling, laughing.

"Oh, man… I can't even imagine what she said. I'm not sure I want to know."

Hugh laughed for the first time in our entire conversation and the rest of the tension in my body melted. I had gone into this ride expecting Jack Davis, with a thorough chewing out. This guy really was different.

"No, you don't want to know. But that's just her frustration right now. She deals with it by trying to be a badass. She tries to project a big attitude to protect herself. But underneath all of that is a fragile, sensitive girl."

The tears sprang back to my eyes. "I desperately want to know that girl." I realized that I said that out loud and blushed.

I watched Hugh take out a scrap piece of paper from a side compartment on the driver's side door. He wrote down a name and handed it to me.

"Listen, Maddie streams on Twitch. You know, the video game streaming website? Her name is 'MakeThisBelievable.' She's going to be on a lot this weekend. If you want to see the real Maddie, away from the armor and the hardened persona, check her out on there."

He could have handed me a billion-dollar check and I wouldn't have been as happy as I was in that moment. "I will, thank you! And thanks for the ride. I'm sorry that she's had another bad day. I hope it gets better for her."

"Me too, Kellan. Keep trying with her. I think you can make progress if you just hang in there. Take care and good luck with your football season. I'll talk to the principal and get on to the school to make it safer for her. She deserves better. Thanks for trying to do their job."

I nodded once and exited the car. I had so many conflicting emotions swirling inside that I didn't know where to start unpacking everything. But I thought all that could wait. I ran inside my house, plopped in front of my computer, and signed up for Twitch. I couldn't really think of a cool name so I just went with MangaGuy06. I would be ready to catch her the next time she streamed.

I reveled in the thought that I would get to see her smile... *really* smile, not just some sad smile that I glimpsed before she cut me in half with her words.

I leaned back in my computer chair and daydreamed of those lips. And then I grabbed my pencil and started drawing.

Chapter 17
Maddie

"So, we know West Time Town is dead. That's a big hint. Eliminates a lot of checks."

After an uneventful rest of the week, I was back on stream with my favorite game: The Legend of Esmerelda: Lenora's Mask. I was playing a randomized version of the game, with all the stuff you need to beat it shuffled throughout Revalda.

I felt cute enough tonight to wear my cosplay outfit of the main character, Lane. It was just a little green tunic that probably didn't cover enough of my legs and basically a hat that looked like Santa's but in green. I had little felt boots to go with it, but nobody could really see that on stream.

The chat was a little slow tonight, with only 30 or so viewers. People chimed in here and there as we found more pieces of the puzzle, but most were in lurk mode, content to sit back and enjoy quietly. That was fine with me.

A quick check of my inventory told me that I'd found enough items to beat Wide Bay Dungeon, so I made my way in that direction. I heard the chat ding and checked it.

MangaGuy06: "Hi, I'm new here. Are those elf ears that you're wearing?"

I swung my sword at a giant dinosaur-looking creature and rushed to collect the gems that his death left behind.

"Hi, Manga. Welcome to my stream! So, these ears are Rylian ears, which are like the humans in The Legend of Esmerelda. I like to play this game in cosplay as Lane, the main character. Are you familiar with the Esmerelda games at all?"

> *MangaGuy06:* "Omg, duh. I'm silly. I was 11 when Cry of the Wild came out and I played that game almost non-stop for three months. I should have known what those ears were. They look really cute on you, and I guess I just wasn't thinking straight."

I hustled my character through a mostly empty green field with a smattering of trees and stone pillars spread throughout. At the time the game was made, my dad was still a cool skater kid in college, and my mom was living up in Sedona, waking up every morning to chant Om at the sun. So, this game was freaking ancient. The overworld was probably considered awesome when it came out, but compared to today's games, it was pretty empty.

I heard the chat ding and checked it.

"Yes, exactly! I was 11 when Cry came out, too. I love that game, but I prefer the older Esmerelda's. Especially Lenora's Mask. We play that a lot here. I hope you enjoy it!"

I always liked having a new follower stop in and chat. Almost every stream brought in at least one new person. My stream was still up and coming, and although I had gained a lot of followers since I started playing in more competitive Minecraft tournaments, I was nowhere near the big leagues. I tried not to get too excited, but I thought if I could just get big enough in the next couple of years, maybe I could make this my full-time job.

I scratched the tip of my nose as I wondered about MangaGuy06. It was the internet, so you could never be sure, but it seemed like he was my age. He said I was cute and liked manga. I started to imagine what he looked like. I'd love to meet a guy in real life who was attractive and shared similar interests.

> *MangaGuy06*: "I've never seen it. It looks like a lot of fun. And not to be a complete idiot, but what exactly is a randomizer? I'm sorry, I don't play many video games."

> *ToryisCute05*: "@MangaGuy06 A randomizer takes the original game but shuffles all the important items around, and sometimes other things, like dungeon entrances, so that each time you play, it's like a new experience."

I read the chat and jumped in.

"Yeah, it's like Tory said. You could also think of it like an always shifting puzzle, where you have to put the pieces together in a different way each time you play, but the end result is the same. So, I have to run around opening chests and do other things that might lead to items, trying to get what I need to beat the game.

"Most of the items are randomized, and the first things I find early on sort of dictate where I can go next. It sounds like it would be linear, but it's actually not. A lot of times, the choices you can make are quite varied... it's fun to try to read the seed and determine what it wants you to do. But the main object of the game remains the same—save Time Town from the moon that is somehow small enough to only crash on it and not anywhere else." I made a sarcastic eye roll and giggled.

> *MangaGuy06*: "That's cool. I bet it took a long time to learn the game enough to be able to complete it with everything randomized."

I read his reply and wondered if he was impressed.

"Oh, man... it took ages to be able to complete one of these fast enough to stream in one sitting. I was in online school last year and had more time on my hands. I spent just about every waking moment for three months deep-diving this game. At the end of that period, I was good enough to beat normal seeds in less than four hours ... oh, by the way, a seed is what each randomized game file is called. So, if I say I 'rolled a seed,' I mean that I used the randomizer program for Lenora's Mask to make an individual game file that has randomized the game based on the chosen settings.

"But yeah, I'm not able to race against other people yet, but I'm improving. We're down to about three hours for a regular seed. And it's fun! I like doing this and being able to relax and chat. My normal streaming is competitive Minecraft PvP stuff. It's harder to talk to you guys when I'm doing that. With this, we can chat more. And I love talking to you guys!"

I made a heart and blew a kiss at the camera.

"So, how did you find my stream, Manga?" I asked, always fascinated by how the algorithms on Twitch work. If he didn't know how video game randomizers worked, why would Twitch suggest me? Was he an LGBTQ kid, too? Or maybe he liked Minecraft.

> *MangaGuy06*: "I'm new on Twitch and this channel
> just happened to be recommended to me."

Huh, that's interesting.

"Oh, cool. I love how Twitch recommends channels to people. It's always so random. This channel is definitely not manga content but I doubt they take your screen name into account when they give recommendations." I laughed.

> *MangaGuy06:* "Yeah, lol. This is great, though. I'm
> glad I found it. I see your tentative schedule on
> Discord. Looks like you've got some big Minecraft
> stuff going on tomorrow?"

I finished solving a puzzle in Wide Bay Dungeon to reach a chest that had the possibility of containing an important item. I opened it to find a whole lot of nothing, just a small amount of money. I groaned and continued forward.

I heard the ding and glanced over at the chat.

I threw my head back in an exaggerated nod. "Oh, yeah. Pretty big tournament tomorrow. Each month, a group of streamers gets together for a bunch of minigames. I've been paired with a good team this month. I think we have a chance of winning. There are no prizes or anything, but it gets competitive. It's a chance to show your skills off to a wider audience and hopefully attract them to your Twitch and YouTube pages. And you get to network with more experienced streamers which can lead to other Minecraft stuff, like SMP servers. I will have officially made it the day I get to network with GeminiTay."

DavidinWales: "Someday, Maddie here is going to have thousands of people watching her streams and millions of subscribers on YouTube. We better enjoy chatting with her while we can!"

I tilted my head with a narrowed eyed smile. "Aww, David, I'll always have time for you guys. That's so sweet! Not going to lie though, it would be super awesome to be a professional streamer. I mean, be able to play video games and skate for a living? Pshhh yeah! I'm in!"

I finished off the boss in the dungeon with a flourish but groaned again when no useful item dropped. "Well, Wide Bay was absolute garbage. That's just gross, game. But it was required, so at least it's out of the way."

MangaGuy06: "So, you said you were in online school earlier. What happened with that? Just wanted to go to regular school?"

I read Manga's reply and I smiled. Most of my followers only talked about the game or wanted to talk about trans rights and stuff like that… which is totally cool! I liked discussing those things. But not many people outside my core group of regulars, like Tory and David, ever asked questions about me. Not that I wanted creepy internet people asking me personal questions, but Manga seemed cool and genuinely interested.

"Online school was okay. I met some kids in a local non-traditional schooling group that I wouldn't have otherwise, including my BFF. And since I had no friends before that, it was a huge plus. But I wanted to take the computer science program at my local public school. I figured it would help me prepare for college. I'd like to be a video game designer if my streaming and skating don't work out."

> *MangaGuy06*: "That's awesome @ video game designer… as a public-school kid myself, I can see how getting to do something different would be a nice change of pace. There are so many classes that I have to sit through that I know will make zero difference in my life, except for the horrible grades that weigh down my GPA lol."
>
> *MangaGuy06*: "So, how are you making out thus far? Are you enjoying it?"

Now I know he definitely hadn't seen the tags below my stream. I paused the game and looked off into space.

"Well, I used to go to this school until the middle of 10th grade. I skipped out over Christmas break for personal reasons and returned for my junior year. And no, I can't say that I am enjoying it. It's been shit for the first two weeks, to say the least. Most of my fans know this... but since you're new, you might not realize something about me. I'm a transgender girl," I said, my voice trailing off and breaking a little. I don't want this to matter to him, or to anyone else for that matter. He saw me as pretty and I wanted him to stay.

Even though I didn't know Manga, I felt like I did when I saw Kellan for the first time in the café. The initial warmth and joy followed by the feeling that I was at the top of a rollercoaster, getting ready to rocket downward. It was eerie. I didn't think I really cared if someone didn't find me attractive because I'm trans—I could live with that. But once I started talking to them, I didn't want everything to be going well and then BOOM! 'Oh, didn't know you were trans, goodbye!' It had happened before while streaming. Thank God I had good mods because I got trolled at least once a month. One of the perks of being queer, I guess!

"So, yeah... you probably see the little tags beneath my stream title, but in case you didn't, yep, I'm trans. I've always been that way, but I've recently chosen to start presenting as female, you know, as me. And I thought maybe I'd slide under the radar at school... but I was recognized almost immediately... and that didn't work out too well."

Waiting for his response felt like being trapped under the ice, unable to breathe, having to feel my way along, praying that there would be a hole to surface through. I hadn't been in that situation before, but I read about it. It sucked, and obviously must feel like this.

> *MangaGuy06*: "No, I couldn't tell. And I didn't see the tags, but I do now. I got lost in the cosplay and how beautiful you are that I didn't notice the rest of it. ;) Being transgender doesn't change the fact that you are still attractive to me! But I'm guessing others at your new school have a different opinion?"

I breathed again. I went from being trapped under ice to standing in a spring meadow with little flowers spread across a carpet of grass, my toes curling into the warm earth.

"Aww, thanks, Manga. That's sweet of you. I feel like I need to hear that right now." I sighed and sagged back into my seat. I knew that like 30 other people were possibly watching and listening, but I felt alone with him, and for some reason, I felt like going deeper.

"Yeah... that's what these first two weeks have been all about. I don't really get it. How do I threaten anybody? I don't see why people feel the need to make fun of me or physically assault me. It's not like I'm doing anything to them. You'd think they'd just have a laugh and then move on. But I've been threatened with all kinds of violence. Sometimes I feel like I've walked into some B-rate horror movie, where everyone is holding up a crucifix when I walk by. It's weird. It's like my life is some kind of a political statement to everyone else...

but to me... it's just... my life, you know? Why does anybody care?"

> *ToryisCute05*: "People 101: Most of them are dicks.
> Aafghfsh I could smack someone for threatening
> you though!"
>
> *MangaGuy06*: "Do you have any friends there?
> Anyone to stand up with you, to try to help you? It
> sounds a little scary. Are you okay?"

I laughed at Tory's comment. "Yeah, people can be crap sometimes... and no, Manga, I don't have any friends at school yet. I should reach out to the LGBTQ club, but I just haven't. But you know what's funny? There has been one person trying to take up for me. And that one person just happens to be the freaking quarterback of the freaking football team. Mr. Jock himself."

I rolled my eyes and stuck my tongue out the side of my mouth.

"So, we live in the same area of town, and he saw me at my café job over the summer. He tried to talk to me practically every day. The kid wouldn't quit. He drew a picture of me before he knew who and what I was. When he found out that I was transgender, he kind of took this self-anointed protector role. I don't understand him. I wish he would just leave me alone and go back to his cheerleaders and football and God knows what else.

> *ToryisCute05*: "Omg can we see the picture?"

DavidinWales: "I was going to ask the same thing as Tory!"

I waited a few seconds to see if Manga was going to respond but he didn't. I sighed and looked to the side. "Sure, I guess I'll show it. Hang on a sec." I got out of my chair and bent down to grab the picture underneath the bed, belatedly realizing I'd probably just shown more of my body than I wanted to. *Oh well.*

"Here it is," I said, standing up and holding the drawing to the camera, moving it back and forth slightly until I saw it come into focus on the monitor. "I guess it does really look like me. He's talented; I didn't expect Mr. Football to be an artist. I wanted to trash the picture so bad, but I just couldn't."

ToryisCute05: "WOW! Maddie!!! That's such a cute picture. Is this guy hot? He might really like you...

I mean, he's trying to be there for you, right?"

I blushed hard and sat the picture to the side. I collapsed back into my chair and looked down.

"Thanks. Umm... yeah, he is attractive. I hate that he is. Oh, God, I hate that he is." I put my hand over my forehead to cover my face. I don't know why I felt embarrassed, but I didn't usually talk like that with anyone but Charlotte and Destiny.

"Physically... well, he's exactly my type. He's masculine, he's got a ton of muscle, and he looks like he could pick me up and throw me across the town. But... it's not just that."

I looked at my hands and blinked a few times, smiling. "He, umm, I don't know, his eyes... they're puppy eyes which look out of place on somebody so big and strong... and he has dimples when he smiles. Made me wonder over the summer if he had back dimples... like, above his butt, you know?" I put both hands over my mouth and nose and looked at the camera for a second before running off screen and laughing.

When I returned to my chair, I giggled at a few of the comments Tory had made concerning his other attributes. They were cheering me on, encouraging me to talk to Kellan, wondering why I was so hesitant.

"But he's a football player, guys. I mean, what would I have in common with him? I don't know about his personality, I haven't really talked to him much, but from all the girls he's been with over the past few years, I can't say I have much hope... and it's really all moot, right? This guy isn't *really* interested in me. His bedroom is like a revolving door for cheerleaders and Barbie automatons. Blah!" I stuck my finger up to my mouth and made a vomiting sound.

I unpaused the game and continued my quest. I'd freak out later at how personal this stream became, but for now, I wanted to forget about it. I would delete the VOD and not upload it to YouTube. Folks, if you wanted to see all of Maddie's legs and butt and hear about her personal life, you shoulda been here live! Tough luck if you missed it!

The ding of the chat snapped me out of my spiraling thoughts. Manga had finally responded. My heart fluttered and I kicked myself for responding so strongly to a name from a stranger in chat.

> *MangaGuy06:* "You never know, Maddie. Maybe you want to give this guy a chance. I mean, at least he draws manga style! :P"

I snickered. "Well, at least there's that. Yeah, I don't know. I pretty much told him today what I think of him. I also told him I wasn't interested and that he wasn't my type, which was a lie... but, whatever. I've probably crushed his feelings. But maybe he'll finally leave me alone."

> *DavidinWales:* "Well, as jealous as I am that I'm stuck in Wales and can't be in Arizona with you, I have to say... why not at least give him a chance? He could be a friend? I mean, I totally understand if you're afraid of new people right now."

"Yeah... I guess I'm just scared of getting heartbroken. Like... I don't know. I've been through so much. I just want to blend in, do the computer science program, and then get out of there. I'm not there for friends or boyfriends. I'd love to have a boyfriend, I mean, that's always the goal, right? But not with some guy who is known for moving from girl to girl. What is gorgeous Mr. Football going to want with a transgender girl? He's just confused. Once he gets over his confusion, he's going to move on and forget that I even exist. I don't think I can handle getting close to someone, even as a friend, and then get left behind. I deserve better than that."

I felt like crying but focused on the game. I looked at my tracker and went through the list of the checks I had left, trying to decide where to head next.

> *MangaGuy06:* "That guy would be an idiot for not opening his heart and mind. I hope that you give him a chance, even if just as a friend, you know? Maybe he's growing. Maybe you've shown him something new about himself and he just needs time to see it."

I read Manga's words and a warm fuzziness settled over me. I was really hoping this guy was cute. I'd never see him in real life, but I hoped that he really meant what he was saying and wasn't just running game. If he meant it, he was incredibly sweet and whatever girl he meets would be really lucky. I tried to imagine his face but just saw Kellan's. I guess that was because we spent the past five minutes talking about him and he was lingering in my mind.

"Not everyone is as kind as you are, Manga. I think this guy just sees what he wants to see. I'm afraid that if things got serious... if I got to that place with anybody... I'm just afraid of being rejected when they see... you know..."

> *MangaGuy06:* "Yeah, I understand. I feel for you, Maddie. You're in a tough situation. Stay open though, the right guy is out there. Could be this guy, could be somebody else... easy to say though, right? I guess I need to take my own advice about

the girl I like. She keeps rejecting me, but I can't stay away. Something so special about her that makes every other girl irrelevant."

I smiled really big. "Got a special somebody, huh?"

MangaGuy06: "She is definitely special. But like I said, she's not interested in me. Basically, she told me what you said to that guy who drew your portrait. Guess that's why I'm kinda rooting for you to give your guy a chance... if he feels like I do, then you might be surprised... and what exactly is happening in the game right now? That is one weird-looking guy!"

I started to respond to the first part of his reply, but then burst out laughing at the second.

"Oh my God, this is like my favorite check in the whole game. It's called the Pamela check. Basically, this girl Pamela's father is a research scientist who is cursed into being a mummy-esque creature. You gotta play this song to heal him, and then he drops an item. In the vanilla game, it's a mask that you can wear to unlock more stuff. And it definitely is a disturbing little cutscene. I love it."

The rest of my stream was light-hearted. I checked the viewer list at one point, and it was mostly bots and my core regulars. As much as I wanted to grow my viewership on Twitch, I loved these intimate streams. I hoped Manga would become one of my regulars. Whatever brought him here, I was grateful. He was nice to talk to.

After the Pamela check, the seed unfolded fairly pre-dictably, and I was able to beat the game just before three hours had elapsed. I thought about streaming something else, but I was tired.

"Welp, that was fun. I'm glad you guys could make it. Maybe we'll do this again tomorrow night if I feel up to it after Minecraft. I hope you can make it to the stream tomorrow, Manga. It was fun talking to you. Good luck with your girl that you are interested in!"

MangaGuy06: "Thanks, Maddie. I'll be here tomorrow! Wouldn't miss it. This has been wonderful."

I beamed. "Goodnight, everybody. See you to-morrow!" I made my signature sign off, a heart with my hands, and blew a kiss.

I shut everything down and was surprised that I didn't feel lonely. Tonight had been one of the best streams I'd ever had. I discovered that I liked getting intimate. I was still going to delete the VOD, but I did enjoy myself. I could talk to Destiny or Charlotte, and that was super helpful. But it was fun to talk to other people, too. I wished I had more friends. It was fun being able to hang out and be accepted as yourself.

I decided to head straight to bed, feeling too lazy to take my makeup off. I'd regret it in the morning when my pillow was inevitably stained with foundation. But I didn't want to risk this good feeling deserting me. It had been a long time since I'd felt this peaceful.

Chapter 18
Kellan

I didn't sleep much after having my first real conversation with Maddie. Granted, calling it "real" might be a bit of a stretch—she didn't know who I was, and it was on the internet, but I was the lucky one who got to hear her voice, and she wasn't trying to push me away. I let myself conveniently forget that she'd probably kill me if she knew I was pretending to be some random kid she didn't know.

But Maddie, if you think I'm going to let you go after getting to see a glimpse of the real you, I'm sorry but that's not happening. You're every bit as awesome as I thought you were.

I got out of bed early and tiptoed to the front door, slipping away as quietly as I could. I wasn't coming back down from the clouds to talk to my drunk mother. I went for a long run, encircling the town and racking up the miles.

In the middle of my jog, a lady in a minivan with two young kids in the backseat almost ran me over by the college campus. She got out of her car in a panic to apologize, but I just laughed and told her everything was great. She looked at me weirdly and I explained my joy.

"The girl of my dreams talked to me yesterday for the first time. Nothing can possibly go wrong now!"

She put her hands over her heart and made a smile-frown, telling me how cute that was, and then joked that she was glad that her distracted driving didn't ruin the second conversation between me and my girl.

My girl.

I laughed and waved at her kids, then jogged toward the café. I didn't think Maddie worked here anymore—I hadn't seen her the last few times I'd been. But I wanted to grab a coffee for the walk home. I checked my watch as I got to the door. 9:51 am.

SHIT! She's streaming at ten!

I jerked my hand off the door, startling the people behind me.

"Sorry!" I yelled as I broke into a full sprint. I laughed as I dodged street signs and other pedestrians. I ran as hard as I could until it felt like I had barbed wire raking across my lungs. I stopped at the corner of a street to catch my breath. I marveled at how bright everything was today, at how the town smelled like spring, not fall. There was a coming to life in the way the place looked. It was as if Rock Canyon stopped being a dusty suburban town and turned into an oasis.

I brushed the sweat from my eyes, thought of Maddie, and checked my watch. It was 10:00 am. I was going to be late. I held her smiling face from last night's stream in my mind, a renewed strength washing over me. I put my head down and took off, quickly closing the remaining distance between me and my computer—between me and her.

When I arrived home a few minutes later, I was soaked from head to toe and gasping for air. I bounded through the front door, ignoring my mother in the living room. I figured she was probably past full awareness by now anyway.

I closed and locked my bedroom door. Nothing would stand in the way of Maddie. I sat down in front of my computer, frantically tapping the space bar to wake it up. I had left the browser open to her Twitch channel, but the page needed reloading. I cursed violently while waiting for an advertisement to finish playing.

Come on, come on, come on!

When the page loaded, I saw her and remembered to breathe. I realized dimly that I was soaking my chair in sweat but I wasn't walking away, not when she was live. I saw the familiar Minecraft graphics that I remembered from playing the education version in middle school. Maddie was wearing a big headset which made her look even tinier and more precious than usual. I wasn't aware that was possible.

I noticed that chat was bumping, with over three hundred people watching her stream. She was in an intense battle with her team, and I could hear their back-and-forth chatter. They were shouting at each other, something about the border of the world would be shrinking again in less than 15 seconds. It seemed to be a very tight match from what I could understand.

"Look out, Councilor, two behind you!" I heard Maddie's unmistakably sexy voice call out.

I watched as she dove into the fray, knocking both would-be attackers off a blocky mountain. She let out a whoop when their avatars died upon hitting the distant ground due to fall damage.

"Yes! Way to go, girl! No one beats Maddie at combat PvP. Kid is straight fire! Let's go!"

Maddie beamed from ear to ear as her older teammates patted her on the back over coms. I was overloaded trying to process seeing her this happy.

"Okay, guys, just one more left, and it's RoseLord," Maddie said. "The border is about to get smaller again. Somewhere RoseLord has found some good loot, though. I caught a glimpse of his diamond ax and it's enchanted. If we each come from a different direction, we should be able to bring him down before he gets all of us."

I was glued to the screen, my heart racing with mounting anticipation. I didn't really understand the game, but Maddie's excitement was infectious. She crouched behind a couple of blocks, while her teammates slowly encircled RoseLord. He was stuck in the middle of the remaining territory as they closed in. I could see their opponent's name above his avatar: TheRoseLord97. He'd backed unknowingly straight into Maddie's position. I couldn't see the name of her avatar but I figured it was because she was crouched and maybe that hid it.

When he got close, someone called out over coms, "Now, Maddie!"

She sprang out from behind the blocks and hacked ferociously at him. She managed to get a few solid hits before he turned his enchanted ax onto her and killed her. My heart fell to the floor when I thought she had been defeated, but bounced back into my chest when she laughed as her team-mates finished him off.

As emotional as I became about anything concerning Maddie, I wished that I understood this game better. I swore that I'd have a heart attack before this was over.

"Heck, yes! FINALLY! I never win at this darn game. Glad I had a good team with me today!"

I relaxed and laughed with Maddie, elated right alongside her. The rest of the stream went similarly well as her team stayed in the top-ranking spot all the way to the final round. The final round was a showdown between the first and second-place finishers.

I watched as a wheel listing over 50 mini-games appeared on the screen after a few minutes of intermission. Maddie told chat that it would be spun by an administrator of the server to determine which game the teams would play against each other. She said it was a luck-of-the-draw kind of thing; your team was either good at the minigame that was chosen, or you weren't. When it landed on 1v1 Arena Combat, Maddie's grin returned.

"This is you, Maddie. Go bring us home that trophy," one of her teammates said.

"Yeah, this is all you, Maddie. Cakewalk. I'm going to go insane when you beat Greg. I'd pay to see this!" another teammate chimed in.

I felt the welling up of emotion that I was used to just before the start of the fourth quarter of a football game when the score was close and the pressure was placed squarely on my shoulders to deliver. That intoxicating mix of fear and excitement taking the form of, "I really don't want to be the one who screws this up," and "nobody but me can take us where we need to go. I got this." I wondered if Maddie relished these types of situations as I did.

"Okay, guys, I'll do my best."

I scrutinized her face as if looking at a fellow competitor. Come on, Maddie, show me your game face. Show me the intensity. Show me that you want this, that you need this. Show me that THIS IS YOURS!

I clenched my fists and bit my lip, waiting for the first round to begin. When I saw her little Viking avatar walk into the arena, I looked at Maddie. I saw the narrowing of her eyes, the lowering of her eyebrows, and her mouth clamped shut like an executioner. *Yes! That's it. Get it. Let's go!*

When the round began, she came out hard, alternating between jumping, blocking, and swinging her ax, and her opponent seemed to be caught off-guard the entire round and was easily defeated.

She's good. She's damn good.

Her health was automatically refilled before the next round. This time, her opponent came charging out. This one seemed determined to go on the offensive with his bow, firing volleys of arrows at Maddie, sending her scurrying behind a little wall at the corner of the arena.

Come on, Maddie. Work your way closer. Get inside of him, where he can't get those arrows off. Where you can swing that ax straight at his blocky face!

Maddie returned fire with her bow, working her way toward a few barricades in the middle of the arena. She faked like she was going left, and then blasted around to the right at full speed, fooling her opponent and getting in close. A few shield blocks and well-timed ax swings, and he was down.

In this mini-game, I learned from the background chatter of Maddie's teammates, you have three lives. With one more kill, Maddie would have won the tournament for her team.

"Dude! It's Greg. Oh my God, this is great! If you beat Greg, you're undisputedly the PvP champion of the Minecraft world. Make me proud, kid," a voice that I'd come to recognize as their team leader, TheCouncilor, said.

Maddie had a morbid grin on her face, and I flash-backed onto that same look from the parking lot a couple of days ago. I didn't think Greg, whoever he was, had a chance.

The final round began with Maddie confusing Greg by rapidly firing arrows from the back of the arena. He had expected her to charge and was caught exposed running toward the middle of the arena. Maddie was able to land three shots before he found cover. She sprinted toward him before he had a chance to regenerate his health and an epic battle ensued.

She landed two more hits before her shield broke. She backed up and brought up the bow from her inventory. Greg took the bait and surged forward. She expertly switched back to the ax as soon as he moved and charged, swiping at him before he had the chance to make an adjustment. Her dangerous strategy paid off as his avatar disappeared under the final blow, and all his items fell into a pile around her feet.

She put her hands up to her face and screamed. The chat went wild, so many people typing at once that I couldn't catch much of what was said. Not that I was really paying attention. I had jumped out of my chair and was fist-pumping about a hundred miles an hour after she defeated Greg, trying not to lose my mind.

When I finally sat back down, I realized I was as happy as I'd ever been. I laughed and tried not to blink, wanting to take in every reaction of hers. It felt so good watching her win after seeing her so dejected and humiliated at school.

If anyone ever did anything to break her smile again...

No, I wasn't going to think about that right now. I was going to celebrate along with her. After the tournament,

Maddie thanked all her fans for their congratulations and donations.

I was shocked that Maddie received almost $100 in donations from this stream alone. Here my stupid friends were making fun of her, and she had over three hundred people watching her play a video game and paying her for it. The joke was on them.

"That was EPIC! That was the most fun I've had in a long, long time. I think beating Greg at his own game was... ahh, I'm definitely clipping that and putting that up on YouTube and TikTok ASAP. Whew! I need to breathe." She giggled, and I couldn't understand why no one else at school could see how beautiful she was.

She talked with chat for a few minutes at the end of her stream. I didn't say anything. I sat back and enjoyed watching her talk. I was sad when she wrapped it up.

"Well, I'm going to head off here. Thanks for coming by to watch all the mayhem and madness. Thanks again to everybody! I truly appreciate your support and your donations. It means the world to me. I can't say it enough. I'm really grateful for everything. I'll most likely be back later tonight for Lenora's Mask. I'll see you guys then. This is Maddie, signing off!"

She did her heart and blowing kiss thing, and I blew her a kiss back and then laughed at myself.

Whoa... this is what being head over heels feels like. Wow. I had no idea. This is... amazing. I have the feeling that if she was trapped on the other side of a brick wall, I could run through it unharmed. Like, nothing could stop me.

I know I've got to make this girl see that I'm the right guy for her. I would be so empty knowing that she existed and I couldn't be her special someone. I don't give a damn what anybody else thinks about her or me or anything else. Screw them, they don't matter.

Because it's always going to be you, Maddie. It was you the first time I saw you flying around the corner on your skateboard. There is no alternative. There's nothing that you are that would stop me from wanting to give you all of myself. Not when it's a choice between being with you or not.

Please, give me a chance. I feel like I've been missing a huge part of myself my entire life... and when I look at you... I know that I've found it.

I flipped through the prepaid credit card options at the nearest grocery store. After the Minecraft stream, I had decided that I wanted to subscribe to Maddie. But since I was 16, with no job and no credit card, I had to search online for alternative options. Luckily, I found out that I could use a special type of prepaid card to subscribe to Twitch streamers. I was about to give up hope of finding it when the last option on the sales rack was exactly what I needed.

YES! I jumped up and down and then noticed a few people staring. I smiled meekly and headed for the checkout counter.

Maddie was scheduled to come back around nine, which left me with a little over seven hours to kill. That seemed like an eternity. I wanted to walk straight from the grocery store to her house and congratulate her on the win. I amused myself thinking of what I would say.

"Hey, Maddie! That was an awesome win today, congrats! You really brought the intensity at the end there. I was on the edge of my seat, rooting so hard for you... Oh? How do I know that you stream on Twitch? Your dad told me when he gave me a ride home from football practice. It's all good, no worries."

I immediately felt myself free-fall as it hit me that she wouldn't be the same Maddie when I saw her again. No more laughs and smiles. She would just scowl if she bothered to look my way at all. Because, to her, I'd be Kellan, the football jock, who she hates and doesn't want anything to do with. I wished that I had retrograde thrusters like in the sci-fi movies because I was coming back to Earth too fast.

I'm just going to have to be patient, I told myself. For once in my life, I was going to have to put in the time, effort, and energy to earn a girl's heart and trust. And I had to accept that there was no guarantee that she'd ever want me. I'd have to give it my all and it was going to be what it was going to be.

I slowed down, no longer in a rush to get anywhere as I contemplated my future with Maddie.

Is this how you feel about the entire world? When you try to be yourself and you have no idea what anyone is going to do or say about it? Do you live with this constant fear that someone will reject you?

I swallowed back the hurt, thinking about how hard it must be for her. I watched the people passing by on foot and in their cars, and I thought about how they had problems, worries and troubles. But when they walked into the store or their workplace, did they have the constant fear that someone might stare at them? Might laugh at them for being different than the accepted norms? Did they fear never being able to find a partner who would accept them for who they were?

I was under no illusions that I understood the full extent of what she'd had to go through, and I didn't think I ever would. But I did understand why she didn't want me to come around. She'd been hurt so much by life... if I was in her shoes, I don't think I'd want to leave my room, let alone talk to a guy who was trying to pursue me.

I'm so impressed by you. I'll do everything I can to make your days better at school.

The rumbling in my stomach reminded me that I hadn't yet eaten and it was already early afternoon. I thought about tempting the wrath of my mom and ordering a pizza for delivery but forgot about it, remembering that Maddie had a YouTube channel with all her past streams. I ran the rest of the way home, not bothering to grab anything to eat as I hurried to my room. I pulled up her Discord and followed the link to her YouTube.

When I opened the page, I was a little kid in the greatest toy store that's ever existed. There were endless rows of Maddie, all waiting to be played with a simple click of the mouse. I clicked a random Lenora's Mask stream from back in July.

With each person that said hi to her, I felt little stabs of jealousy. I wished that I could have spent my summer nights watching her. It was funny though; while she was streaming, I was drawing her a couple of blocks away.

While watching the streams, I felt that her community was like the family I'd always wanted. They shared their thoughts and feelings with each other, mostly about mundane things such as the game, current events, or even about food and clothes. But occasionally, the conversations got deep. I realized I could learn a ton about Maddie by watching these old VODs.

I pulled out a piece of paper and started making notes. If I could learn enough about her, I figured I could leverage my effort in a meaningful direction. She'd see that we shared interests and maybe that would nudge her a little my way. And it wouldn't be a lie because what she was interested in, I was interested in. And if I ever got the chance to take her on a date, I'd know just what to do to make it the most special night of her life.

I sat in my computer chair from a little after two until eight that night, watching two Lenora's Mask streams. I laughed, I answered her questions out loud, and I pined hard for the girl in the green cosplay outfit. Sometimes I moved to the bed, laying back and half paying attention while I let myself dream about being with her.

In six hours, I had compiled quite the list:

-You're Vegan – I had suspected this at the café but wasn't sure

-Melodic Death Metal is your favorite music; favorite bands are Dark Tranquillity and Amon Amarth, the latter of which will be coming to Phoenix in October, and you'd love to go (and I'd love to take you)

-You also like lo-fi chill, indie rock, and some electronic music. Didn't expect you to be normal there, either. I approve.

-You're a bit morbid, but not enough to be strange… well, maybe the right kind of strange? I find this hot for reasons that aren't entirely clear to me

-You suffered with self-injury issues but are determined not to go back to that. God, I hope these past couple of weeks haven't pushed you over the edge

-Your favorite movie is Interstellar because it's ultimately a story about a father and a daughter, and you liked how Cooper, played by Matthew McConaughey, stopped at nothing in his struggle to get home. You also liked his willingness to put

himself in harm's way for a crewmate. And you
especially loved the otherworldly pipe organ blaring
incessantly in the background
-Skating is your passion and you like collecting
vintage skating shirts. Your favorite is a skeleton
on a skateboard. If you thought you could be good
enough, you'd pursue it as a career.
-Your favorite meal is a Sofritoes and Guac burrito
at Chipotle. You can only eat half before feeling
completely stuffed... which is hilarious because I
could probably eat two of them if they're vegan. But
you're a sexy little, tiny thing so, yeah, I guess that
makes sense
-Your style is retro mid-2000s, called "Scene." You
love the big hair, skinny jeans, and emo makeup. I
didn't know what it was called—I just thought it was
your own because it seems made for you
-Your biggest hope is meeting the right person and
your biggest fear is being alone. Well, hello, my
name's Kellan, nice to meet you!

I put my list down and stared at the ceiling, feeling both drained and exhilarated. I rubbed my eyes and flinched when I heard my phone say, "Bruh."

The noise brought me crashing out of my fantasy world. The jolt of frustration almost made me throw my phone against the wall. Instead, I sighed and picked it up.

Ty: Bruh, what's good? You free tonight?

I threw my head back onto my pillow, feeling intruded upon. *No, I'm not. I'm never going to be free again. I have 97 YouTube videos to watch that average about three hours each. Plus, all her new streams in between. And there's always the pipedream that maybe she'll actually let me be her friend in real life, in which case... it was nice knowing you.*

I laughed at my monologue. I loved Tyrell, and would always want to hang out with him, but I was so locked into Maddie right now. I had spent all summer wanting to get to know her. And now I had my chance... even if it was through YouTube of all places. But I couldn't walk away for this, not even for a second.

There was simply no way I was missing her stream tonight. I'd have to think of some excuse.

I paced the room, running my hands through my hair before thrusting them forward and grunting. *Why do they care what I'm doing? What's so special about me being at some party?*

The lyrics from the Beach House song "Other People," ran through my mind and I finally understood it. Why did people always need to keep in touch? What about sharing experiences with one group of people made you want to start telling everyone else about it? All they would do is post every stupid moment from the night on social media as if anybody else actually cared.

I grabbed my phone off my bed. I'd just have to tell him the truth—I didn't feel like coming out. I didn't have to tell him the whole truth, which was that I was probably never coming out again. I'd hang out with Ty, but I was done forever with those people who made fun of Maddie.

Kellan: Hey, man, I'm hanging in tonight. Everything good?

Ty responded a couple of minutes later.

Ty: Yeah, man, just seeing if you wanted to head out to a little party at Jessica's. Going to be like ten of us, thought maybe I'd pick you up on my way back from my grandma's.

Kellan: I'm good, man. Enjoy yourself. Don't break too many hearts.

Ty: You already know I am. Get at you later.

Sometimes I was glad that he was so self-absorbed or he'd be calling me out and wondering what was going on.

I used what time I had left before her next stream to shower and finally eat. I waited impatiently for Maddie to go live, laying on my bed and tossing a little plush football at the ceiling. At 15 minutes past when she said she'd be on, I began to panic. What if she was too tired to stream or didn't feel like it? I tried to let my mounting disappointment go; the world wasn't going to end if she didn't stream again tonight.

Feeling disappointed, I hopped off my bed and started to click another YouTube video from the summer, but when I reached my computer, she was there. I was the first one in chat. For a few seconds, it was just me and Maddie, alone in the same digital space. And everything was okay again.

Chapter 19
Maddie

DING! DONG!

I stretched and groaned as the doorbell woke me up from my nap. I zombie walked out of my room to the top of the stairs, hearing Charlotte speaking to someone. Then an arrow struck deep into my chest when I heard Kellan's voice responding.

The bottom of our stairs lined up almost directly in front of the front door, spilling out into the living room. I was secluded from my current vantage point, but if I took one more step, Kellan would be able to see me.

"...no, you wouldn't know me. I'm Charlotte, Maddie's twin sister. We've never gone to the same school until this year. But I know you. I mean, everyone knows you at school." I imagined her twirling her hair with her pursed lips. Ugh, gross.

"Plus, we've talked about you here," she continued in her syrupy sweet voice. "Your portrait of Maddie caused quite the stir." She laughed and I imagined Kellan flashing her one of his million-dollar smiles.

"Do you mind if I talk to her?" Huh, didn't sound like he was flirting back. Just sounded urgent.

"Oh, sorry, come in. I'll go get her, though I can't promise she's going to want to see you."

This time, Kellan laughed. "Don't I know that already."

I quickly tiptoed back into my room, closing the door quietly. I looked around my room, wondering the best place to look disinterested, and then feign surprise at our guest. Gaming chair? No... nothing is turned on, will look weird to be sitting in the middle of a quiet room doing nothing. Maybe the bed—

I heard Charlotte knock. I hurried to the bed and made myself look like I was just waking up.

"Come in," I said, using my best groggy voice. She entered, closed the door, and then leaned back against it, a mischievous smile playing across her face.

"You have someone here to see you."

I'm not going to be that easy, Char. "Oh, is it one of the kids from the skatepark or theatre class?" I asked innocently.

"Nope. It's none of those people." She really played it up, wiggling her eyebrows up and down.

You little brat, you love this.

"Umm... wait a second... it's him, isn't it? Please tell me it isn't him." I might as well play it up a little bit, too. It's only fair.

"Uh-huh. In the flesh. Downstairs in our living room as we stand here and speak." She accentuated the last word with a resounding *k* sound. *I swear that girl is getting the lead in the play this year. If she doesn't, I'll punch somebody.*

"Just run him off, tell him anything you want. I've tried to tell him five different ways that I'm not interested. I just want him to go away."

Her jaw fell open and she made an indignant puffing sound. I was having fun playing this little game, but now I was starting to get pissed. I thought she'd be happy I didn't want to come down, the way I could hear her flirting with him at the door. I could see her winding up a speech so I sat back and waited for it.

"You're serious? He shows up here, and you're just going to sit in your bedroom and sulk? I thought you've crushed on him since you were little? What the hell, Maddie? What's wrong with you?" She breathed hard after her little outburst. A part of me knew that she was right, but I wasn't about to listen to that part.

"Well, if he's so great, why don't *you* date him? He's not my type anyway and we both know he doesn't actually want me. He wants something that he thinks I am. I don't want a guy who is an idiot."

She pushed off the door and put her hand on her hips, facing me.

"I think he wants you as you are, Maddie. Why would he come here otherwise?"

"I don't know, because, like I already said, he's an idiot? Ugh! He needs to get it through his thick jock skull that I don't want anything to do with him. I'm not into him, I don't want to be his friend, I don't want to see his face. Ever. I wish he would go try to charm some other girl with it." I flung myself to the side, away from Charlotte.

I'd been thinking about Kellan since I described him on stream and if I could reach into my brain and rip out my memories of him, I would. I was tired of wishing things were different. They weren't and he needed to move on.

"Fine. Be that way. It's not my loss. I'll express your sentiments to him," she said with a sassy wave of her hand.

I heard her grab the doorknob but didn't feel the slight rattle of the wall that usually accompanied the door being shut. I looked up and saw her still standing there, lips pursed in that typical Charlotte "I'm smarter than you are" pose.

"I want you to know something before I go, little missy. He's not going to believe you anymore than I do. Because you're a terrible liar."

She slammed the door before she saw my middle finger flick in her direction. I wasn't mad at her... I just didn't like how close to the truth she was getting. I didn't want to sort through this. I wouldn't have to if he went away.

I moved to my gaming chair, threw my FXPAK pro cartridge into my Super Nintendo, and fired up Star Ocean. I had the vague thought that I should wait to play this on stream, but I needed a distraction right now. I needed the warmth of 16-bit graphics on an old CRT the way some people needed a chocolate cookie or a slice of pizza—it was my comfort food.

Before I knew it, half an hour had passed and I was getting into the story and starting to level up my characters. I paused the game when I heard a knock at the door, expecting Charlotte to try again.

"Sure, come in," I said, spinning around in my chair.

My dad walked in with a stern look on his face. "Maddie, why didn't you come down to say hello to Kellan?"

I responded sarcastically. "Because I told him not to come here ever again? And he wasn't invited? Why would I say hello?"

Dad sat down on my bed. There was no sign of any humor on his face and, for once, I was a little scared. Usually, he tried to make jokes about things, or go out of his way to be super supportive. He just looked angry right now. I hadn't seen that from him in almost a year... not since I burned my grandmother's Bible in the backyard. I hadn't done that because I was against everything it said, but because of how she used it against me. She deserved it. Dad eventually admitted that he agreed and even found it funny. I thought he was the greatest dad in the world at that moment, even though he stuck with his punishment of one week of no skating.

"Maddie, I know you have a hard time and you're very protective of yourself. No one understands that more than me and your mother. But what I don't get is that you have someone showing up here trying to be your friend and you're acting like a spoiled brat. Why? Would you like to explain the part that I'm missing?"

I shrugged. "Not really."

"Humor me," he volleyed back.

"Well... I don't know. He badgered me all summer, trying to get me to hang out with him, and then he made fun of me with his friends the moment he found out the truth. You know all this. Why do you expect me to be nice to him?"

Dad looked away and shook his head. I could feel the frustration oozing out of him with every sharp exhale. When he looked back at me, I could tell how he made it to VP of Sales for a Fortune 1000 tech company. He was all business, seeing through my charades as if I were a new sales recruit fresh out of college.

"I don't buy it, Maddie. He apologized to you. He drew you a picture. He took up for you at school. He's made every effort to make amends and he's still doing everything he can to be your friend. What else is going on here? What are you scared of?"

I spun my chair around, facing away from him. "I don't want to talk about it," I mumbled.

I heard the creak of my bed as Dad stood up. "You know what? Fine. I respect your right to your privacy. But he's coming to dinner—" I spun back around and Dad held up his hand before I could say a word. "He's coming to dinner, Maddie, it doesn't matter whether you like it or not. And when he gets back from a walk with Charlotte, I'd like you to come down and at least be cordial."

"They *what?!* I knew it! I knew she wanted to date him! That little—"

"ENOUGH!" he snapped, and I cowered, making myself as small as I could in my chair. My parents had been so gentle around me since my accident last year that I forgot what it felt like to be yelled at. I could feel the pinpricks fighting around my eyes, threatening to fall at any second.

Dad took a deep breath and softened, his eyebrows returning to a horizontal position. "Charlotte is being friendly to him, the same thing that you should be doing. I guarantee that he'd rather be on that walk with you, but you're sitting up here acting like you're too good to say hi. When we call you for dinner, you can either come down or you can give me your skateboard for a month, it's your choice."

My head fell forward and I wanted to throw myself on the ground but thought better of it. When he left, I stomped over to my makeup bag and started putting on the basics. If I was going to have to see him, he wasn't going to see me like this.

After putting on my makeup, I waited at the window in the hallway just outside my room for them to get back. When they did, I stood quietly at the top of the stairs, trying to gather my courage. I listened to them as they plopped down on the big L-shaped couch in our living room.

"And Maddie…" I heard Charlotte start laughing so hard she couldn't finish the sentence. "You should have seen her going off on this kid. She was not having any of it. It was great!"

"I think I can visualize this one fairly clearly, especially after my recent experiences," I heard Kellan say with a lot less humor.

"Kellan, I hope you are staying for dinner," I heard my dad say. He must have poked his head through the archway that opened into the kitchen from the living room. I quickly started making my way down the stairs, trying to head this off.

"Yes, I'm going to stay, as long as it's okay with Maddie," Kellan replied.

"It's not okay with Maddie. At all," I said, crossing my arms and standing in front of the stairway.

Kellan wheeled toward the stairs. His eyes wide, I saw him involuntarily checking me out, then realized I had come downstairs in a black tank top and short shorts. Oops.

"Nonsense, Maddie," Dad snapped. "Kellan's joining us and that's that. Perfect timing because dinner's ready. Go grab your little brother out back and drop your attitude."

I glared at Kellan from underneath my hair before walking to the backyard and yelling for my brother, Ryan, to come to dinner.

When I got to the dining room, I was overjoyed to see that my mom had set a place for Kellan between me and Charlotte.

I could feel him glancing at me from time to time as we ate dinner, but I didn't bother to look up from my plate. It was surreal to hear him making small talk with the rest of my family in between bites.

Just as I thought I had made it through dinner, Ryan turned to Kellan and said, "Did you know my sister used to be my brother?"

I dropped my fork onto my plate with a loud clang. Nobody said a word. My mom's breathing turned shallow and rapid, sounding like a basketball being inflated.

I snuck a peek at Kellan and saw that he was smiling at my brother. "Wow! That's amazing! Your sister is a magical superhero, Ryan! I don't think I've ever met anybody as cool as her. You're really lucky, huh?" Kellan said.

"Yeah!" Ryan enthusiastically agreed.

Kellan turned to me and I glanced back down.

"Can I go?" I whispered.

"No, it's family game night. Kellan, would you like to play with us? We usually just play simple card and board games," Mom said, and I could already tell she was taken by him.

"Wait, WHAT? You're inviting him to that, too?" I exclaimed, the irritation raw in my voice.

"I really don't have to stay. I don't want to upset you." I glanced at him and wished I hadn't. Those puppy eyes were pleading.

"Maddie, you're being rude. He wants to be your friend and you're acting like a small child. You're doing exactly what other people do to YOU that you hate and always complain about," Dad said.

Well, it seemed we were bringing our private conversations to the kitchen table. Nothing like being 16 and getting treated like you're 6.

"Let's play Crazy Bananas. That'll be fun with Kellan," Charlotte said excitedly. I repeated her laughter sarcastically and inwardly smiled when Kellan laughed.

"I've never played Crazy Bananas. How do you play?" he asked. Of course, Charlotte responded immediately.

"So, you draw a card, and it will either have a question to answer, or you have to, like, do something, like ask another person an embarrassing question, or maybe do charades, or play 20 questions. It's just, like, a social game, I guess. A lot of random things to do or say. It's silly but it's fun!"

I should have brought a trash can to the table. I was going to need to hurl if she kept acting so peppy.

Ryan demanded to go first, and my mom obliged. He pulled the first card off the top of the deck.

"Tell everyone your favorite sport and then defend it if someone disagrees," he read. "That's easy! Football!"

"Well, you'll like him then," I muttered, thrusting my thumb toward Kellan. No one disagreed with Ryan, so it was Charlotte's turn next.

She drew a 20 questions card. It was my mom's turn to ask the first question. "Is your person, place, or thing larger than something I can hold in my hands?"

Charlotte giggled. "Yes." Dad was up next.

"Is it tall?"

"Yep!"

It was my turn but I waved it off, so Ryan went.

"Is it scary?" he asked, scrunching up his face.

"Not to most people," Charlotte said, glancing at me.

Mom started to ask another question but Dad interrupted her. "Maddie, you need to participate. Ask your sister a question."

"Ugh, fine. I think I know what it is without needing any clues. It's Kellan, right?"

Charlotte's jaw dropped for a second, and then she leaned in front of Kellan and said, "Yes, it's Kellan. You must be psychic." She stuck her tongue out at me and I rolled my eyes.

"No, I just know how you are. I knew when you said what the card was exactly what you would pick."

Everyone was quiet for a few moments before Kellan said, "It's my turn, right?"

He drew his card and read it quietly to himself. Ten seconds passed. Then 20. I squirmed as I felt him looking at me.

"Well, what's the card say, Kellan?" I said, the saltiness in my voice earning me a frown from my dad.

"It says to say something nice to the person sitting to the left of you. The person to my left is... well... you."

Chapter 20
Kellan

Everyone was silent at the table. Even Ryan was quiet, picking up on the tenseness of his parents.

I was quiet for probably no longer than a minute, but it felt like an eternity. I couldn't make my mind up about what I wanted to say. A part of me just wanted to make a throwaway statement, just to get it out of the way and keep the game going. But another part of me wanted to go all-in and pour my heart out.

As soon as I thought about pouring my heart out, I knew that's what I was going to do. I couldn't half-ass things with Maddie. The intensity of my feelings were far beyond that.

So, screw it. I decided that I was making a stand. I was putting the ball in the air. That's what I did best. I figured I was about as far away from the end zone as I could be. I had nowhere to go but closer.

I turned my body to face her and spoke slowly and gently. I wanted to make sure she took in every word, straight from my soul.

"Maddie, I think you're the most beautiful girl I've ever seen. When you smiled at me the other day in the parking lot, even though it wasn't a happy smile, my whole world just stopped. It was the first time I saw you smile. I'd kill to see it again. The way your eyes glowed... it took me to places inside of myself that I didn't know existed.

"And I just want you to know that I think you're awesome. And brave. A true fighter. I respect you for sticking it out in school, refusing to back down. It's incredibly attractive. I just... want you to know that someone notices you for who you really are. The amazing girl that's underneath—"

Maddie's head swung up and I flinched backwards at the sight of her gritted teeth.

"Underneath of WHAT, Kellan? This male body?"

I crumbled, feeling as helpless as I did in a dream I had a few nights ago. In the dream, Maddie kept slashing me into a thousand pieces with a giant sword and then magically putting me back together, only to do it all over again. At least in the dream, I was able to hear her angelic laughter as she taunted me.

"That's not what I was going to say. I was going to say underneath all of that armor you put on to protect yourself. The amazing girl underneath that."

Maddie brought her fists up to her face and I braced to be punched, knowing I was not going to block her.

If this is what it takes for you to touch me, go ahead. Give me your best.

"Why do you insist on pursuing me? Why do you feel this way about me? WHY?" she shouted.

I held her gaze, searching for any sign that she didn't completely and utterly hate me. I found none.

"Why do you insist on being so cruel to me?" I whispered.

Her mouth dropped open and her body sagged back into the chair. Her fists fell to her sides. I could see the tears streaming down her face and it took literally everything I had to keep from dropping to one knee and wiping them away.

It's okay, just let me in. Just let me be your friend.

I was about to reach out to her, to hold her hand in mine, but the next thing I knew she was a blur of motion. She flew out of her chair and bounded up the stairs.

I sat there staring at her empty chair for what felt like an agonizingly long time. I kept playing the scene over and over in my head, wondering where I went wrong.

I felt a lot like I did last year when I threw my only interception of the season. I analyzed it over and over again for five days straight until I knew exactly what I had done wrong. That was just a simple football play. I had no idea if I'd ever know what I was doing wrong with Maddie.

"I'm sorry... if I said too much," I finally said. *Or maybe not enough.*

Her mom got up and scurried over to my chair, wrapping me in a hug. She rubbed my back and sniffled.

"I'm sorry, Kellan. I don't understand her sometimes," she whispered.

I closed my eyes and almost forgot about the pain. It had been so long since my mom really hugged me. I didn't know I needed this. I wanted to stay in this until all the years of hurt had washed away, but I knew I couldn't.

I opened my eyes and glanced at Charlotte. She was squeezing her long blonde braid between both hands, a sympathetic smile on her face that made little dimples on the ends of her lips. I smiled weakly in return.

"I think... I think I need to go," I said after Daisy released me. "Thanks for dinner and the games. I enjoyed the meal, it was wonderful." I couldn't meet her parents' eyes.

"Kellan, you are welcome here any time. I hope she comes around... I don't know what to say about her. I wish I did," Daisy said as she walked me to the door. She was taking this personally. Maybe that's what good parents did. But I knew Maddie enough to know that she was fiercely independent, that there was nothing her parents could possibly do to change her.

"It's okay. Maybe she'll come around, maybe she won't. I don't think I can stop trying. If she'd just let me in..." I looked out at the street, noticing that the sun had sunk low. It reminded me of the time of day when Maddie would skate by. It saddened me that she probably wouldn't be tonight.

"Well, thanks again. Goodnight, Mrs. Martin." I started walking away, not waiting for her reply. If I stayed any longer, I knew I would disintegrate in front of her parents.

I had all the space in the world to fall apart at home. That's exactly what I planned to do.

I awakened early the next morning. I rolled over in bed and stared at the dark ceiling. It had been a rough night, there would be no denying that. But at some point in the brutally honest hours of the early morning, sadness had been replaced by the bittersweet feeling of acceptance.

There was no moving on. There was only hope and patience. It was a very poor substitute for being her friend, but that wasn't up to me. I felt grateful that at least I had her on Twitch. That was better than nothing. I figured if she wouldn't come around, I guess I'd just be alone. The way I saw it, there was no replacing her.

A quiet peace fell onto my morning routine. I didn't rush myself but took my time drinking my coffee. I tried to ignore my mom's cans piling up next to the sliding glass door. I guess she couldn't make it the extra ten feet to the side yard to put them in the recycling. She'd been off the past few days, and I could tell she'd made the most of it, downing at least two 30 packs.

I was going to have to do something about that soon. Either hurry up and turn 18 or try an intervention. But I didn't have anybody to help me intervene... and if it was just me, she'd just get pissed and keep drinking anyway.

I looked away and shifted my thoughts back to the day ahead. I decided I was going to leave Maddie alone for a while. I'd finish my manga book and give it to her when I was done. And maybe enough time would have passed that she'd at least be open to being friends. I glued that idea to my mind, afraid to let it go—it was all I had.

I glanced at the clock and saw that school started in about 45 minutes. I texted Tyrell and told him that I was going to walk to school. It was a cooler morning, at least for Arizona, and I wasn't feeling very social.

I quickly dressed and put another cup of coffee in a travel cup. I took the scenic route toward school, avoiding Maddie's house. There was a chance she'd be at the bus stop, and as much as I'd like to see her, I also wanted her to know that I respected her space.

About halfway to school, I realized I'd developed a curious habit of late. I'd begun imagining how Maddie would act if we were together. How she would look walking next to me, what she might say, the things she might notice. I enjoyed that. If I thought about it, I felt a little childish for pretending that she was there. So, I decided not to think about it. Instead, I enjoyed the thought of her small hand in mine, and what she would say about this beautiful morning.

It's funny, when I walked into the school building, after deciding to leave her alone, she was the first thing I saw. She was walking toward her locker and I felt proud of her. She wasn't letting any of these other assholes stop her from trying to have a normal high school life. I looked away and saw Ty approaching, and I laughed inwardly when I realized our paths were going to cross less than ten feet from Maddie.

"Bruh, what's going on with you? You didn't come out at all this weekend. You good?" he asked. I glanced at Maddie but her back was facing us. She hadn't noticed me yet.

"Hey, Ty. I had some things that were very important to me this weekend so I couldn't make it out." I watched Maddie flinch when she heard my voice.

"What are you talking about? You sitting home getting high or something? Is this about this mysterious girl that you told me you're in love with? She finally sees how handsome you are?"

I laughed as he framed his face with his hands and fluttered his eyelashes.

"Eh, something like that. It was about her but she still isn't giving me the time of day. But I'm trying."

"Man, who is this girl? Does she go to this school? Or South Rock Canyon? Or wait! Is she homeschooled? You know her mom is going to be watching her like a hawk, bruh. I can't recommend that. I tried it."

He was in rare form this morning, gesturing so wildly that his long arm span was dominating the hallway. The warning bell for first period rang and I started backpedaling slowly away from him, looking deliberately at Maddie for a few seconds, and then back to him.

"It's a mystery, bruh. I'll see you at practice later," I said, winking.

Ty looked at Maddie, a question mark on his face. When he looked back to me, his eyes were wide. I thought I would have felt terror in this moment, and I might have a couple of weeks ago. But I didn't care anymore, I was past all that. Besides, Tyrell had been my best friend since I was seven—he had my back.

"Wait… Kellan, you don't mean her?" He pointed. She still wasn't looking, but I could only surmise that she knew he was pointing at her. "You're kidding me, right? Bruh… you're telling me about this at practice later. And quit joking around! You're making me think crazy things that I know aren't true!"

I laughed and spun around, holding out a thumbs up as I headed to my first-period class.

I sailed through the day. I kept mostly to myself, lost in my inner world of Maddie. I was finally feeling okay with everything. I ached inside, knowing we might never be, but at least

I had chosen her. That meant more to me than I thought it would.

In moments between classes, I played "Oatmello — Thinking of You" on loop in my earbuds. It was a simple little lo-fi song, but it made me think of her smiling on my computer screen.

I had forgotten all about my conversation with Tyrell, but he obviously had not. He was leaning against the wall outside the locker room, his arms crossed. I started to smile but stopped when he noticed me and lowered his eyebrows.

"Bruh… you got me all kinds of worked up. Are you telling me that you're in love with a guy? Or were you just joking? What's up, man, be straight with me."

I looked off across the field, having the distinct feeling that I was about to end one phase of my life and begin another. My life had seemed almost boringly predictable until I met Maddie. Now every moment seemed to bring a new experience.

I looked at him and allowed myself to hope. *He's going to understand me. He's my best friend.*

I went for it.

"She's transgender if you're talking about Maddie. And if you mean, am I in love with her and does she have a male body, then the answer is yes. But she's not a guy, okay? She's a girl."

Ty's jaw dropped and he took a step back. He ran his hand quickly across the top of his head and I couldn't stop watching the way his lips twitched. It was as if I'd attached little electrodes next to his mouth and kept shocking him. If the positions were reversed, I'd be floored, too. I'd have 15 million questions rushing forth at once.

I waited for some sort of regret or worry to rise within me, but it didn't. I chuckled softly, watching Ty's mind on overload. I moved to sit on a nearby bench, waiting patiently. He stumbled after me.

"So… hold on, bruh… what are you even saying? Female inside? How can you be female and yet… have a penis…? I'm not following, dude."

I took a deep breath. I'd talked with Hugh, researched transgender stuff online, and thought a ton about Maddie, but I felt woefully unqualified to answer those questions. I was fascinated by all that I had learned, and I felt a world of compassion for the people who were born this way… but I was so wrapped up in Maddie that I didn't really pay too much attention to the wider situation. I could write volumes about my love for Maddie, but I didn't know if I could explain what she was. I'd have to trust the understanding that had found its way into my heart.

"Being transgender means that you aren't the gender of the body that you were born into. So, you could be in a female body, and yet actually be male, in the mind or soul or whatever you want to call it. Or you could even be neither gender, feeling like a mix between the two. In Maddie's case, she was a female born into a male's body.

You and I take who we are for granted... we've always felt like guys and we have a dude's body. But Maddie?" I started to choke up and bit my lip. "She's had a hell of a time, Ty. She's always had to live in a body that didn't feel right to her. And not just that it was too fat, or too skinny, or too tall or short... but too male.

"Can you imagine feeling that way? Feeling like you're one gender, and yet having a body that tells another story? I've tried. It wasn't even real to me but it was awful. I'm 6'4, over 230 pounds, with broad shoulders and legs wider than my hips... where the hell would I get clothes? How would I ever look like a girl? But there are people going through this. I don't know how they make it through a day. And that's just what's going on inside of them... then you have people staring at you, judging you, making fun of you." I stood up and paced a few steps away, struggling with my composure. I reminded myself that I was here in this moment for Maddie, to help bring understanding to other people. I took a deep breath before walking back to Tyrell and resting a hand on his shoulder for a second before continuing.

"Ty, just step into her shoes for a minute before you judge her. You can't possibly think that it would be easy to be anything other than what you are. What if you were told you had to be a baseball player instead of a football player? You loved football, knew you could be great at it, but you were never allowed to play.

"Look, it's not a perfect analogy, Ty. Not being able to play a sport is not the same as being transgender. But I'm trying to get you to understand what she feels like on the inside... so that you don't judge her. Because, yeah, I'm in love with her. I want her to be my girlfriend."

I haven't seen Ty look so flabbergasted since we came home from practice one day to see his mom kissing a white guy on the couch. I laughed so hard as he freaked out in his bedroom. I tried to show him that he had a double standard, that he dated all sorts of girls, but he wasn't having any of it. Later that night, after I thought he was asleep, he told me quietly that it wasn't because the guy was white, but because it was his mom. He felt like after his dad had abandoned them, he didn't want to see her get hurt again.

He kept looking up at me, only to glance back down in confusion. Some of the other players were starting to come out of the locker room, so I stepped closer to him and spoke quietly.

"I struggled inside when I found out. It really took me for a ride. I asked all these questions to myself a thousand times... what it meant, was I gay, or something else, and did I really want her or just what I thought she was. And I pounded my mind day and night for answers... but in the end, all I could see was her. And I realized that was the answer. I didn't need a label, I just needed her. I don't care what any of this means... I'm just going to give her everything I've got because I've never felt like this about anybody else before."

I could tell that Tyrell still hadn't recovered. Heck, I wasn't even sure if he was hearing me. He looked at me like I'd just told him I was quitting the football team to join the chess club.

"Bruh... are you gay?"

I laughed. "I'm into Maddie. As I said, I'm beyond caring what I am and am not. I'll let others make the labels for me. I spent many nights agonizing over all this. I would be so confused... and then I'd see her, and the confusion would evaporate. Gone. So, whatever I am, I am. I love myself. And I love her. And that's enough."

I looked at Ty and realized that for the first moment in my life, I felt like a complete person. The trickle of acceptance I had begun to feel in the early morning hours was now a waterfall of warmth, swirling around my body and erupting in my heart. I had seen through my deeper fears, and I had been honest to another human being about what I felt for Maddie.

"And you know what, Ty? While we're having this conversation, I want you to know I'm not changing for anybody else. People are either going to support me or they're not. And to tell you the truth? I couldn't care less." I slapped him gently across the back. "Come on, bruh. Let's go make idiots out of our defense."

I left him standing there and jogged onto the field, feeling for the first time that I had earned the right to hold my head high.

Thank you, Maddie. Even if you never look at me again, you've given me the strength to look deeper inside of myself. I'll never be able to thank you enough for that.

Tyrell kept his distance at practice as we went through the preliminary walkthrough ahead of Friday's game.

I felt at ease that afternoon. With a couple of games under our belt, I was settling into the season and had never been more sure of myself on the football field. It's like the game was slowing down, and I was playing in slow motion. When I lined up under center, I could see exactly what the defense was going to do before they did it. Now that I had answers to the rest of my life, football clicked into place.

In the locker room afterward, Ty was distant. We shared a locker next to each other and often chatted about anything and everything—tonight he didn't even look at me.

I didn't mind that too much. He needed time to digest everything. I watched him, detached, as he quickly went through the motions of getting his stuff together. A couple of weeks ago, I would have withered inside thinking that my best friend wouldn't accept me, that he would turn his back on me as I discovered deeper truths about myself.

Now? Only Maddie's acceptance mattered. Only her love counted. If Ty came around, that would be great. I would prefer that. But if he didn't, that was okay, too. I meant it when I said I wasn't going to change for him or anyone else. I had done that all my life and it had gotten me nowhere.

I took my time getting my stuff together, enjoying the new glow that had made a home in my mind. I walked slowly out of the locker room, listening for the telltale bass. When I didn't hear it, I knew that Ty had left without me.

Is it going to be like that then, bruh? I understand. Can't say it doesn't sting a little, but she's worth it. And if that means I walk home alone, so be it.

I was past hurrying; having nothing to hurry to. I allowed myself to be mindful of each step, feeling the uneven pavement beneath my feet. I listened to the evening birds chirp-chirp while enjoying the last red tendrils of light as the sun hung as heavy as an atlas stone at the edge of our desert town.

I wasn't alone, though. She walked with me. She was quiet, content to enjoy our sacred space together. I closed my eyes and reached out to hold her invisible hand. I talked to her without speaking, sharing my thoughts directly.

Were you proud of me back there? Were you happy that I finally admitted out loud what I know is true in my heart?

I pretended that I would hear an answer any moment. When none was forthcoming, I smiled and squeezed the hand of my little ghost.

Please answer me, Maddie. I want to hear your voice say something nice to me, just once.

Realizing that my imagination wasn't going to respond, I opened my eyes and looked to the west. The light was blurry and I stopped short of the next intersection and stared, wondering why Earth suddenly had three suns. I rubbed my eyes and discovered that my cheeks were soaked, long strands of moisture reaching down to the stubble across my jawline. I hadn't realized I'd been crying—I didn't feel sad, but rather unusually calm.

I turned the page, didn't I? The feeling of craving approval from outside of myself had always been a giant anchor cinched tight around my waist. At some point while falling in love with Maddie, it had slipped its knot and fell away. I no longer needed someone else to write my script, to tell me my life's path. I could follow my own truth, listen to my own mind.

What was that dumb Shakespeare play we had to read that said: To thine own self be true? I didn't understand much of the rest of it, but that part resounded in the caverns of my being. I've always needed to hear that.

Come on, Maddie. To hell with everyone else. Give us a chance. Let them say what they want; we'll have each other. It'll be enough. We'll snatch life from the jaws of death that surrounds us. I'd give up anything for you if it meant always feeling this alive.

I showered when I arrived home to an empty house, standing still and letting the water bead and slowly roll off my body. I wrapped a towel around my waist afterward, hesitating in the hallway as I considered eating before bed. I decided that I didn't have much of an appetite, and even though it was early, I climbed into bed.

She wasn't streaming tonight and I didn't feel like doing anything else. I put on one of her old streams, the volume turned just high enough to hear her voice like a whisper in my ear.

As I laid in bed, the room slowly becoming dimmer as the sun receded deeper below the horizon, it struck me how conditional everyone was. They shifted in the wind like palm trees, blowing in any direction commanded of them. Tyrell had seemed to be there for me no matter what until he thought I was gay. Then he couldn't even bother to give me a ride home.

Everyone else had always been the same way. If I stayed in the little box that was created for me, meeting the expectations of those around me, they were happy to support me. If I stepped outside of that box and wanted something different for myself, the support was removed.

Then there was Maddie. She had the support of her parents, but she didn't have much else. She certainly didn't have a support network at school, however flimsy I was learning my own to be. But unlike me, she didn't give a damn. Sure, she got hurt and embarrassed, but did that stop her from being herself? From showing up every day the way she wanted, even in the face of physical threat?

No. Maddie didn't bend like everyone else I knew. She didn't yield. She was true to herself and was willing to pay whatever price was necessary to live authentically.

I shot up in bed, my clenched fist raised above my head. *Don't you ever give up, Maddie! Don't quit being you!*

In a shallow sea of half-truths and constantly shifting currents, you're the ocean beyond. I'm learning how to swim, and hopefully, someday, I can come and join you.

I talked to her as I fell asleep, just like I talked to her on the way home from practice. I told her how strange it was that the world had it all backward—that a girl who the world saw as a boy was actually the most authentic person anyone could ever meet. I laughed when I discovered I was still hopeful of a response.

Tomorrow, Maddie. Tomorrow, you're going to talk to me. Tomorrow, we begin.

Chapter 21

Maddie

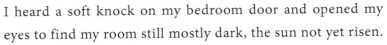

I heard a soft knock on my bedroom door and opened my eyes to find my room still mostly dark, the sun not yet risen.

I heard the door open and considered pretending to still be asleep. I was not ready for such a ghastly thing as Tuesday morning just yet. People hated Mondays; but Tuesday was the really awful day. On Monday, you at least were coming off a weekend break; on Tuesday, it was the second day of the school week with three entire days left *after* it was over before the weekend began again.

I wasn't a fan, and whoever had the balls to interrupt the last moments of my sleep were risking their health and well-being.

"Hey," Charlotte whispered.

I sighed audibly and sat up. *If she's waking me up this early, she must have something important on her mind.*

"Come in," I croaked, frowning at how deep my voice sounded in the morning before coffee.

She tiptoed in, closing the door gently behind her. I felt her climbing into my bed, so I scooted over and offered her some of the covers. She got under but kept fidgeting, her legs moving up and down like a metronome. Now awake and growing increasingly annoyed by what seemed to be an unnecessary intrusion into my morning routine, I rolled toward her.

"Is there a reason you shaved an hour of sleep off my day or are you just feeling especially cruel lately?"

The fidgeting stopped. Thank God. "What do you mean especially cruel lately?" she said softly, and the guilt was instantaneous.

"Well, after your little adventure with Kellan around the neighborhood last weekend, I can only surmise that you've woken me up to tell me that you want to date him. I saw how excited you were at the table. It's not like I don't know what you're thinking—"

"Ow! What the hell?" I yelped, rubbing my freshly kicked leg. I was about to shove her out of my bed when I saw the tears in her eyes and became confused. I put my hand on her arm but she spoke first.

"Maddie... I love you. I'm never going to take something away from you that I know you want... even if you don't know you want it, okay? This isn't about Kellan... it's about something else..."

She trailed off and I waited patiently, trying to ignore the part of myself that agreed with her about wanting Kellan.

"Okay, well what was important enough to wake me up? What's wrong?" I asked, more conscious of the way I was speaking. Pre-coffee conversations were never my strong suit, especially after becoming seriously addicted to the liquid essence of joy over the summer.

"I'm... I don't think I can say this. I'm not as brave as you are," she said, turning away from me.

"Whatever it is, you know I'm here for you. You've always been there for me... even though I haven't deserved it. You can tell me anything. I'm not going to judge you, Char." I reached out and brushed her hair with my fingers.

She sniffled and everything came pouring out at once, her voice sounding like a YouTube video being played at 4x speed. "I'm gay. That's why I asked you for that book and it's why I'm always trying to hang around when Destiny is here, and it's why I wanted to vomit when I kissed Trevor Parks over the summer and he felt me up and it was just so unbelievably disgusting, but when I think about kissing a girl, my heart does backflips and—"

I sprang to her, crushing her in an embrace. "Shh, it's okay, I understand. It's nothing to be ashamed of." I paused, trying to think of what Mark would say. Coming out had always been about me and never about anyone else. I hadn't considered that since I was queer, people might feel comfortable sharing with me. My sister trusted me enough to start her journey here. I'd never felt so close to her. I tried to focus so I wouldn't ruin what I knew from experience was a huge moment that she'd never forget.

"Hey, I'm honored that you chose me to come out to first. I'm really proud of you for having the courage to discover yourself and be honest about it. I didn't see this coming... at all. I'm so sorry that I'm always so wrapped in my own shit," I heard her sniffling and paused. "Hey, I love you and everything is okay. You're perfect the way you are."

Oh my God, I'm terrible at this. I'm failing at being queer right now.

Through her tears, she said, "Well, to be honest, I sorta kinda came out to Reddit first... but it's only because I was questioning! I wanted to talk to other girls who felt the same way. This isn't some stupid 'I just want to kiss my friend to see what it feels like' kind of thing. I literally dream about being with girls every night," she paused and bit her lip. She smiled and I wiped the tears away from her closed eyes.

"And I mean literally dream. Every night in my sleep there is this girl in like a warrior's outfit and she's climbing this giant tower to reach me where I'm imprisoned. It's like Rapunzel but weird. The only part that sucks is that every time we kiss, I wake up. It's not fair!"

We giggled together and I twirled a piece of her hair between my fingertips. I felt so much joy toward her that I was afraid if I didn't stop hugging her, I'd squeeze her to death. I flopped back over on my back.

"I can understand wanting to hang around Destiny if you're gay. Inside and out, you don't get much hotter than her."

I felt Charlotte sigh as she curled into a tighter ball. "Yeah, that's been one crush among many I've had the past couple of years. All of my crushes are probably straight girls." She put her hands up. "Don't worry, I've read all about the hazards of crushing on straight girls. But, I mean, it's not like you can control these things. Most people aren't gay and I haven't the first idea of how to notice the possibilities." She slumped against me.

I smiled so big in the darkness that I was surprised the room didn't light up. "Who exactly said that Destiny is straight?"

I felt her go still. In that adorable little voice of hers that was full of hope, she said, "She's not straight?"

"No, she's pan. I don't think she's ever been with a girl, at least not that she's told me. But we have talked about sexuality and gender. I mean, obviously we would. So, don't write off Destiny yet."

"Pan? What does that mean?" she asked, turning to face me.

I laughed. "You really do need a queer education. After school today, we're doing Queer 101. It'll be your own private AMA with me, your resident Super Queer!" I made a jubilant thumbs up at the ceiling.

"But, yeah, pan means that you're not so concerned with the outer wrapper as much as you are the person inside. She likes boys, girls, non-binaries... Destiny doesn't discriminate."

"Oh... okay... that's cool." I could hear the hope in her voice as the wheels started turning in my head.

"Why don't you text her and ask her to hang out? It doesn't have to become a relationship. I have no idea what Destiny thinks of you. But you're both 16. You both like ridiculous house music. I don't know. You could at least hang out, see if there is a little spark there?"

Charlotte looked as if I'd told her she could play my Super Nintendo. (For the record, don't touch it unless you want to die).

"You would... let me? You hate when I try to hang around her."

I arched my back before flopping back to the bed with an exaggerated groan. "Okay, look, I think we've established that I'm kind of an ass. I'll work on it. I'm sorry about the Kellan thing. I'm going to say this once and only once— you're right about my feelings. And I need to process that before I completely drive him away.

"But as far as Destiny is concerned? If my sister has a crush on my best friend, I'm not going to stand in the way. I'd be so happy for you both! I'd have to kill her if she ever broke your heart... that part would suck... but whatever, we'll cross that bridge when we get there. And you'll have to work your own magic, I'm not saying a word to her. And maybe you can just start as friends with her. You obviously need queer friends. So, yeah, I'm all for it."

The sun began to rise and the room was bright enough to make out Charlotte's wide smile as she looked at me. She pecked me on the cheek and then I swore I could see smoke trailing her as she rocketed for the door.

"Oh my God! What am I going to wear when we hang out? I have no idea! Help me!"

I pulled the covers up to my chin, giggling. "You haven't even texted her yet! Get out of here! I've got like ten minutes left to rest and I plan on using it!"

I was still smiling minutes after she left as I regretfully made my bed and began getting ready for school. I was thrilled for Charlotte because I knew how much it meant to come out to a trusted person.

She also helped me look at Kellan differently. He had opened my eyes in the hallway yesterday when he had as good as confessed to his best friend that he was into me. I didn't see that coming. I thought it was something he would want to keep private. The fact that I was wrong about that made me think I might be wrong about a lot of things.

I groped around in my closet and found my favorite Amon Amarth t-shirt. I paired it with leggings, plopped on my normal makeup, and headed downstairs. Breakfast flew by in its normal chaotic way, with everyone bumping into each other as we grabbed our food.

For the first time since I could remember, I was in a good mood as I walked into the school. I looked down the hallway and easily spotted Kellan standing head and shoulders above almost everyone else. He was at the far end, and I thought that if he approached me, I'd say hi… or something. I'd at least be nice. I felt a pang of fear that maybe I'd gone too far and had pushed him away already, but the smile in his eyes when he saw me told me otherwise.

I lost sight of him as I made my way through the crowd. As I was about to reach my locker, I felt someone tap my shoulder.

"I just don't understand. Are you male or female? Or do you choose each morning?" Like a shark smelling blood, a bully could sense a good mood. I turned and saw two tall boys sneering down at me. I tried walking around them, but they kept blocking my path.

"Nope, wrong way! Nope, not that way either, freak!"

I was not prepared for this today. My edge was completely gone after Charlotte's confession and my opening toward Kellan. I didn't have it to fight. All I wanted was the semblance of a normal school day… or whatever cisgender kids experienced at school.

I looked past the boys and noticed Kellan quickly approaching. A solitary tear fell down my cheek.

"What's wrong, are we hurting your precious little feelings? Do you have PMS? Or wait… you can't, can you?" the boy on the right said.

Kellan kept moving in and out of view as he got closer. I knew he could hear what they were saying because it had become a lot quieter around us. Kellan stepped quietly behind the boys and we locked eyes. When he saw me crying,

I could tell something was snapping deep inside of him. His face became pure rage, his brow lowered almost over his eyes, his upper lip curled. I could see him trembling and I wasn't sure what was going to happen next.

I tried to take one more step around the boys, hoping that maybe they'd had their fun and I could get on with my day.

"Why can't you just be a normal faggot instead of pretending to be a girl?" one of the boys said with a laughing sneer.

I don't know why but that broke me, broke everything I had inside. It had taken me over two weeks to feel comfortable in this school, and the first moment I did, I got bullied hard. I didn't even know these kids.

Tears spurted out of my eyes as I looked up at their laughing faces. I glanced back at Kellan, but he was already a blur of motion.

He let out a deep roar as he launched himself at the guy that called me a faggot, slamming him into the lockers. I watched, horrified, as the boy ricocheted off the metal like a pinball. He stumbled back toward Kellan, his body bent in half, the wind knocked clean out of him. Kellan let out another scream as he bent down and swung as hard as he could, connecting an uppercut into the boy's ribs, the sickening sound of shattering bone causing a gasp throughout the rapidly forming crowd.

Kellan watched him fall to the ground and then turned toward the kid's friend. The boy looked at him as if he'd seen a ghost and tried to run away. Kellan sprinted after him, needing all of five steps before he caught him by the collar of his shirt. His head snapped back so hard, I knew he'd have whiplash. Kellan tightened his arm around the boy's throat in a chokehold.

"Kellan, don't!" I yelled, my own voice frightening me. I was afraid that he was so far gone that he'd kill this kid if I didn't stop him. He shoved him to the ground and I watched him hit the concrete floor, roll, and then scramble away.

I could see Kellan turning back to me out of the corner of my vision as I stood shaking, looking at the kid laying destroyed by my feet. The boy was moaning something, but I couldn't make out his words. I felt strong hands touch my shoulders and I looked up.

"Are you okay?" Kellan half-whispered into the hushed hall. I nodded yes and he wiped the tears off my cheeks. I didn't fight him but closed my eyes. The memories of all the years spent wishing that Kellan would look at me, would touch me, would want to be with me came bursting forth. His touch felt like the core of a dream come true. His fingertips only brushed across my cheeks for maybe a second, but all my focus went rushing to the contact, and I was left fighting not to beg for more. I wanted to lean into him and ask him to carry me out of here before anything could hurt me again.

He released my shoulders and spun around slowly, looking at the gathered crowd.

"I told every single one of you. I warned you. If you mess with her, there will be consequences." He motioned toward the kid next to his feet.

"Take a good look. That's you if you mess with her. I don't care who you are. You mess with her; you're messing with me. I will find you. And I will hurt you. LEAVE. HER. ALONE!"

I saw him lock eyes with his best friend, Tyrell, but from his closed face, I could tell that they weren't exactly on speaking terms right now. Was that because of me? I saw Charlotte peek-a-booing a few rows back in the crowd, the concern evident on her face. I mouthed to her, "I'm okay," and looked back to Kellan.

I watched as he finally broke off his staring contest with Tyrell and shook his head. When he looked back at me, his eyes were softer, and I let myself release into them for the first time. The tension flowed out of my body like air from a slashed tire. When I smiled at him, a real, genuine smile, he looked transfigured as if light was beaming out of every pore.

There had always been tension between us ever since the first day he walked into the café. But that tension felt like repulsion, of wanting to scream and kick and punch until he finally left me alone. This tension was different. There was a warmth between us and I felt like we were standing in our own little bubble, shielded from the cold and dark surrounding us.

The walls and roof recede and fall away, and then the people beyond the bubble disappear. We stand alone, the empty darkness beyond forming a tight circle, the only light seeming to emanate from our bodies. He closes the distance between us and takes my hands into his. I feel so small this close to him.

Kellan looked as if he was about to say something, but the school cop cut through the crowd and my daydream and placed her hand firmly on Kellan's arm. He shrugged it off and stared her down for a second.

"Kellan, follow me now!" she said.

When he looked back at me, I was waiting for him. I hadn't looked away.

"Your smile... it's everything to me..." he whispered before walking slowly backward. I heard the nurse as she whirled past me to reach the kid sprawled on the concrete floor. I didn't bother to look—he had gotten what he deserved. He hadn't cared if he took a knife and slashed the inside of my soul, so why should I care what became of him?

I kept my eyes on Kellan's back and didn't move until he had disappeared around the far corner. I was brought out of the trance he had put me in when Charlotte wrapped her arm around me and asked if I was okay.

"Are you alright, Maddie? That was pretty intense. I only saw the end of it, but I could gather that someone bullied you and Kellan snapped."

"Yeah... yeah, it was intense," I said, my eyes dreamy as I stared through Charlotte as if she wasn't there. "His eyes...

they really are just for me, aren't they? The way he looked at me... I thought I was going to melt and turn into a puddle."

"What? No, I meant... oh," she smiled. "Yeah, I guess that was intense, too." She grabbed my arm and ushered me away from the scene. When we had rounded the hall and we were alone, she put both her hands on my shoulders.

"Are you really okay, Maddie? We need to get to class but I wanted to make sure you're okay before I leave you alone."

Still lost in a haze of wonder, I nodded. "Yeah. I've never been better."

Chapter 22
Kellan

"Well, this escalated quickly, Kellan." Dr. Walker was in a foul mood and made no effort to conceal who she blamed.

I sat slouched to one side in the chair opposite her, a lazy grin pasted across my face. It took a concerted effort to hear what she was saying—it was almost impossible to care.

I was still in that hallway, where I had the strangest and most wonderful sensation of it being just the two of us. I was still holding the hands of the angelic little figure who had singlehandedly reached inside my heart and beaten back the dark emptiness that I didn't realize was there, leaving me suffused in her sublime light.

"Well? What do you have to say for yourself?"

I flicked my eyes to Dr. Walker's. "She got bullied and no one was there to protect her," I started, nonchalant. "I warned you, told you what was happening, and nothing changed. The adults in the room couldn't do the job. You failed. So, I did the job for you. The blame for what happened in the hallway is with YOU. But don't worry, Maddie will be safe, one way or the other."

I laughed when Dr. Walker's head snapped back. She looked as if she'd been electrocuted.

"Who do you think you are, coming in here speaking to me like this? After what you did to those boys? After that little speech you gave afterward? Are you aware that you *could* be expelled for the threats you made? Do you know what disciplinary consequences you are facing, young man?"

I slouched further into the chair, allowing my head to come to rest in my hand.

"I haven't the faintest idea. Enlighten me."

"For openers, I SHOULD kick you off the football team. You're looking at a minimum one-game suspension. And you're going home for the rest of this week, that's non-negotiable."

I didn't bother to respond. I could live with a one-game suspension. Coach Baker would be pissed, but it was what it was.

"Do you see the seriousness of what you've done? And what you could lose?"

"Yes."

"Then, you're sorry for what you've done?" she asked expectantly.

"No. I'm sorry for the despicable lack of action this school has taken to protect Maddie. I'll never be sorry for protecting her."

Dr. Walker leaned back in her chair, her voice finding a lower range I didn't know she had. "Kellan, I am suspending you from school for the rest of the week. And you're off the football team for two games. I don't care what Coach Baker says. This might be a big joke to you, but it's not for me. It's going to be a nightmare trying to explain to that kid's parents why he has broken ribs and possibly a concussion, maybe even internal bleeding."

I was playing with fire, but I didn't care. Whatever happened to that kid didn't matter. He laughed when he saw Maddie crying. I wasn't going to sit here and feel bad for him or his parents.

"Actually, I think that will be the easiest part of your day. I can do it for you if you'd like. It's simple: he told the girl that I'm in love with that she should be a normal faggot. Whatever happened to him next makes perfect sense, don't you think? His parents should feel lucky that he still has a pulse."

Dr. Walker abruptly stood. "Please sit in the front office until a parent or guardian comes to retrieve you. That will be all."

I nodded slowly. When I stood up, I made a point of silently towering over her for a few seconds before walking to the door.

You're nothing but a paper-pushing coward. All those years in school to get to this position... for what? To sit here like a little tyrant? You should have helped her.

I stopped at the doorway. "You know, it's hard doing the right thing until you actually do it. Then it's the easiest thing in the world. You ought to give it a try sometime."

I didn't wait for her response. I walked, head high, back to the front office and flopped down into an old couch in the corner. I got comfortable, figuring that it'd be a while before my mom would be sober enough to answer the phone.

In the eerie calm of the office, I contemplated my punishment. The rest of the week off from school was a gift. I was at a crucial part of my manga book, and now had the hope that maybe Maddie would actually want to see it.

The football games would sting when my adrenaline wore off. Two games weren't the end of the world—it wouldn't sacrifice our ability to win states. But those were two games that the scouts would be attending and I wouldn't be there. Two opportunities to showcase myself. Two more steps out of this town.

Coach was definitely going to be hot. That wasn't going to be fun, but I'd live. Nothing was going to dampen the warmth that had spread to every cell in my body.

We held hands. She smiled. Nothing else matters.

I closed my eyes, holding Maddie's smile in the hallway, basking in the triumphant gleam in her eyes.

I must have drifted off at some point because when I opened my eyes, I saw my father standing in the office, staring blankly.

What the hell was he doing here? I returned his stare, searching for subtle clues as to his current level of inebriation. Was this going to be happy dad or angry dad?

Doesn't look wasted yet. I thought you were out of town, Dad, hauling up and down the east coast. I didn't realize you had come back already. Lucky me.

Dad broke the silence between us after the secretary awkwardly left the room.

"They called me. Guess they couldn't get a hold of your mother. Come on, Kellan, let's go. We'll talk about this back at my place," he drawled.

His truck carried the same liquor and stale tobacco smell that had turned my stomach since I was a little kid. Thankfully, the radio was country instead of talk. The combination of talk radio and drinking brought the worst out of my dad.

His trailer was way outside of town, and on the ride out, I realized I hadn't been there since last Christmas. I let myself escape into the vistas opening before us as we left Rock Canyon. The desert is mesmerizing once you get a few miles outside of town. Only the occasional cluster of cacti and desert grass interrupted the rock and sand.

I didn't even attempt small talk. If Jack Davis had something to say, he'd say it one way or the other. He didn't seem too upset, but if I said one thing the wrong way, it'd be game over.

When we pulled up next to his trailer, I noticed a second car parked in the driveway adjacent to the faded "Make America Great Again" sign.

Well, this should be interesting.

I expected to see a woman on the couch or in the kitchen when I walked in, but no one was there.

"She's probably still asleep or I'd have her say hello. Don't worry, you didn't interrupt anything this morning. We did all that last night." I arched my eyebrow and my dad chuckled.

He sat down in his recliner across the room and I sat on the couch. I didn't want my clothes to wreak and avoided leaning back into the worn-in cushions. Dad pulled out a pack of cigarettes and I felt like my effort was futile. He plucked one in his mouth and fished around his pocket for a lighter, grunting when he came up empty. He sat the pack down and cleared his throat.

"So, they tell me you've been suspended for the rest of the week and you're going to miss two football games. What in the hell was worth all that?"

He smiled, and I could tell he was looking for some war story to be able to tell his road buddies, to pretend somehow like he had something to do with it.

Alright, Dad, you want a good story to tell? Try this on for size.

"A couple of kids were picking on a girl that I like. I've talked to the principal about it before, I've even made a speech about bullying in front of the entire school. And yet, here these kids were, picking on this girl. I saw her crying and I snapped."

Dad furrowed. "Why were they picking on this girl? Doesn't sound like the kind of girl you'd be hanging out with.

I've seen the girls that are all over you after your football games. I don't think anybody is going to make fun of them."

I held his eyes, waiting for his laughter to die down, and took a terrible chance.

"This girl is transgender."

Dad's face went stone cold. His cheeks were pulled tight, the lines running across like a road map from years of substance abuse. He moved to the edge of the recliner, and I was suddenly aware of how quiet it was out here. The steady ticking of an old clock behind me was the only thing that filled the vacuum of silence.

"What does that mean? Transgender..." I clenched my fists at the way he said the last word. I became conscious of my breathing, fighting to stay in control. I was juggling fire now, and one small mistake would be it all it took to get burned.

"In her specific case, it means that she is a female who was born in a male's body. But it can mean quite a few different things, depending on the person."

I watched my old man's face distort into an ugliness that I had expected. Still, it hurt, and I could feel the surge within, riding on a wave of years of repressed anger.

"So, let me get this straight. You defended a queer who thinks he's a girl, and that was worth losing two football games for? When you've got scouts from all the major college football programs coming to see you? Is this some kind of a joke? Because I'm not laughing, son."

I saw the slightest hint of an off-ramp, a way to defuse this situation, tell him it really was just a sick joke. But I wasn't interested in that. I was done hiding and done lying. If I was ever to deserve Maddie, I couldn't run from her when she wasn't around.

"It's not a joke, Dad. And, yes, she is queer, I guess, but not in the sense that you mean it. She is a transgender female."

He got that whiny tone in his voice that he usually gets when he's drunk and indignant about something on Fox News. "I don't care how woke you want to make it, she's a he where it counts, right?"

"She has a male body, yes. What does that matter? Should kids be allowed to pick on her just because they want to? Is she barred from deserving dignity because she's not what everyone else wants her to be?"

His eyes narrowed, his lips parting slightly. He kept leaning forward, inch by inch, until I thought he was going to fall off the chair. I knew this look, and I knew it well. I tensed, preparing myself for when he jumped. I wasn't going to take it today. Not about her.

"You said you liked her. What exactly did you mean by that, boy?" he said, his tone turning rougher with each word. I knew what I would say next would push him past the edge.

I was about to respond to him when I noticed a sliver of sun falling in through a window behind him. The contrast of light cutting through the dingy pallor of the living room reminded me of Maddie in the hallway. I imagined her sitting next to me, holding me in her vision, waiting to see if I could proclaim my true feelings for her even in the middle of hell. I wrapped our hands together.

"I mean, that I am in love with her."

The clock behind me ticked on steadily, and I wondered which tick would be the final one I'd ever hear.

"Are you telling me that my son is gay?"

"I'm telling you that I like her. I don't know the answer to any of the rest of it. What's it to you? It's not like it's your business anyway."

That did it. He sprung up out of his chair.

"You son of a bitch! You don't talk to me that way! I didn't raise no fuckin' queer!"

I stood, feeling calm but ready for anything.

"You didn't raise me at all. The only thing you raised were aluminum cans, one after the other, until you beat either me or my mother."

I saw him reach into his pocket. Ever since I was a little kid, I remembered that he carried a switchblade. He would tell me that it came in handy as a truck driver in case somebody crossed him late at night at a rest stop.

I didn't hesitate to make the first move. I lowered my shoulder and plowed him back into the recliner. The chair tipped over, the table with the cigarettes falling sideways onto his face.

"You fucker, I'm gonna—"

I didn't stick around to hear him finish. Instead, I bolted for the door, throwing it open and sprinting away from the trailer.

Thinking quickly, I planned to stay on the road, getting as far as I could until I saw his truck pursuing. I had hunted with my dad out here before, and I wasn't really interested in trying to make my way back to town through the open desert. It was easy to lose your sense of direction in the monotonous rolling landscape.

I ran as hard as I could until my body gave out. I slowed to a walk and said a small prayer as I reached into my pocket. I felt the hard plastic case and sighed with relief.

Thank God I was carrying my phone with me. The miles between my dad's trailer and Rock Canyon had never been more imposing, and with no water, I'd dehydrate before I made it back to civilization.

I opened my phone and blanked. Who was I going to call at this time of day? Mom would still be passed out, and I didn't have any other family in the area. All my friends, if I had any left, were still at school.

I scrolled through my contacts, looking for anything, and stopped when I saw "Hugh Martin."

I clicked on the contact, my fingers trembling. I thought about it for a minute, and with nothing to lose, hit the call button. The phone rang three times and then I heard the gentle voice of Maddie's father.

"Kellan? Is everything okay?"

"No, it's not. It's a long story, I can fill you in later. For now, I need a ride if at all possible. I'm way out on Saguaro Road, walking back toward Rock Canyon. Maybe, I don't know, ten miles out. I wouldn't have bothered you, but I didn't have anyone else to call."

The line went dead silent, and I pulled the phone away from my ear, checking to see if I still had reception. The call was still active.

Had I pushed him too far? I hadn't stopped to think much about it before the call, but this was seriously out of left field. He probably expected this to be about something happening at school... which, it was, but it had become a little more complicated than that.

"Are you still there?" I asked. I heard the distant sound of a chair creaking and he sighed.

"Yeah, I'm here. Are you alone? Is Maddie with you?"

"No, it's just me," and I wanted to laugh, thinking that interrupting any time I had alone with Maddie would be the last thing I'd ever do. If she was with me, I'd call when we were on the verge of passing out from dehydration. Maybe.

Hugh muttered something to himself that I didn't catch. I waited, considered explaining myself more, and then he finally responded again.

"Okay. I'm leaving now."

"Thanks, I appreciate it." I hung up and looked back toward the trailer, searching for my father's truck. Not seeing anything, I wiped the sweat from my face and kept walking.

I could see Hugh's Volvo a good mile up the road before it reached me. The heat shimmered off the black hood and I thought maybe all this was just a mirage, or maybe a wild dream.

I should stop and enjoy this because it has to end soon, right? I mean, she didn't really smile at me, did she?

When the car reached me, Hugh slowed, and I climbed into the passenger seat. Hugh put the car in park and looked at me for a long moment. I thought I saw the hint of humor in those dark eyes, but I couldn't be certain. He removed a water bottle from the cup holder and handed it to me. I opened it immediately and started guzzling. I could hear him drumming his fingers on the steering wheel as he waited for me to finish drinking.

I drained the contents and then glanced at him. "Sorry for sweating all over your car. I'll clean it up when we get back to town."

He waved me off. "Don't worry about it. But how about telling me why we're ten miles outside of town before noon on a school day?"

I chuckled and put the empty water bottle between my legs. "My father lives a few miles away from here. I was suspended from school this morning for the rest of the week, and since my mother was probably too drunk to answer her phone when the school called, my dad got the honors of picking me up. And then when I told him why I was suspended, he went for his switchblade. I tackled him before he had the chance to use it, then bolted. And here we are."

The humor in Hugh's eyes evaporated. His face fell and he took his hand off the gearshift. He kept opening and closing his mouth like he wanted to say something but didn't. I didn't realize how screwed up my father's actions were until watching Hugh's reaction.

You probably think I come from the worst white trash west of the Mississippi. Well... you're not wrong!

Hugh scratched at his cheek before shaking his head and putting the car in drive and turning us around.

"I guess you had better start from the beginning, Kellan. What happened today? I have the feeling that somehow this is tied to Maddie." He snorted and shook his head again.

I adjusted the seat as best as I could and drank in the cinnamon cookie smell.

"Alright... from the beginning..." I told him every-thing, concluding with the principal's office. "All the fun I've had today earned me a vacation for the rest of the week. And two football games."

Hugh had stayed quiet while listening, but midway through I had started to pick up on his growing agitation. When I finished, he could no longer hold it back.

"Kellan! My God, why did you do that? You didn't have to do that! That could have been handled differently. You can't go around beating up everybody who makes fun of her. That's the problem with this world, everything is an eye for an eye!" He banged the steering wheel.

I nodded, not to him in particular, but because I could see his point. But it was hard for me to step back and see the bigger picture... not when I had stood in that hallway and felt like I was standing inside her mind, watching the gaping wound those ignorant kids had sliced open, the hemorrhaging of her anguish running like an angry red river from horizon to horizon.

I knew that I did what I had to for Maddie. Hugh wasn't there, he didn't see the sorrow on her face. He didn't feel the sting of watching her vulnerable and alone, the wolves encircling.

"I did have to do that," I said forcefully. "The school wasn't doing anything to protect her. So, I did. And I'd gladly do it again."

I looked away, out the window at the desert landscape. There were a few housing developments sprouting up here and there as we neared town.

"You know what though? It was worth it. Whatever the consequences, it was completely worth it... she finally smiled at me. We had a breakthrough. In front of the entire school, I was able to prove my feelings for her. It was glorious."

Hugh puffed his face and let out a rush of air.

"Kellan… I don't know what I'd do if you were my kid. I don't condone the violence. There is always another way… but I know your feelings for Maddie. Look, where am I taking you? Home to your mother's?"

I looked down at my hands and grinned.

"You can take me to my mom's, I guess. She's probably still passed out. I don't know where else I'd even go. It's fine, though. I can just go to my room and… I don't know. I have no idea what. But I'll be fine."

I could sense Hugh wanting to get into lecture mode but feeling that it wasn't his place. I actually hoped that he would, just to see what it felt like to have a real parent.

"Kellan, why don't you come back to our house? I'll fix you some lunch. I'd like to talk about this more if that's okay with you? I can't make you come, I can't make you listen, but I would appreciate it if you would."

I didn't hesitate. "Alright, that's fine with me."

As we turned into our neighborhood, I realized that I might be at her house when she got home. Would things be different now?

Will you be happy to see me? Have you let me in a little now? Or will it still be the way it was? Whatever it is… I'll still be here. Waiting for you. Ready to be… whatever you want me to be.

When we pulled into the garage at Maddie's house, Hugh put the car in park, shut it off, and looked at me.

"Is your father going to try to find you? Will he wonder where you are?"

I blinked, having forgotten about him. "Huh… I hadn't really thought about that. I don't think so. You know, it's awful enough, what he did. But it's worse that he didn't even follow, and probably won't even call." I shrugged. "I'm not worried about him. If it's up to me, I'm never seeing him again. Not after the way he reacted to Maddie."

Hugh started to say something, then patted my arm.

"Let's get inside, I'll fix us some burgers."

I followed him quietly into the kitchen, standing awkwardly while he gathered ingredients from the refrigerator. He sat a package of meat on the counter and laughed as he went back to grab onions and condiments.

"You have to sneak these in when Maddie's not here. You eat meat in front of her and you'll never hear the end of it. I've been forced to watch videos on YouTube, showcasing all the horrors of modern agriculture. I try to tell her this is grass-fed meat and the cow's life isn't so bad but… well, it's Maddie. She doesn't compromise. I've always admired her for how pure she is."

I smiled and meandered out into the living room. I was too nervous to get a look the first time I was here. The big L-shaped couch that sat in the center of the room looked cozy. I imagined the family gathering around to watch TV or play video games.

The walls were covered by the kid's artwork throughout the years, with stick figure drawings and blobs of paint that

only a parent could cherish. On the sloping wall of the staircase, the family names were connected via oversized letter
tiles.

Maddie's house made me feel like I did when I was a kid
watching the Disney channel. I would look at our broken
family and wonder why we weren't like the families in the shows.

I lingered in the living room, looking for the little
touches of her. I noticed a framed handprint made from
finger-paint and moved closer to see if it was hers. In messy
handwriting, it said, "For my mommy. Happy birthday!" A
name had been scratched out and in much cleaner handwriting, "Maddie" was written underneath.

I started to put my hand up to the handprint but
stopped when I noticed Hugh watching from the archway.
Blushing, I backed away.

"I remember doing stuff like this as a kid. If my mom
still has mine, it's probably shoved in the attic."

I continued to look at each thing she had made over the
years. I found a poem she wrote in elementary school about
a warrior princess who could fly:

> I soar above all the boys below
> With my cape that is pink and can glow
> I save the day with my magic staff
> Sprinkling my spells all along the winding paths
> I'm a warrior princess, don't you know?
> They sing my name throughout the land, whether
> friend or foe.

I read the date below the poem. She had written it when she was seven. She must have known even then.

I smiled at a gift certificate Hugh made her when she had hit 50 subscribers on Twitch. I took in the rest of Maddie's creations over the years, and had almost made it around the room when Hugh called me into the kitchen for lunch.

I joined him at a booth in the corner of their kitchen. It was pretty cool that they had an actual booth. I said something to Hugh about it.

"It's called a breakfast nook. When we built this house a decade ago, Daisy insisted on this. Extra cost aside, I have to say, it's become one of my favorite things about the house. It's a nice spot with these corner glass windows overlooking the backyard."

I nodded and took a bite of my burger. *Hole-lee-crap.* "Wow, these are amazing!"

Hugh looked at me conspiratorially. "You learn to make them count when you don't get many opportunities."

I laughed with him, imagining Maddie giving her parents a hard time. I doubted that the girl ever gave ground on something she cared about.

When we finished, Hugh suggested we sit in the living room and talk about what happened.

"I've got a Zoom meeting for work in about ten minutes, but I'd like to talk for a second before I have to get ready. Kellan... I know how you feel about Maddie. It's obvious that you're serious about her. And, trust me, from firsthand experience, I know how much it hurts watching her struggle. But you can't beat up the world every time it doesn't accept her. There are other ways of dealing with ignorance. For starters, I'm going to keep pushing the school to ensure her safety. It's their job, and it's my tax dollars paying their salaries. God knows I pay enough for them to do something."

His phone beeped and he clicked a button to ignore it.

"Look, I better get back to work. But listen… if you're open to it, here's what I'd like you to do next time this happens. You have my number. You can text me anytime you see something that isn't quite right. Better yet, record it so we have evidence. I'll contact the school right away and they'll have to deal with it… and in the meantime, instead of fighting, go up to Maddie and stand with her. Be a witness and an ally to her. Make your presence felt and pull her away from the bullying. You can be there without bloodying every kid who looks cross at her.

"And if you really want to help her, do what you can to make her feel loved and wanted on the inside… that's what she's struggling with. You can help to blot out the nasty things that she hears every day. You can make her forget about all that and get lost in something better. That's your role, Kellan, if you're going to be her boyfriend. You can create a better world for her. That's going to matter to her more over the long haul than how many people you fight. There's no end to the madness of the world... but you can be her little slice of paradise."

He got up and walked around the couch, stopping behind me. He squeezed my shoulder.

"Just give what I've said some thought. I have to get to this meeting, but you're welcome to stay and wait for Maddie. Feel free to play video games or whatever you want to do. You're not grounded."

I glanced back at him and he winked before walking to his office. When the door closed, I looked around at the room, still reeling from what he had said. It felt so natural getting advice from Hugh... as if that's how it was supposed to be for a kid. You make a choice or take an action, and then a responsible and caring adult helps you see what you did right and what you could do better next time.

I stared at the handprint on the wall. Hugh was ultimately right; beating up that kid might impress her temporarily, and it may have shown her that I really do care. But no amount of busted heads would take the sting away of having to hear the mean comments circle around her mind when she's alone. I can't bash the head in of every person who judges her; there isn't enough time in the day.

But I could be there for her... I could hold her hand and we could face the challenges together. I could fill her with love and hope that it was enough to wash away the hate.

"That's your role as her boyfriend."

That's optimistic, Hugh. That'll be the day. When I reach that milestone, you'll have to print me out one of those certificates like you did for Maddie.

I spied a Nintendo 64 sitting next to the Nintendo Switch. I'd seen her playing it on stream. I decided to give it a try, figuring it was either hang out here or go back to my bedroom and wrack my brain wondering if she would talk to me now. I'd rather wait and get my answer in a few hours.

Yep, think I'll stay here and play your video games, Maddie.

A cartridge was in the dock with the title "Everdrive 64." I fired it up and clicked on a menu option marked "Games." Cycling through the games, I stopped when I saw "Lenora's Mask — Vanilla Game."

Let's give this a try. It looked like fun when I watched her playing it.

It was funny—I lost all sense of time playing a game that was explicitly about managing time. I threw my hands up in frustration at least a dozen times trying to figure out what to do and when, only to discover that most of the rewards were only health capacity upgrades.

I fought for over two hours, figuring out the janky controls and the general lay of the land to reach the first dungeon. As I was entering the dungeon, I heard the door behind me open.

I jumped off the couch and spun around and looked into Maddie's startled eyes.

Chapter 23
Maddie

When I was a little girl, I used to watch my dad play old Super Nintendo RPGs. It would take weeks just to finish one. Mom thought I was nuts for enjoying even the parts where my dad would spend hours "grinding levels," or fighting enemies over and over again to earn experience points so that he could beat a tough boss. I loved everything about the experience—the art, the music, and especially the tough challenges that needed to be overcome so that a small group of teens with cool hair could save the world.

But my favorite part? The moment just after the final boss was beaten. I wouldn't be able to move as I read the text of the characters as they wrapped up their journeys. If anyone spoke during these primitive cutscenes, I'd flip out. There was something about going through the most excruciating challenges and coming out the other side that, even at that age, enraptured me.

Afterward, I would close my eyes and imagine myself there with my favorite characters, trying to get closer to their world to feel what they were feeling.

I tilted my head, staring at the Python script on the monitor in front of me, remembering the last time I had felt something close to this. I looked around the room at the rows of computers and the kids staring half-interested and I could have sworn that none of it was real.

I wasn't supposed to be in computer science right now. I was supposed to be wherever he was, seeing whatever he was seeing, touching whatever he was touching, feeling whatever he was feeling.

I placed my hand over my chest and thought of his eyes holding mine. *He really meant it. He... likes me.*

I kept saying this over and over to myself, trying to find a way not to trust it, but unable to deny it any longer.

In the hallway after class, I looked for him but then felt ridiculous, knowing that the principal wouldn't just release him after what he did to that kid.

The clouds I had been floating over dissipated, and I rushed back into reality. I started to panic, thinking about what would happen to him. Would they suspend him? Or worse?

By the end of the final period, my hands were shaking as I walked to the bus. I needed to know what happened to him. Charlotte picked up right away on my apprehension when I sat next to her on the bus. She grabbed my hands, trying to still them.

"Hey, what's wrong? Is everything okay? Were you bullied again?" she asked.

"Yeah, I mean, no, I mean… I don't know! I'm worried about Kellan. What do you think happened to him?"

Charlotte's hands moved to her heart as relief flooded across her face. "Aww, this is so cute! You finally admit to yourself that you like him, and that he is serious!"

I made a shrugging motion with my hands. "Well, obviously. He just defended me in front of a good chunk of the school. And… I don't want to run from it anymore. I just want to know if he's okay." I bounced in little jerky movements, unable to calm down.

"Aww, it's going to be okay! Why don't you skate over to his house and knock on his door? It'll probably make his life."

I glanced at her sideways and bit my lip. Could I really do that? Just go knock on his door? After everything I put him through?

"I guess that's one option… do you have any others?" I raised my eyebrows in a nervous smile.

"Wait, hold on a second. Lemme get this straight. Maddie, Ms. Cocky herself, is now suddenly too shy to go and knock on a boy's door that she wasn't scared to tell off multiple times? In front of our parents no less?"

I swatted at her shoulder. "It's different. This is… new. I don't know how to do this. I don't know what to say." I fidgeted with my thumb ring and noticed that we were almost at our bus stop. I had wished for this moment all day and now I was terrified.

"He likes you for who you are. You just... be you. For some reason, he likes that."

I smirked at her, then gathered my pack off the floor as the bus slowed to a stop.

"I guess I'll fix my makeup and then go over there." I swallowed hard, racking my brain for what I would say when he answered the door.

"Don't make it more than it is. He'll be thrilled to see you. Trust me, after watching him the other night, I can assure you he's going to go out of his way to make you comfortable. He literally worships you, Maddie. You rejected him all summer, told him you weren't interested, that he wasn't your type, you screamed in his face and almost punched him and—"

"Okay, okay, I'm a monster, I get it. Jeez, you're making me feel awful." I scratched at my arm absentmindedly, wondering if I should change my clothes before I leave.

Charlotte opened the door and I followed after her.

"Besides, you—"

I looked at Charlotte, curious as to why she stopped abruptly and then noticed movement out of the corner of my eyes. It was Kellan. He was holding my Nintendo 64 controller in his hands. He made it look so tiny.

"Or maybe you won't have to skate to his house. He could just be standing in our living room waiting for you." I could hear the smile in her voice.

"Hi," he said, not bothering to look at Charlotte.

"Hi," I responded, trying to force my mouth closed.

"So, there's a story for why I'm here. But I can leave if you want me to. Please don't be upset," he hastily said, and I cringed inwardly, remembering what Charlotte had said on the bus.

"No, please... I'd really like it if you stayed."

I breathed again as I watched him relaxing.

"Hey, Char, will you give us a minute?" I waved her away without taking my eyes off Kellan. When I didn't hear her move, I looked back.

The little brat was holding her phone out, recording us. I snatched it out of her hands and scowled.

"What? No way! Hand it back! This is getting good! I was getting ready to go make some popcorn!"

I pushed her playfully and thrust the phone at her.

"Go. Away. Now!" I said.

"Okay, okay, I'm going. But if you want to sleep tonight, you'll be giving me details. Or else I'll lay on top of you until you tell me what happened!"

I rolled my eyes and waited until she was up the stairs before turning back to Kellan. My heart thundered. This was so much easier when I was convinced that he didn't really like me. What would I say to him now? *Think!*

"Umm... so... you like Lenora's Mask?" I motioned toward the TV.

He blinked and glanced behind him.

"Oh, yeah, that... yeah, it's cool. I mean, I'm failing miserably at it right now, but it's fun. Finally made it out of

Time Town after two hours of running around. There's so much going on in that little town." He scratched his cheek.

"I could help you with that. I'm pretty good at this game if I do say so myself."

Kellan smiled at me the way he had all summer, but for the first time, I let myself enjoy it, my eyes naturally drawn to his full lips.

"Oh, I'm sure you could, but how about we take a walk and I'll tell you about my not very unique, supernormal day?" he asked, his deep-set eyes obscured in laughter.

I smiled and gazed at my shoes. "Sure."

"Oh, and grab your skateboard. Not because I like seeing you on it or anything."

I glanced up under my eyelids, unable to conceal the delight spreading across my face.

"Okay."

I was conscious of every movement I made as he followed me through the house to the garage. I hadn't been this nervous since the first day I presented as female. I felt daring enough to risk running a hand through my hair and wondered how that made him feel.

I grabbed my skateboard and pressed the button to open the garage door. "So, where are we going?"

"How about Mayfield Park at the end of the subdivision?"

I nodded and fell in beside him as we reached the sidewalk.

"Hey, go ahead, skate. Before this dream is over, I want to see this in person. Well, more than just you zooming past my house, pretending not to notice me."

I looked at him, ready to volley, but got lost in the gleam in his eye. I shook my head and giggled, throwing down my skateboard and jumping on. I skated back and forth on the road, feeling special when Kellan would walk backward so that he could watch me. I totally showed off, performing ollies and grinding the lip of the sidewalk.

"How long have you been a skater?" he asked as I slowed beside him.

I inclined my head. It felt like I was born with a skateboard. "Since I was six. Tony Hawk Pro Skater was like the first video game I played by myself. I played for hours and hours and just had to have one. I begged my dad and finally he bought me a skateboard for Christmas. I haven't stopped since. It was really helpful the last few years with everything. If I was feeling rough, I could just grab it and get lost for a couple of hours. I've skated so much that sometimes when I lay in bed and close my eyes, I feel like I'm still on my board, rolling across the pavement."

This close to Kellan, I smelled a mix of sandalwood and that musty teenage boy smell of body oil and sweat. It was wonderful.

"That's neat. You know, I thought about seeing if you went to the skate park over the summer." I must have shot him a funny look because he backed away with his hands up. "Hey, it's not like I went! I respected what you said. I only harassed you at work." He grinned and I rolled my eyes.

"But I bet you own the skate park. I'd love to see you there sometime. I've never actually skated before. I guess when you're a tall kid, you don't think about getting on a little board with wheels and trying to control it."

I giggled. "Yeah, well, thankfully, I never had that problem. I can teach you, it's not that hard. Can't promise you won't fall on your ass a lot, but it's fun."

"I'll take you up on that. You might have to hold my hand at first, though." He smiled coyly.

I smirked and sped away from him, the park just ahead. I was glad it was mostly empty. Kellan jogged after me and caught me at the entrance.

"Do you come here a lot?" I asked him, surveying the map of the trails just inside the gate. It was a tiny park but it seemed to make the most of the few acres it had with twisting and winding trails.

"Only when I get rejected by hot baristas."

I busted out laughing despite myself. So, he was a corny, witty kind of guy. I liked it.

"No, seriously," he continued, "I haven't been here in a couple of years. Not since my mom made me give up Baxter, my dog. I used to bring him here and throw a tennis ball for him until my arm felt like it was going to fall off. We had so much fun." Kellan looked away, a sad smile on his face, and I felt like squeezing his hand but didn't.

"Mom works nights as a nurse and was tired of being woken up all day. I used to enjoy sitting on this little bench in the corner of the park. It's nestled in a dense grove of desert willow trees. I'd like to check it out if that's cool with you?"

"Yeah, that sounds good." I felt an inner smile bloom across my heart. There was a sensitive side to Kellan. In all my thinking about him, I hadn't considered that he might be different than what he seemed like on the surface.

We walked in silence, the sounds of little kids playing on the playground blowing to us in the breeze. I hadn't been inside this park since... ever, I guess. I liked the cute little stone pathways that wound around clusters of trees and playgrounds. Mom was always complaining about the H.O.A. fees but at least they used the money for something cool like this park.

Kellan led the way. We would occasionally brush against each other, his hand bumping into my elbow. I tried to imagine how we would hold hands and walk together. I was so short and he was so tall. It would probably be comical to anyone watching.

Kellan flopped down on the bench. I sat and swung my feet up on the bench, facing Kellan, wrapping my arms around my legs.

"So, I had an interesting day. How about you?" he asked.

I rested my chin against my knees and snickered. "Yeah, can't say it was my usual experience."

I remembered the hallway and warmth washed over me.

"Hey, I just wanted to say thanks for what you did for me today. What those kids said to me... I've heard some mean things these last two weeks, but they really cut deep."

A streak of sunlight had pierced the canopy of desert willow and reflected in Kellan's eyes as if it was the middle of the day. I looked away and saw his face in the hallway, blazing with a fire that cut through all my doubts.

"No one has ever stood up for me like that. It was... amazing." I started to laugh. "You know, I'm almost sorry I stopped you with the second kid. But I had no idea what you were going to do. I didn't want you to like... kill him or something."

Kellan thrust his chin out. "Yes, I was quite something to behold." I pushed him gently on his shoulder and he rolled his head and smiled. "I wish your dad shared your feelings. He didn't find it awesome at all. He thought I should have filmed the bullying so we could use it to show the school the extent of what you're going through. But I think he misses the part where you smiled at me afterward in front of practically the entire school. It's lost on him." Kellan threw his hands out to the side and shrugged.

I groaned through my laughter. "Yeah, that sounds like Dad. By the way, how did he get involved in all this? What happened to you today? I was worried about you."

Kellan leaned back and wrapped his long arms around the bench.

"I got a suspension from school for the rest of the week and lost two football games. And since my mom is a drunk, they called my dad to pick me up. When we got back to his trailer and I told him why I was suspended, he went for his switchblade." I sat up, my jaw coming to rest against my chest. Kellan didn't see me, or he probably would have stopped.

"My dad lives way the hell out of town, so I took off running in the general direction of Rock Canyon. I knew I couldn't walk the entire 13 miles to town, so I grabbed my phone and searched through my contacts. I saw your dad's name and remembered he gave me his phone number at some point. He picked me up, we had lunch and talked. And I didn't really feel like going home... not when I could just sit and play video games and see you."

When he looked back at me, his expression instantly shifted. He reached out and touched my hand, and even through my shock, I felt heat ripple up my arm.

"Did I say something wrong?"

I shook my head. "No, it's not that. It's... you went through all that? Your dad pulled a *knife* on you? Oh my God, Kellan, why?"

Kellan's carefree smile returned, his shoulders sagging back into the bench. "Oh, that. I told him why the kids were picking on you. And then I told him I liked you. He said he didn't raise a queer and went for the knife. Just normal white-trash stuff, no big deal."

I looked away at the ground, not quite comprehending that a parent would pull a knife on their child because they liked someone. I thought of my parents and my heart sank for Kellan.

"You went through all that just because you like me?" I half-whispered, still not able to look at him. He reached his hand out again, this time letting it linger on mine.

"Yeah, but don't be sad. Remember when you, Maddie Martin, actually smiled at me, Kellan Davis? I mean, it's almost surreal after the past few months we've had, so if I'm not quite remembering it right, please correct me. But I think I am. And whatever I had to go through today, it was worth it."

He cracked his knuckles. "If I have to punch a few jerks each day to see that, I'm up for it. Might not be good for my throwing hand, though... but, hey! I'm not going to be needing that for a couple of weeks, so we're good."

I looked up at him, the smile unable to reach my eyes. I couldn't stop thinking about if the roles were reversed—if I had Kellan's parents. My dad had always been so supportive of me, no matter what. Kellan's dad would have probably tried something horrible like conversion therapy. I definitely had my challenges in this world and probably always would. But I was finding out I wasn't the only one.

"I'm really sorry that you're going to miss your football games. I'm sure that means a lot to you."

The first hint of shadow crept onto his face. "Yeah, I'm not going to lie, that sucks. I can easily take a vacation from school. But football... that's the only way I get to college." He sighed and rested his head in his hands. I wished that I hadn't said anything.

"Those guys are going to be distant from me now anyway. I don't... whatever. I don't care about most of them. You saw how they acted on the first day of school. But Tyrell... I didn't expect that. I told him about you at practice last night. He didn't take it well... but you know how it is, I don't have to explain it to you."

He looked at me like he understood and I nodded slowly, a small lump forming in my throat. Why did it always feel like when it came to me, people had to make a choice? I didn't really understand why who I was represented an ultimatum. It sucked that Kellan suffered because he liked me.

He must have sensed my apprehension because his voice got quieter. I leaned instinctively toward its deep softness. "Maddie... as far as I'm concerned, they can think what they want, cut me out of their lives, have nothing to do with me. Whatever. I don't care because I don't want to be a part of something that doesn't accept you. You'll see that if you let me stick around."

I felt like I was being tugged closer to him as his eyes bored into mine. He licked his lips and I wondered if he was going to kiss me. I didn't have to wonder if I wanted it.

He put his hand on my knee. "Hey, want to head back and play some games at your house? I saw Mario Kart in there. Think you can beat a dumb jock?"

I blinked, caught off guard, then laughed. "Oh my God... aww I'm sorry I called you that. I don't think you're dumb. But, uhh, yeah, I think I can beat you at Mario Kart. In fact, I know that I can."

He poked me on the arm. "Oh, yeah? Guess you'll just have to prove it. Come on, let's go." He snatched my skateboard up before I could react. "Give me that skateboard, I want to try."

He took off running and I followed him giggling. He was way too fast for me, and by the time I reached the road, he was already skating. He did okay going forward, but when he tried to turn around to avoid a car, he misjudged how much space he needed and slammed into the sidewalk. His big body spilled across it but his head fell in the grass.

"Kellan! Are you okay?" I yelled as I sprinted to catch up to him. He roared hysterically and I could hear him tell the driver who had slowed to check on him that he was okay. When I caught up to him, his face was covered in dust.

"That was fun. And umm... not as easy as it looks." He sat up and brushed himself off. "Should have probably waited for those lessons from the pro, huh?"

I crossed my arms. "Yeah, that was no way to impress a girl the first time you hang out with her. And you're going to get beat at Mario Kart, too. Man... it's not looking too good for you right now. Are you going to be okay tonight? It's going to be pretty rough. Sure you want to go through with all this?"

Kellan stood up, towering over me with a smirk.

"Save your trash-talking for the game. You might look really silly when Yoshi is way out in front of you on the bullet bike."

Oh no you don't. "Uh-uh, no way! I always play as Yoshi!"

"Sorry, I'm your guest. You HAVE to let me choose my character. Fair is fair!" He smiled at me sweetly and I wanted to slug him for being so cute and stubborn. That was my role.

"Let's get one thing straight. You're not my guest, you're my dad's guest. I had nothing to do with you being at my house today. Remember, I'm the one that's been trying to keep you out of it. So, yep. I'm playing as Yoshi. End of story." I leaned in and poked him lightly on the chest. "You wouldn't really try to bully me, would you?"

I made the cutest eyes I could, fluttering my lashes shamelessly. I watched Kellan's balance falter for a second and I knew I had won this round.

"So, that's how it's going to be then? I bust some heads in your honor, but nooooo, you have nothing to do with me getting an early exit from school, huh?" He backed up, pressing his lips into a smile. He looked away for a moment, then looked back to me with a mischievous smile. "Okay, tell you what. I'll play as Dry Bones. And, by the way, STILL beat you. But we got to make a bet, make this interesting."

"Like what kind of a bet? Like you and I each pick something that the other person has to do if we win?" I asked.

"Exactly. You pick first."

I tapped my fingers against my lips.

"Okay, if I win, you have to draw me another picture... but this time of yourself."

Kellan tilted his head. "Oh, like what you see, then?"

I shoved him, my breath catching when I felt the muscles of his stomach. "And in case I pass out during the race or something, and you somehow... I don't want to say win... but your character through no fault of mine just happens to finish before mine... what do you get?"

He took a step toward me and tucked a stray piece of hair behind my ear. "I get to kiss you."

He had to have seen my knees buckle, and I was certain he could see me blushing. It felt right that Kellan would be the first guy to touch me tenderly like that since he was the guy I most often... thought about since I was younger.

I looked at my skateboard laying at my feet and pretended to consider his offer. I already knew what I was going to say but I didn't want him to think it was such an easy choice. I moved my lips to one side of my face, playing it up. I wondered if his heart raced while waiting for my response. I hoped so. I twirled my hair between my fingertips and looked at him.

"Okay, deal. You're going to have a lot of time sitting at home this week to draw the perfect picture for me."

"We'll see about that."

The rest of the walk back to my house was mostly quiet, with the occasional stolen glance at each other. I could feel the tension of the hallway returning and growing ever stronger as we walked inside.

The sounds of the outdoors that had provided a buffer against my pounding thoughts shattered into silence as I went to set up the game. I expected it to feel awkward, but it felt more like waiting for the shower to heat up, knowing that, eventually, it would get so hot that it would burn if I wasn't careful.

"You know, that booth in your kitchen would be a cute spot for a first kiss."

I spun around to see him lounged across two couch cushions, a controller already in his hand.

"I'm glad you got a tour of my house when I wasn't here. You might want to focus more on sharpening your pencils, Kellan. I'll have a list of demands for this picture. Might be best to think about what you're actually going to be doing than what you'd like to be doing, hmm?"

I turned back around and grinned to myself. I heard footsteps on the stairs but didn't have to turn around to know it was Charlotte. I knew she'd check in on us at the first opportunity.

"Oh, cool! Mario Kart. Can I play the winner?" she asked, plopping down next to Kellan.

"Sure. We've made a bet. If I win, he has to draw me another picture, but this time, of himself. He's not going to win so it doesn't really matter what he would get."

"What do you get? Tell me!" she asked Kellan, bouncing up and down.

"I get to kiss her," he said, and then laughed when Charlotte jumped off the couch, her hand covering her mouth. She looked back and forth between us.

"Well, I think I know who I'm rooting for! Come on, play! Pick something short and quick that you suck at, Maddie."

"Pfft, you know I don't suck at this game. I think I'll pick—"

"Pick a random track, Maddie," Kellan interrupted. "No cheesing it by picking one of your favorites. I want a real chance at those lips."

"Fine with me. I'll beat you on any track, any time of the day."

The match started close—each of us taking turns in first place during the first two laps. I was surprised that he was good at this game. I had a hard time imagining Kellan playing anything Nintendo. I figured he was all Fortnite or Madden or whatever else jock kids played. *What other surprises do you have for me?*

At the start of the final lap, he was right behind me.

"Just slow down a little bit. I know you want me to win. You like my prize better," he said.

"Uh-uh, no way I'm losing to you. You want it, you gotta earn it."

He grunted. "Oh, don't I know it."

I ran through a question block and got three green shells out of it even though I was already in first place. It was admittedly a super lucky haul, but I wasn't telling Kellan that.

The green shells rotated around my bike, and one by one, I started firing them back toward Kellan. The first two barely missed, but the third connected, stopping him dead in his tracks.

"Ha! I told you. You're not beating me at this game, or any other game for that matter." I stuck my tongue out at him.

Kellan sighed, handing Charlotte his controller. She looked as disappointed as he did. His puppy dog eyes turned up to max as he looked at me.

"Be honest. You're disappointed. You're going to have to wait for our first kiss. It's not like I can give it to you now. And I was really wondering if your lips would taste as good as you smell."

I heard Charlotte gasp but ignored it. I brushed the hair out of my face with a quick flick of my head.

"What do I smell like?" I asked, my voice a lot quieter than it was during the game when we were trash-talking.

"Cinnamon cookies. With lots of sugar." His honey-brown eyes narrowed in a challenge.

I looked away, my heart somehow feeling like it was beating in every cell of my body. I flinched when my parent's bedroom door opened. My mom took one look at Kellan and burst open like a flower in spring.

"Oh! Kellan! It's great to see you again. Oh, Maddie, I'm so happy that you've come around."

Thanks for embarrassing me, Mom. At least you picked a good time to do it.

"You guys hungry? I haven't eaten a thing all day. I was so busy at Ryan's school that I didn't even stop for lunch. How about pizza, guys? I pulled the dough out this morning." Mom turned to Kellan. "Maddie usually makes us pizza at least once a week. She keeps us all healthy with her vegan cooking. We always make two pizzas and have plenty of leftovers. Stay for dinner! We'd love to have you," my mom finished with a smile.

"Oh, man, that sounds great. I'll help you make it," he said, standing and motioning toward the kitchen.

"You cook?" I tried to imagine him coming home from football practice and opening up a recipe book. Couldn't see it.

"No, I like microwaves and delivery. But it would be fun to cook with you. It'll probably go as well as my skateboarding and Mario Karting."

I giggled as Charlotte moaned.

"I can already tell that I'm going to regret telling you to be nice to him."

Mom frowned at Charlotte. "Leave them alone, Char. Go ahead, you two. Any time you're ready. I'm starving! I've got to grab your brother from his after-school program and then we'll be back."

Kellan followed me into the kitchen. I grabbed a homemade sauce out of the fridge, along with a bundle of vegetables.

"So, vegan pizza... what's that look like?"

I pulled up a recipe on the iPad stationed at the corner of the kitchen island. We usually left it there because I was always trying new recipes.

"So, the pizzas I usually like to make are loaded with veggies and use a cashew cream sauce instead of tomato sauce. Check it out." I pointed to the screen. Kellan moved to look closer but bumped his head on the fan hood mounted over the gas range. It was positioned a little lower than it would have been over a normal stove range because it was in the middle of the kitchen. I suppressed a laugh as he rubbed his forehead.

"Broccoli, corn, cherry tomatoes, onions, jalapenos, and sun-dried tomatoes... wow, this is a ton of chopping, isn't it?"

I pointed to my arms. "Yeah, well, I'm pretty good with a knife, I can handle it."

Kellan sucked in a gulp of air and looked like he was going to faint as his eyes tried to avoid the scars running every which way on my arms. I busted out laughing and swiped his concern away with my hand.

"I'm just kidding. I haven't self-injured since... it's been a long while. They look fresh because I don't half-ass anything, but trust me, they're old wounds at this point."

"Maddie, I love your sense of humor but that's... I mean..." He shook his head, his eyes even more adorable when they were sad.

I grabbed the dough from the fridge that had been left to rise. "Hey, it's either laugh or cry. I choose to laugh. It's in the past now and I might as well dance on its grave."

He took a deep breath, his shoulders sagging forward. I was surprised that he was so sensitive about me. I liked it.

"Okay, so what can I help with? Want me to smooth out the dough?"

I arched an eyebrow. "Have you ever done that before?"

"No, help me get started."

I grabbed my favorite spatula hanging from a storage rack mounted on the wall. I placed a little bit of flour on it and scooped out a piece of dough that was resting on a baking sheet. I sprinkled a little bit of flour on the kitchen island where we would be working the dough so it wouldn't get stuck, before placing it down.

"Come here, let me show you what to do with your hands."

I slid in front of him and felt his breath gently tickle my neck as he wrapped his arms around me to reach the dough.

"Put your hand down and start pounding until you go all the way around..." He started pounding the dough like it was another bully to be crushed. "No, no! Not like that! That's too rough. Here, put your hand down, and let me guide you."

I started to put my hand on top of his but flinched when we touched. I forced my hand down, swallowing hard, and focused on showing him just the right amount of pressure to apply. I felt him wrap closer around me, his head coming to rest just above my shoulder.

"What's next?" he whispered inches from my ear. I closed my eyes, drunk, my knees suddenly made of puddy.

"Cup your hands like this, lightly," I said, my voice betraying me. *If you kiss me right now, I won't stop you.*

I tilted my head slightly toward him, not daring to meet his eyes. "Now, we're going to stretch the dough between the tips of our fingers, going down and out. Be careful not to touch the rim, that will become the crust."

I watched him slowly stretching the pizza, the muscles in his hands flexing as he made little circles. I imagined those hands running over my body. *That's perfect, Kellan. Just like that.*

"That's good," I said, locking eyes with him. His hands slowly moved from the dough to rest on mine. I let the moment linger, and then scooted away from him. "Stand back a little, I'll show you how to throw the dough to stretch it a little further."

He hesitated but did as I asked. I grabbed the dough, tossing it between both hands a few times before inspecting it for any holes.

"Stretch, throw, stretch, throw, check for any tears. There isn't much to it," I said.

Kellan watched in fascination. He seemed genuinely impressed. "When I watch you doing something, I get the feeling that there isn't anything you can't do, if you're interested in it."

"Oh, I don't know. I'm just good with my hands, I guess."

His eyes twinkled with a hint of mischief as he looked at me sideways.

"Oh my gosh, Kellan! That's not what I meant!" I punched him in the ribs and danced out of the way when he moved to grab me.

"Too slow!" I giggled, grabbing the dough and placing it back on the baking sheet. "We just have to put the dough in the oven for about five minutes or so before we put anything else on it," I said. "You can just watch me cut the veggies. I wouldn't want you to slice your pinky off or anything."

Kellan laughed and grabbed the cashew cream sauce.

"Wow, this smells surprisingly good. When you said what it was, I thought I'd be eating one piece and then pretending to be full."

"Yeah, it's amazing. You don't even want tomato sauce after you've had that."

"I don't doubt it. You made this yourself?"

"Mm-hmm," I said, getting into a groove chopping the broccoli. "I've been cooking since I could walk."

I liked having him watch me while I cooked. This was usually something I preferred to do in private. It whisked me away from my thoughts and troubles and I didn't want anyone to interrupt that. But it was nice having Kellan here. He was impressed with me in a way that no one had ever been before.

"So, when did you become vegan?" he asked.

"I've been vegan since I was nine. I saw this awful video on YouTube and I just couldn't do it anymore. At first, it was hard. Not going to lie, I loved chicken nuggets. Like, obsessed. There was a definite withdrawal period," I laughed. "But I learned how to make replacement foods and get enough vitamins and minerals. It's been fun learning how to cook and all the neat things you can do with plants."

"I'm excited to try those things with you. I mostly eat meat at home. Lots of burgers. Guess it's just something you do when you don't think about it."

I poked him in the chest. "Well, we can work on that together. I will make you a plant burger so good you'll never want another beef burger." I wrinkled my nose in disgust.

"Oh, did your dad teach you how to make burgers?"

Kellan facepalmed and turned away quickly.

"What do you mean? No, I learned from a recipe. Why would my dad... wait... what did you guys have for lunch?" I opened the trash can, searching for evidence. "He's been making burgers again, hasn't he?"

Kellan didn't answer, instead, pretending to study the recipe on the iPad.

"Kellan, what did you have for lunch today?" I moved close to him and asked him sweetly. He looked down at me with an exaggerated smile.

"Umm, I don't really remember. Can we just talk about something else?"

I put my hands on my hips. "He made burgers for lunch, didn't he? I *knew* he was hiding meat in the fridge."

Kellan stepped toward me, touching me lightly on the arm.

"Please don't say anything. I feel awful for outing him. They were... so good," he moaned.

I swung at him but he jumped out of the way, laughing.

"If that's as good as you can do, I think we've found something I can easily beat you at."

I leaped after him, undeterred as he put his hands up and cowered into the corner, landing punches on his arms and sides, his giggles touching every part of me and making me feel like I was going to turn into a mushy ball.

"That's what you get for eating meat in my house before we're even officially friends." I stomped my foot, letting my hair remain splayed across my face.

"So, we're friends now?" he asked, angling his head sideways.

The oven time dinged just in time to dodge the question of what we were. I grabbed the dough and spread the sauce and vegetables on top of the pizza, then put it back in the oven for another 15 minutes. I drummed my fingers a few times on top of the kitchen island.

"So… we have a little bit of time until that's ready. What should we do?"

"Well, we could have been making out… but somebody HAD to be Yoshi and was determined to win. So, guess we'll have to pick something else."

Before I could respond, I heard a voice say, "Bruh." Kellan reached in his pocket for his phone.

"I'm going to have to change that sound. That was a running joke for Tyrell because it's all he ever says. Now that he's not around anymore…"

He opened his phone screen and his face fell. "Oh no. It's my coach. He's texted me asking me to call him. Do you mind if I just get this over with?"

"Sure, no problem. I'll wait in the living room." I slipped out, my hand coming to rest on my chest when he could no longer see me. I didn't know what we were going to do for that 15 minutes and I was glad to be saved.

I wanted to kiss Kellan… but I was scared. It would be my first kiss. I wanted it to be the right moment. I wanted a romantic, foot-popping, we'll remember this together in 20 years kind of kiss. Waiting for a pizza to be done cooking wasn't that moment.

I also wasn't ready to show him my room. If he saw all the streaming equipment, he'd naturally ask questions. My stream was my safe space and I didn't want him there yet. If we stayed friends, or became more, I'd tell him about it. Eventually. Just... not yet.

I glanced over and saw the Switch controller sitting on the couch and considered playing another track or two while waiting for Kellan but stopped when I heard a barking voice through his phone. I tiptoed back to the edge of the kitchen and listened in.

Chapter 24
Kellan

I read the text again from Coach Baker.

"Davis! Call me ASAP!"

This isn't going to be pretty. He's probably heard the reason for my suspension, and he's going to be pissed.

I pressed call from the text message screen and didn't have to wait more than a single ring for Coach Baker to answer.

"Davis! What's this I hear about you punching a couple of kids out in the hallway today?"

Yeah, this is going to be bumpy.

"Coach, it was one kid. And he earned it. It sucks that they stripped me of two games instead of just one, but I don't know that I can do anything about it."

Coach huffed. "Story is that you were defending that little queer who calls himself Maddie. Said that you like him."

I glanced toward the archway separating the kitchen from the living room and noticed a shadow moving ever so slightly. I hoped it wasn't Maddie listening in. I stepped toward the glass doors leading to the backyard.

I leaned my forehead against the glass door, trying to gather my thoughts and steel my resolve.

I can't let him talk about Maddie that way, whether she can hear or not.

"Coach, I'm going to give you one chance to take that back and apologize, or I quit." My voice was raw, and I was surprised to find myself trembling with anger.

The line went silent. I closed my eyes and images of my future rushed to greet me.

I saw myself sitting at home, watching my mother drink herself closer to an early grave as I tried to eke out decent grades at the local community college, hoping and praying that they would be good enough to get into an art school... any art school. With no scholarships for washed-up high school jocks turned wannabe-anime artists, I'd have to take out student loans and hope that I could afford to pay them back when they came due.

"Davis, are you joking with me?"

I saw my past, all the work I had put in since I first picked up a football at seven years old. All the people who had told me that I'd be a star in the NFL someday. All the times my dad made me train until I almost puked, telling me that there was somebody out there working harder than me, that I'd never be good enough if I didn't listen to him. And I'd grunt and keep pushing harder, determined to earn my ticket out of here, to blast out of town and never come back.

"No, sir, I don't joke about Maddie. And it's not him. It's her."

I remembered the nights sitting in front of my sketchpad, wishing desperately that my drawing was why everyone kept looking at me with adoration. I didn't understand what people expected of me. Just because I could throw a football didn't make me a god. Why did grown men gleam at me when talking of my future? Is that what they wanted when they were growing up?

All I wanted was more time with my art. I was never able to focus on it like I wanted to. But that was because I knew the only thing that was going to get me away from this hell was football. So, I doubled down, studied extra film, lifted more weights, threw more balls to Tyrell.

And I stuffed my passion down as far as I could. I hid from myself, pretending that I was doing what I loved when it was slowly becoming what I hated.

I don't know how the phone stayed in my hand. I felt the pressure behind my eyes growing stronger. I didn't know why this was happening to me. Why, when I did something for myself that I actually wanted, was the world condemning me? I liked Maddie. Why did it matter what she was? And why did I get in trouble when I was only defending her?

Darkness swept into my mind as I considered that she might not even want me the way I wanted her. I was preparing myself to walk away from my only salvation and I didn't even know if she felt the same way.

I saw our possible future together. She became my girlfriend, my everything. We were inseparable and life felt complete. And then high school winds around and it's time for college. She's in honors everything and has a full scholarship somewhere far away, and her parents want her to take it, and she wants to take it, but I can't really follow. I can't get into the school she's going to, so I can't get a dorm room, I'd have to rent somewhere, and how would I afford to live?

So, we break up. She leaves, and I'm alone, stuck in Rock Canyon.

"Let me get this crystal clear. You think defending a gay kid who wears makeup is more important than preparing for your college football career? What the hell, Davis? You're letting us all down."

I glanced back toward the archway. I froze. Maddie was standing there, hand over her mouth, her eyes wide. And then I realized how easy the decision really was.

I see the girl behind the café counter, her black hair concealing the eyebrow that I know is arched in annoyance. I see her sitting in the booth, hunched over her journal, softly biting her tongue, writing ferociously. I see her crouched low on her skateboard, fists clenched, jaw set, gathering speed on the hill in front of my house.

And I see her now. The pink, blue, and white trans-pride colored nails on the hand that feels like heaven when it touches mine, the magnificent little legs wrapped in tight denim, and the eyes... the eyes that my heart can't say no to.

I turned and faced her. If I was going to do this, I wanted her to see it. I wanted her to know that *if it's just this day or the rest of our lives, I choose you. I'll always choose you.*

"No, Coach, you're letting yourselves down. If that's how you're going to talk about her, I can't do this. Maddie means more to me than playing football. I quit."

I hung up, looked at the phone for a second, and then put it in my pocket. I glanced up at Maddie, not quite able to see her face. I felt dizzy and stumbled toward the breakfast nook, managing to find the edge of the booth to sit down.

I just walked away from everything I've ever known. I wanted to vomit. I knew I made the right choice, but after it was done, the reality was already sinking in. I looked toward Maddie but not quite at her. I didn't want her to see me this upset, even though I knew it was impossible to hide.

"I… I'm sorry… I don't want to be hurting from this. Like, I don't care about football if they don't know how to accept you. But it's all I've ever known, you know? I feel selfish for thinking about it after the things that he just said, that you probably heard him say, but it's what I was going to do, at least to get into college.

"I've heard for years that I've 'got what it takes.' Well, I guess I don't have what it takes to ignore people when they make fun of you. And I can't pretend that I can be around people who think and feel as they do. I won't do it. I haven't minded being judged by others the past couple of days, but I don't like when they turn their hate onto you. Like it's your fault. Like you've done something wrong, when all you've done is be yourself.

"But… I just can't help shaking the feeling that I've lost my purpose. Like what else can I do besides throw a football? That was my only hope…" I trailed off and looked away from Maddie, out the large glass window facing her backyard.

"After winning states last year, I had college scouts giving me their phone numbers, telling me to come and visit their programs. I feel like I have a shot at the NFL someday. And now…" I felt my voice catch and sighed deeply, sinking my face deep into my hands.

Don't lose it in front of her. She goes through enough— she doesn't need your shit.

I rubbed my eyes. "Hey, look, I'm really sorry for burdening you and unloading. This just hit me really hard. It's been a long couple of days and it's so silly. It's either people thinking that you're a punching bag for their insecurities or because they're too closed-minded to accept you for who you are. Well, I'm not. And I won't dignify their bullshit by enabling them. If I can't play football anymore, so be it. I'll figure something else out. I choose you. And you don't have to choose me back or anything, I just…"

I trailed off when I heard Maddie's hushed footsteps racing across the stone floor, my whole world slamming into me and pushing me back into the booth.

"Slide over, Kellan," she whispered, her hands frantically pushing on my shoulders.

I slid back, eyes wide as she followed me into the booth, crawling into my lap. She rested her hands on my chest and slowly moved them to my face. She leaned in, stopping when our eyes were mere inches apart. My hands sprung to life, running up her back as she closed the gap between our lips.

The heaviness evaporated, and as our breath became one, I was only aware of lightness buzzing in every pore. Her hair falling on my face was everything I thought it'd be, and I grabbed a fist full of it, tipping her head back and kissing the space between her neck and collarbone softly. I made my way slowly back to her mouth, worshipping every spot along the way. When I began moving away to kiss the other side of her neck, she grabbed my chin and fought her way back to my mouth, biting my bottom lip.

I wrapped my arms around her and squeezed her against my body. I felt an urgency with her that I'd never felt with anyone else. I thought I knew how much I wanted this, but I had no idea the depth of my yearning, of how I needed to feel her responding to my touch.

"This smells great! I'm really hun—"

I saw Charlotte's blonde braid whirl in the corner of my vision, but neither one of us looked away from each other. Maddie closed her eyes, a lazy smile on her already swollen lips.

"Oh… I'm sorry," Charlotte muttered before scurrying out of the room with a giggle.

Maddie scooted off my lap and sagged down into the booth, her body nooked into mine, her eyes hidden behind a lattice of tussled hair.

"Are all kisses like that?" she asked breathlessly.

"Only if they feel like you're travelling faster than the speed of light across the universe, to arrive at a home that you never knew you had but instantly recognize."

Maddie ran her finger slowly across the top of my hand, tracing each knuckle. "So, that'd be a no?"

I moved to get closer to her again, my body vibrating as I brushed her hair away from her mouth and moved toward it.

Beep! Beep! Beep!

I cursed the oven and the engineers that designed it. "Guess we'll have to put that on pause."

Maddie slid across my lap slowly, pausing at the edge of the booth to look at me over her shoulder. If I could have hit rewind on the transcendental explosion that was our first kiss, I think I would have set it to replay on loop. And never turned it off.

I rested my head against the back of the booth, unable to take my eyes off her, watching as she pulled the pizza out of the oven. Not long after, the entire family filed into the kitchen, and I tried to keep up with the small talk that was directed at me.

Everything felt like slow-motion—it was one of those moments in life that you know as it's happening you'll remember it always in the most vivid detail. I drank her in, my eyes locked on the little wood fairy flittering across my vision. She kept looking back at me in a way that I had spent nights praying was possible. Someone tapped on my arm and I finally looked away.

"Hi, Kellan. I thought my sister screamed at you and didn't want you here," her little brother, Ryan, said. I chuckled and looked back at a smiling Maddie.

"She changed her mind. Maddie decided that I wasn't so bad after all. Always remember this, Ryan... girls can be weird. You have to learn to live with it," I said.

"Hey!" Maddie and Charlotte turned at me like identical twins, their furrowed smiles bringing laughter to the entire family.

I watched Maddie cut the pizza and make everyone a plate. I loved that her multicolored nails matched the trans-pride bracelet around her wrist. She was proud of who she was and I admired that. I wanted to get one of those bracelets for myself as soon as possible.

Maddie and I lingered in the kitchen and stole a quick kiss before we grabbed our plates and joined the others in the dining room.

When we're alone again, I'm going to explore every inch of your skin.

I noticed that my chair next to Maddie was much closer than it was the last time I was here. I wondered if she did this on purpose. From the way her foot kept finding ways to touch my leg during dinner, my guess was that it was intentional.

When I took my first bite of the pizza, I wasn't expecting much considering it was vegan. Since Maddie cooked it, I should have known better.

"This is amazing! Wow, I totally didn't expect this to be good, not gonna lie."

She winked at me. "You'll learn."

When dinner was over, Maddie walked me out to the front porch.

"I hate that we have to say goodnight, but I have a stupid English paper to finish. Last-minute and all that." She rolled her eyes. I grabbed her hand and held it in mine.

"Well, that's what you get for taking honors classes. Hey, when can I see you again? I'm pretty much free all week." I made a show of checking my phone for the calendar I didn't use. "Suspended from school... no football... yep! Cleared my schedule."

Maddie shook her head and laughed. "Umm, I have a thing tomorrow night. But how about Thursday after school? Maybe we can go to The Resca, get some coffee—" we both heard a noise at the door and looked up in time to see Charlotte peeping out of the window. Maddie sighed. "And also get away from family interruptions."

I laughed. "That'll be fun. You know I'm going to be counting the minutes until I see you again, right? Oh, hey, can I have your number? I just realized that we've never exchanged numbers. That was one place I didn't have the privilege of badgering you at."

Maddie smirked as I pulled out my phone. The setting sun wrapped us in an embrace as we stood in the quintessential pose of young people hunched exchanging numbers.

Maddie ran a finger down my arm, making me almost shiver with pleasure. "Hey... don't forget you owe me a picture. Now that you have all this time on your hands, I expect nothing less than the best. I did give you two kisses that you didn't earn tonight, after all."

I moved too quickly for her to react, wrapping my hands around her heart-shaped face, and slowly kissing her lips. When I managed to pull away, I tucked her hair behind both ears.

"Third time's a charm," I whispered. I grinned and started walking backward down the sidewalk.

"Just thought I'd get a little deeper in debt with you. You'll have to think of all the ways that I can make it up."

She didn't say anything, just held her hands together in front of her chest and watched me walk away. The last image I had of her that night was the first I planned to draw when I got home—the way the evening light splashed across her. It was like light reflecting on crystal; all the colors of the rainbow sprinkled and shattered across her radiant face.

I broke into a sprint, feeling brand new as I rushed home.

Chapter 25
Maddie

When he disappeared, I lingered for another minute, staring at the last place I could see him. I felt like my smile was permanent as I walked in a slow daze to my bedroom, closing and leaning against the door. When I looked in the mirror, it was as shocking as the first moment Destiny let me see myself after doing my makeup.

Is this me? Is this what Kellan looks like on me?

I looked at this new stranger and decided that I liked her even better than the girl with the makeup. This girl looked happy, and I didn't remember ever seeing her before.

That night, in the shower, I found myself at my waterfall. I felt a presence and looked over my shoulder, surprised to see Kellan instead of my magical stranger. He was naked, walking toward me, the water droplets falling off the hard planes of his chest.

He sank to his knees behind me, touching me ever so slowly at the small of my back, his hands working their way around to the front of my body. I could feel my excitement throbbing.

Yes, Kellan, touch me. Right... there... yes... just like that.

In my safe spaces, I was always in a female body and dreaded opening my eyes and having to shatter the illusion. But as soon as the thought encroached, I always opened my eyes. Tonight, it came faster than I wanted it to. I blinked open, looked down, and frowned at the form of attraction that I wish wasn't there.

Don't do this tonight. Just let it go. Don't crumble, don't fall, focus on what went right today. He stood up for you, he kissed you, he's into you. Just for one stupid night, let go.

I closed my eyes again, trying to recapture the moment, but it was lost. I felt the anger surge upward and I stood up, shaking. Just as I was about to spiral, I heard a guitar riff and stood puzzled for a few seconds before realizing it was my text message notification. I didn't get many texts aside from Destiny, and she usually video called.

Kellan?

I hurried out of the shower and grabbed my phone, dripping water all over the screen.

It was Kellan. I dried off and dressed in record time, bursting out of the bathroom. I ran straight to my room, leaping into the bed.

> *Kellan:* Hey, Maddie, it's Kellan. You know, the boy you kissed tonight? Anyway, I left something at your house, I was wondering if you could bring it to me on Thursday when we hang out.

Oh my God! My first cute text from a boy!

Maddie: Hmm, I don't know if I remember these kisses with a Kellan. ;) Haha! What did you forget?

Kellan: My heart. Make sure you bring it back.

I could see him typing as soon as my messages were delivered. I liked that he didn't try to seem cool by waiting for a few minutes to pass.

Maddie: Omg that's so cheesy... but I like it! :P

Kellan: LOL! Hey, thanks for everything tonight. Thanks for being there for me. You're the best. I didn't mean to get so mopey about football, especially after everything you go through on a daily basis. :(

Maddie: No, Kellan, please don't think like that. You stood up for me. To like the entire world. And you lost everything because of it. We didn't have a chance to really get into that, but I'm very sorry. I understand how you feel.

Kellan: I didn't lose everything though.

My head snapped back a little. *Huh? Of course you did. All your friends abandoned you, you quit football because your transphobe coach is a douche, not to mention your dad and what he did.*

Maddie: Your friends, football, whatever your dad was to you...

Kellan: Yeah, well, that stuff, sure. But I thought I gained everything that really matters. We're friends

now. And we're friends that kiss each other. Who
cares about that other stuff?

Maddie: Lol, aww yeah, I know but those things
were your life before me, and I know it might hit
you later. And it might hurt. Like mega hurt. So,
I'm sorry for that. And I'm here if you want to talk
about it.

I started pacing the room, watching the little text at the
bottom of my phone screen that told me he was still typing.
He was either writing a novel or the message was broken. I
tapped my lips and they felt sore. I rubbed them, closing my
eyes and sliding back into the booth in my memories. I fell
into my gaming chair with a smile and opened my eyes when
I heard the guitar riff.

Kellan: Anybody who doesn't like you is an asshat
and was never really my friend to begin with.
People like Ty will either come around or they
won't. And football? Yeah, okay, it does hurt. And
it probably will continue to hurt, especially when
I think about what I'm going to do with the rest of
my life. But I don't want to be around people who
are closed-minded about who I like. And hey, I'm
learning what it feels like to walk in your shoes.
You do this every day. Your strength is amazing. I
feel like I would be crushed if I had the first two
weeks of school that you've had.

You obviously haven't seen me freak out enough yet.

Maddie: Thanks. I don't know how strong I am. But knowing you're there, that you're for real and you genuinely care? That helps. Like a lot. I'm sorry I didn't trust you before. I didn't think it was possible for someone to feel that way about me. I thought you just saw what you wanted to see so I kept pushing you away.

Kellan: I do care. And I understand why you didn't trust me. I wouldn't have trusted me either. I was prepared to be as patient as I had to be to prove to you I was for real. Haha, I kind of expected you to lose your mind when you saw me standing in your living room today!

Maddie: LOL! Not after the hallway, silly. I mean, what do you think I am, a monster?

Kellan: Umm, yes? But maybe a really cute monster?

Maddie: :P Yeah, I guess I had my moments over the past couple of weeks. Oops!

Kellan: Oh, man. Did you ever. "And Kellan? You're definitely not my type."

Well, that snarky little comment didn't age well, did it?

Maddie: Yeahhhh... so, about that. Turns out I was lying. :) Tell you what, I'll take one kiss off the debt that you owe me. I still want that picture of you though! Cuz you're kinda sorta EXACTLY my type. ;)

I felt so pretty typing these flirty texts. I didn't know I wanted this so much. I kept running my hands across the tops of my thighs, feeling like the most beautiful girl in the world.

> *Kellan:* I'll get you that picture. I'm drawing you tonight, though. There was a certain moment that I'd like to capture.

I think I know which moment you're talking about. Although, you don't have to capture that moment on paper; you can capture it in my arms on Thursday.

> *Maddie:* Oh? You'll have to show me all the pictures you've drawn of me sometime. :) Hey, I want to ask you something serious. Okay?

I sent the text and then immediately regretted it. We were having fun, enjoying what felt like a couple's banter. Why the hell would I turn this into something it didn't have to be? *Because I'm me, that's why.*

> *Kellan:* Go ahead. Ask me anything. Except to be vegan all the time.

> *Maddie:* Well, that, too! But you do realize what I'm going to look like naked, right?

Why did I send that text? It's been one night. We kissed three times. I'm not even remotely ready for anything more. Why does it matter right now?

Because it does and always will. It matters because if I'm going to get my heart broken, I might as well do it now instead of later when I'm really attached... as if I'm not already.

Kellan: Yes. I know. Look, Maddie, I know you
think I'm a dumb jock and everything, but I'm not
THAT stupid. ;)

Maddie: You know I don't think you're a dumb
jock. I'm being serious. You know what pursuing
me means, right? And, hey, I'm not ready for
anything more than kissing right now. I want to be
clear about that. But I don't want to get my heart
broken later, okay?

When I didn't see him typing right away, I fired off
another text.

Maddie: I'm sorry, I just get nervous.

I left my phone sitting in the chair and threw myself
on the floor, face-down, in my favorite freak-out position.
I stayed like this for all of three seconds, unable to bear not
looking at my phone screen any longer. I grabbed the phone
off the chair and stared at the notification that told me he
was typing.

He typed for what seemed like forever and I thought
by the time he responded I was going to win records for how
long I could hold my breath.

Kellan: I perfectly understand where you are
coming from. I can put myself in your shoes and
totally get how you feel. That's why I said you're
so strong. I'd probably still be hiding. That's one
of the many things that's hot about you. And yes,
I know what I'm going to see when you take off

your clothes. If that mattered to me, I wouldn't pursue you. I would never play with your heart that way. And as far as what it means to pursue you? It means I've fallen so hard for you. What else could it mean? I like and accept every part of you. Period.

Maddie: Really? You do?

Kellan: Yeah, I do. I'm into you. All of you, exactly as you are. And I'm fine with kissing for now. I don't want to rush, either. I want you to be comfortable. I can't take you running away from me again. I'll do things if that happens. Like, I don't know, but things!

Maddie: LOL, okay. Thanks, this means a lot to me. Sorry for being so ridiculous. It's just been so hard for a long time. I kind of feel like I need this reassurance to feel comfortable. I just never expected you of all people to be into somebody like me. Sorry!

Kellan: Maddie, if you say sorry one more time, I'm going to run back to your house and smother you. I know it's been hard for you. I'm going to do everything I can to make it better.

Maddie: Awww <3 thanks. I'm tempted to say it, btw. Just to see if you'll actually run back here.

Kellan: LOL! Don't try me! You know after today what I'm capable of!

Maddie: Mmm, yes, I do! Hey, I'm going to put my phone on silent in a sec and get some sleep. I'd say see you tomorrow in school, but since you're such a bad boy, I'll see you on Thursday, waiting for me on my front porch, yes?

Kellan: I'll be wherever you tell me to be.

Goodnight, Maddie Pie. Sleep well.

I'll admit: instant swoon that he already had a pet name for me. This boy...

Maddie: Maddie Pie?

Kellan: Yeah, I like it. I think it's #fire. You like?

Maddie: I love it <3!! I feel special! My first nickname. Hey, text me tomorrow and don't forget my picture!

Kellan: I won't! -hugs- -kisses-

I sat my phone down on my nightstand and clicked the lights off. I lay still for a few minutes, not quite sure how to be in the face of this new reality I'd stumbled into.

Kellan Davis would be anywhere I wanted him to be. I closed my eyes and gently touched my face as he did earlier on my front porch. I thought of his smile with the dimples and his strong hands as I wrapped myself in a tight ball, imagining what it would feel like to have him behind me.

How would it feel to have him pressing into me? Where would he touch me? What parts of my body would be his favorites?

I lost myself in a sea of Kellan, falling asleep surrounded by him.

Chapter 26

Kellan

I woke up early the next day. It's funny how that works—you get a day all to yourself, no worries, no pressures, no schedule, and yet you find yourself ready to go bright and early. Why couldn't I feel like that on a normal day?

It's not like I could relax and sleep much anyway, not after kissing Maddie. I kept waking up with the cheesiest grin. At one point, I had so much trouble going back to sleep that I went into the backyard and sat under the stars. I felt like one of those animations from a lo-fi music station on YouTube, minus the obligatory cat.

I watched the handful of stars that were visible from Rock Canyon wheel across the sky and found my mind expanding as I pondered existence. I thought about how it wasn't possible to have a beginning or an end to life—you could always imagine that there would be something before or after. And in the vastness of creation, with however many universes spread across an infinity of time, I was here at this moment with Maddie. Somewhere, somehow, I had earned a blessing that I didn't deserve.

I sat up in my bed, hearing my mom rustling about in the kitchen. I yawned and lazily threw open my curtain as far as it would go without having to move any further from the warmth of the bed. I hadn't told my mom about my suspension, but I assumed she had listened to her voicemails last night once she sobered up for work. While I wasn't looking forward to that discussion, I could get through it. I doubted she cared too much about the suspension, but the football would be a different story.

I tossed the covers back and allowed myself to put one foot in front of the other toward the kitchen. Mom was leaning back against the counter, arms crossed, a beer resting next to her. From the smug smile on her face, I could see that she had listened to the voicemails.

"Heard you got the week off. Going on a vacation? Any good plans?"

I ignored her tone and moved for the coffee pot. I had a lot of drawing planned for today and needed the fuel. I intended to finish the manga book I had made about Maddie, putting the picture she requested of me as one of the last scenes. I probably wouldn't eat between now and then, the thought of handing her the finished book making me feel like it was two seconds before the start of a big game.

"Did they tell you what happened?" I asked over my shoulder as I fumbled with the controls of the coffee pot.

"I didn't have a chance to speak with the principal yet. Planned on calling her back today. All it said was that you were in a fight and would be suspended for the rest of the week. The second voicemail said they had reached your father and he would be picking you up. I figured seeing your father was probably punishment enough, so I've decided not to punish you any further." She chuckled and then took a large swig of the beer.

I considered telling her about what happened after he picked me up but let it go. "Yeah, well, a couple of kids were picking on a girl I liked. They were saying the nastiest things and I unloaded on one of them."

Mom made an expression that I hadn't seen in a while—a look of inquisitiveness that told me she wasn't fully drunk yet. "What kind of things did they say that made you so angry?"

I clicked the button marked BOLD on the machine and turned to face her. "She's transgender."

Mom's beer was in motion toward her face and abruptly stopped, returning to the counter quietly. She looked at me, her eyes traveling around my face as if searching for an answer that might be there. She finally nodded, looking away and out the kitchen window.

"Okay, that makes sense why you got upset. Is that where you were last night, with her?" she finally said. Of all the reactions, this wasn't the one I expected.

"Yeah, I was at her house. Mom, you do understand what transgender means, right?

She looked back at me with a sneer. "Kellan, how dumb do you think I am? I'm not even 40 yet, and I'm a nurse. I know exactly what transgender means."

"And you're okay with the fact that I like a trans girl?"

"I'm not your father, Kellan. Who you like is your business, not mine. But I think it's really stupid that you beat up somebody because of what they said. You could have just ignored it. People are always going to say shit about something, but you don't have to listen to it."

I didn't really hear much of what she said past the part where she said she didn't care that I liked Maddie. I gave her a hug when she was finished, ignoring her acrid breath, and she laughed. It had been so long since we legit hugged that I had to turn around quickly to hide my emotion.

I grabbed a mug and filled it with coffee, not bothering with cream or sugar.

"So, what did your coach say about all this? I can't imagine that asshole had anything good to say."

And here I thought I was going to get out of this one easily.

"Umm, no, he didn't take it too well. Actually, they suspended me from the team for two games."

Her eyes bugged as she stepped toward me. "WHAT?"

"And, uhh… Coach said some really nasty things on the phone about Maddie, so I quit."

She breathed out so hard that I smelled her breath across the kitchen. "You're fucking kidding me!? You quit the goddamn football team?"

"All my friends from the team have basically abandoned me, and then coach said—"

"I don't care what he said! Christ, Kellan, you can't quit the team just because somebody said something about your girlfriend. This is your life, your future. You want to end up like your father? Like... me?"

I sunk back into the counter, crossing my arms. I hadn't really stopped and thought about anything since my conversation with Coach Baker. It wasn't two minutes after hanging up my phone that Maddie's lips were entwined with mine. Thoughts about anything other than her had been impossible since.

"I—"

"You can't do this, Kellan. You can't quit. You aren't capable of doing anything else. I've never cared about your grades because I knew that you'd be getting a full ride to the place of your choice for football. But without football, what the hell are you going to do? Have you thought any of this through?"

I remembered seeing Maddie standing in the kitchen archway, hand over her mouth, hearing every word the coach said, and feeling desperate to make any pain that she felt go away. I remembered her eagerness as we kissed, the final chains breaking loose in her heart as she embraced me.

If I thought about it a million times, I would never even have considered another decision.

"Yeah, I have. I chose her."

Mom slammed her hand down on the counter, letting out a sarcastic laugh. "How long have you known this girl?"

"I met her over the summer."

"You met her over the summer. Well, this is rich." She shook her head. "You're an idiot. She could dump you tomorrow, just like you've dumped the last 15 girls you were with. You catch a few lousy feelings and you're ready to walk out on the rest of your life. You're not thinking with the right head. You can't run away every time something isn't just the way you want it to be. Are you going to quit everything that involves people you don't like? Every time somebody says something ignorant?"

"Are you going to keep drinking yourself to death just because life didn't turn out the way you wanted it to?" I volleyed back and then gasped, realizing what I'd said.

I put up my hands, trying to back further into the corner. I knew I had crossed the line. Her face turned to ice, her mouth a thin line of contempt.

"Mom, I'm sorry, I—"

"How dare you talk to me that way!" She picked up her beer and threw it at me. I ducked at the last second, hearing the can smack against the cabinets behind me. I bolted for my bedroom, barely avoiding her outstretched hand trying to grab me by my shirt. I heard her yelling after me down the hallway.

"This conversation is not over, Kellan!"

I locked my door and barricaded it with my dresser. Maybe I had misjudged how much she had drank and I didn't know what to do if she came after me. I knew better than to challenge her about her drinking, but the way she told me, her own kid, that without football I was worthless… it hurt. Because somewhere deep inside, I agreed.

I slumped in front of my dresser, the magic of yesterday all but evaporated. I listened for my mom but didn't hear anything. Eventually, I got up and gathered my sketchpad and drawing supplies, stuffing them in my backpack, and grabbed an old pair of shoes out of my closet. I snuck out my bedroom window, planning to head to The Resca.

I wasn't staying around here for round two when she was completely wasted. I was going to finish the manga book for Maddie one way or the other. I shifted my pack to a comfortable position on my back, and walked through the gate in the backyard, down the alley, and out toward the street.

I spent all day at the café. I settled in and immediately began drawing Maddie as she looked after our first kiss, her tussled hair mostly concealing her face, the beautiful features peek-a-booing here and there. I guessed what she'd say to me if she could see me.

"Kellan, you're supposed to be drawing yourself, not me!"

I know, Maddie. But that's so boring when I can draw you.

I drank way too much coffee and didn't bother to eat anything. I didn't have the money. The manager stopped at my booth during a dead moment in the café and admired my art, saying that the girl looked exactly like somebody he knew. I recognized him from my many failures with Maddie over the summer.

"Yeah, it's Maddie," I said, looking at a drawing of her slaying an alien.

"Ah, really? I thought it might be. Are you a friend or? I'm Mark, by the way, but of course, you can read the tag," he said, sliding into the seat across from me.

"I'm Kellan, Maddie's boyfriend," I said, then grimaced. "Well, I hope so anyway. We kissed last night and then texted a bunch. I feel like more than her friend and I hope she feels the same way about me."

Mark laughed, looking delighted. "Kellan, huh? I remember hearing all about a Kellan over the summer when she worked here. So, you've finally made it through the fortress and stormed the castle, eh?"

I blushed as red as the table I was now staring at. "Yeah, it wasn't easy but it was definitely worth it."

He nodded, the glow in his eyes telling me all I needed to know about his feelings toward Maddie.

"So, what brings you to our fine establishment in the middle of a school day?"

I told him my saga and he arched his eyebrows, whistling softly when I was finished. "And I thought I was being metaphorical about the castle. I suppose I shouldn't say this, being a responsible adult and all," he rolled his eyes dramatically, "but I'm glad you were there to take up for Maddie. I can't believe she's suffering this bad at school. I thought it was rough when I went to NRCH."

We shared a few moments of silence, the café quiet this time of day. Mark asked if he could look through my finished pages and I handed over what I'd done. I'd never seen somebody so animated, other than maybe Maddie's sister. His hands were flying everywhere, his face seemed made of playdoh, able to project any emotion in an instant.

"Whoa, you've really captured her. Has she seen this?" He looked up at me eagerly.

"No, I'm going to finish it before our date tomorrow night. We'll actually be coming here. Her idea."

Mark smiled and pointed toward a corner booth. "Something tells me that booth will be closed for 'maintenance' until just about the time you arrive here. It's a nice cozy spot for a first date." He winked and I knew I liked this guy.

"Thanks, that's really kind of you." I gathered up my drawings and tapped them against the table, putting them back in a neat stack. "I hope she likes it. I've spent months working on it. It's a little goofy, but my heart's in it."

Mark waved me off. "Oh, darling, she's going to love it! Maddie adores manga. You didn't know that? You couldn't have picked a better present for her."

A group of college students walked in and Mark slid out of the booth, tapping me on my shoulder as he walked to the counter.

I looked up at the clouds through the large, tinted glass windows. I felt like I was walking on them, drifting from one puffy blob to the next. The things my mom had said still lingered in the back of my mind, but they didn't seem real. The girl on the pages was reality.

I spent a few more hours at the café, finally accepting Mark's offer of food, apologizing profusely that I didn't have the money. He wouldn't hear any of it, making sure I left with a full belly.

I left when I thought my mom would have already gone to work, wanting to avoid that conversation until at least tomorrow morning. Maddie would be streaming soon, and I planned on settling down in my bed and watching.

Is it still okay to watch? Or is that just weird? Shouldn't I tell her that I know first?

I slowed, feeling my chest sink to my knees. This was going to be a problem, wasn't it? I couldn't just keep talking to her as MangaGuy06 and pretending to be somebody that I wasn't—that would be lying. I also couldn't just pretend like

I didn't know about her streaming when she eventually told me about it. I couldn't keep the secret that I'd known about it and talked to her on there.

Tick-tock, tick-tock. I could hear the bomb waiting to explode. I couldn't see the timer, but I knew the minutes were married to numbers that were getting smaller every second.

Perhaps the easiest thing to do was to tell her now. Just call her or text or whatever, and say something like, "Hey, I don't want any secrets between us, your dad gave me your Twitch info, please don't be mad."

But what if she was mad? What if the fairy tale we were living in evaporated, and I had just walked away from everything I'd ever known, mortgaging my entire future because I fell in love with her... only to have her walk away after one day because of some stupid thing I knew about.

So much for walking on clouds. I'd have to figure this out and fast, or else everything my mom said would be right.

I decided to watch the stream. I was going to try not to chat anymore—there was no way I could explain that away when I told her I knew. But I still felt horrible watching. I was wrestling back and forth with whether I should turn it off or not when I heard a sharp knock at the front door.

Startled, I tiptoed down the hallway, avoiding the line of sight at the top of the door. I peeked out the window and saw Tyrell's car. My heart instantly found itself on a treadmill heading for the max setting.

Shit! I don't want to deal with this.

"Kellan, I know you're in there. That's the only place you ever are anymore. Open up, we need to talk."

I sighed, slapping my hand against my thigh. I couldn't ignore him forever. I could wait until Monday and face him and everyone else from the team at school, or we could do this right now. In private.

I walked to the front door, glanced at him through the window, and opened it.

"Hey, Ty, what's up?" He barged past me, taking a few strides toward the kitchen before turning and pointing a long finger in my face.

"What the hell is wrong with you, bruh? I don't understand why you're attracted to that *girl* but that's fine. That's your business. Look, I get why you punched that kid out yesterday. To be honest, I'd still be pissed at you for getting kicked off the team for two games, but we'd survive. There would still be plenty of time for both of us to shine in front of the scouts and win states again." He took a step back, bashing his fist into his hand.

"But to quit the team? What happened that was so bad that you're going to walk away? Kellan, we've been dreaming together since before we even had a full set of teeth. You need to help me understand why I shouldn't just punch you right in the mouth."

I took a step forward. "Because, first of all, I'd kick your ass and you know it."

"Pfft you—"

"SECOND OF ALL... you didn't hear what Coach said to me on the phone."

He shrugged. "It's words, Kel. What the fuck? Somebody hurts your feelings and you quit?"

"It's not *just* words, Tyrell. They're about a girl who is really special to me. You all act like she doesn't count because she's different than the rest of us. Well, she's a human being. With feelings just like you and me. And I'm not spending one second of my time around somebody who talked about her like that. He was no better than that kid in the hallway yesterday. If he would have said that shit to my face, he would have regretted it."

My breath became more shallow as I felt the anger coursing through my body thinking about how many people must have judged me in the past two days. I could see their texts, their calls, their laughs, their excitement and I couldn't hold back.

"You know what? I'm glad you stopped by because you're right. We do need to talk. Where the hell were you yesterday? You're supposed to be my best friend and you didn't even text or anything. You don't really care about me or about how I feel about Maddie. You feel the same as the rest of them about her. You probably laughed and joked right along with them.

"You know, you got some balls coming here acting righteous, like you've got a claim on my life. Who says I have to play football?" I threw my hands up, angling my head trying to catch his eyes as he scowled at the floor. "Huh? Who says? And if you've got something to say about Maddie, you can say it right to my face!"

I was hot, my fists and teeth clenched as I waited for his response. I could understand his disappointment that I had quit. Maybe it seemed rash to him. But he wasn't even trying to see things from my perspective. He waited a day and a half before saying anything to me. It gutted me that it seemed like the only thing he cared about was football.

Tyrell finally met my eyes. "Bruh, you're only thinking about yourself," he said quietly.

"You're goddamn right I am!" Startled, his eyes shot open and he took a step back. "Everybody has always told me what I was going to be, what I should be, what path I was going to take, and here you are just like the rest of them, telling me what I ought to be doing. Well, screw you, Ty. If you can't be my friend when I choose not to play a stupid game, then why don't you get the fuck out!"

I opened the door with a rush, holding my hand out. He lingered, his sad eyes holding mine. I expected him to be angry, to push back, to strike out. He did none of that.

He merely stood there, his hands in his pockets, looking bewildered.

"Go on, Ty. Don't come back unless you're ready to be a real friend."

He shuffled to the door and stopped on the front porch, his back to me. "Kellan, it's not about Maddie. I don't understand it but I don't care about it. I do care about our future. Before you throw it all away, think about it. That's all."

I watched him walk slowly to his car, the anger ebbing away. I closed the door and plopped on the couch, the room turning a sickly white as the security light flashed on outside with the dying of the day. I didn't bother to close the curtains, my mind elsewhere, trying to make sense of everything.

Was I seeing this all wrong? Should I have just taken my two games and put up with whatever Coach had to say? Would she have still respected me if I did that?

Or, maybe an even more important question… would I still respect myself? No. I had to walk away, even if she didn't overhear the conversation. Hugh told me Maddie didn't compromise and I intended to match her. She deserved nothing less from her boyfriend, and that's what I wanted to become. I could live with the consequences.

The silent house didn't argue back as I heated up frozen Chicken Parmesan. I looked at the wrapper as I waited for the microwave to finish cooking, laughing at how Maddie would punch me for eating this. I pulled my phone from my pocket and sent her a text.

> *Kellan:* Help! I need vegan recipes! LOL! Whatcha up to?

I knew she was streaming and wouldn't be responding any time soon, but I felt warm looking at her name on my phone. I had added a <3 styled heart next to her name, trying to match her name tag from the café.

Whatever anyone else thought, it didn't matter. There would be no peace when I lay in bed at night if I had wavered in my dedication to Maddie.

All the other voices in my life, from Ty to Coach to my mom... they spoke from the head.

I chose to listen to my heart. I could live with that.

Chapter 27

Maddie

I was a blur dressed in all black, rocketing down the sidewalk, smiling wide in anticipation of seeing Kellan again.

I skillfully navigated around pedestrians, stopping with a flourish just before almost crashing into the café door. All in a day's work. I kicked the skateboard up, snatched it out of the air, and walked in.

Kellan was leaned against the trash can near the front door, his smile matching mine. My insides became a furnace.

"Hey! I missed you," he said.

"I missed you too! I'm surprised I'm not a little tired though. Mr. Suspended kept me up until after midnight texting." I poked him in the ribs.

"Yeah, well, I'm getting to know you. And I want to know everything. Still reeling about that love for Metal Gear Solid. Didn't see that coming," he said. His eyes kept roving from head to toe. Guess he liked the yoga pants?

"Kojima is only like the greatest video game creator alive, soooo, yeah," I said.

Kellan laughed. "I'll assume that's the guy who made the game and roll with it."

I flipped my hair back and noticed he was holding a cylinder in his hand.

"Is that my drawing?" I asked excitedly.

"Umm, yeah, in a way. It's kind of a surprise, actually. A pretty big one. Let's grab some drinks and get settled into a booth and I'll show you."

I threw my head back and groaned. "I can't wait that long! I need to know now!"

Kellan rubbed my back lightly as we moved toward the register. Being in public with Kellan felt natural, like this was always meant to be and we had both waited all our lives just for this.

"What are you getting?" he asked me as he scanned the menu.

"You mean what are *we* getting. I want to share a drink together, it'll be cute. And what we're getting is a pumpkin spice latte with almond milk. Special, off-the-menu, Maddie-sized. It's cold enough in here today that we can pretend like we actually get Autumn here."

"Ooh, pumpkin spice. That sounds good. Not that I have much of a choice."

I flashed him a sassy smile and turned to see an amused Mark, obviously beside himself to see me with a date.

"Hey, Mark. You know someday I'm going to dye my hair pink. But I love my black hair so much that it's hard to want to change."

Mark twirled his pink locks. "Hon, that punk rock angst look you've got going on looks so good on you. Reminds me of when I was a teenager. I was the cutest little scene boy in Rock Canyon, you better believe it. And if you don't, I've kept the pictures! And HEY! You've got to let me be the only cutie with neon pink hair in Rock Canyon. Don't be encroaching on my style, girl!"

I smirked. "Eh, I'm going to dye it pink someday. We'll have to share the spotlight together. Hey, can we get a Maddie-sized pumpkin spice latte with almond milk? In a to-go cup, please, in case we want to walk before we're done."

"Sure can, sweetie, even though I know you'll have it finished before you sit down." He looked up at Kellan and arched his eyebrows. "And, Kellan, I'm a man of my word. I've saved the special booth in the corner just for my favorite young love birds."

I looked back and forth between them, my mouth agape. They both looked at me mischievously before Kellan flashed his signature grin.

"I spent yesterday here working on my surprise for you. I told Mark our little saga and that we'd be here this afternoon for our first official date as boyfriend and girlfriend. And he suggested the corner booth."

"Boyfriend?" I said incredulously.

"Yeah, boyfriend." He rolled his tongue around in his cheek, trying and failing to conceal a smile.

"So, you're my boyfriend?"

"Yes. Or do you want to say otherwise? Be kind of rude now, don't you think?"

I looked at my feet. *That means I'm Kellan's girlfriend.* Euphoria rocketed over, around, and through me, making it hard to stand. Kellan's arms slipped around my shoulders, and he kissed me on the top of my head softly.

"So, now that we've got that sorted, who's buying today?" Mark asked with a toothy grin. Kellan started to move toward the credit card machine, but I slid in front of him like a ninja.

"I am," I said, inserting my card before Kellan had a chance to object. I may have been permanently swept off my feet, but I wasn't about to turn this into a scene from *Happy Days.*

"Hey! Your boyfriend is supposed to buy stuff for you, not the other way around," he pouted.

"It's the 2020s, Kellan. Deal with it," I said.

"You're hurting my pride, girl." He crossed his arms and feigned hurt. All three of us laughed, and then I thanked Mark, moving with Kellan to wait at the drink pickup area.

Kellan's fingers entwined around mine and closed tightly. My breath caught and I felt too shy to look at him. We had kissed, sure, and he had rubbed my back, but holding hands in public? It felt so intimate, so special, like a siren blaring that said, "I'm taken and I'm happy."

"Am I your first real girlfriend?" I asked.

"Yeah… you are," He looked at me curiously and then turned serious. "And that doesn't add any pressure for, you know, I just want you to know that I'm committed to you. This is a serious relationship to me. I don't want to just be your friend. I mean, at first, I thought that would be my way in the door. But I don't have time for that. I want to be the only one for you. Because that's what you are to me."

I scooted closer, wanting to feel every piece of him against my body.

Mark handed us our drink and we snuggled together on one side of our special booth in the corner, facing away from the rest of the world.

I immediately started devouring the coffee, much to Kellan's amusement.

"Geez, the way you ate the other night… I would have thought you'd take three sips of this and I'd get the rest."

"Nope. I drink lattes like they're my life." Kellan squeezed me tighter as I giggled into the coffee, dribbling a little on my lips.

"As much as I think sharing a drink is cute, I'm not sure this was such a good idea." He wrestled the cup away from me, laughing.

A memory of the kid in the hallway flashed across my mind. Something he said made me think about how all summer I was scared that Kellan would only want what he had seen—that he wouldn't like me if it wasn't for all the makeup. Swallowing hard, I decided to ask him.

"Hey, Kellan, there's something I wanted to talk to you about. I've been thinking about what the kid in the hallway said the other day, and I'm wondering if it was true."

Kellan had the latte halfway to his mouth before he set it back down, his brow furrowed.

"Is everything okay? Did he say something that I missed?"

I made a dismissive gesture with my hand. "No, no, it's nothing like that. I just... remember when he said that I shouldn't pretend to be a girl?"

Kellan's hand balled into a fist. "I knew I should have hit him again while he was on the floor."

"No, I'm serious. Like, I don't know. Would you still like me without the makeup if I looked less like a girl?"

Kellan's face crumbled and he took a deep breath. I'd never forget how sad he looked when he turned to me. Guilt pangs raced through my body. I knew this was the second reassurance I'd asked for in almost as many days, but this was all new to me. I wanted to be liked for me.

"Yes, of course I would like you, but only if it was authentic to you. If it wasn't, then, no, I wouldn't. I love your style. It's what I thought attracted me to you first. But now that I've gotten to know you, I don't think that's true. You're so much different than everyone else, and I'm not talking about being trans. I'm talking about your authenticity. You're so real. I wouldn't leave if you changed. The way I feel about you is deeper than how you look. It's… what I feel when I'm around you."

He sighed and searched for the right words. "Maybe I can explain it another way because thinking about this reminds me of something your dad said about you. He said that you don't compromise at anything. He said you're pure. I haven't known you for long, but I agree. It's obvious. And I think that authenticity is the most attractive thing about you. Even though the world sees a contradiction when they look at you, I don't. You don't compromise, you don't contradict, you're just you, take it or leave it. And that's the closest I can come with words to describe why I fell for you from the first moment I saw you. For the first time in my life, I laid eyes on someone who was 100% real, no bullshit, no games. I might not have known that in words, but I felt it. And that's what kept me coming back again and again, unable to let you go.

"And look, I'm not going to lie, you're as sexy as anything the way you are now. But if you want to change your style or whatever, that's not going to change my feelings for you. You're allowed to evolve and grow… as long as you're being true to yourself. The only thing you're not allowed to do is change your feelings toward me. That's off-limits."

He nudged me and grinned. Overwhelmed, I couldn't hold his eyes.

"Kellan?"

"Yes?"

"You're messing up my eyeliner, you big, cute jerk."

Kellan laughed and gently tipped my chin upward. He kissed my tears with slow, feather-soft pecks, and then moved to my lips, pumpkin spice and cinnamon wrapping around our tongues as they slowly danced together. He pulled me into a hug and whispered in my ear.

"I'm sorry that you have to hear the awful things that people say to you. I'm sorry that they replay in your mind sometimes. I wish I could take those things away."

I leaned into him, resting my head on his chest. "Yeah, me too. You know, sometimes I don't know what to be or not be. It's confusing. I know who I am at my core, but I don't always know the best way to express that... to express it in this body, I guess. I feel like I'm on my own and there are so many people who hate me for being different. I don't understand it. When I tell them I'm transgender, they seem to have me all figured out instantly... but how can they? When I'm still struggling to learn and understand myself."

Kellan grabbed my hands, his arms still wrapped around me. "Meeting you has shown me how ignorant I am of what other people go through. It's stupid to assume what's right and wrong for another person. How can we know when we've never walked in their shoes?

"Over the past few days, I've had the smallest taste of your daily life. Maddie, I hurt so hard for you and how you suffer. But I'm thankful that you're not entirely alone. You've got amazing, supportive parents. Charlotte seems nice. And maybe the best part? You have me now! So, things are looking way up."

I knocked my head gently against his chest. He grabbed the cup and held it in front of me.

"Hey, since you've had like at least three-quarters of this drink, you might as well have the last sip."

I sat up and ripped it out of his hands. "Aww, you're so sweet." I made mocking eyes at him and drained the cup.

"I'm just glad you don't want to share food. I'd probably die of hunger within a week."

We both laughed. The cylinder laying on edge of the table caught my eye.

"Oh! I almost forgot! I want to see your surprise!"

Kellan grabbed it and blushed. "So, I started this not long after I first saw you over the summer." An eternity passed waiting for him to open the container, my thoughts stilled, every cell in my body tensed waiting to see what he'd spent so much time on. "I hope you like it."

He unfurled a stack of oversized drawing sheets. At a loss for words, I flipped through each page. He had made a manga book with yours truly as the main character. Awed at the detail, his love for me was blindingly obvious in every pencil stroke.

"Are you giving me this?" I finally managed, continuing to flip through the pages in a state of rapture.

"Of course. That was always my plan. I was going to give it to you even if you still weren't talking to me. I thought if you saw this, you would understand what I feel for you."

I came to the final page, and there was my requested drawing of him. He was shirtless, abs glistening with sweat, samurai sword in hand, my arms wrapped around his waist. We were fighting the leader of the evil aliens that were evidently corrupting the youth of North Rock Canyon High. Ironically, we were in the same hallway as the fight from two days ago.

"So, I don't have abs like this. But creative license, you know?"

I kissed him. I kissed him like no one had ever been kissed before, his head snapping back under the force. I put all of my barely one hundred pounds into it. His hands came up to my shoulders, pushing me back as he laughed into my mouth.

"I take it you approve?" I nodded and found his mouth again, my hands framing his face. I was forced to come up for air at some point and I slid down next to him, feeling a sweet deja vu.

"I was so unbelievably wrong about you. I guess there's a first time for everything, right?"

He tickled my belly and we laughed together as I flipped back through the book again. I flashed on the beginnings of my crush on Kellan and was surprised that I hadn't thought of it the first time we actually talked.

"Hey, I just had a memory of us from a few years ago," I said after finishing a second pass through the book.

Kellan pointed between us. "What? Us? When? I don't remember."

"You probably wouldn't. It was 8th grade. Biology class. I wasn't presenting as female then. I was still hiding, trying to figure out what everything meant. But we were lab partners. Does that bring back anything?"

Kellan gazed out the window for a few moments, looking confused. Suddenly, his eyes lighted and he turned to me.

"Oh my God! That was you?"

"Yup! Sure was! I felt so lucky that they assigned me as your lab partner. I had the biggest crush on you. I used to think about you all the time."

Kellan smacked back into the booth. "Wow. I had no idea..." He shook his head quickly and sat up, intently staring at me. "And what do you mean you thought of me all the time?"

"Like, you know, I was into you. I knew you weren't going to look twice at me, especially then. But I would write your name in my journal and fantasize about what it would be like if you did look at me." I bit my lip and looked away.

"Oh, that sounds interesting. Tell me about this fantasizing. Did that involve—"

I put my hand over his mouth. "You know what, I can see that this was probably a big mistake." I playfully poked him in the stomach, rolled up the manga book, and put it back into the cylinder. I slid out of the booth, grabbing my skateboard and heading for the exit. Undaunted, Kellan was right on my heels.

"No way, I want to know. Tell me. I need to know, Maddie. Tell me, tell me, tell me."

I stuck my tongue out at him over my shoulder and slammed the door open.

"Nope. We're done here. Come on, follow me and try to keep up. I want to take you to the skatepark and introduce you to a few kids I know there. Here, carry this for me."

I tossed him the container. He caught it in stride as he hurried behind. "What do you mean 'keep up'? Is this a race?"

"No. It's a slaughter. Hope you know your way there!"

Chapter 28
Kellan

She slammed her skateboard down and quickly shot off. I couldn't help but stand and watch her for a moment, her recklessness briefly reminded me of Ty. I shook off the thought and started sprinting after her.

I passed her on the grass as she was stuck on the sidewalk trying to get around a group of moms with strollers. I spun around, running backward, and blew her a kiss.

Okay, skatepark. It's about ten blocks south of here, maybe a few blocks over this way, to the east.

I veered to the right, widening the space between us. I glanced back and noticed she kept going straight. Knowing that she'd probably left work and went to the skatepark many times over the summer, I was sure I'd made a mistake.

I lowered my head and pumped my legs, finding a higher gear. After zigzagging a few blocks to the east, I turned south on 8th, and as I was about to cross the street, Maddie came flying around the corner, cutting me off, hair blowing everywhere in the wind, rock fingers stuck high in the air.

No, you don't.

I spied a shortcut just to my left, an alleyway behind an older house that I knew would take me to 9th street, and if I remembered correctly, the skatepark would be a few blocks down on the right. I dashed across a lawn, waving to the old man sitting on the front porch.

"Sorry!" I yelled as I ran down a small hill, leaping over the little creek at the bottom and sprinting up the other side to reach the alley. I crossed over without bothering to look for traffic, blasting my way through another yard, finally popping out onto 9th street. When I got to the pavement she was less than 20 feet behind me.

Damn, she's fast.

There was a long, gently sloping hill in front of us, and I knew she was going to pass me. I heard her gaining, and watched her zoom past. She was picking up too much speed—all I could think was what would happen if she crashed without a helmet going this fast.

"Maddie! You're going too fast! And this hill is cheating!" I yelled after her, but that just seemed to encourage her to crouch lower on her skateboard. I was scared but I couldn't help but admire her devil may care attitude. I snapped a mental picture for my sketchpad later.

As I came to the final block, my lung was about to collapse but I ignored it and pushed myself as if my life depended on it. I saw the park looming ahead and I knew I would need a prayer to beat her there. I made the split-second decision that I didn't need to follow her, that she'd be okay. I shot down another alley, hoping it was just what I needed to close the gap. A little clearing between the back of an office building and an apartment complex gave me a last glimmer of hope. The skatepark was just ahead. If I gave it everything I had, I thought I might just beat her. It'd be a photo finish.

I emptied my tank, squeezing every ounce of energy I had left, flying across the open ground. As I approached the last one hundred feet or so, I chanced a glance to my left. I watched Maddie riding out her momentum from the hill, soaring past me, and knew I had lost.

I slowed to a jog, fatigue already welcoming me. When I got to her, she was standing with three other people. All eyes were on me as I walked the last few feet and then collapsed on the ground beside her.

"I will... eventually... beat you... at something," I said between snatches of air and laughter, my arms spread across the dirt.

"Who is this?" a lanky kid in an old Sex Pistols t-shirt asked.

"My boyfriend," she said and dropped to her knees. She gave me an upside-down kiss before adding, "And I don't think so. I like beating you."

"If it wasn't for that hill... I would have had you."

She kissed me again and then bounced a finger off the tip of my nose. "Woulda coulda shoulda. Hey, let me introduce you to my friends."

She pointed up at the lanky kid first. "That's Paul, that's Julian, and that's Marie."

"Hey, I'm Kellan, I'm just out for a jog, how're you all doing?"

Marie spoke first. "I'm okay, I guess. Wow, a lot has changed for you since the weekend, Maddie. Boyfriend?" The other kids were too dumbfounded to even speak.

"Yep. He punched a kid out who called me a faggot and I took pity on him."

I busted out laughing, doubling over. "You could have let me believe for a little while longer that we actually had something here. My ego is on life support."

I rolled over and stood up slowly. I already ached and knew that I'd be sore tomorrow. I wrapped my arms around Maddie.

"So, you guys go to South Rock Canyon?"

"Yeah," Paul said, avoiding eye contact.

"That's too bad. We both could use more friends at North Rock Canyon. Especially after this week. I think we've alienated the entire school."

Maddie laughed. "Ah, who cares. Hey, Julian, how's your boneless coming? You pull one off yet?"

"ABD, Maddie. Check it out." He walked to the rim of the nearest halfpipe, hopped on the board, and slid gracefully down, making his way into an open area of the arena. He slowed a little and then took his front foot off the skateboard, grabbed it with his hand, and then jumped up with his back foot still connected to the board before placing his front foot back down and landing.

"WOW!" I exclaimed, genuinely impressed. "That was awesome, dude!"

Julian looked at me with arched eyebrows and a friendly smile. "Yeah? Thanks, man! How about you, Maddie? You think you can land a laser flip today? You were so close last time."

Maddie glanced at me before answering. "I don't know. I don't have any pads, so this is going to hurt if I don't. Guess I have no choice but to land it."

I started to protest when I heard 'no pads,' not quite sure what she was going to try, but she was already gone, zooming down the halfpipe. She circled around the skatepark arena before moving back toward us. She let the board slow a little, positioning her left foot in the center, toward the outer edge of the board. She maneuvered her right foot on the back of the board. Then, she was up in the air, the board spinning beneath her. A seatbelt clicked around everything inside of me as I held on tight and prayed. Just when I thought she was going to crash, the board miraculously lined up beneath her feet and she violently landed it, holding on to her balance and riding out the momentum.

"Oh my GOD! She did it!" Paul shouted, suddenly losing his shyness, his hands firing forward in spastic waves.

"I knew she would. She was so close last weekend. Dude!" Julian said.

I didn't know what to say, standing there with my hand over my mouth. It was one of the most incredible things I'd ever seen. If she was showing off, I couldn't tell. She made it look like it was something she could do in her sleep.

She rode up the halfpipe, never taking her eyes off me as she grabbed her board and walked toward me.

"Are you impressed?"

"Impressed? I'm way beyond impressed. That was the most amazing thing I think I've ever seen. I'm not joking. That was absolutely EPIC! You're so talented at this! Damn! And that was called a laser flip? Should be renamed a Maddie flip. You owned that!"

Maddie looked like she was going to burst into a brilliant ray of light at my barrage of compliments.

"Do you have time to work on the varial heel underflip with me?" Julian asked excitedly.

"Nah, I don't think we can stay much longer. Besides, I need pads before I'm messing around with anything else. We've got a decent walk back, and I've got stupid homework. We'll catch you guys later."

We said our goodbyes, and when we were out of earshot of the group, I turned to Maddie.

"Here, let me carry your skateboard. That was... what can't you do, Maddie Pie? You're wonderful."

She winked at me and took my hand. It's the first time she had been the one to grab my hand and my body responded in a way that made it hard to walk.

"Everything I try, I succeed at… don't cha know?"

I laughed. "Well, I'm eternally impressed. I love watching you out there. I hope we come back soon. I could watch you all day. Something about a hot girl on a skateboard. I didn't know that was a thing for me until I met you."

"So, any girl would do it for you? As long as she skated?" Maddie asked, an innocent look on her face that I knew wasn't real.

I facepalmed. "I totally walked into that one. Let me backpedal." I made a screeching sound like an old tape rewinding. "The sight of YOU on a skateboard does it for me. Yeah, that's exactly what I meant. That's much better."

Maddie tilted her head back. "Much better, indeed."

We held hands the rest of the way back to Maddie's house, swinging them back and forth, talking and laughing. When we got to her house, I handed her the skateboard and the cylinder.

"Oh, I almost forgot. My friend, Destiny, texted me yesterday and we're going over there tomorrow night. Charlotte came out to me and has a huge crush on her, and yeah, the four of us are going to hang out and play games with her family."

I stepped back, bewildered. "That was quite the info dump. You have a best friend named Destiny and your sister is gay. Do I know you?" I joked.

"Oh my God, I know, I'm sorry. We've been so wrapped up in each other the past two days. And I wouldn't change it! But yeah, I met Destiny last year after I was taken out of school. She helped me so much. I'm so excited for you to meet her, she means the world to me.

"And Charlotte... yeah that hit me out of left field. I didn't see that coming. I thought she liked you!"

I nodded. "Yeah, I kind of did, too. But I always assume girls like me, you know? I'm so handsome and charming and all that."

"Oh, shut up, Kellan." She undid our hands and slapped me playfully. "Anyway, while I know Charlotte wouldn't mind you knowing, maybe don't say anything to her? Just until she's comfortable being out. We haven't really had that conversation yet."

I nodded. "Yeah, absolutely. I'm looking forward to meeting your friend. It'll be different to spend a Friday night hanging out with friends instead of sweating on a field somewhere."

She stepped up on her tippy-toes and kissed me on my cheek. "I'll make sure you don't miss it one bit."

I melted and smiled.

"So, what are you doing with your day off tomorrow? Any good plans?" she asked.

"I think I'll head to the university gym. It's been a few days and I'm itching to get back to the weights. Maybe some squats, pull-ups, and dips until I can't walk anymore."

"That sounds... fun?" She wrinkled her nose. "Nah, it sounds boring, not gonna lie. Hey, what's squatting? That sounds like pretending to poop with weights."

I roared, putting my hand on Maddie's shoulder. In my world, I took it for granted that everyone knew what squatting was. "I love that you have no idea what squatting is. That's perfect. I wouldn't want that any other way. So, let me see if I can explain it. I guess it's kind of like sitting back into a pooping position, if you want to stick with that metaphor. Just imagine holding a barbell loaded with weight on each side across the top of your back and then bending your knees until you are parallel to the ground, and then standing back up. Rinse and repeat."

Maddie grimaced. "People go out of their way to do this? Like, voluntarily? Why?"

"It builds a lot of strength and muscle. It's good for athletes or someone who wants to impress their girlfriend with a nice, hard body."

Maddie nodded. "Ah, okay. I approve of this squatting, then. Continue to pretend to poop with lots of weight across your back."

I shook my head laughing. "Will do. Well, as much as I don't want to, I guess I should say goodbye so you can do your homework and be a good little girl."

I looked up at the house in time to see Charlotte standing behind the front door. I waved and she quickly waved back before stepping out of view.

"Looks like we're being watched. She probably wants to catch us kissing again," Maddie said.

"Well, let's not disappoint her." I kissed her passionately, exaggerating my movements by running my hand slowly up her back and into her hair. She moaned into my mouth, and if we weren't in open view of everyone else, I would have kept going.

"That'll give her something to chew on," I said when we were finished.

Maddie purred. "Meet me off the bus again tomorrow, 'kay? Destiny lives close to The Resca, so maybe I'll buy you another drink on the way if you're lucky."

"Oh no you don't! I buy this time." I thrusted my thumb at my chest.

"We'll see about that. Text me later, too! Send me cute things... umm wait, that sounds wrong, that didn't quite come out the way I meant." She scrunched up her face as I giggled.

"I know what you mean, and I will."

I blew her a kiss, both of us walking backward, unwilling to look away until I passed out of view.

Chapter 29

Maddie

I stretched and yawned. The angle of the sun blasting into my room reminded me that I didn't have school today. Sleeping in was my second favorite thing in the world, just after Kellan.

I glanced at my phone, noting that it was already going to be Halloween next week. Where had the time gone? Kellan and I had been so wrapped in each other the past six weeks that I hadn't stopped to pause and breathe. The only thing that I cared about was getting to the end of each day and into his arms. We hadn't done more than kiss yet, but when we kissed? We. Kissed.

Kellan would put on something relaxing like lo-fi, and we'd curl up in his bed and he'd whisper the sweetest things to me as we cuddled. I'd read that it's impossible for a human mind to understand infinity but maybe whoever wrote that just hadn't spent a quiet afternoon with their beloved.

Nothing and everything existed at once in his little bedroom. We were shut off from the world and yet wide open to the universe, the current of our love carrying us through eternity.

Aside from the bliss palace that was our extracurricular activities in his bedroom, things had gotten better in school. Kellan talked me into joining the LGBTQ club with him. We instantly clicked with the group, and we all started going to the café together on the weekends.

Mark had become our unofficial group elder, stopping by to dispense his wisdom. I was grateful that Kellan had begged me to join the group with him—I started to feel more comfortable at school now that I had friends.

As I was rolled over to melt into my thoughts about how great life had become, a little bird with a voice three times its size landed on my window and looked at me, chittering.

Alright, alright, I'm getting up, I told it in my head.

Throwing the covers off my body, I quickly ran downstairs, grabbed some coffee, and then changed into my Lane cosplay outfit. I had a stream scheduled for that morning. I wanted to hang out with some of my online friends from Europe that I played Minecraft with, but never seemed to catch because I couldn't get on until they were already asleep.

I did my makeup on only half a cup of coffee, and fortunately, it didn't show. Not long after I got on, David joined me and we started talking.

> *DavidinWales:* So, you've been with your boyfriend
> for about six weeks now, right? How's everything
> going?

"It's been wonderful. I'm really glad that I got over myself and gave him a chance. We have so much fun together. I was thinking last night about how I never had a friend as a kid, and I missed out on like playing and stuff, you know? Like, after school yesterday, Kellan came over and I left a note with a toy sword by the front door that said, 'No kisses until you can find and defeat me.' It was goofy, I know, but he played along and tried to sneak through my house to find me. You guys haven't seen Kellan yet but the thought of him sneaking would be hilarious if you have. He's a freaking block of muscle that's taller than my house.

"Anyway, I was hiding right in the living room as he walked in, and I sprung at him and he ended up catching me in midair, and we tumbled to the ground. Let's just say he got his kisses sooner than I had planned."

I narrowed my eyes in a cheeky little grin, as David always called it. I was taking the opportunity to have a chilled stream, focusing more on chat while playing Jets of Time, a Chrono Trigger randomizer.

DavidinWales: "I need to get out of the house more and meet a Maddie or a Kellan of my own… when do we get to meet him?"

You probably already should have. I paused the game, sitting the controller down and crossing my legs. This had been bothering me the past week. It was really weird not telling Kellan. I told him everything else, and I mean everything. There was nothing about me that the boy didn't know. But I kept this one secret from him. *Why?*

"I don't know. I should tell him… I've *planned* on telling him, but then I just don't. I don't know what my problem is. I don't want this to change anything between us. Like, I don't know what it would change, but I feel like everything would." I tussled my hair roughly, stifling a groan. "I need to just make myself tell him before it becomes more awkward. I'm going to tell him… soon-ish?" I did my best to smile but it ended up more of a grimace. I unpaused the game and focused way too much on watching Chrono run through Magus' castle, trying to forget about the one glaring hole in my relationship with Kellan.

TheWayFaringSock: "So, what are you guys up to this weekend? Anything special?"

Hmm, this weekend? Probably pretending that I'm going to finally tell Kellan about my streaming and then not doing it.

"Well, since Loverface quit the football team because they're a bunch of bigots, we're totally skipping homecoming and hanging out at my friend's house. Going to be lazy, drink pumpkin spice lattes, play with makeup, watch stupid stuff on YouTube… the usual. How about you guys? Anybody doing anything crazy this weekend?"

The rest of the stream was good, but the nagging feeling that I was lying to Kellan kept coming back. I caught a glimpse of myself in the mirror at one point and recoiled, not wanting to look into my own eyes.

Ironically, I didn't have to wait long for the truth to come out, but it didn't happen as I expected. Kellan and

I had spent the evening at Destiny's and we were walking home late, not bothering to hurry, holding hands and stopping for a kiss every so often. I asked Kellan if he missed being the star quarterback at the homecoming game and he laughed.

"Nah, that part I don't miss at all. I miss football, but not all that silly stuff that came with it. Frankly, I'm actually relieved that we're not going to homecoming tomorrow night. I hate those dances. With my old group of friends, it was like any other weekend, except, instead of wearing normal clothes and getting wasted, you got dressed up to drink and act like idiots," Kellan said.

I caught his profile for a second as we passed under a streetlamp and imagined him in a snazzy three-piece suit. I hadn't known that I wanted to see that until then, and now I knew it'd be all I thought about.

"If it weren't for the kids that we went to school with, I would have begged you to take me. I want to get dressed up really pretty and have you escort me somewhere fancy. Wouldn't you like to see me in a little black dress?" I stepped in front of him and twirled like a ballerina.

I heard him quietly gasp. "Oh, one hundred percent, yes!" He stopped, and I knew he was getting excited. He always leaned forward a little, his hands coming up around his chest, gesturing wildly. "Hey, we could do that! We don't need homecoming. I know you can't tomorrow but next weekend we could plan something."

I cocked my hip and furrowed. "Why can't we tomorrow? I never said I was busy."

"Yeah, but don't you have the Minecraf—"

His face turned to pure horror, his hands quickly wrapping around his cheeks as he stepped closer to me.

"Oh, no. Maddie, I—"

Wait… he knows I stream? All this time I've been stressing about it and he already knew? Has he been watching me?

I started back peddling away from him, trying to breathe but feeling like I was on Mars, gasping for air but suffocating. "You know about that? You know that I stream? How long have you known about that?" He tried to touch me but I recoiled.

Kellan rubbed his eyes and looked as if he was going to cry any second. "Maddie Pie, listen—"

I took another step back and stomped my foot. "Don't you Maddie Pie me. Tell me how long you've known. NOW!"

I was back at the kitchen table that first night he came over, looking into puppy eyes that looked beaten and bruised. *But he lied to me! He knew and didn't tell me!*

"Look… your dad picked me up from practice the night after the assembly when I made that speech. While he drove me home, I shared my feelings for you and everything… and well, I guess he wanted me to get to see another side of you. I—"

I started running away from him as if my life depended on it. I heard him behind me as he easily caught up, and I shoved him just as he drew apace with me.

"GET AWAY FROM ME! YOU LIAR!" I pounded my fists at him, feeling them connect with his chest and arms. He tried to grab my wrists.

"Maddie, stop it, let's talk about this!"

NO! I'm never talking to you again! I tried to get the words out but there was a golf ball in my throat. I shoved him away and took off running, my house in view.

He raced after me, leaping over the fence as I opened the gate to my sidewalk and ran for the front door. I'd be impressed if he wasn't such a creepy asshole. I wanted to vomit thinking about him looking at my stream without telling me.

"MADDIE, STOP!" he screamed, and I whirled toward him, my finger already outstretched and pointing in his face.

"You watched me when I didn't know it. You bastard, I bet you watched every stream since we met. I said things about you... things that YOU weren't intended to hear. You saw me... oh my God... you saw me sharing your picture..." I burst into tears, my face scrunched tight. The pain was so hot that any moment I expected my body to rip open. I wheezed, trying to force air into my lungs, but I was beyond being embarrassed. I gathered myself for long enough to ask the question that I knew would haunt me forever.

"Did you... did you talk to me on there? Don't lie to me twice. I swear to God, I'll kill you and no one will ever find your body."

"Just calm down, will you? Yes, I've watched every stream since we met. You think I'd miss one? I'm in love with you, remember? I just didn't know how to tell you… and I think you can understand why." He leaned forward with a patronizing smile on his face.

He means because I'd freak out if he told me, doesn't he?

"So, this is my fault, huh? Okay, cool." I turned toward the door. "Goodbye, Kellan. Hope you have a nice life." My hand touched the doorknob as the final piece of my world imploded.

"I'm MangaGuy06."

I froze, my foot resting on the landing in front of the door. The night was eerily quiet for a moment as if the entire world was holding its breath. I sagged forward, unable to stop the ocean from falling down my cheeks. I remembered my conversations with MangaGuy06, and how sweet I thought he was. He had disappeared for most of the last six weeks, and now it all made sense. I heard Kellan approaching and turned to face him.

"Is that supposed to make this better? That makes it worse," I said quietly, already feeling like my parents were probably watching. We had both screamed at each other; they had to have heard.

"I can't believe you. I trusted you! Even after all my fears, I let you in. And… I thought you were something special. Why, Kellan? Why didn't you just tell me? Why did you keep going behind my back? And you kept talking to me like you were someone else? What the hell is wrong with

you? What kind of a creep are you? I don't even know you…"
I wrapped my arms around myself, feeling cold even though
the desert night was warm.

Kellan took another step, reaching the front porch. I
stood with my eyes closed, trying not to completely lose it. I
knew I was one thread away from a full-blown freakout.

"Maddie… I don't… look, I meant every word I said on
there. If you remember the things I said, you can see how I
felt about you, even before you would talk to me IRL. I just
never knew how to tell you. I missed you on the nights we
weren't together when you were streaming. I don't know what
to say about my still talking to you on there a few times. I
don't know why I did that. I… can't you just forgive me? Look
at everything else we are. Look at what I've—"

I shook my head emphatically, cutting him off. "No,
I won't forgive you. You're not who I thought you were. I
thought you were different than everybody else. I was beginning to think we were soulmates. I fell in love with you. And
then I find out that all you are is a stupid liar. How could you
do this to me? How could you watch me and talk to me…?
You're not my boyfriend anymore. I hate you. I hate that I
love you. Don't ever speak to me again. Don't look at me.
Don't think about me. Just go fall on a sword and die."

I grabbed the knob and blasted through the door,
slamming it behind me as hard as I could. I was face to face
with my parents, who didn't try to even hide that they were
watching.

"I don't want to talk about it." I bounded up the stairs and locked myself in my room. Kellan's pictures were hanging all around my bed, and I ripped them down, throwing them under my bed before turning out the light. I grabbed my sheet, pulled it up over my head, and drowned my sorrows into my pillow.

Chapter 30
Kellan

STOP! This is crazy. She's not going to talk to me again tonight, and it's awkward to keep appearing in front of her house. She'd just as soon throw me off Chase Tower than listen to another word I have to say.

Over a half-hour had passed since Maddie slammed the door on me, and I was still out on the street. I'd almost made it home three times, only to walk back to Maddie's and stand on the sidewalk. I wanted to kick the front door in and make her talk to me.

How did this happen so quickly? I don't even feel like I had a chance to explain. And knowing Maddie, I might not get one.

I shook my head like a dog trying to dry off, hoping to jar myself loose from these thoughts. I couldn't afford to think like this. I'd never make it through the night if I thought we were over for good.

No, she just needed space to see that I wasn't the awful person she told me I was. Yes, it was a mistake that I didn't tell her sooner, and... yeah, I had to admit that it was creepy that I kept talking to her on Twitch. But it wasn't often, only a couple of times, and it was about the game, nothing personal. I wanted to cheer her on when she played Minecraft stuff. I was her boyfriend. I cared.

Although it was still relatively early on a Friday night, the only sound were my shoes scuffling on the pavement. I was sulking, not really wanting to go home and stare at my bedroom walls full of Maddie. I didn't want to lay on the sheets that we'd tangled up together just the day before. I didn't want to smell cinnamon cookies on my pillow.

Because when I did, I'd die.

I stepped onto my porch, which was wrapped in shadow. I had left the light off and it was just as well. I didn't want to see anything. I wanted to sit in the chair and try to pretend that it was only a fight, that every couple had fights, and this was our first. Maddie was an exploder, and maybe that's how she needed to deal with me. She'd come around.

An hour later, I wasn't convinced. I resigned myself to the impending implosion and went inside. That was a huge mistake.

"Hey, Kel, thought you'd be out with your girly friend. Whatcha home early for?"

There were no lights on in the house and my mom's car was gone. But she was most certainly here. I could smell the acrid tang of Jack Daniels as soon as I opened the front door.

"Mom? What are you doing home?" I said hesitantly.

She belched and laughed, her laughter almost drawling out like a car that was trying to start but wouldn't turn over.

"I showed up to work slightly inebriated and Carla took my keys and drove me home. You know she had the nerve to suspend me for two weeks?"

I rubbed my eyes, almost convinced I'd heard her wrong.

"You showed up to work drunk? Is that what you're saying?"

I saw her slam a shot back and sit the bottle down on the table.

"I had a shot of Jack and a beer. I wouldn't call it drunk. But they smelled it and that was that. Now I've got to get the damn car in the morning. Oh well. I could use a vacation."

I'm going to get stuck with you now, aren't I? I'm going to get stuck here trying to go to college, taking classes I don't care about, working bullshit jobs to pay the bills because you chose to throw your life away.

"So, what are you doing home early anyway? Why don't you grab a beer and talk to me," she patted the couch cushion next to her. "You're old enough. If you want to have one or two, I won't stop you."

My face fell. "Mom, I don't want a beer. I'm tired, I'm going to head to bed." I turned to go but she called me back.

"No, seriously, what are you home for? I figured you'd be out later than this. It's only nine. You usually don't get home until 11, and doesn't her dad, Hugo, or whatever give you a ride?"

"It's Hugh, and yeah. We had a fight and I'm tired, okay? I'm just going to go to bed."

The discordant sound of her alcohol-ridden laughter washing over me made me want to take the bottle and smash it to pieces over the kitchen counter. Then I remembered my mom doing the same thing the night before my dad left forever.

"It's only been six weeks? And you had a fight? And you quit everything for that girl. Doesn't she know that? What did you do that was so bad that she kicked you out early? I would have thought she would have worshipped you for giving her a chance as a trans girl. She ought to feel lucky you even looked twice."

I marched into the living room. "How dare you! She doesn't have to worship me for giving her a chance! She gave ME a chance!"

She laughed even harder. "Kel, it wasn't like the girl had many options. What did you do? Come on, tell me. Did you sleep with someone else?"

"No, Mom, I didn't sleep with anyone else. It's complicated, but it'll probably pass. She needs time, that's all. It's the first fight. We'll make it through." My voice faltered at the end, and I knew I wasn't convincing anyone, least of all myself.

"You gave up everything for her. I hope it was worth it," she said, her glazed eyes condescending.

"She was definitely worth it," I said, then realized I had spoken of our relationship in the past tense. I could feel the rising pressure and tried to push it away. I'd have to let the emotion run at some point, but I wasn't going to do it in front of my liquored-up mother.

"Worth giving up football and your future career for? Come on, Kellan. I was right and you were wrong. Admit it."

I turned toward the hallway. "I'm not doing this right now. I'm not ever doing this. It's none of your business."

I heard her stagger to her feet and could imagine the spittle flying from her lips. "My son is my business. You need to come to your goddamn senses and go talk to your coach. You've got a couple of games left this year, and an entire season next year. You can still get a scholarship and stay on track. Otherwise, you're going to end up a failure. Just like your washed-up father! All for a fucking girl!"

I moved quickly, grabbed the bottle, and hurled it against the far wall. I got up in her face, teeth gritted. "How much have you had to drink? Huh? Quit pushing me on my girlfriend and my choices. It's none of your business. Your business is to be a mom and show up to work sober so you can pay the bills!" I stepped back and pointed down the hallway. "Go look at yourself in the mirror! You're an absolute wreck. You're disgusting. You're the one who's become Dad! IT MAKES ME SICK!"

I saw stars before the sting of her closed hand bashing into my ear reached my awareness. I stumbled sideways.

"Don't you ever tell me I'm like him again!" she said in the nastiest voice I'd ever heard in my life. It was like something from Resident Evil.

"Then stop acting like him and start acting like my mom! Quit being an idiot who drinks every second she's awake! You're a waste of life!" She moved to strike me again and I blocked her, pushing her back into the couch and running for my room. I quickly pushed my dresser in front of the door. She was there a second later, beating her fists so hard into the door, I was afraid it was going to splinter and crack.

"Open this goddamn door, Kellan!" I didn't respond to her demands, instead, I grabbed my headphones and hit refresh on the lo-fi girl radio tab I had left open on Chrome. I turned the volume up as loud as I could stand it and let it drown her out.

I had a funny image of what this would look like if it were a game, like the Sims. I saw this scene as if my perspective was top-down, my drunk ass mom banging on my bedroom door, having completely lost control, while I sat in my room listening to relaxing beats, staring at pictures of what I had to assume was my ex-girlfriend. It was like Sims: White Trash DLC.

Wait... my... ex-girlfriend? That realization did it. I crumpled to a fetal position on the floor and began sobbing. I pulled my phone out of my pocket, knowing this was a terrible idea. I called her four times in a row to the soundtrack of my mom coughing and screaming behind my bedroom door. No answer.

I started texting. One text after another, each one more emo than the last until, finally, I was outright begging her just to tell me we could at least still be friends.

Many hours later, long after my mom had stopped trying to get me to open the door, with still no response from Maddie, I fell asleep on the floor, my head resting against the wet carpet. I found no respite in my dreams, only a beautiful raven-haired girl who kept screaming in my face, insisting that I was nothing but a liar.

Chapter 31
Maddie

MangaGuy06: "No, I couldn't tell. And I didn't see the tags, but I do now. I got lost in the cosplay and how beautiful you are that I didn't notice the rest of it. ;)... Being transgender doesn't change the fact that you are still attractive to me! But I'm guessing others at your new school have a different opinion?"

I wrapped the towel tighter around my shoulders, having moved beyond tissues at some point yesterday, and clicked pause on the recording of my old stream. I had planned to delete it the night it was recorded because of how personal it became, but I guess I had forgotten. In some sick way, I was grateful. I could sit here and relive the first time Kellan spoke to me on stream.

It was Sunday afternoon, and I'd now watched all of my old VODs at least twice. I'd been holed up in my room, not eating, barely remembering to drink water. Yet somehow my body was still producing fresh tears, every hour on the hour. I would be fascinated if it didn't hurt so much.

I kept staring at his name tag. MangaGuy06. I kept asking it the same question over and over again. *Why didn't you just tell me? You could have told me the first night we hung out.*

I could hear his voice telling me that he was afraid that I'd freak out, that he didn't want to ruin us after we just started. And I could see waiting maybe a few days, but six weeks? And to talk to me multiple times as if he was somebody else? That was unacceptable. I couldn't forgive him for that.

The sun had moved its way into my windows and I shuttered most of the curtains, leaving me sitting in a weird pool of semi-darkness, watching the dust swirl in the single strand of light still piercing through.

I braced myself and cycled through to the next video. This was the one that hurt the most. It was the video where Kellan had subscribed to me.

> *MangaGuy06:* I'm happy to be able to support.
> You know, being 16, and trying to subscribe to a
> channel on here, it's not easy! I had to go down to
> the nearest grocery store and find like a specific
> prepaid card that Twitch will accept.

I held the towel up to my eyes as I shuddered violently.

You went to all that trouble just to subscribe to me, only to have me almost punch you the next day. And then you still kept coming back... so why were you so freaking weird about not telling me that you knew about Twitch? You could have told me who you were and it would have meant so much to me. What was your game, Kellan? Why did you keep it a secret and keep talking to me?

Receiving no answers, I shuffled to my bed, collapsing with the towel over my head. I didn't bother to move it. I heard footsteps pounding up the stairs, louder than anyone in my family.

Is it him?

I thought about diving under the bed. I didn't have any makeup on, I hadn't slept, and I didn't want to ever see him again, anyway.

The knock was loud, sharp, and continuous.

"NO! I don't want to see you ever again!" I yelled, my voice broken and raw.

"Girl, that's no way to talk to your best friend. You better open this door or I'm going to break it down. You've got five seconds. Four. Three. Two—"

I opened the door and collapsed into Destiny, sobbing against her chest. She wrapped me in the tightest hug ever, immediately rubbing my head and consoling me.

"Shh, it's okay. Let's go sit on your bed." I held her hand like it was the only thing stopping me from falling into an abyss. In a way, it was. Charlotte followed close behind. We all settled into the bed, pulling the covers over us. Destiny spooned me, and Charlotte spooned Destiny. I really wish I could have taken a picture of us, I bet it was so cute. Destiny squeezed me tight against her.

"First off," she began in that authoritative boom of hers that I loved. "It shouldn't have taken your sister texting me to tell me what you're going through, but I'll beat you up for that later when you're feeling better. Second, if you want to talk about it, I'll listen. But I came here to try to cheer you up. You need comfort food, girl. I brought you carrot cake and got us all mocha lattes at The Resca. You need to get out of this bed and do something. I can smell you—you haven't even showered, girl!"

I giggled a little bit before the ache in my heart reminded me that I couldn't be happy. Destiny's fingers raked through my hair, and for a moment, I thought it was Kellan and felt a warmth beat back the cold that had settled in my body before realizing he would never touch me again. I curled up tighter and tried to choke back the tears.

"So, are you going to come down and hang out with us or what? We can chill and play Nintendo. You can bring your towel and cry, it's all good. Mario gets me sometimes, too, not gonna lie. No shame."

I appreciated that she was trying to cheer me up. It was sweet, but it tipped me over the edge again, and I sobbed into my fists.

"I can't... right now. Everything... hurts. Everything... is him."

Destiny sat up and tapped my arm. "Aww, let's talk about it then. Maybe if you get some of it out of your head, it'll help."

I rolled over to face them. "He lied to me. Dad told him about Twitch before we were together and Kellan never told me. He kept... kept watching... and never told me," I leaned forward, spilling onto her lap, wailing. I had no idea how I was going to make it to school the next week.

"Yeah, Char told me. That sucks. I mean, I like Kellan. I think you guys are great together. But that's a pretty big no-no. He definitely should have said something. Have you guys talked about it yet?"

"No. I'm never talking to him again. We're done," I said, and Charlotte frowned.

"Seriously, Maddie? You're not even going to let him try to apologize to you? I agree that what he did was out of bounds, but aren't you at least going to hear him out? He worships you. Everything else he did was all about you. He made a huge mistake but it's not something you guys can't come back from."

I scowled at her, noticing her lip gloss, booty shorts, tank top, and pigtails. She was really making a play for Destiny. For a second, I wondered if she was using my situation as an excuse to get her over here, but I shook off the thought as me just being an ass.

"How long was he going to do it, Char? A year? Forever? It's messed up. I don't want to be with someone like that. You know how I am about liars. You get one chance and if you lie, that's it. Goodbye!"

Charlotte crossed her arms. "Maddie, you're so stubborn. People aren't perfect. What did you expect? Kellan to be like some character in a book? Say all the right things, do all the right things, put up with all your bullshit but have none of his own? You went, what, almost two months without telling him you stream? Coming up with all kinds of weird excuses of why he couldn't see your bedroom. You should be thankful he knew about your streaming because, otherwise, he would have probably been freaking out."

I threw my pillow at her face. "Get out!"

She huffed and stormed out of the room. Destiny looked at me sadly, her lips pressed together. The room was eerily quiet after Char had slammed the door. I kept waiting for Destiny to say something, but she wouldn't.

"What? Do you agree with her?" I finally asked.

"Maddie… I'm not getting in the middle of two sisters fighting. I'm here to support you."

I grabbed Mark's "Human" pillow he gave me and clutched it against my chest. I tried to resist giving in to the anger that bubbled when Charlotte challenged me, knowing that if I spoke from it, I'd regret it, but I felt my lips opening and moving and I couldn't stop myself.

"You know she likes you, right? She's probably more interested in hanging out with you than being there for me."

Destiny stood up and furrowed. "I can see the signs, Maddie, but it wasn't your place to tell me. That wasn't fair to Charlotte. If she wants me to know, she'll tell me. And if I want to act on her signs, I'll act on them."

She started to walk toward the door and I felt myself slipping into the abyss below. She stopped and I felt my nails grasping to hold on. *Please don't leave!*

"And, Maddie... your sister is right. Not everyone is perfect. Not even you. Before you write this guy off, you might want to look in the mirror. I love you, girl, but you aren't always the easiest person to deal with. And that boy loves even those parts of you. Think about that." She smiled and then looked away. "I'll be here for a while hanging out with Charlotte, and I'm always a short walk away, so text me if you need me."

She left quietly and I fell, sinking hard and fast, finding no end to the depth of devastation washing over me. Old memories of how I used to deal with this pain flashed hot and fast across my mind, and I involuntarily began wondering if I'd stashed any knives in my room that my parents never found.

NO! I jumped off the bed and held my fists at my sides. *No, it's not going to be like this. I'm not falling that far again.* I sank to my knees and let myself go. I let myself feel whatever was coming up in that exact moment, fighting to keep my awareness on the crest of the wave. I learned in therapy that I could surf these massive thought disturbances and I'd ride out the other side better for it.

I felt a million tendrils wrapping and snaking and constricting in my stomach, but I stayed right in the moment, ignoring everything else. If I wanted to change the feelings I was experiencing, if I resisted even for a second, I'd lose my edge and crumble back into old patterns.

It could have been minutes of skating on the razor's edge of agony, and it may have been hours—I really didn't know. At some point, the energy must have run its course because the next thing I woke up to was my dad rubbing my back.

"Hey, sweetheart. I'm sorry I woke you up, but I wanted to talk to you for a few minutes, okay?"

Usually, I would have been annoyed with him, but his gentle voice was soothing. I nodded my head meekly and sat up, my mouth making a nasty clicking sound. I rubbed my eyes and looked around. It was still light outside, but it was definitely evening. Dad moved to my gaming chair and sat down patiently, waiting for me to get my bearings.

"Did Destiny leave?" I asked, scooting over to rest my back against my bedframe.

"Yeah, she left a little while ago. She seems to be getting close to Charlotte." My eyes shot to my dad but I didn't see anything there but his normal smile. I looked away, toward the edges of the sunset.

"I suppose you know what's happened between me and Kellan by now. I'm sorry that I was rude yesterday. I didn't mean what I said to you."

He nodded, steepling his hands under his chin. "I understand your frustration. I didn't take it personally, though you know I'd prefer if you didn't use such strong language." He winked at me and I relaxed into something resembling a smile. Under the circumstances, getting my lips to go anywhere but straight down was a small miracle. It was almost as hard as getting Charlotte to shut up about Destiny.

Oh, shit. I was a jerk earlier to her, too. I'm going to have some cleaning up to do.

"Yeah, look, I'm sorry. It's been the worst weekend of my life. It wasn't your fault he didn't tell me about Twitch. I know why you told him. And I don't mind that. But he should have told me, you know?"

Dad moved a finger to his lips. "Yes, I agree that Kellan didn't make the wisest choice. And for whatever it's worth to you, I think he should have told you a lot sooner." He shuffled in the seat, clearing his throat.

"I'm not going to try to tell you what to do or not do. If you want advice, you'll ask for it. I trust you to look into your heart for the right answer. I really like Kellan, and I hope to see him again. But if it's not what you want, I respect that."

He motioned toward the old CRT with the Super Nintendo sitting in front of it. "What are you playing these days?"

"Chrono Trigger randomizer. I've even streamed a few over the past few weeks. I thought you checked up on me to make sure I was being safe online and all that parenty stuff?"

Dad laughed. "I usually do, but lately I've gotten so wrapped in my work that I haven't made much time for anything else. It seems like ages since you and I sat down and played a video game together. Remember how much fun we had playing all the old RPGs? It must be at least two years since we've done any of that stuff together. Where does all the time go?"

I looked at one of Kellan's pictures he drew of me on my wall that I had forgotten to tear down the other night. "Yeah. I miss that. I miss a lot of things right now."

I heard the chair creak and looked to see him rolling toward the TV. "Why don't we play now? Show me this randomizer. You can make fun of me when I stink at it. Come on, it'll be a blast."

I don't know why, but a lot of things flashed in front of my mind at that moment. Being little, snuggling up to my dad and waiting with bated breath to see what would happen after he beat the final boss... realizing that I was 16 and would be headed to college before I knew it, on my own as an adult, a trans woman alone to face life's challenges... and then I saw Kellan, sitting in his room, lazily sprawled across his bed, talking about life between making out with me... and I ran for my dad's arms, jumping in his lap.

"Why did he lie to me, Dad? Why did he ruin everything?"

He wrapped me against him, holding me while I shuddered. He kept whispering, "It's okay," over and over again, and I wanted to believe him. I wanted to believe that this would pass and Kellan would be back and I'd be able to forgive him. But I knew I couldn't. I'd never be able to feel the same about him again—the magic would be gone.

"I hate to see you so heartbroken, angel. It eats me alive. I wish I knew how I could help you feel better." I closed my eyes and let myself feel like a little girl again, protected by her dad. It was the first time all weekend I felt safe. I never wanted to let go. It was as if a bubble had formed around us, all my problems circling around it but unable to penetrate.

He held me until it was almost completely dark in my room. I kept yawning and he finally told me I should get myself ready for bed. That sounded good to me since I hadn't slept much at all the past two nights. I didn't want to miss any school, even knowing I'd probably have to face Kellan there. We were in the middle of a group project in computer science, so one way or the other, I was going.

I brushed my teeth, avoided my reflection, and climbed into bed, happy to find Mark's pillow resting under my covers. I closed my eyes and was soon fast asleep.

Chapter 32

Kellan

"I see that you and your boyfriend must have broken up." Kate smiled down her nose at Maddie before turning to me. "Was it worth it, Kellan? No one will touch you now. You've been with another *guy*. You're queer. You're tainted," she said, flicking her tongue suggestively. If she thought I missed any part of her sluttiness, she was sorely mistaken.

Maddie had managed to avoid me for almost the first two days of school. When I finally caught up to her as she was walking to her bus, Kate intercepted us.

I didn't care what she said, I was beyond that. I stared at her blankly at first, and then a smile slowly spread across my face as I thought of the most wonderful six weeks of my life with Maddie.

"I don't know anything about being tainted," I began as if talking to a child. "I do know that I don't want anyone else, so if that's what I am? Okay, cool." I spread my arms and shrugged. "But for the record, it was totally worth it. She's the exact opposite of you and everyone else in this school.

She's authentic and true to herself and not worried about what everyone else thinks. She taught me so much. I wish I had been able to be with her sooner." I paused and glanced at Maddie. Her eyes held mine but I didn't see the usual sparkle. There was only an infinite sadness, the puffiness not quite hidden behind her makeup. I stifled the urge to hug her, knowing that's not what she wanted from me.

I looked down for a moment and looked back into Kate's rapidly calculating eyes. She kept darting between our faces, obviously enjoying herself. "Maddie's not like you, Kate," I said softly. "She wouldn't stand here and enjoy someone else's suffering. But you? You feed on it. You're like an energy vampire, waiting to suck someone dry so that you don't have to face the ugliness of who you really are.

"But what am I saying? You wouldn't know anything about what it's like to have a conscience, Kate. You probably don't even understand the concept of integrity."

I looked back at Maddie and I could see a hint of emotion in her breath, her chest rising and falling faster. *Feel us again, sweetheart. How it was to be in each other's arms. I'm so sorry I hurt you.*

A sea of people shuffled and murmured around us as they headed for the exit, their heads still snapping back for another look. This had become normal over the past six weeks, something we enjoyed and even laughed at. But that was then, when we had been one. This was now, when we were two lonely islands, a gulf spreading out between us.

I felt the familiar tendrils of electricity snapping between our hands now that we were only a couple of feet apart. I wanted to reach out and grab hers, but I resisted. I didn't want to ruin this moment. I settled for tracing her precious face slowly with my eyes, remembering what it felt like to do it with my fingers.

"Maddie, you're the most beautiful girl in the world, inside and out. I can't believe I wasted any of my time with anyone else." I turned toward Kate. "I don't want to be touched by any of you, ever again. So please, consider me so tainted that I'm radioactive and never speak to me again."

I walked away, feeling myself tearing apart inside, but I didn't look back. It would be so easy to fall into desperation and start begging her to take me back. That's not what either of us wanted. I didn't mind begging, but I wanted her to be comfortable. I knew Maddie like the back of my hand—she needed time if I was to have a shot at all. While that hurt, I had no choice but to wait.

I dodged through a few remaining clumps of students near the door, heading for the sidewalk. Without my own car, or someone to give me a ride, I was walking to and from school. I had been riding the bus with Maddie but figured she'd want space, at least for now. So, walking it was.

I put my earbuds in and turned up Beach House. It was a beautiful afternoon, temperatures in the mid-70s, birds chirping, people smiling. I passed the athletic fields, not bothering to look. I knew all my old friends would be out there, preparing for their next game. There was what, two left? I didn't even know what their record was. I stopped paying attention long ago. I didn't want to start thinking about football right now. If I started missing that...

Anyway, I only had one thing on my mind. *How do I win you back?*

I shifted my pack and looked at the sky. Our bus passed me and I could taste the diesel as I watched my heart speeding away.

What am I going to start writing country music songs now? I laughed at my sappiness and then wrestled with my mind about how I could get her back.

If I just show up, she'll slam the door. Obviously can't talk to her on her stream, that would be the final nail in the coffin. I need a <u>Moment</u>. I need something so big she couldn't say no. But what?

I inventoried everything I knew about her. The things she dreamed of doing. And then I remembered the notes I had taken while watching her old streams.

The notes! If there's a god, please let me have kept those somewhere!

I took off my backpack and held it between my hands as I ran like a lovesick fool, not stopping until I was home, blasting past my mother and locking myself in my room.

I ransacked my room, piling clothes and papers everywhere until, finally, I found the notes. I sat down in the middle of the mess, quickly tossing a stack of old drawings out of the way.

I searched carefully through the list. For the first time since Friday night, I felt the flickering of hope. Never in my life had I put my mind 100% to something and failed. I scrolled through the list and stopped on an entry about music.

Her favorite band, Amon Amarth, was coming to Phoenix in October to an open-air metal festival. I knee-walked over to my computer, pulling up the calendar. There was one weekend left in October. *Please let it be this weekend.*

I didn't bother to hop up into my chair, staying on my knees and searching for the event. It was this weekend!

"WOOO!" I yelled, performing the all-time fastest Google search for tickets.

"Tickets for this event have been sold out," the official event page stated. Unfazed, I scoured the internet looking for tickets to the sold-out event, coming up empty, even on the major third-party ticket resellers.

I snapped my head back and groaned. How could this possibly be happening to me? I needed this more than anyone else in the world. As a last-ditch effort, I pulled up Facebook Marketplace. One person had two VIP tickets to the event. The tickets were early access general admission with backstage passes.

Oh. My. God. She'd SHIT if she got to meet the band. This is it! This is what I need to win her back.

The computer screen became blurry as I rapid-fired a message to the seller. I was bawling my eyes out and didn't give a damn. I missed her and now I had a chance. That's all I could ask for. I hoped that I wouldn't have to wait long for a response. Thankfully, the seller responded right away.

"Hi, this is for two tickets with two backstage passes. I bought them for a lot more than what I'm selling them for, but since I can't go, I figured I might as well at least get something back. I'll sell them to you for $500. With that, you'll get signed merch, get to talk to the band for a few minutes, and a photo op. The tickets themselves are early access general admission."

I swallowed and grabbed my lockbox. That was a lot of money, and I'd never worked, too busy with sports. I had saved what little I could here and there. It amounted to just over $550. Barely enough for the concert and dinner.

Without thinking about how I'd get us there, or if Maddie would even go, I messaged the seller back, agreeing to the price. One problem at a time.

"Okay, bring cash tonight at 7 pm. Meet you at the McDonald's on West Chandler Boulevard in South Phoenix."

I agreed and then began figuring out how I was going to get to South Phoenix without a car. It didn't take long to figure out my only option.

I reached for my phone, found the right contact, and pressed the call button. It rang four times before Hugh answered.

"Hey, Kellan. Is everything okay?"

It almost is just hearing your voice. I miss you guys.

"Hey, Hugh. No, Maddie doesn't talk to me anymore, my life is already over. But I have a plan to win her back and I need your help if you're available tonight. Are you busy?"

The line went quiet for a few seconds. By now, I was used to Hugh's patience. Someday, I hoped to be like him. I daydreamed a few times over the past month about what it would be like to have kids with Maddie someday. I vowed to be a father like Hugh, offering my kids something I never had—a steady, supporting presence no matter what.

"I'm scared already," he finally said with a soft chuckle. "No, I can't say I have anything in particular going on. Why? What do you need?"

"I need to be in South Phoenix at seven tonight. I'm supposed to meet someone at a McDonald's to buy two Amon Amarth tickets and backstage passes for Friday night. I know I need to connect on a Hail Mary pass to have a shot at winning Maddie back and I thought maybe this would be just the thing."

I closed my eyes and listened to the joyful laughter of Hugh. I had focused on Maddie so much the past few days that I forgot about the other one billion things I was going to miss if I couldn't get her back.

"How come I get the privilege of being Uber for you?"

I laughed. "Because you're cheaper, and this is going to cost me every dollar I have. I'll have enough left for us to eat Chipotle on the way... oh, and yeah, I'll also need to borrow your car on Friday night, preferably with the gas tank full... and, uh, you need to let me take your daughter to a heavy metal concert, but I swear that's all!"

Hugh laughed even harder. "You sure? Why stop there? If you're going to ask for the moon, might as well throw in a few stars while you're at it."

"Maddie is the moon, the sun, and the stars. And someday, I hope to have the honor of asking you for your daughter's hand in marriage, but for right now, this will be all."

Hugh inhaled sharply and then let it out with a rush. I replayed what I'd said, and then blushed harder than I ever had. It just kind of came out, like things usually did when I was with Hugh. But I meant it. Every word.

"Well... listen... I can't make her go, as much as I'd like to see her back with you. She's been moping around here all week, either crying or just staring numbly out of a window. Don't let her fool you, she misses you. With a passion. But the girl has her mother's pride, so good luck getting her to go. But if you can, it's fine with me. And you can borrow the car. What time is this concert?"

I fist-pumped about 20 times, accidentally dropping my phone. "Oops, sorry, dropped the phone. Umm, it's at eight. It's pretty cool because it's geared more for all ages. I'll totally make sure we get home at a decent time. And thanks... I appreciate it. I just want to see her smile. I didn't mean to hurt her; I just didn't know how to tell her I knew about her streaming. I should have said something much sooner. I've been thinking about it all week and I know that she's right. I hope she'll accept this as an apology."

I could almost see Hugh sitting in his office chair, slowly nodding, listening to every word like no one else I knew did.

"Well, as I said, Kellan, she's extremely stubborn and gets it honest. But... you know what? This might just work. What time would you be coming by to pick her up?"

"I was thinking I'd come over around 4:30, take her out for her favorite dinner, and then we'd head over to the festival to meet the band before they play."

Hugh chuckled and I smiled quietly, realizing I felt like myself again.

"Alright, Kellan. You know I'll help you. I'll pick you up shortly so we can grab those tickets."

"Thanks, Hugh. I owe you like, everything. This means the world to me." I wanted to say more about how he felt like a father to me but stopped, not quite trusting my emotions.

"It's no problem. I'll see you in a little while."

I hung up and sat my phone down with a smile, then furrowed, wondering how I'd tell Maddie about Friday night. I knew that she wouldn't see me, and I didn't want to go through Charlotte or Destiny. I'd have to slip a message along with Hugh.

But it wasn't going to be any old message. It was going to be an epic love letter. Everything I had was on the line—all my money, all my dignity, and all my heart.

I sat down at my desk, writing quickly but with a furious intensity. I poured all my love for her into the pages of the letter, leaving nothing to chance. I had no guarantee she'd read it; heck, it was more likely that she'd burn it, but if she did read it, she'd know that nobody else would ever love her as I do.

I ended with details of the special date I had planned, telling her to call me, yes or no. I didn't think she'd walk away from Amon Amarth, even if it meant having to spend the night being nice to me.

But it's just like our beginnings, Maddie. Once I get my foot in the door, you won't want me to leave. You'll remember all the great things about us, and you'll look past the one stupid mistake I made. And I promise I won't make any more... because God knows I can't afford this ever again.

I sealed the letter in an envelope as Hugh pulled into the driveway. Thankfully, my mom was already in her bedroom. I didn't know how to explain to her what I was doing, especially since we hadn't spoken since last Friday night. I left quietly, double-checking my pockets to make sure I didn't forget the cash.

I slid into the passenger seat of Hugh's Volvo, nodding my head and smiling. I felt as if I'd had six shots of espresso. Hugh looked amused.

"I hope Daisy feels the same way about me as you do about Maddie."

I shook my head. "I don't think anybody feels like I do. I can't even explain it. It just is. But who knows, maybe Mrs. Martin will surprise you someday with tickets to a heavy metal concert."

Hugh roared as we pulled out into the street. "I'd be much happier with a little jazz bar, a nice juicy steak away from the prying eyes of my daughter, and an early night in. To each his own."

The ride to Phoenix with Hugh was the first bright spot in days. I almost forgot that Maddie wouldn't talk to me, letting myself pretend that we were going somewhere to pick up Maddie and the past few days weren't real.

Almost an hour later, we pulled into the McDonald's. Hugh put the car in park and turned to me with one of his fatherly looks that I missed.

"Kellan, I don't mind taking you to buy these tickets, or letting you borrow my car on Friday night. But I want you to know that I can't make her go with you. If she doesn't want to go, you're out whatever these things cost. Are you sure you want to go through with this?"

I didn't hesitate. "I'm absolutely positive. I know how much this band means to her. And I know how much she means to me. If there is even a 1% chance she'll go, it's worth it. I have to do this. I'll regret it for the rest of my life if I don't buy the tickets, whether she comes or not."

He held my gaze, seemed to be considering something, then waved it off. "Okay. Let's go get the tickets. I hope this works for you."

The restaurant was mostly empty inside, and a bald guy in the corner waved us over. After a few pleasantries, he got out the tickets and I pulled out the cash. I noticed Hugh's eyes widen at the amount, but he didn't say anything.

The ride back was quieter. I got lost contemplating whether she'd go or not. As the bright and soaring lights of the city gave way to the lower, more subdued lights of the suburbs, I wished I had a fast-forward button. I needed to know if she was going to go or not before I completely freaked out. I almost wanted to ask Hugh if I could ask her straight away, but I knew better than that. I fingered the letter in my pocket and knew this was the best way.

As we pulled into my driveway, I took the letter out. "Would you pass this along to Maddie and see that she at least takes it out of your hands? I know she might destroy it upon contact, but I'm hoping that she at least reads it. It has the details about the concert and everything in it. I'm sorry for involving you again, and I hope she wasn't too hard on you about the Twitch stuff. It wasn't your fault."

Hugh rested a hand on my shoulder. "No worries, I'll see that she gets it, and I'll tell her that it's important that she reads it."

I looked down at my hands, barely seeing them in the dim glow of the interior lighting. Once I left this car, it was back to being alone. No friends, no real semblance of a family, no warmth. I'd sleep in their basement just to avoid going back to my bedroom.

"Thanks, for everything tonight. I wouldn't have been able to do this without you. I know Maddie would kill us both if she knew we did this."

Hugh grinned. "It's really not a problem, Kellan. I'm glad to help. I'll be avoiding telling her that we did this, at least until you get your answer. I think if she knew I was involved, it would taint her response and not in the direction you want. But good luck, okay? I hope to see you on Friday. Oh, and before I forget! Daisy sends her best and says she misses you. She hopes to see you on Friday as well."

I got out of the car, the tears already threatening. I'd been extremely emotional since I met Maddie. It made me wonder what I was before. Like, did I not even feel? Or did I run from one thing to the next and never have time to process what was going on inside of me? Either way, so much had changed in the last few months. I'd gained and lost an entirely new family.

I pretended to walk toward the house, but lingered, wanting to watch Hugh drive away. The euphoria of the night was already long gone by the time he pulled away. I stepped inside, staggered down the hallway, and fell into a heap on my bed, staring at my computer, knowing it was a streaming night, but not daring to see if she was live. She probably wasn't streaming anyway, but it was none of my business until she said it was. It might be too late but I was going to honor what I should have been doing all along. Maybe if she opened the letter, I'd be welcomed back someday.

Open the letter, Maddie. Please, just open the letter. If you read that letter, we can get back to being us. I'm so sorry that I hurt you. You know I love you. Come on, sweetie. Let's move past this.

I waited… my phone turned all the way up. My clock went from four digits to three as morning arrived. I kept seeing her burning the letter, smiling as the flames lapped at the handwritten pages, my heart blowing away in bits of smoke and charred paper.

That's fine. I understand. You can burn it, trash it, do whatever you want with it. If it made you smile, it was worth it. But I'm still coming over to your house on Friday. I'm not letting you go without fighting with everything I've got.

The clock kept marching forward and even though I knew the call wasn't going to come, not at those hours, I still sat vigil, swiping the screen open every so often, seeing her face staring back at me from the screen. I closed my phone for the final time shortly after four am, surrendering from this world of nightmares to the ones in my dreams.

Chapter 33

Maddie

I flung myself down on our living room couch with a sigh. It was finally Friday afternoon. No more longing looks from Kellan in the hallway until Monday. It was exhausting trying to avoid the kid. He was everywhere at once. I still hadn't figured out what I wanted or even if I could forgive him. I needed space and school obviously wasn't the place for that.

I went to grab my skateboard, but Dad poked his head out of his office. "Hey, sit tight for a little while, we've got dinner plans."

I groaned, stomping my feet as loud as I could up the stairs. *Figures. I finally feel good enough to hang out with my friends at the skatepark and I can't go.*

I fired up my Super Nintendo, playing yet another Jets of Time Chrono Trigger seed. It must have been at least my twentieth of the week. It took me away from the pain for a little while, helping me almost forget about Kellan.

After about an hour, I kept hearing weird noises outside my door. At first, I thought it was Charlotte going to the bathroom, but I kept hearing soft creaks like someone was walking back and forth. I paused the game and crept over to the door to check it out.

It would stop for a moment, and then start again. I swung the door open and bumped right into Kellan. I shrieked and jumped back in my room, frightened. He took a step back, hands up, eyes wider than I'd ever seen them.

"I was going to knock... I just..."

"What are you doing here!?" I said as if we were still together. The shock of seeing him standing outside my room, a place he had never been, caught me off guard.

Charlotte's bedroom door opened and she ran out into the hallway, her hand over her mouth. As I recovered from my shock, a boiling rage came over me, watching his greedy eyes darting behind me, examining my room. *Like you haven't already seen enough of it on stream!* I closed the door and stood in front of it, my arms crossed.

"Can I come in and talk to you alone?" His eyes nervously darted between me and Charlotte, before handing me two black roses. I snorted, accepted them, and promptly dropped them on the floor and smushed them. I cocked my hip and clenched my jaw. Two roses, even if they were black, were not going to cut it. Not even close.

"No. Say whatever it is you wanted to say and then get out. I don't have anything to say to you. You lied to me. I knew you were going to break my heart from the start. I should have listened to myself." I made a pointed face at Charlotte that she didn't deserve before looking back up at him under my eyelids.

Kellan put his hands in his pockets and shifted his weight to the side. I wasn't used to seeing him so out of place.

"So, I saw my letter sitting on your desk unopened. I guess you have no idea why I'm here or what I've planned for us, do you?"

"Yep. Didn't read it. Didn't want to. Don't care what you've planned. You've got one more minute before I drag you out by your ear and slam the door in your face."

I could see him start to get angry under the surface, those honey-brown eyes flaring up like a furnace on a clear night. Good. I didn't like this insecure version of Kellan. If he had any chance, he needed to be stronger than this.

He lowered his brow and bore his eyes into mine. "Fine, we'll do this in front of an audience, if that's what you want. Okay, Maddie, I lied to you. I'll name it—I didn't tell you I knew about your streaming. I watched and pretended to be somebody I wasn't. And it was absolutely wrong. I'll own it.

"But you know why it started? You wouldn't talk to me. In the beginning, you wouldn't even give me the time of day. So, yes, I spent time with you in the only way I could, on Twitch. Do I regret that part? Hell, no! Because that's where I got to know the real you. That's where I fell in love with you. I was into you before Twitch, but I wasn't certain yet... but I remember the exact moment I was watching you and all that fell away. It was the first minute of the very first stream I watched. Why? Because I saw you happy for the first time. I'll never forget that as long as I live. I had only seen you

scared or angry up to that moment… then I saw you smile."
He closed his eyes and took a deep breath.

"I remember thinking how cool you were, with your cosplay and your sexy face. I remember thinking I'd never met anyone like you… ever, Maddie, ever. There's just no one like you, you're so special… and I know that if I don't do everything I can to be your boyfriend again, I'm going to regret it for the rest of my life."

I looked down at my feet. He'd already started to melt me, but I didn't want him to see it yet.

"So, I watched, and I chatted, and I rooted so hard for you during your Minecraft stuff." He took a step back and started shaking his fists excitedly. "Oh my God, sweetheart, if you could have seen me bouncing around my bedroom when I watched you, like a little kid at Christmas… especially that moment that you beat that Greg guy one on one. I lost my freaking mind jumping up and down. I've wanted to celebrate stuff like that with you every day, but we can't… because I was a coward who couldn't tell you the truth.

"And I want to tell you what I've done every. Single. Day since I knew you were a streamer. I climb into my bed at night and put on one of your YouTube videos. I love to close my eyes and listen to your husky, sultry voice in my headphones. Every single night, Maddie, I've done that, just to feel like you were there with me. I always want to feel you there with me. And, oh, I liked adding a little extra bass to the audio settings because it gave you such a nice little purr."

I let out a little giggle and bit my lip. I tilted my head and looked into his eyes. I wanted to think about anything other than how hot he was when he was wound up. I failed. Miserably.

He stepped closer to me, his voice softening. "So, yeah, screw it, I lied to you. I'm an asshole. But I just didn't want you to lose your mind on me and stop talking to me. I know that was quite the 200IQ decision on my behalf. It's worked out real well for me, let me tell you." He laughed and I let myself be wrapped in its deep timbre.

"In retrospect, I should have told you like the first week. I just... dammit, Maddie, I didn't want us to end. I'll admit it, as much as I don't want to. I was scared. Terrified. It hurt so hard to think that I would lose you after I just found you. Do you have any idea how much you mean to me?"

I looked down, unable to answer.

"Well, I'm going to tell you. The days before you, I was just another teenager. I thought I was so cool with all my friends and girls and football, and I didn't think life could get any better. Then, I met you. Everything else seemed like a joke because it was a joke. If you think it was hard for me to lose my friends and football, you should have seen me the past week after losing you. Some nights I can't even breathe...

"I don't want to be away from you anymore. I don't think you want things like this, either. I know you're hurt. I'm sorry. I'm... way beyond sorry. I made a mistake. I should have told you. You're right, and I'm wrong.

"But I'm here to make it up to you. I have an epic date planned. I'm going to sweep you off your feet. And I have a deal to make with you."

I looked up and melted even further as he gently wiped away a tear at the corner of my eye.

"Okay, I'm listening," I said, sniffling slightly.

"Go with me on the best date that anyone has ever planned for their girlfriend. If by the end of the night, I haven't made it up to you, and you don't want to be with me, I'll leave you alone. Forever. I promise. I'll go home, I'll cry by myself, and I'll sleep under my bed, hoping that it breaks and crashes on top of me, smothering and stabbing me to death."

I wiped my eyes and burst into laughter. "Are you always this morbid?"

Kellan blinked and then I saw his recognition of when he first asked me that same question back in the parking lot. He grinned wide, tossing his hair dramatically to one side.

"I don't know. Why do you care?" he said, and then we both laughed together, his hand reaching out and touching mine.

Home.

I tapped my lips, knowing it drove Kellan wild when I did this.

"So, do I get a preview of this epic date, or do I just have to say yes or no?"

Kellan looked smug and I knew somewhere along the way I had lost this battle and he had won. If this was what he was finally going to beat me at, I was the luckiest loser in the world.

"You get a preview. Here goes. So, I paid attention during your streams." He winked at me in the corniest way ever. "In fact, I even took notes before you'd talk to me, making lists of all your interests that you shared on stream so that IF you ever gave me a chance, I'd be ready. I didn't want to blow any opportunities—I was determined to be prepared. It's the quarterback in me. And I choose to think of this as romantic behavior, but if you want to think of it as creepy, be my guest. I'm in love with you and I just didn't want to forget anything about you. And, lucky for me, you like creepy.

"So, this date starts with your favorite dinner. Chipotle. Sofritos, cilantro rice, white corn salsa, guac. You'll only eat half because you get stuffed. And, no, I'm not sharing the other half with you. Look at me... I need an entire burrito.

"Then... well, just hold out your arm and close your eyes."

I made a questioning face.

"Just do it. Trust me," he said.

"Okay... I guess I'll trust you... *again*," I said, scowling at him before closing my eyes and holding out my hand.

Kellan wrapped something around my wrists and the disappointment was immediate. *Jewelry, Kellan? Do you not even know me?*

"Open your eyes."

I squinted at the bracelet, trying not to cringe before looking at Kellan. "What is this? Not gonna lie, I thought the jewelry would be cheesy, but this is like cardboard. I'm so confused right now."

Kellan didn't bat an eye as he pulled a couple of folded sheets of paper out of his back pocket.

"I didn't buy you jewelry, Maddie Pie. I know you better than that. The goofy bracelets go with this." He held the printout confirmation of Amon Amarth eTickets in front of him.

I put my hands over my nose and stared at them. Then I looked at Kellan. He was so eager to see me happy, his expectant smile half-formed, waiting to celebrate with me.

I love you.

I jumped into his arms, knocking us both backward into the closet door opposite my room. My mouth found his as hungry as mine, and my hands framed his face. I felt his hands slide to my butt and lift me higher.

"I guess she said yes," I heard Dad saying from the top of the stairs as a chorus of clapping erupted.

Kellan pulled away and glanced at my entire family watching from the top of the staircase. He turned as red as I'd ever seen him, and that made him all the cuter. I was sure he was thinking about what he'd said and how they'd been there watching, but I didn't care. He was my boyfriend and they shouldn't expect any less drama from something concerning me.

I tried to return to his lips but he laughed and sat me down. And then I totally lost my mind because I was about to meet Amon Amarth.

I leaped over to Charlotte and grabbed her by the shirt.

"Oh my God, oh my God, oh my God, he's taking me to see Amon Amarth!" I jumped over to my mom. "And we have backstage passes! I'm going to get to meet the band! What shirt do I wear? Oh my God, I'm going to have to get ready!" I whirled back to Kellan, striding right over and getting in his face... or chest, I guess. But I looked up!

"Why didn't you tell me this right away?"

He reached out and tucked my disheveled hair behind my ear. "Because I wanted you to come just for me. But I figured it was nice to have a solid safety net. I'd like to pretend I care whether or not you would have taken me back, just for me. But I don't. Whatever it takes, you know?"

I smirked, poking him hard in the chest, forgetting how wonderfully firm it was. I'd have to refresh my memory more later. "Well, *Manga*, you needed something big after your behavior. This most definitely will suffice. How did you get these tickets anyway?"

Still blushing, Kellan grinned. "Facebook Market-place, after much scouring. I looked everywhere, finding nothing, then struck gold when I remembered to check there. I had to ask your father to drive me to the other side of Phoenix to get the backstage passes, but it seems like it was worth it."

I glanced back at Dad, a shit-eating grin on his face.

"By the way, this night represents just about every dollar I had, sooooo… yeah. Enjoy this date. Because the next, like, 20 are not going to live up to this."

I put my hand on his heart, splaying my fingers and tapping lightly. "Kellan… promise me you'll never keep anything from me again. And I promise you I won't freak out or anything. Deal?"

"I promise." He lifted me up and spun me around before planting a soft kiss on the corner of my mouth.

My family clapped again, and my dad slapped Kellan on the back. Kellan blushed an even deeper crimson. I looked at him sideways, an eyebrow arched.

"Hey, how exactly are we getting to this dinner and concert? You got a car I don't know about, too?"

Kellan shook his head and then looked at my dad. "Nope, no secret car. I'll admit to being boring and only keeping one secret from you. Your dad drove me to buy the tickets on Wednesday night, and he has been gracious enough to let me borrow the Volvo for an evening of romance."

I rolled my eyes at my dad. "I should have figured you were in on this. Sometimes I think you like him more than me."

Kellan made a big show of looking surprised. "Well, now really, Maddie, can you blame him? Who doesn't love themselves some Kellan?"

Everyone laughed, especially my mom. If I didn't love Kellan so much, I'd hate him for the way my family fawned over him. But I understood it. He seemed born to impress people.

He put his hands on my shoulders and steered me back toward my room. "Go! I want to make sure we have time to eat. Now that we're back together, I am suddenly starving. I haven't eaten like all week."

"Right! I've got to pick out my shirt and match my makeup, and oh my God, do we have enough time?"

Kellan picked me up and carried me into my room.

"Finally, I get to walk in here. Could have done this sooner since I already knew about your streaming six weeks ago." I smacked him on the arm. "Too soon? Yeah, probably is." He pushed his lips up and nodded before laughing. "I'll wait downstairs. Just… start somewhere and don't worry about everything, just throw a shirt on, pick out your makeup real fast, and let's go. I don't want you to be late to meet your favorite band!"

I hurried over to my makeup area and yelled back at him. "You're such a guy, Kellan. This is so much to think about. Arghhhh! We're going to meet Amon freaking Amarth! Can you believe it?" I screamed.

"Yes, since I was the one who bought the tickets," Kellan yelled as he descended the stairs. "Come on, Maddie, let's go!"

I hurried to my closet, rifled through my t-shirts, and grabbed my Shieldmaiden tank top. I kept my black skinny jeans I was already wearing but swapped out my purple

Converse for my custom trans-pride colored high-tops I ordered on Etsy.

I quickly wiped away my standard purple eyeshadow and decided to go bold. I made a red star over one eye, and a black star over the other. Black lipstick. Red bow in my hair. Black sleeves on my forearms.

I peeked at myself in the full-length mirror on my closet door. If there was a cuter girl at the concert, I wanted to meet her. I looked older, wilder, more ferocious. More like me. *Kellan's going to lose it.*

I floated out of my room, my feet barely touching the ground. I was on cloud nine, back with my boyfriend and headed to my first concert. I hopped my butt up on the stair railing, sliding down, catching Kellan's eyes halfway to the bottom.

His lips parted, his hand moving involuntarily over his heart, and I knew I'd stolen his breath.

"This is so cute! I want to take pictures, but I know you'll kill me and you're already late," Mom said.

Kellan was still lost, his eyes dancing over me, unable to decide which part he liked best. I ate it up, catching his gaze every few moments with a coy smile.

"I wish I had made a video of your little speech to Maddie to post on TikTok. #Feels. That was serious. If she didn't go with you on the date, I was going to disown her," Charlotte said.

Kellan didn't take his eyes off me. "Look at how wonderful she is..." he said before blinking and glancing at the others. "I'm just glad we're back together. I don't know how I feel about an hour of this music but I know it'll make her happy and she'll never forget it. And since she'll never forget about me watching her streaming without her blessing, at least there will be good memories associated with all this."

Everyone laughed and talked over each other, trying to one-up their "Maddie was so depressed this week" stories. He nodded to them occasionally, but mostly we looked at each other.

"I'm glad I wasn't the only one staying at Hotel Rock Bottom," Kellan said when he finally had a chance to speak.

"So, how do I look?" I asked, batting my blackened eyelashes. I already had all the answers I needed the moment we locked eyes as I was rocketing down the stair railing, but I wanted to hear it, too.

"Well, you know we missed homecoming last week. And I know you were excited to wear a pretty dress. And we should totally still do that... but honestly? This is so much better. It's so you. You look like a heavy metal princess. It's, umm... well, I'll tell you how I feel about it when your parents aren't standing right here."

My mom wrapped her arm around Kellan, laughing. "We all know how you feel about Maddie. You can't hide it, Kellan."

Kellan's eyes fell to the floor as he laughed, thrusting his hands in his pockets like he always did when he was nervous.

"Alright, you two have a good time. Be safe and text me updates! Don't make me worry. I've worried enough for one lifetime," Mom said.

We said our goodbyes to everybody as my dad handed Kellan the keys and made a silly joke about having me back on time. I think he was as worried about Kellan as he was about me.

When we walked to the car, I could tell that the way I looked was affecting Kellan. He seemed nervous as he kept stealing sideways glances. I was happy to let him suffer.

He bumped his head getting into the car. "Ow!"

"Pffttttt! Might want to adjust the seat before getting in, smart guy," I said.

"No, you think? I forgot how short your dad is. This car wasn't really built for big blockheads like me."

I smiled sweetly at him. "You should be glad he's so short. That means I won't grow that much more, either. I'll always fit right in your pocket."

Kellan beamed, putting his hand on my thigh. "It's been almost a week since I've seen you look at me like that. I missed that. Do it again," he said.

I smirked and pointed at the clock. "Yeah, well, I'm going to go back to angry Maddie if you don't throw this car in reverse and get us to the concert on time!"

I attached my phone to the car and turned on a melodic death metal station and cranked the volume up.

"You're the only girl in this world pretty enough to make me able to tolerate this. I love you!" he yelled over the growling guitars and blast beats.

He stole a kiss and then backed us out of the driveway.

Chapter 34
Kellan

Maddie walked in front of me as we hurried into Chipotle. Watching her walk was like watching an ax being swung by an expert warrior. She was so tiny but she moved her body like a sharpened servant of the battlefield. I could feel my heartbeat synchronize with the swinging of her hips, and smell her hair on the soft breeze.

She turned back at me abruptly and stopped. "Whatcha lookin' at?" she said far too innocently.

"Umm, honestly? Your butt. And I'm not sorry."

She spun around, giggling, and then stopped me inside before we ordered. She put a hand up to my chest and then moved a finger to my lips.

"Hey, you're not getting steak here, okay? You're eating the sofritos with me."

I laughed. "Maddie, I've eaten vegan since we started dating. Promise. And I never took off the trans-pride bracelet your mom made me. I've been nothing but yours."

I have to admit, I was scared about the sofritos, but when we sat down at the table and I had my first bite, they were actually pretty good.

"Hey, this isn't too bad," I said in between bites. "It's not the steak, but it's not bad."

Maddie looked straight ahead with that intense glare that I'd missed. If her face wasn't covered in war paint, I'd kiss her cheek. "At least it didn't have to suffer and bleed to get in your stomach. If you add that into the equation, then it's way better than the steak."

"What about grass-fed beef? Hugh said—"

She turned on me, serious. "Don't believe his propaganda. He just wants to enjoy his burgers without guilt. As long as I'm around, that's not happening."

I rubbed the small of her back and laughed.

"Don't ever change. Not even a little bit," I whispered in her ear.

Traffic was heavy; it was Phoenix after all, but we didn't encounter any jams. For a Friday night, I thought we were lucky. I had never driven with Maddie before, and it felt like we were older. It was like a preview of what life would be like in the years to come. I would find stuff she loved to do, and we'd go have a blast together. The only difference was that we'd have an electric car because, you know... Maddie.

On the way to the concert, she reached over, turned off the music, and grabbed my hand.

"Hey, I'm sorry about the roses. That was really emo and unnecessary. I was hurt and... I'm sorry. It was sweet of you to bring them. I wish I would have kept them and put them in my hair."

I shook my head. "Oh, don't worry about it. I don't care if you soak the petals in propane and light them on fire, as long as you're my girlfriend, we're good." I squeezed her hand and admired her delicate little mouth as she smiled at me.

"I am and always will be your girlfriend... but watch the road!"

I quickly looked back to the road and noticed that we'd drifted over the white line toward the railing on the highway. Crashing probably wouldn't be a great way to impress Hugh the first time he let me borrow the car.

"Oops. Guess you shouldn't have looked so hot tonight. Then maybe I could have kept my eyes on the road and not on you," I said, trying to hide my embarrassment.

"There will be plenty of time later for your eyes to be focused on me. When we're alone. In your room." She patted the top of my leg and I stirred. *What does that mean?* I wanted to ask but she spoke first.

"Hey, I wanted to tell you... I watched back all the old VODs where you talked to me as MangaGuy06."

I tensed and forced myself to take a deep breath.

"You know, I still think you should have told me, but the things you said to me... you were so sweet. Did you really have to walk down to Safe Foods to find a prepaid card to subscribe to?" she asked.

Relief washed over me. I had wanted her to see this about the streaming; that while I shouldn't have done what I did, I loved her with a passion that couldn't be explained, and all I was trying to do was connect with her.

"I did. I had to try not to jump up and down in the store when I finally found the right card."

"And then the night after that, I'm screaming in your face and doing everything I can to drive you away."

I glanced at the navigation as it beeped, the AI lady telling me in a posh British accent to turn right in two miles. *Nice touch, Hugh.*

"That's okay. I knew I just had to keep working to crack open that shell, that once you saw me for who I really was, you'd let me in and it would all have been worth it. And it was."

Maddie sat back in her seat and looked at her hands in her lap. When she got silent like that, I knew she was feeling either sad or embarrassed. I tried to soothe her. To me, the past was the past—I wanted to make the most of us now.

"But, yeah, I'm glad you didn't punch me that night. I thought for sure you were going to take a swing. I wasn't going to block you. I thought maybe if you got out your anger, it might help loosen things between us." I rubbed my chin. I hadn't shaven all week. I hoped she found it sexy.

"No, I was never going to punch you. I don't want to mess up that face."

I laughed and double-checked the navigation, making sure I had the right exit. It was less than five hundred feet away. Thankfully, I had already merged into the right lane. I wasn't used to driving much into the city—in fact, this was only like my third or fourth time.

"Hey, Kellan… would you still be trying if I hadn't come around yet?"

I checked the rearview mirror, picked one of the two exit lanes, and brought us down the off-ramp. "Yes, of course. Is that a joke question? It was always going to be you, Maddie." I glanced over at her as I came to a red light. "But don't get all sentimental. I really like those stars around your eyes. Think about how much of a jerk I was not telling you about Twitch. I want you to look your best when you meet the band. I know how much this means to you."

Maddie busted out laughing. "I'm done thinking of you as a jerk. And it looks like we're close! AHHHHHHH!!!!"

I laughed, fighting to keep my focus on the road as she bounced up and down in the passenger's seat.

I never thought I'd get to see you like this again. Please, if there is anything close to something resembling a god, don't let me screw this up. Give me the grace to always be here for this girl and make her happy.

We parked as close as we could to the festival and followed the signs saying, "Backstage pass patrons this way," to an area with row after row of trailers and campers. It was a lot less glamorous than I imagined it would be, but I figured because it was outdoors, I shouldn't have expected much more.

The wind picked up as the sun sank lower. The temperature would be cooler than we thought it would be, and I hoped Maddie would be warm enough in her tank top.

Everyone we passed complimented Maddie on her makeup, and a few people asked if she bought her shirt on Grimfrost. I had no idea what they meant, but that was okay because Maddie did most of the talking, firing off more words per minute than I could keep up with. I'd never seen her this hyper before.

After having our backstage passes verified, we were led by a friendly security guard to a giant white tent, and when we got inside, there were a few people mulling about, but not much else going on. In the corner, I spotted a tall guy who looked like he might have just stepped off a Viking longship, his blonde hair flowing around a chiseled face. He was surrounded by what I assumed was the rest of the band.

My assumption was correct. Maddie noticed them and went absolutely bananas, jumping up and down and screaming in their direction. She shook my hand away and ran over to them, speaking so fast that there was no way they could understand her. *I* couldn't even understand her.

For their part, the band was very gracious, answering all her questions, posing for multiple pictures, and showering Maddie with merch. I knew my last-second effort to win her back had paid off. To see her this happy was everything I'd ever wanted.

The tall blonde man finally turned to me and said hello, asking me if I was also a fan.

"The only thing I know about you guys is how much she loves you," I pointed to Maddie, who was getting her picture taken with another member of the band. "She's my girlfriend and I bought these tickets and backstage passes because I hurt her feelings and had to win her back. It took every dime I had, but it seems to be working! So, you know what? The answer is yes! I am a huge fan!"

I shared a hearty laugh with the guy, and I beamed when he told Maddie what an awesome boyfriend I was.

The band wished us a good time at the show and asked us to hashtag them with our pictures from the show on social media. When our time was up, I thought I'd have a hard time dragging Maddie out of there, but she hugged everybody, gushed one more time, and then walked out with me.

We ran back to the car to stash the merch before the show. Maddie was in rare form after meeting the band. She kept tugging on my arm and jumping up and down. You would have thought we were at Disney World, and she was five.

"How do you have all this energy?" I asked her, shaking my head and laughing. "You eat like four bites of food a day."

She thrust rock fingers in my face. "I live on metal and coffee. It's all I need to lift off! WOOOOOO!"

The concert was in a giant open field, and I kept seeing several drones buzz back and forth over the growing crowd. I didn't know what to expect before we got here, but it wasn't this. There would be tens of thousands of people packed into this one area. All raving metal fans, probably as hyper as Maddie was. I hoped we didn't happen to pick the one spot where the mosh pit would break out.

What the hell did I sign myself up for? I thought as people began to fill up the field.

When the concert began, Maddie complained that she couldn't see a thing over the people in front of us. With our early access tickets, we managed to get close to the front row, but there was still a throng of humanity in between us and the stage.

I squatted down to her vantage point and realized there was no way she'd ever see anything. I bent down and picked her up, and she looked at me, eyes wide. I stole a quick kiss, then yelled in her ear.

"Climb up around my shoulders, I'll hold you for the show! You owe me a big massage later!" Somehow, she heard me, though how anyone could hear a thing over the overdriven guitars and blast beats was beyond me.

After a few songs, I found that I liked the band and how they engaged with their fans, and the energy of the music was awesome. I especially loved the way it uplifted Maddie. I imagined that when she listened to this alone, it unleashed her from the pain and agony that she'd suffered through.

She bounced on my shoulders the entire concert, occasionally leaning down to flash rock fingers in my face and scream. She was adorable.

For the last song of the show, I watched the tall blonde guy emerge with Thor's hammer, or at least that's what I thought Maddie yelled in my ear. He smashed something on stage with it, timed perfectly with flashes of fire shooting in front of the band. I grabbed Maddie from my shoulders as the song reverberated into the night and slid her down so that her legs were wrapped around me. She kissed me wildly, and I thought that this was how metal kids must slow dance.

When it was over, I carried her all the way back to the car, her legs still wrapped around me. She kept smiling at me, the now smudged black lipstick (my fault) and cool stars around her eyes as entrancing as they were the first moment I saw them.

When we got to the car, my ears were still ringing from the cacophony of thousands of screaming fans and death metal played at infinite decibels.

"That was... the best night of my life," Maddie said. "I can't believe you did this for me. I never thought I would get a chance to see Amon Amarth live, let alone meet the band. You have no idea how many nights that music gave me the strength to make it to the next sunrise."

I held her hand as I saw her sitting in her room alone, trying to understand her identity and who she was. I vowed that she'd never have to do that alone again.

"Then I'm glad we did this together. We should do more stuff like this... and maybe let Hugh pay for it. Sound good?"

Maddie rubbed my cheek and giggled. "Sounds perfect."

It was dark when we got back to the highway. The city lights looked like false daylight against the blackened sky. It was as if it were noon on an asteroid. I put on a Purrple Cat mix for the ride home. Every cell in my body felt like it was ready to charge into war after all that metal, and I was ready to chill.

Maddie was unusually quiet. After how hyper she'd been, bouncing and flinging herself around on my shoulders for most of the concert, I expected her to be amped up for the ride home. Instead, she was sitting quietly in the seat, staring straight ahead, fidgeting with her hands.

I wasn't complaining though. We were back and I was content to cruise in peaceful silence, feeling the last lingering remnants of the painful week drift away in the rearview mirror.

About half an hour later she spoke, and I jumped, bumping my head against the roof of the car.

"Something just occurred to me." The hint of smokiness in her voice aroused me. It was a little hoarse after all the yelling, growling, and screaming she did at the concert.

I turned down the music. "What's that, Maddie Pie?"

"If you have my dad's car, that means your mom is working tonight, right?"

"No, she was suspended for two weeks from work. But she left a note saying she'd be gone this weekend, up at my aunt's place in Flagstaff. Why?"

Maddie moved her hand quietly to my leg. She touched it gently at first, near the knee. She slowly dragged her finger up my thigh, making lazy, looping circles.

"You know, Kellan, earlier I said you would have plenty of time to look at me when we were alone, in your room. Do you remember that?" she said, the husky voice shifting even lower. I could feel the pressure growing in the center of my body. I glanced at her, thinking my racing heart had to be telling me a lie.

But the way she's biting her lip tells me that maybe it's telling me the truth. But she couldn't mean...

"Oh? Would like to go to my house on the way home?" I concentrated on keeping both hands on the wheel and looked at the navigation. Two more exits to go, and then we'd be sliding into Rock Canyon.

"Yeah," she almost purred, her hand reaching the top of my jeans and squeezing. "I think it's time for us." She'd never touched me there before, and it was all I could do to make the exit. She traced her finger back and forth over me and I had to fight to keep my eyes open.

"Take me to your bedroom, Kellan."

If I could have recorded the way she said that to me, I would play it back a million times.

Is she suggesting... us... tonight?

I found myself driving Hugh's car a little faster than I would like, but with her teasing, I couldn't seem to get home fast enough.

She didn't let up, and when we finally arrived, we both jumped out of the car, running for the door. Maddie giggled as I fumbled with the keys, dropping them once and cursing sharply. When I got the door unlocked, I kicked it open and picked up Maddie, carrying her over the threshold, using her dangling legs to kick the door closed.

I stopped in the hallway, pushed her gently into the wall, cupped her butt with my hands as her legs wrapped around my waist and our hungry lips found each other.

Chapter 35
Maddie

I ran my lips down his neck, smelling the desert night mixing with his sandalwood essence, and sank my teeth into his shoulder. He stumbled and we fell to the ground, with me on top.

I bit his ear gently and laughed. "Oops! Too much for you to handle? Mmm, but I do like the lipstick mark on your neck. It says I own you."

He growled and scooped me up as if I was a doll, carrying me to his bed. He threw me down next to his open sketchpad. The drawing of me on the page was one I hadn't seen before. I was wearing a long t-shirt and nothing else, both hands in my hair, with a suggestive smile on my face. He tried to move the sketchpad out of the way, but I grabbed it.

"Uh-uh. Leave it right there. I want to see this the entire time. Get out of those clothes. I want to run my hands all over your body," I said.

I could tell from his wide eyes that he wasn't used to this type of aggressiveness from a girl. I was glad. This was my first time and I wanted it to feel like his, too.

He got up and cut the lights in the room. The only light that remained was the soft glow of the screensaver from his computer.

He lost his shirt somewhere behind him before climbing back on top of me. He kissed me slowly and I ran my hands up the V shape of his back. I dug my nails into the side of his head when he moved to my neck, going right for the spot he knew I loved most.

After a few minutes, he sat up and tried to take my shirt off, but I went stiff. I had forgotten about the part where I'd have to be naked in front of him. My blood ran cold as I thought about what he'd think once he saw me without my clothes.

He pulled back and sat beside me, rubbing my arm.

"Maddie..." he said gently. "You asked us to come here. I don't want to get the wrong idea and make you uncomfortable. Were you asking for us to have our first time together? If you've changed your mind, that's okay. But I want to be on the same page."

I felt safe with Kellan, and I wasn't scared about the actual having sex part, but... I don't know, I was terrified of watching him look at me naked. What if he rejected me? What if all this time he thought he wanted me but when we actually got to the moment of truth, he freaked out? How could I live with that?

I curled into a ball, facing away from him. "I was asking for our first time... and I do want it. I... I'm sorry... I wasn't nervous until it hit me that I'm going to have to be naked too. I was excited to see you. I'm terrified for you to see me. I'm sorry."

Kellan nuzzled up against me, wrapping me in his arms.

"Maddie, I just want you to feel comfortable. I'm not attached to whether we make love or not. If you're not ready, I understand. I will never try to force you. It's always your decision, each step of the way. I'll always be here, and when you're ready, I'll make sure our first time is as amazing as it can be."

When I didn't say anything, Kellan stood up and I could hear the rustling of clothes.

"Hey, you were excited to touch me. Here I am. It's all yours. No pressure for anything more."

I rolled over slowly, my eyes pouring over his now naked body. He laid beside me on his back and I felt a fire between my legs. I licked my lips, unable to hide the way his body made me feel. I slowly reached out with my hand, beginning with his chest and stomach, feeling the muscles rise and fall with each breath. I had touched him like this before when we made out, but he always had a shirt on. That was like looking out the window at a beautiful scene, and this was like being immersed in the middle of it.

I moved my hand to his ribs and then slid it lower, patiently, lingering on his hip bones, suddenly feeling the urge to bite them.

I started to move down his leg, but then stopped, retracing my steps, my fingers crawling over his skin. I let my hand reach for him, hesitantly at first, just touching a fingertip softly and running it up and down his length before finally wrapping him in my hand. I held him still for a few moments, feeling his heartbeat pulsing against my palm.

I started to move my hand slowly, a small motion at first, and when he moaned, I forgot all about being nervous. I sped up, my fingers dancing up and down as his breathing became increasingly shallow.

The desperate look of pleasure in his eyes as I stroked him made me feel as if he was plugged into me and I was his source of power. I lightly swung my hair back and forth, letting it fall in his face, and that seemed to have fanned the flames. He leaned up and grabbed the back of my head, bringing it down to his, our tongues quickly finding each other.

I released him and laughed as instant frustration flashed across his handsome face.

"Why did you stop?" he asked, panting and looking as if he was going to die if I didn't continue.

I gave him one more squeeze. "Because I think I'm ready to take my clothes off." I stood up, facing away from him. I looked over my shoulder, seeing him propped up on his elbows with an eager grin.

I took my tank top off first, and then stripped out of my jeans and underwear. All that remained on my skin was my trans pride bracelet.

The fear gripped me again as I was about to turn around. I felt as if someone had placed a spell on me, and I was doomed to stand there in his room like a statue, facing away from him.

Please let him still want me.

"Kellan… when I turn around, I hope you accept what you see. I don't think I can take it if you don't."

I heard him scoot forward to the edge of his bed before I let out a sharp gasp as I went slamming back into his body. He held me tight with one arm wrapped around my torso. I trembled as the moment I'd feared for years was staring me right in the face. A guy I liked was about to see me naked. And it wasn't just any guy, it was Kellan—my eternal crush, my soulmate. Would he accept me?

He kissed my shoulder and ran his hand down to my butt, and I could almost feel him smiling as he cupped a cheek in his hand.

He reached up and grabbed my hair, snapping my head back so that his lips were next to my ear, and ran a finger slowly down my throat.

"What if—" he began, his finger moving slowly down between my petite breasts, "I like—" his finger now trailed down my stomach, "every part—" moving lower and lower until he wrapped his hand around me, "of my girlfriend."

He paused for a moment, kissing the back of my head gently as I expanded into his hand.

"What if I not only accept it," he whispered into my ear, as he began stroking my growing excitement, "but I love it? And it's actually what I want to find when I see you naked?"

I threw my head back into him, turning into his face, moaning. "Then take it. All of it."

He picked me up, moving me forward with ease, making room so he could stand behind me, so that both his hands could explore. I closed my eyes, surrendering to his touch.

"I've imagined this for so long," I whispered. "Only, I was always a biological girl. But this... this is perfect. You make me feel as if I'm beautiful, just the way I am. Please touch me there again. Please wrap your big hand around me. Don't make me beg for it, Kellan. Just hold me in every possible way, make me feel a love that I've been dying to feel for so long."

He slowly spun me around and guided me down to the bed. When he pulled back, he must have seen the concern flash in my eyes.

"I'm not stopping, just let me get a towel real quick, I don't want to get the lube everywhere when we... you know."

I angled my head sideways, my eyebrows forming a question mark. "Wait... you were prepared for this?"

"Umm... yeah, I Googled. Like when we first met. I have water-based lube and condoms, so we're safe. The water-based lube won't break down the latex condom as an oil-based one would. You have a smart and caring boyfriend. Aren't you lucky?"

Kellan reached down and brushed a stray piece of hair that had fallen across my face.

"You've got that look of curiosity that I know needs to be satisfied before we move on. Go ahead, ask your questions." We both giggled and then I watched as he got lube and a condom out of a drawer next to his bed.

"When did you get this stuff? Did you have it... before me?" I asked. I know it was irrational, but if he answered yes, it would break my heart.

"Oh, no! Definitely not. I mean, the lube part, no. But... umm... I may have bought it way sooner after finding out that you were trans than I want to admit right now. Maybe we can talk about that later? I've been embarrassed enough this week and you are looking so adorable right now."

I swallowed, relieved. I narrowed my eyes. "Hmm... I guess I'll let you off the hook. Go get the towel," I said, giggling as I watched the muscles in Kellan's butt tighten and untighten as he walked away.

When he returned with the towel, I slid out of the way and then watched amused as he applied the lube to himself.

"I don't really know what I'm doing, in the spirit of perfect honesty. This is a new experience for us both."

I laughed and pointed. "Well, it's obvious that it's an experience you're excited about."

Kellan looked at me, serious. "Yes. Making love to you means everything to me. This is the first time this has ever felt sacred... actually, nothing felt sacred to me until I met you. Now everything does. I want to be inside of you, to feel one together."

"I want that, too. I love you, Kellan. Forever."

It's the first time I've ever said that out loud to him, and I couldn't have picked a worse time. He stopped everything and bent over to kiss me, and I had to push him back.

"Oh my God, don't get that stuff in my hair!" I laughed.

He smiled and went back to concentrating on applying the lube to himself and then to me. I reached out when he was finished, tipping his chin up so that our eyes met.

"Hey... start really slow, okay? Maybe just a little bit at a time and rest. You're... not small. I'm kinda nervous. And maybe you should wipe your hand on the edge of the towel. I really don't want that stuff in my hair."

He wiped his hand and moved to rest between my legs.

"Of course, Maddie Pie. I'll be very gentle. Any time you want to stop, just tell me. We're learning this together."

He began slowly, a fraction of an inch at a time, as we looked into each other's eyes, our lips brushing together occasionally like tree branches in the wind.

"Just breathe. Relax and open. I want this to feel so good for you. I want to fill you up and rest together," he whispered.

I felt him deeper and deeper until I motioned for him to stop. We stayed like this, no movement necessary. I felt anchored to Kellan and it was like we were back in that school hallway again, the world falling away around us, with only our love to illuminate the space that remained. I felt the urge to cry as my heart opened wide for him.

After a few minutes of slow and soft kissing, Kellan asked if I would be comfortable switching positions.

"Let me lay down and you get on top, with your back against my chest. I want to hold you like that."

We moved quietly, and Kellan moaned a little bit when my hair fell against his chest. We took our time getting back inside. Then we lay still again, content to drift together, the intimacy its own reward.

The subtle movements of breath created the tiniest amount of motion back and forth, and I felt so in tune with Kellan, like I was inside of his mind. I could feel him growing and getting closer to the point of no return. He reached down and wrapped me in his hand again, beginning to very lightly stroke me. He leaned forward and ever so softly kissed the top of my head.

My soft moans quickly brought Kellan right up to the edge, and he whispered in my ear. "Let's go together, my little angel... I love you... so much... oh, Maddie!" I felt shrink-wrapped against him as he squeezed me tight, pulsing inside of me. I looked over at the picture of myself on the sketchpad and I felt myself soar, the expansion just before release wrapping my brain in a momentary oneness as he continued to caress me, and on the edge of what remained of my consciousness, as I passed through the lights beyond the sky, exploding into the universe, I heard myself screaming. I crested that magnificent towering peak that only two devoted lovers ever reach, the blissful waves emanating from within and without, an ecstasy so pure it was almost painful as all my thoughts ceased, leaving only the steady rhythm of him emptying inside of me as a reminder that I was still on Earth.

Chapter 36
Kellan

We lay together afterward, the only sounds our breathing and a rare Arizona rain plinking against the window. I pulled out gently after a few minutes and moved to lay next to Maddie.

As I twirled her hair between my fingers, I sank deeper into what we had just shared, the depths of our souls entwining together for a moment as we rested at the core of our beingness.

When the two of us become one... everything else becomes a shadow in our light.

"Let's take a shower together, my love," I said, picking her up and carrying her into the bathroom. She looked so peaceful as her face kept moving in and out of my vision in the patches of dim light. I couldn't stop staring at her; I'd never seen her this beautiful. The freckles in her eyes seemed to have a lifeforce of their own, flittering like fireflies in a summer field of blue cornflowers.

"You're so pretty, Maddie Pie," I whispered, kissing the tip of her nose.

I sat her down next to the shower and discarded the condom in the trash can. "We need that for safety but it definitely makes for an awkward moment buster afterward."

Maddie just laughed softly and rubbed my back. I loved that she always seemed to genuinely appreciate my silly commentary. I started up the shower for us, making sure it was nice and warm before picking her back up and placing her gently in the running water. I stepped in behind her, grabbing the bar of soap and lathering up a washcloth. The mist moistened my face as the water splashed on Maddie's body.

"Sorry, I don't have any fancy shower gels. Just this boring sandalwood soap that my mom buys me to try to hide what she calls my 'awful teenage boy' smell. Hope you don't mind smelling like me."

Maddie faced me and put a hand on my chest. "Oh, God, Kellan, I love the way you smell, even when it does have a bit of teenage boy wang to it. I want to wrap myself in it forever."

I smiled and sank to my knees. I began washing her, lathering and caressing one foot at a time. I rinsed them off and kissed the tops gently.

"What are you doing?" she asked, looking at me with a confused smile. I had to get underneath her face to stay out of the shower spray. The water cascading around her head made it feel like I was standing in a dry spot in the middle of a waterfall.

"I'm taking the time to love each part of you. It might be goofy, but I want to care for each little scar on your body. I know you suffered for so long, not understanding yourself, and hating what you saw in the mirror. I want to appreciate you, show you that you are wonderful just the way you are. I want to nurture you, Maddie, always. You deserve it."

She put both hands to her heart and joined me on her knees. Her makeup was washing away, and it was the first time I had ever seen her without it. She wouldn't believe me, so I didn't say anything, but I thought she was even more radiant without it.

"I love you, Kellan. I don't know what my life would be like without you. Thanks for fighting for me, every step of the way. You've been there. And I know you'll always be there."

I squinted through the water beating down on the top of my head. Maddie's hair was now soaked and clung to the sides of her face, falling in little snake-like strands to her shoulders. I brought my forehead to hers, and then she brought her mouth to mine. Water droplets raced down our faces and mingled between our lips.

I thought of how late it was getting and pulled away. "Hey, we better get back before your parents get worried. I have one more thing planned for our date. But don't get too excited because nothing is going to top what we've already done together tonight."

"Aww, what is it? Tell me!" Maddie took the towel I handed her and began drying herself.

"Cuddling on your couch and watching a Shoujo stream. I know she's your favorite streamer and I personally verified on Discord to the woman herself that she would be streaming tonight. Looks like she's playing a randomizer."

"You're so thoughtful and sweet, I—" She caught herself in the mirror and I could see that she realized that her makeup washed away. She turned away from me and covered her face.

"Hey, it's okay," I said, coming up behind her and trying to turn her gently toward me.

"No, don't! My makeup washed off in the shower. I don't want you to see me like this."

I put a hand softly on her the small of her back. "Maddie, what do you think I saw in the shower the entire time we were in there? Do you think I'm really going to find you less attractive because you don't have any makeup on? Sorry, but you're wrong."

"But I look less like a girl," she cried, still refusing to turn around.

"That's not true. And who cares anyway? It's you. You're hot with or without it. I can prove it. We just made love, and yet here I am, still obviously physically attracted to you. You have no makeup on, and I'm still game for round two. Not that we have time, but just sayin.'"

She glanced back and smiled at my "proof." She sighed and turned to face me, still obviously uncomfortable.

"When are you going to stop being so perfect? It's going to get boring at some point, you know," she said.

I shook my head. "Oh, I wouldn't say I'm perfect. Don't worry, I can throw in a weird thing like watching you secretly on Twitch here and there. Just to keep you on your toes."

She punched me in the shoulder. I hadn't been punched by her in like a week. It felt great.

"Oh, shut up, you big goofball! And... maybe you can keep me on my toes ... in other ways." She winked at me.

I finished drying off and hung the towel over the shower.

"Let's get dressed and get out of here. Your mother has probably had three heart attacks by now. It's like 11:30 and we were definitely supposed to be back before now."

We rushed to my room and got dressed. Maddie checked her phone as we walked out.

"Oh, crap. Six texts and four missed calls. We're in for an earful."

We hurried to the car and climbed in. I fired it up but paused before backing out. We were thinking that we would be in trouble for being late, but we had a much bigger problem.

"Is something wrong?" Maddie asked, leaning forward to catch my eye.

"Yeah... I'm wondering how we explain your not-so-perfectly-straightened hair and lack of makeup."

"Oh... oh shit! Umm... you know what? You can solve this. I have faith in you. You've been the one with all the good ideas this week. So, yeah... whadda ya got?"

I banged my head against the steering wheel repeatedly. "We're screwed. I don't know how to explain why you would have taken a shower at my house instead of going home to do it."

Maddie made her signature throwing away gesture with her hand. "Ahh, screw it. We're just gonna go in there and blind them with confidence. It's my parents. What are they going to do? I've put them through absolute hell the past three years. I've been in and out of the psych ward multiple times for goodness sake. I mean, if one night I did normal teenager stuff, like slept with my boyfriend at his house and then took a shower... I can live with that. In fact, I feel like they should celebrate that I've downgraded my rebellious streak from self-injury to sex. And I was hygienic afterward. I mean, I really should get extra points." She nodded briskly, looking proud of herself. "If they ask, I'll do the talking. But they probably won't. Let's just see what happens."

I considered her plan, and lacking any ideas for a better one, we began the short drive back to Maddie's.

Her parents were waiting for us in the living room as we entered. I expected that. Would have been weird if they weren't, but it was still unnerving.

Daisy chastised Maddie but looked relieved that we were okay. It didn't seem like she had any idea what might have happened after the concert. Hugh, however, was a different story.

Maddie put on her best innocent daughter voice. "Sorry, Mom, I didn't mean to scare you by not texting back. The concert was awesome, and we were having such a great time. I just forgot to check my phone."

You can sound so sweet when you want to. I'm making a note of that.

"It's fine. I've grown accustomed to going gray early. I was so worried about you kids driving through the city at night. Was traffic alright? I had all sorts of horrible thoughts. I'm just glad you had a good time and you're home safe," she said, hugging us both.

Hugh didn't say anything, sitting stoically at the corner of their large L-shaped couch, his eyes narrowed as he searched our faces.

"We did. It was the best night ever. Thanks for letting me go... hey, Mom, Kellan and I were going to watch a stream and chill on the couch. Is that cool?"

I felt a nervous pit in my stomach, thinking that her parents were going to expect me to say goodnight to Maddie. I wasn't ready to be without her, not after what we'd shared.

"Yes, of course. If you'd like, I'll fix you guys some hot chocolate," Daisy said.

I breathed a sigh of relief and almost laughed at my stomach's instant response to the idea of putting something in it. It growled so loud I was surprised no one else heard it.

I didn't realize how hungry holding Maddie all night... and, of course, the stuff afterward, had made me.

"That sounds great," I said, putting my hand up to the side of my mouth pretending to whisper, "but please make it two cups because Maddie will drink it all if we have to share."

Maddie elbowed me in the side. She was so pretty with her disheveled hair and natural face. I had to resist the urge to scoop her up and hold her.

Daisy laughed, turning toward the kitchen. "Yeah, that sounds like Maddie. She won't eat, but she'll drink coffee or hot chocolate in the time it takes me to blink."

Maddie and I both looked awkwardly at Hugh after Daisy disappeared into the kitchen. I braced myself, holding my breath and waiting for the inevitable interrogation. Somehow, I'd always escaped the fathers of the girls I'd been with, but I didn't want to avoid Hugh. I just hoped he wasn't angry. It was obvious we loved each other. Would that count for something? Or had I finally found my way onto his bad side?

He stared at us for a few moments and then got up slowly, walking into his bedroom, shaking his head. I hoped my face was at least a shade lighter than the blood-red throw pillows on the couch.

"He totally knows," I whispered to Maddie. She shrugged.

"Dad seems to be on to something, but he didn't say anything about it. I mean, we are 16. It's not like it would be shocking. But... I think we're out of the woods."

After realizing that the shower might not be the huge deal I had projected it to be, we snuggled together happily watching the stream and drinking hot chocolate.

"Would you like it if I wore Yoshi hats like Shoujo?" Maddie asked, drawing figure eights on my thigh with her finger.

"She is really cute, but I like those little Rylian ears you wear. It doesn't get much better than that."

When we looked at each other, there was a little something more there now. It was as if our love had deepened in our most intimate of moments. It was hard to look away from her—nothing else felt real.

When she started to yawn, I stretched across the couch and whispered for her to lie on top of me. She curled into a little ball, her head resting beneath mine. I didn't know how much time we had before her parents would ask me to leave, but I was in no hurry to find out. She put her head over my heartbeat and quickly fell asleep. I stretched, careful not to wake her, and turned the volume down. I rested with my eyes half-open, listening to her sleeping almost like a meditation.

About half an hour later, Hugh emerged from her parent's bedroom. He stood by the couch to the side of me, talking quietly so as not to wake her. I almost shuddered as the fear ripped through me, expecting him to finally address the elephant in the room.

He brushed her hair with his hand and smiled tiredly. "I don't think I've ever seen her as happy as she was tonight," he began. "You've fought through her layers and shined a light into her darkest corners. You've helped her see a different view of life, a different view of herself. You've made her feel beautiful. I don't want to know exactly what you've done these past few weeks… or tonight, for that matter," he said, and I felt my face tingling as I flushed, "but you're exactly what she needed. Daisy and I are both thankful that you're her boyfriend. We couldn't ask for anyone better." He moved his hand to my shoulder.

I fought to hold back the emotion, completely unprepared for this heart-to-heart. This wasn't the conversation I expected… but it was the one I would have wanted.

"All I've ever wanted to do is make her aware of how amazing she is, and to see her smile. I'm glad she has given me a second chance," I said.

Hugh brushed her hair again. "I've always wanted her to be happy, but as her father, I felt powerless sometimes. I know she wants love, like we all do, and I know it was hard for her to imagine that someone like you would come along… but here you are. She never talked about it with me, but I know she's always wanted somebody like you."

I've had thousands of people cheering for me as I came running off a football field, but that was nothing compared to Hugh's acknowledgment of my value to his daughter. I sat mesmerized as he continued.

"You've illuminated her, Kellan, made her feel things inside that Daisy and I never could. You've brought a life into her that I never thought I'd see again. I didn't realize how much I've missed her these last few years."

Hugh looked away, lost in thought.

"She was so full of spunk as a kid, and then she hit about 11, maybe 12, and that's when I think it really hit her that she was different than most of the other kids. She had to deal with the awful feeling of being trapped in a body that didn't feel right... and when she finally embraced herself, she had to suffer rejection from the world for one reason or another."

Hugh clenched and unclenched his jaw. I wondered what he'd had to go through... what challenges—legal and otherwise—he'd had to stomach, watching kids like his get discriminated against across the country. Maddie and I had talked briefly about it, but I was so focused on her that a lot of it flew over my head.

"It's been so hard to take, Kellan. I didn't tell you this that day I picked you up from your father's, but I understand how you felt in the hallway when those kids were bullying her. I understand why you did it. I've lived through this for years. In quiet moments... it eats you alive. You want to rage against the world, demanding to know why they won't accept your child for who they are. She's just a kid. She just wants... to be happy."

He looked away, choking off his words. I'd never seen Hugh this emotional. He was always so calm that I had just come to expect that from him. He gathered himself and turned back to me, his eyes red.

"But you came... and provided a refuge against that. You brought a new world to Maddie and allowed her to experience life as a kid should. I know you two are young, and a lot can happen. But I'm rooting for both of you. I hope you face the challenges ahead together, allowing them to strengthen your bond, growing stronger as a team. You both deserve the best. You're perfect for each other."

He put his hand back on my shoulder and nodded toward the stairs. "Why don't you carry her up to bed. You can spend the night. I don't think Daisy will mind either."

My jaw dropped, almost banging into Maddie's head. "Are you serious right now?"

He chuckled. "Go on before I come to my senses and change my mind."

I didn't need to be told another time. I wrapped Maddie up in an embrace and moved toward the stairs, careful not to jostle her too much. She'd had a long week and I wanted her to sleep peacefully. I stopped at the bottom and looked back to Hugh, Maddie's poem she wrote when she was seven framed just behind his head.

"Thank you... you're..." I stopped and sighed. I couldn't do this right now. "Look, if I didn't think I'd crumble in front of you, I'd tell you what everything you've done for me means. I didn't really have a family before meeting you guys and... now I feel like I have one. But that's all I can say because I'm not going to have a breakdown in front of my girlfriend's father."

Hugh looked at me with a knowing glance. "I'm glad to be here. For both of you."

When I closed the door to Maddie's room, she whispered to me.

"I heard everything."

I smiled in the darkness. "I thought you were sleeping. But I'm glad you heard it."

"My dad loves you. I'm almost jealous," she said. I laid her in her bed and kissed her forehead.

"Yeah, well, I'm lovable, you have to admit," I said, ripping off my shirt and lying next to her. "But honestly, he loves me because of what I am to you. He's a great guy, and I love him too, but he'd kick me out if he thought I was hurting you. He's got your back, Maddie. Remember that's why you like Interstellar so much? You felt like you had that type of relationship with your dad."

Maddie put a hand on my cheek, rolling to her side to face me.

"You really did watch like every single stream I ever did, didn't you?"

"I did. I enjoyed every second of them. I never wanted to feel like I was without you, so I would just put one on and end up getting sucked into it. I especially loved the cosplay," I said as I trailed a thumb across her lips. "You think maybe you could wear that just for me sometime?"

She kissed my thumb and snuggled into me.

"I'll wear it in the morning, just for you. Well, and for the stream I planned on doing tomorrow night, too. But you'll be there for this one. Sitting right next to me. Or maybe I'll just sit in your lap."

She wiggled even deeper into our embrace and I imagined that she was probably biting her lip right now, like she did when she took the initiative.

"I'm looking forward to that. You know, it killed me this week but if you streamed, I didn't know about it. I unfollowed you because I figured that's what you'd want. I'll have to refollow. And subscribe. And... maybe you can make me a moderator or at least a VIP."

"Aww, sure! I'd love that. And hey... you know how you always call me Maddie Pie?" she said.

"Yeah... you do like that, right? Maddie Pie," I whispered as I nibbled on her ear.

"Mmm, yes, I do. But I've been thinking of names for you. I think I like... Kelly Bean. You know, like Jelly Bean? But Kelly Bean."

I stopped and rolled onto my back. *Kelly Bean?*

"Do you... like that at all?" she asked in a small voice.

"I think if anyone ever called me that aside from you, I would gladly kick them where it hurts," I said.

Maddie threw her leg over me and snuggled her head into my neck. "But what about when I call you Kelly Bean?" she said in her best little girl voice.

I leaned down and met her lips. "I like it."

"Good. Because I was going to start calling you that anyway."

"I figured you would." I tickled her and she laughed. "Hey, this is our first sleepover. I think your parents should let us make this a habit. I'll come home with you every Friday after school, and then leave late Sunday night."

I could sense Maddie's indignant furrow without having to see it. "Oh, we're not asking them. We're just going to do it. And hey, are you tired at all? Because I am so wiped after this week. I know I made a big display earlier like I didn't care, but I basically sat up every night and cried my eyes out thinking about us," she said.

"Aww, I'm sorry... I did the same thing. Let's just never have a week like that again. I'll get my stuff together, promise," I said, and we both giggled together. "I'm excited to put that behind us. Let me hold you all night and make it up."

"Okay," she said softly. "I love you, Kelly Bean."

"I love you, too, Maddie Pie. Goodnight, my little angel."

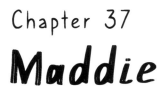

Chapter 37

Maddie

When I opened my eyes, it was just starting to get bright in my room. Kellan's arms were still wrapped around me, and I turned my head as quietly as possible to watch him sleep for a few minutes.

As long as you're here, everything is always going to be okay.

I placed my lips against his and held them there. Within a few seconds, he was moving his against mine, and our hands were reaching for each other.

"Kellan."

We stopped kissing and I giggled. "You kept the text message alert I made for you?"

He smiled meekly. "Well, yeah, it sounds really hot, don't you think? But if that's not you texting me, who is? Because no one else really texts me anymore, except maybe one of the kids from the LGBTQ club at school. Were we supposed to meet them at the café today?"

He reached over to my nightstand and grabbed his phone. From his ashen expression, I doubted it was one of those kids.

"Oh, no. It's my mom. She wants to talk this morning." He looked at me and his sad face broke my heart. "I have to go, but I'll come right back, I promise."

I looked down at the small space between our bodies, the little rainbow unicorns on my sheets smiling at me.

"Hey," I said in a tiny voice. "Can I... come with you?"

I felt him tense. "Are you sure? My mom isn't like your parents. It's..." I glanced up and his eyes were shut, a deep crease running across his forehead. "It's not the same. She could be drunk for all I know. I have no idea what she really wants, or why she's back in town already."

I touched his cheek. "I know, we've talked about it a little bit. And I know what I might be walking into. But you walk into everything with me without blinking. I want to be there for you. Let me come, okay?"

He opened his eyes and swallowed. "Okay. I'll tell her we'll be there in an hour. I know you need time for your makeup and everything."

I kissed him for being a sweetie. "Aww, you know me so well. An hour isn't much, but I can work with that. I'll meet you downstairs."

I showered quickly and then straightened my hair, con- templating my makeup and outfit the entire time. I decided on wearing a little beige dress and pairing it with leggings and flats. I never wore this kind of crap but I knew I'd get a rise out of Kellan and that always felt good. Plus, even I had to admit going girly girl here and there was fun, and it was my first time meeting Kellan's mom. She'd get plenty of my metalhead look later on.

I throttled back on my normal gallon of eyeliner, half a palette of eyeshadow approach, opting instead for what Destiny called the feminine routine—heavy on the contour, light on the accessories. I chose a copper eyeshadow that Kellan had never seen me in before, and a brown eyeliner I'd never used. I finished off with a dab of highlighter down the center of my nose and looked in the mirror.

I looked more feminine than I ever had before and the intense euphoria shocked me. I still preferred my metal look because that was authentically me, but I'd keep this in my back pocket. I could see me in this style for a fancy dinner with Kellan or for opening night at one of Charlotte's plays.

Kellan and Charlotte were sitting on the couch playing Super Smash Bros. when I came down the stairs. They didn't hear me approach.

"Who's winning?" I asked. Kellan turned to me and dropped his controller along with his jaw.

"Thanks for the distraction, sis. Beatcha again! Ha! Ohhh… wow, Maddie, clean up good much?" Charlotte said.

Kellan got up, banging his knee on the corner of the couch as he came closer to me, his eyes never leaving me. He looked me slowly up and down.

"Whoa," he whispered.

I soaked it in, not gonna lie. "You like, huh?"

He nodded eagerly. "Yeah…"

"Well, good. But don't get too used to it because it's a once-in-a-while thing. I feel naked without my skinny jeans."

"Maddie, you look like a little American Girl doll. You're so cute! Can I take a picture?" Charlotte asked.

I batted my eyelashes at her. "Why, of course."

We had our fun, taking way too many ridiculous pictures together, which I was sure went straight to Char's Instagram feed in less than ten seconds after we left. Even my mom made a big fuss about how cute she thought I was. I wished I could start every morning with that kind of pampering.

Kellan kept beaming at me the entire time, not saying too many words. I didn't think making him tongue-tied would ever get old. He finally regained some composure as we reached the sidewalk.

"I was so focused on you that I forgot that this would be the first time you meet my mom. Are you sure about this?"

I grabbed his hand and entwined our fingers together. "Of course, Kelly Bean. Whatever happens, it's fine. I don't have any expectations. If she outright rejects me, I'm not going to hold it against her. I'll get her back when her son is home alone." I said with a sly grin and he nervously laughed.

"Okay… well, let's do this, I guess," he said. We walked quietly to his house. The sunlight was starting to get a richer orange as we entered autumn, and the temperatures were still reasonable at this time of day. I felt genuinely pretty holding his hand and a part of me wanted to keep right on walking past his house, making our way to the café and spend a lazy couple of hours tucked into a booth.

When we reached his door, he paused. "If at any point you want to leave, it won't hurt my feelings, just let me know."

"Hey, it's really okay. None of whatever is behind this door is a reflection on you. Let's just see what happens. Come on." I motioned toward the keys in his hands. He sighed and reluctantly unlocked it.

I stepped in and was greeted with a sad, tired smile by a woman sitting on the couch who looked a lot like Kellan.

Chapter 38
Kellan

I peered into the living room and saw my mom slouched on the couch. I was getting ready to explode but stopped when I saw the coffee mug in her hand. She looked up at us, her eyes going wide for a second at the sight of Maddie. She looked exhausted, the puffiness under her eyes resembling a dirty sponge. I heard Maddie close the door behind us and I walked to the edge of the living room.

"Hi, Mom. Umm, this is Maddie, my girlfriend. We got back together yesterday."

I expected my mom to smirk, but instead, she smiled. "Hi, Maddie. It's nice to meet you. I'm Suzanne. I'd offer you a seat, but I really need to talk to Kellan about something important, if you don't mind giving us a few minutes."

No way. You'll talk to me with her or not at all.

"Mom, anything that you want to say to me you can say in front of Maddie. I'm just going to tell her anyway."

Mom nodded, looked out the window for a moment, and then looked embarrassingly at Maddie.

"Maddie, I'm sorry I look like hell and the place is a mess. It's been a long night… a long life actually." She arched her eyebrows in a slow, lazy motion.

"No, please, it's fine," Maddie said. "I caught you off guard. You didn't know Kellan was bringing a guest. My room looks like this most of the time."

A hint of a smile touched my mom's face before she shifted in her seat, attempting to straighten up.

"Please sit down for a minute, Kel, this is really important." She nodded toward the loveseat opposite the couch. I took Maddie's hand and we crossed the room, the silence still feeling incredibly awkward. Maddie smushed up next to me and kept my hand squeezed tight in hers.

I still couldn't get over how beautiful she was in a dress. Just when I thought my mind had blown as far open as it would go, Maddie seemed to find just the right kind of dynamite to blast it open further.

Mom opened her mouth a few times as if she was going to speak, and kept adjusting her blouse.

"What did you want to talk about, Mom?" I said, fighting to keep the roughness out of my voice.

She looked down at the coffee table. "I started to head up to Aunt Sally's last night, but I made it as far as Lucky's instead."

I leaned forward, the one hand that Maddie wasn't suffocating clenched. "Jesus Christ, Mom! What the hell is wrong with you?" I yelled.

Maddie dropped my hand and dug her nails into my thigh, trying to calm me down I guess. Mom just smiled tiredly, her head drooping to her chest.

"I'm trying to find out what isn't wrong, Kel. But I know this. I don't care how much it hurts; I'm not touching another drop of alcohol so long as I live. I've thought a lot about our conversation earlier this week, and I'm sorry for the things I said to you. No mother should ever say those things to her child. I'll never forgive myself for how I've been, but I'm going to try to make it better.

"I'm going to drag myself to A.A. meetings every day that I can. I'm going to kick this. I'm sorry that I'm not who I used to be. It's been a long road since your father left, I'm not going to pull any punches.

"I thought it would be different, once he was gone, but I've just been spiraling downwards for years. I'm so sorry, Kel, I don't know how I let it get this far. If I've said some things to you... while intoxicated... I don't really remember much these last few months... I'm sorry."

She started to cry, and then I watched dumbstruck as Maddie got up and joined my mom on the couch, consoling her in an embrace. Not 24 hours earlier, I wasn't sure if Maddie would ever speak to me again. Now she was hugging my mom.

After the initial shock, I was both touched and amused— touched because of Maddie's sweetness and amused because she was so tiny that her arms barely fit around my mom. My mom responded back, swallowing Maddie in a hug.

And then my soulmate made an impassioned speech to my mom that I never would've expected.

"Don't be hard on yourself, Mrs. Davis," she started, pulling back from the embrace. "It's tough when you get into an addictive pattern. I suffered from self-injury over the past few years." Maddie held out her scarred arms. "There were so many nights that I knew I needed to stop. I almost killed myself once by accident, and then deliberately tried to a month later.

"You would think I would have been able to click my fingers and stop after the first near-miss. But it's not that easy. We can't stop these patterns because we're harming ourselves or others. We can only stop them when we have a strong reason why we want to change."

Maddie watched as my mom dabbed at her eyes with a tissue. She had her hands resting against my mom's arm.

"What were your reasons, Maddie? How did you stop?" she said, sniffling as she wiped her cheeks.

"I realized that I wanted more. I didn't care if I hurt myself, obviously, and that was never going to be a reason for me to quit. And as crappy as it sounds, my parents suffering was not a good enough reason to quit, either. I quit because I realized it made me miserable. I knew that my life would never improve if I kept hurting myself and having to deal with the consequences that came with that. I wanted to stop hating my body for being something that I didn't feel like I belonged in. I wanted to have a boyfriend and go to college, and maybe be a professional streamer. And I couldn't do these things if I was slicing myself to pieces every other night.

"So, ultimately, I quit for me. And it was so hard for a long time. I would get the most insane urges. I would be doing something like watching TV, feeling okay, and suddenly, I would feel that it was imperative that I grab a knife and run it across my skin. I would feel like I needed to see the blood running down my body or I wouldn't be okay. I still feel that a little bit to this day, but it's been over six months since I last hurt myself. And my life is so much better. I met the greatest boyfriend ever."

She looked over at me, and for the millionth time, I wondered what I'd done to deserve her. Maddie radiated love from every pore as she smiled at me before turning back to my mom.

"I read this quote somewhere by this old dead guy and it stuck with me and got me through the darkest nights. 'He who has a *why* to live can bear almost any *how*.'

"Let me tell you, I journaled until my hands cramped, trying to discover my *whys*. They've changed since I first journaled; Kellan is my biggest *why* now, but I found enough early on to keep pushing through when the urges begged me to turn back. But I didn't turn back. And you can do the same thing, too. You've got this, Mrs. Davis. I know you do."

Mom looked at her with an expression I'd never seen on her face. She looked awed. I couldn't remember a time when I'd seen even the smallest hint of a meaningful moment grace her face; I vaguely thought I'd like to sketch her like this.

"Maddie, what you've said really means a lot to me. You walk in my house, and you say exactly what I needed to hear this morning. Thank you. I've been out of it for a while. I knew Kellan had a girlfriend, and I thought you two had broken up. I'm grateful you didn't. I'm glad I've gotten the chance to meet you." She turned to me. "I don't know if you're still willing to take advice from your mother, and I don't blame you if you don't listen. But do everything you can to keep this girl. She's a winner."

Maddie giggled and hugged my mom again, and my heart opened seeing the joy finally reaching my mom's eyes. It'd been years since she looked genuinely happy. I moved to join them at the foot of the couch, dropping to my knees and wrapping my arms around them.

"I'm really grateful that you're going to get help, Mom. If there is anything I can do, anything at all, please let me know. I want to see you heal. I... I miss you, you know?" I choked up on the last couple of words and closed my eyes. I felt my mom's hand grab mine.

"I know. I'm sorry. And there's nothing you can do to help me. Like Maddie said, this is my road to travel. I need to figure out what I need to do to bring lasting change to my life. I think I'll start with a journal, like you suggested, sweetie." She patted

Maddie on the arm. "That's a good first step. And I've got my A.A. meetings, and I'll have a sponsor who's been through this before. Maybe when I get over my initial withdrawal, we can all do something together. I'd like to get to know you better."

"I'd love that," Maddie said, folding her hands in her lap and beaming.

There was a sharp sound at the door and all three of us turned our heads. I poked my head out the living room window and saw Ty's car parked in the driveway.

"It's Tyrell. We can just ignore it."

Maddie stood up. "No way, he's your friend, Kellan. Let's see what he wants."

"My friend? I don't think so."

She shook her head. "Come on, Kellan. People make mistakes. At least hear what he has to say. He wouldn't come here just to yell at you."

"She's right, Kellan," Ty's muffled voice said as he peered through the top of the door. "Let me in. It's cool, bruh. I just want to talk to you."

I looked at my mom. "We really need a new front door." I moved to unlock it and Ty smiled.

"Come in, I guess," I said.

"Hi, Tyrell, how're you? It's been a while," Mom said.

Ty moved into the living room and hugged my mom and wasted no time in turning to Maddie.

"I owe you an apology. I'm sorry for the things I said about you to Kellan, and for not having both of your backs.

That was wrong. Kellan's my best friend, and what makes him happy, makes me happy. I'd appreciate it if you'd give me a second chance. I'm not a bad guy, it just took me a little while to grow up."

Maddie waved him off. "I understand. Apology accepted. How about we just start over? Clean slate." She held out a fist and Ty bumped it, a warm smile on his face.

"And me?" I said roughly, earning a scowl from Maddie.

Ty put his hands in his pockets. "Well, first off, I miss you, bruh. Life isn't the same without you."

"Yeah?" the hard edge still in my voice. Maddie walked over and not so discreetly pinched me in the side as hard as she could. I looked down at her with a frown and she made bug eyes at me as if to say, "Get it together, Kellan."

I blinked, glanced down, and then looked back at Tyrell. "Yeah... yeah, okay, I missed you too. But you didn't have my back with Maddie. That stung hard, dude. I know that it might have been shocking and confusing to you when it all went down, but we were best friends. What the hell, Ty?"

There was a rare look of concern on Tyrell's face.

"Yeah, I know. I'm ashamed, believe me. I should have been there for you. I've come to say I'm sorry. To both of you. I had some growing to do, and some soul searching, okay? But it's all good now. I'm very sorry to both of you. I know you've had a lot to deal with this year. You didn't deserve us all piling on top of that just because we didn't bother to try and understand." He put his arm around Maddie. "Like your beautiful girlfriend said, I'd like to start over. I'd like to have both of your backs from now on."

Maddie smiled. "Everyone deserves second chances, right, Kellan?"

I was more than agitated that she was so quick to forgive him.

"There's one more thing," Tyrell started, and I braced myself. "I want you to come back to the team."

I snorted. "I knew it. You're not really sorry, you just need me to help you look good for the college scouts, you—"

"Bruh, bruh, it's not like that." He walked toward me with his hands out. "Man, don't insult me. Whether you come back or not, I still want to be friends again. With both of you. Football is a separate issue. It's just that it's time-sensitive... we've got three days until our do-or-die playoff game. It's Tuesday night and it's for the last playoff spot."

Maddie walked over and grabbed my hand "Hey, Kelly Bean, hear him out. For me, okay?"

I looked at my adorable little angel and softened. I glanced up at Tyrell and shrugged. "Look, Baker is never going to take me back, even if I wanted to play, which I'm not saying that I do. His pride—"

"Good news then. It isn't Baker's call to make. He's gone." Ty bounced on his heels.

"WHAT?" I almost shouted.

"Yup. He was caught with Kate. In his office. During school hours. It was bad, bruh. He's got bigger problems than football now."

"Oh my God, not the same Kate he used to have over here?" Mom said, and then flushed. "Oh, crap... I'm sorry, Kel." She buried her face in her coffee.

Maddie, to her credit, giggled. "Oh, I know about her. Like I said, we all make mistakes, right, Kellan?"

I was too stunned to comment, not quite sure whether to laugh, cry, be angry, or none of the above.

But if Baker was gone... maybe...

"So, what, is Pinketts running the team now?" I asked.

"Nah, they wanted fresh blood. Ms. Bishop is now the head coach of the Scorpions."

"Wow, no kidding? The art teacher... I mean, I like her a lot and everything, but... does she know anything about football?"

"No, she's just there to manage, make sure nothing else like this is happening, I guess. I don't know, dude, it's over my head. I just want to make plays and defend our championship. Pinketts is still calling the shots on offense and she's game for you to come back. In fact, she'd beg you herself, but I figured I'd come alone and get our stuff straight first and then see where you stood."

I nodded slowly. "Alright, so what exactly are you wanting from me?"

Tyrell looked at me like I was an idiot. "Are you serious right now, bruh? Isn't that obvious? I want you to strap that helmet on and come light up that scoreboard with me. Look, I don't know if you've been following the team—"

"I haven't. I stopped caring long ago," I cut him off.

"Well, we're 6-3," he said.

"Wow, what happened? We were 10-0 last year. I mean, 6-3 isn't terrible... but that's a far cry from undefeated."

"You know exactly what happened. We lost you at quarterback and that put Kyle under center. He's a nice kid, decent arm, but he doesn't make decisions like you do. He doesn't see the entire field. He runs the play and executes it. That's all. No sense of awareness when things aren't working. So, we're backed up at home on Friday night against the Bears. They're 6-3, bruh. No joke. They lost their best player for the first three games of the year, and haven't lost since he returned. So, they might as well be considered undefeated."

I looked away, not wanting to feel this eager about the thought of suiting up again. I wanted to seize Tyrell by the collar and drive straight to the field and start warming up together. I was already running through the plays I thought Pinketts would open the game with.

"Ty, I haven't touched a football for over six weeks, except to throw her little brother passes in the backyard. I'm rusty. And I've probably lost like ten pounds since she made me go vegan, and then you have no idea how many things as a boyfriend that you can do wrong and not even know it. It gets stressful, man."

"HEY! I'm right here!" She elbowed me hard, and everyone laughed.

"I know. And you'll always be right there," I held her eyes for a moment before looking back at Tyrell. "Don't let me kid you, it's 100% worth it. But it's been a hot minute since I've touched a football. I don't know how much I could help you on Tuesday night."

Tyrell looked pained and pressed his lips together before backing up and gyrating with his hands in front of his chest like he did when he had a serious point to make.

"Alright, Kel, I'm going to say this to your face one time and one time only. So, you better listen, bruh. It's you, okay? You're the best player on the team. You're probably the best high school quarterback in the country. All the scouts ask me where you went. That's their first question before they want to talk about me. You were born for football. If you want to play on Sunday, you will. You're gonna make it, Kellan. You have a chance to be a legend. I just want you to be that legend for at least one more game with me. Come on, man, strap on that helmet, and let's go make music."

Maddie looked intently at Tyrell, and I flashbacked to watching her play competitive Minecraft on stream. I remembered her intensity and determination to win, and I wanted to show her mine, too.

I do want to play on Sunday someday. With her in the front row of a packed house, cheering me on with home-field advantage throughout the playoffs on the line. There's no place I'd rather be.

Shit… I know I'm going to do this.

"What do you think?" I asked Maddie, already knowing the answer.

She didn't even blink. "I think you should play."

"Don't you remember how they treated you? They—"

Ty cut in, floating toward us like a boxer dancing in the ring. "Bruh, ain't nobody saying shit. Oh! I'm sorry, excuse me, Ms. Davis." Mom smiled and waved him off. "But for real, nobody is saying nothing to you, that I can promise. I held a team meeting last night. I can't change their hearts and minds, Kel, but I can promise you that mine has changed. I've got you, bruh, and you too, Maddie."

I looked theatrically from Mom to Maddie, and finally back to Ty. I knew I was going to do this, and I might as well enjoy the moment. "So, why are we still standing here, then?"

"What do you mean?" Tyrell asked, the excitement in his voice palpable.

"Unless you're too tired, let's head to the field right now and shake out this rust. We've got a game to win, don't we?"

Tyrell grabbed me and pulled me into a hug. I wasn't used to someone as strong as him grabbing me. I went flying into him with a hearty laugh. "I got an infinite tank, bruh,"

I heard him yelling in my ear before he pulled away. "Come on, let's go. I got my cleats in the car. I'll go all day and night if you want."

He hopped toward the front door, but I called out to him.

"Ty, hold up." He walked back and I stuck my hand out for our secret handshake. When we finished, Ty grabbed me for another hug.

"It's good to have you back. You're like a brother to me. I love you," he said and looked away. I was going to respond in kind but Maddie leaped in between us, tapping her hands together in front of her chest.

"That was so cute! I want to learn that handshake!"

Ty wrapped us all in a hug. "I'll teach you, but I've got to get to that field before I lose my mind. Kellan will tell you, once I get energized, I've got to burn it off or I'll literally bounce off these walls."

We all laughed and my mom stood up. "You guys have fun, I'm going to go lay down and take a nap. It was nice seeing you, Ty, and really nice meeting you, Maddie. I hope to see you again soon."

Maddie hugged my mom and then we both ran after Tyrell, laughing as he jumped and leaped and laughed his way to his car.

Chapter 39
Kellan

When I walked onto the field for the late afternoon start, I was amazed at how many people had turned out to watch. It was only 5:30 pm, but the bleachers on both sides were packed full, and there was a standing crowd at least ten rows deep by each endzone. The entire town seemed to come out for the big game, knowing what was at stake.

Maddie was in the front row looking so hot, her face painted in school colors. She was already yelling and screaming. Next to her were Charlotte and Destiny, and if I wasn't mistaken, Charlotte had her arm wrapped around her. Flanked on each side of the girls were our families. I was thrilled to see my mom standing with Maddie's parents. She seemed to already be doing better.

I flashed Maddie a heart and she returned it.

This one is for you, Maddie Pie. Let me show you what I can do. You've showed me all your talents, now it's my chance to show you mine.

We got the ball first, and I took the field, calling the

first play. Simple down and out to Tyrell, hoping to pick up an easy first down and get the chains moving.

I took the snap, quickly surveyed the field, and fired right to Tyrell. The defender was one step ahead of me and snatched the ball out of the air just before it reached Tyrell's hands, intercepting the pass and easily cruising into the endzone for a touchdown.

It felt like he walked up to me with a sledgehammer and smashed me in the groin. When I got to the sidelines, I sat on the edge of the bench, staring at the ground, ripping at my hair, trying to understand what just happened. Tyrell joined me, surprisingly upbeat.

"This is great, bruh. We'll get that first mistake out of the way. We're going to cash in on that later. He's going to bite again, and we know what to do with that."

The first three quarters were a slugfest. We punched back and forth, and I knew I was still shaking off the rust. I was hanging in there, making some good plays, but I was missing a lot of opportunities, too. We would have had these guys buried by now if I had my best stuff.

I buckled down after the start of the fourth quarter, letting all the noise around me die down and becoming one with the field. When we got the ball, we quickly closed the gap. I hit Ty with a long pass to bring us within four.

"We just need a good defensive stop. Let's make 'em pay if they play it safe," I said to Ty, feeling the game slowing down again.

I spotted you guys an early touchdown with my sloppiness. It's time to get that back.

The other team did indeed play it safe, opting to run the ball and churn the clock, whittling away at the time left for a comeback. They got a few first downs thanks to our suspect defense, but we finally stopped them at midfield, forcing them to punt.

Their punter angled his kick just right, and the ball bounced out of bounds at our own five-yard line.

Well, nobody said it was going to be easy. But we can do this.

I looked at the clock, noting we had just a little over two minutes left to keep our season alive.

Before running onto the field, I looked at Maddie in the stands. She was biting her nails and I could see her shaking all the way from the sidelines.

Now you know how I felt during your Minecraft streams. I wanted to jump through that computer and help you any way I could. But you know what? You're helping me right now. I look at you and gather a strength that makes me unstoppable.

I felt like with the last drive and the quick scoring pass to Tyrell, that the rust was gone. It was time to finish this team off.

I huddled the guys on the sideline, discussing our plans for our final drive of the game, if not the season. We wouldn't have time to waste once we got on the field—we needed to iron everything out now.

"Okay, let's go silent count to open the drive. We get set, everybody moves on two Mississippi. Let's keep it simple, get open. If it's running play, we'll run off Big Rude to the left. Give Byron a hole he could drive a truck through, big man."

I slapped Big Rude on the arm, not waiting for his response and then looked around at the rest of the guys. The guys had all been distant but that didn't matter to me. I wasn't here for them. I was here for me.

"Alright, If I hold up one finger, we pass, two, we run. I don't care if they know what's coming. We're the best on this field and we're going to play like it. Let's go!"

From their five-yard line, I began to engineer the most important drive of my young career.

The team executed the silent count flawlessly, and I took the snap, catching our opponents off guard. I quickly went through my progressions, looking for an open teammate. When I flashed to Tyrell, I spotted him breaking away from his defender. The opponents had expected all passes to be to the outside so that we could get out of bounds and stop the clock. Tyrell used that to his advantage, faking outside and then cutting in. I lit him up, firing a pass as hard as I could into his chest. Tyrell caught it and secured it just before a defender slammed into him, jarring him to the ground. He held on to the ball and we picked up 20 yards.

I held up two fingers. I took the snap and quickly stuffed the ball into Byron's gut, watching as he cut around Big Rude for a five-yard gain.

The next two plays were incomplete passes, and we faced our first do-or-die, fourth down. I held up one finger and the team quickly ran to the line of scrimmage.

I noticed that the right side of the field was emptier than usual. The Bears had rolled their coverage to the left, deciding to place three men on Tyrell for this play.

You're going to pay for that.

I yelled hike, grabbed the ball from the center's hands and looked deliberately Tyrell's way, with no intention of throwing him the ball. I pump-faked, pretending like I was going to throw the ball his way, and then pulled it down at the last second. The entire defense bit and shuffled toward that side of the field. With their ankles moving left, I took off running to the right, easily dodging two defenders and hurtling over a third.

Open ocean, I thought, as I cut toward the sideline, gobbling up yards. Through the roar of the crowd, I swore I could hear my sweetheart yelling my name. I knew in that moment that I was running faster than I ever had before. By the time I was caught and shoved out of bounds by a defender, I'd chewed up over 50 yards.

I looked at the clock... 46 seconds to go. Plenty of time. We were down to the 30-yard line.

Let's hurry up and go, keep the pedal to the metal.

I brought the team quickly to the line of scrimmage, holding up two fingers, hoping to catch the other team off guard with a running play.

I watched as Byron dodged and weaved, trying to find space through the defense. He made it about seven yards before being brought down.

It took way too long for the pile to disperse after Byron was tackled.

Tick, tick, tick! Tick, tick, tick! Come on, come on, come on! Get up, let's go!

When I could finally take the next snap, I spiked the ball hard into the dirt, stopping the clock with only six seconds remaining.

Those cheaters took their time getting out of the pile. We lost 20 seconds because of that... well, it is what it is, Kellan. Make the best of it. One final play. One chance to complete this comeback.

I looked over at Maddie, drawing as much strength as I could. I could barely see her from the distance, all the way down near the goal-line. She was yelling, her precious little face covered in the blues of and yellows of our school colors, urging us on to the endzone.

Here we go, Maddie Pie. One more play. Lift me up and carry me home.

I held up one finger, not bothering to huddle the team and call a play.

It's been backyard football all the way down the field. We're not stopping now. We've got them on the edge of the ring. It's time for the knockout blow.

I took the final snap of the game, and immediately started rolling to the right side of the field as a blitzing defender immediately collapsed the pocket. As I was moving right, Tyrell was moving left, across the field. And he had a step on his man.

For what felt like an infinite flash of a second, I could see Tyrell at eight-years-old, standing in the end-zone, grinning ear-to-ear. I had just thrown him the winning pass at a peewee flag football game. I clearly remembered the look on his face, after the game, as he smiled wide, the two gaps where his adult front teeth had not yet appeared, as he told me that we were unstoppable as long as we were together.

A quick glance down at the field and I realized I was running out of real estate. I jumped in the air, launching the pass across my body, toward a streaking Tyrell. Just as the ball left my hands, I felt a defender slam into me. I didn't see if Tyrell caught the ball in the back of the endzone.

But I heard the roar of the crowd. I knew my pass found its way home in Ty's hands. I relaxed on the ground, grunting when the defender pushed off me.

We did it, Maddie. We're going to the playoffs. We marched 95 yards down the field in just over two minutes to win this. Maddie, we did it! Together!

I rolled my head, looking back toward the endzone for Ty but saw nothing but a pile of white moving toward me. The next thing I knew, I was lifted off the ground, and onto an impossibly wide set of shoulders.

I looked down, astonished to be riding on top of Big Rude. Before I could say anything to him, Tyrell was jumping circles around us.

"Did you see that catch, bruh? Did you see it? Davante Adams would be proud! Wait… he ain't got nothin' on me!"

I laughed and shook my head. "No, I was busy getting the wind knocked out of me. Tell me about it, bruh."

Tyrell laughed manically. "WE DID IT, BRUH! WE'RE GOING TO THE PLAYOFFS! AHHHHHH! YOU BETTER BELIEVE WE'RE GOING TO REPEAT!"

He took off running toward the stands and I followed him with my eyes, a question in my mind, but I shook it off when I remembered where I was. I looked down.

"How strong are you, dude? I'm glad we didn't fight earlier this year."

"I do okay. And yeah, me too. I'm sorry and all that. Let's bury that stuff and just celebrate."

I reached down and patted him on the back. "Alright, that sounds good."

I scanned back toward the bleachers, looking once again for her. I was surprised to see Ty standing next to her, beckoning her to come over the fence. The next thing I knew, he was lifting her onto his shoulders.

Chapter 40
Maddie

I held my breath when I saw Kellan running across the football field, my eyes going wide when he jumped into the air, launching the ball toward Tyrell. When Ty caught that pass, all of us—Mom, Dad, Kellan's mom, Destiny, Charlotte—we all jumped up and down and screamed.

"Is that it? Did they win?" I asked everyone around me.

"Yes, that's it!" Dad said, leaning toward me. "Kellan just took the team right down the field in what amounts to one of the most impressive drives I've ever seen. Your boyfriend just threw the game-winning pass. That was something else. I've seen a decent amount of football, but that was something for the ages. He's really talented, Maddie."

I must have looked like a spotlight, beaming everywhere.

"That's my boyfriend, Dad. What else did you expect?"

I laughed with everybody, hugging Destiny and Charlotte and then looked back to the field when I heard someone calling my name.

"Maddie, quick, climb over this fence!" Tyrell said, motioning rapidly with his hands.

"What? Why?" I laughed at him, thinking that maybe he was always hyper and goofy.

"I'm going to put you up on my shoulders and carry you to your prince. Come on, hurry up!" He shook his hands even faster, if that was possible, and I didn't waste another second.

I bounded over the fence as fast as I could, jumping down after cresting the top. Tyrell bent over and I climbed onto his shoulders.

He cocked his head sideways. "Girl, you don't weigh anything. You need to eat. I'm taking us all out to dinner after this and I'm not leaving until I see you eat some food. Let's go find Kellan."

We both looked back toward the field and laughed simultaneously as we saw Kellan being paraded around on Big Rude's shoulders.

"Well, that was easy," Tyrell said.

When we reached Kellan, he had taken his helmet off and his hair was matted in 15 different places, the sweat dripping down his face and dropping onto his uniform. He had that million-dollar smile plastered across his face, and he looked so much older in his football uniform.

"Hi," I said shyly, soaking in his honey-brown eyes.

"Hey," he said.

"Dad said that was a 'drive for the ages,' whatever that means."

Kellan laughed. "Yeah, that was epic. Did you see Tyrell's catch? He claims it was sensational. I'm going to have to see that on film."

"Believe me, bruh, it was legendary."

"Alright, Kellan, you're coming down. Hunting season starts soon, and I need my shoulders," Big Rude said.

I told Tyrell to sit me down and he leaned forward, dumping me onto the field. Big Rude started to walk away but then came back and strode right up to me. I saw Kellan start to move between us, but then stopped when Big Rude spoke.

"I'm sorry for my behavior in school. I know I hurt your feelings and it was wrong. You have the right to be who you are whether or not I understand it."

I nodded, genuinely moved. I didn't expect this. "Thanks. Don't worry about it. Past is the past."

Big Rude returned the nod and then walked away.

"Well, that was something I didn't expect to see," Tyrell said once he was out of earshot.

"Hey, you left us."

We all turned to see Destiny and Charlotte standing behind us, hands on their hips, looking up at Tyrell.

"Oh, I was coming back to get that phone number, don't you worry, shorty. Figured we'd all be hanging out a lot together now that we're all friends." He wrapped his arm around Destiny but Charlotte peeled it away.

"Oh no you don't! She's my date to this game. I'm hoping she's going to become my girlfriend, so you better watch out!"

Tyrell backed up with a smile. "Oh... okay. I'm sorry. I just saw an opportunity, that's all. I like the way you stick up for your girl, though."

Kellan shook his head at them as they walked back toward the sideline, their voices growing distant. He pulled me close and I looked up into his eyes.

"Well, we've got time for one more cliché high school moment before this is all over."

I tilted my head. "Oh yeah? What's that moment?"

"It's the one where the high school quarterback kisses his transgender girlfriend after throwing the game-winning touchdown."

I mock furrowed, tapping my lips. "I can't say I've seen that one. Thought the normal cliché was always the girl next door instead of the cheerleader. Don't you think this is a bit of a reach?"

"Nah. The world's primed for this. And while you may not be just next door—that would be awesome, by the way— you're only a couple of blocks from me. So, it's close enough," Kellan said.

A slight breeze picked up and I brushed the hair out of my eyes.

"Well, you have to admit, it is a little bit of a script change. But I think people can handle it. So, if you could change anything else about this moment, anything at all, what would it be? Maybe something about me?" I asked, arching an eyebrow.

Kellan framed my face with his hands.

"No. I wouldn't change a thing about you. And do you know why?"

I stepped closer to him. "I think I know what you're gonna say. Because...

Chapter 41
Maddie & Kellan

"I love you just the way you are."

Author's Note

If you made this far, I have to assume that you've read the entire novel. For that, I am eternally grateful. If you enjoyed this book, please leave a review :). It helps tickle the algorithms and get this book into more hands and hearts. You can also join my mailing list @ rileyrianbooks.com to get updates on all future books. Plus, when you join my mailing list, you'll get Kellan's love letter to Maddie. I had a lot of fun writing it, but it didn't end up making it into an already long book. I'd love to share with you.

I didn't know where any of this was going on the first night of my egg-cracking in early fall 2021. This intense little trans-girl popped into my head, said hello, and promptly told me her name was Maddie. I was instantly in love because I knew she was a part of me I'd long ago buried.

I spent many nights awake while crafting this story, taking notes as it unfolded to me in her voice. Often I cried. I cried for what happened in the story, and I cried for what happened to me over the years... and I cried because I knew I wasn't alone; there were others like me all across the world who faced the same challenges and obstacles to authentic, genuine expression—beginning with the ultimate challenge: discovering one's own identity.

In my case, I was so unconscious about who I was that I didn't even know the word transgender until I stumbled into a "banned books" display at my local library (which is ironic because this book is destined for the same fate if I can get enough libraries to carry it). Now, after months of immersing myself in the transgender community, I know there's been an ongoing national discussion for years. But I'm rural, secluded, and didn't have any social media other than a YouTube account. Heck, I didn't even know what TikTok was until late last year! However, by the time you've read this, you'll find my thirsty ass posting videos on there at least twice a week. But until the day that my egg-cracked, my wife and I were raising our son, going about our business, and living a pretty sheltered existence.

And then I saw those books and my life changed forever. It brought an immediate flashback of one of my earliest memories that I hadn't thought of in years: I'm 4 years old, wearing white high heels that belong to the cute teenage girl who is in charge of my daycare room. I'm looking down at them, admiring the pointed toes, seeing my little feet swallowed up by the twice as large shoes, and grinning from ear to ear.

Later that night, just as Maddie was introducing herself to me, I flashed on a variety of memories that should have told me I was more than 'simply' pansexual, as I've always thought. I saw myself in middle school, pretending that a wash cloth was a skirt in the shower, and loving the way my legs looked. I remembered when I had a long-distance girlfriend in Nova Scotia in my late teens, and the half dozen times I drove up there I enjoyed nothing more than having her do my makeup and getting dressed up in feminine clothing before going to the mall with our friends.

Then... at some point... poof! It's like I forgot who I was and became this adult dude. I mean, the accelerated 'male' patterned baldness in my early 20s didn't help things (thank you, Manic Panic!). But I guess getting laughed at one too many times when I was just trying to be myself forced me to let go of my authenticity and retreat.

So when I found those banned books, and Maddie showed up, I started writing, without having the first clue about how to write a book. And I didn't know where this would go. But I'm glad I took the ride because I got ME back. The girl that I am is here to stay. And I have no idea what I'll do about it on the outside... I'm still figuring that part out. I've started with non-binary labels, even though I'm almost certain about my femininity... but that's okay, I'm not in a rush or too concerned with finding the proper label beyond transgender... because I'm happy. I have a super supportive wife, a loving son, and I'm not conflicted anymore. I'm not religious, but I feel blessed. I know how hard it is for some people on this planet to find out where their next meal is coming from; so I'm not worried about dotting my I's and crossing my T's with proper labels; I'm just grateful to be coming to a greater understanding of myself. The rest will come with time.

My primary focus is on giving back and helping the next generations live in a more open, more inclusive world. This book is step one of what I hope is a journey of endless steps. My intention is to continue writing books that deal with topics near and dear to the LGBTQ+ community I'm so honored to be a part of. I'm so stoked by what the younger generation currently coming of age is all about. The increased inclusivity is incredibly heart-warming to those of us who can remember a much darker age not that long ago.

But we've still got work to do. The hundreds of bills that circulated through state houses in the U.S. in 2022 show us that the battle for the future has only just begun. I don't know about you, but I'm ready to dig my heels in and give everything I am to help all kids grow up safely and be able to enjoy natural self-expression. I don't want to just 'say gay.' Oh, no. I want to scream it. I want every kid, regardless of their zip code, gender, skin color, or sexual orientation, to grow up with dignity, a full belly, and a full heart. They deserve it.

I'm going to close with one of the most moving pieces of writing I've ever read. It's from the beautiful Samantha Riedel in a column for Them.Us in February 2022 (link below).

I read it often as it stirs my soul and keeps my heart lifted above the fray. I hope it moves you as it moves me.

"...Since then, queer people from all walks of life have organized, grown stronger together by sharing our stories and experiences, and are taking the first steps towards intergenerational healing and ensuring that we never have to hide our identities again. That's what terrifies conservatives, and what drives them to silence us and destroy the work our writers and artists create.

But those who want to cosplay like it's 1933, to burn our history and what freedoms we've scraped together since, to kill our children and call it mercy — you really should know: we're stronger than you, even our children. And we will not be reduced to rubble again."

https://tinyurl.com/yubyv5ua

Acknowledgments

There are so many people who helped make this "self-published" book a reality.

Falynn. My twin-flame, my wife, my everything. Without her, this doesn't matter or exist. Thank you for continuing to grow with me in this transcendent relationship of ours.

Ellie Rose, who might be reading this to you right now if you purchased the audiobook. I am lucky enough to have an extremely talented young woman that lives right down the street from me with recording experience. When I first heard her rough cuts, I knew she had to be the one to read this book. I'll probably never be able to hire her again if this book does even moderately well, because she's going to get swamped with offers from traditional publishers waving fat checks! But... I secretly hope she gets the offers. She deserves it.

Amy Ewing, NY Times best-selling author and writer extraordinaire. She gave me one hell of a developmental edit when this book was just a piece a crap written in third-person POV. She made me think about a lot more than just writing with her succinct notes. Thank you, Amy. You made me a better writer and helped bring this story to life. Go check her books out wherever outstanding books are sold. You can also hire her as an editor on Reedsy.

Laura Wilkinson, who provided the copy-editing (except for this author stuff in the back. That's me and ProWritingAid... so if it sucks, blame the AI). Your feedback on the final manuscript was uplifting after spending months in seclusion hammering this story out. You can find her on Fiverr: ImWilkinson.

Sarah Lahay for the formatting and cover design... but maybe most importantly for letting me pretend that a Big 5 publisher has published my book. You can find Sarah on Reedsy.

To the marketing team at Novel Cause for helping me actually find an audience... that seems kind of important, I think. I appreciate all that you guys did for me on this book!

To Amon Amarth and Metal Blade Records for not suing me because I used you in the book. My wife and I are head-over-heels for your music and I couldn't imagine Maddie going to any other concert. It couldn't have been a fictional band; it had to be Amon Amarth. Period. (If you want to give me some backstage passes... well... I wouldn't say no ;))

To Beach House for their amazing and one-of-a-kind music. It's cool to be from the same state as the greatest band that's ever existed. Please never stop making music. Please?

To Purrple Cat, Oatmello and all the music that Lo-fi girl studies to... what the hell would angsty writers do without you guys?

And to you, the reader. Thanks once again for reading this book. I hope it touched you in some way.

Riley x

Made in the USA
Middletown, DE
12 July 2022

69039920R00300